The Adve[illegible] ther Cases

Sir Arthur Conan Doyle (1859–1930) was born in Edinburgh and studied medicine at the university, after an education in Jesuit schools in Lancashire and Austria. He had an active career as a doctor and ophthalmologist, including volunteering in Bloemfontein during the Boer War, but also in the public sphere as Deputy-Lieutenant of Surrey, writer of widely read historical works and political pamphlets, vociferous opponent of miscarriages of justice and twice parliamentary candidate (although he was never elected). Yet it was for his brilliant creation of the first scientific detective, Sherlock Holmes, that he achieved great fame – so great that after he killed Holmes off to concentrate on his historical work, he was forced to bring the character back to life. In later life, Conan Doyle was converted to Spiritualism, writing works such as *The Coming of the Fairies*, and was a friend of the magician Houdini. He died of a heart attack in 1930, at the age of seventy-one.

The Adventure of the Six Napoleons and Other Cases

ARTHUR CONAN DOYLE

PENGUIN ENGLISH
LIBRARY

PENGUIN BOOKS

UK | USA | Canada | Ireland | Australia
India | New Zealand | South Africa

Penguin Books is part of the Penguin Random House group of companies
whose addresses can be found at global.penguinrandomhouse.com

Penguin
Random House
UK

The Adventures of Sherlock Holmes first published 1892
The Memoirs of Sherlock Holmes first published 1894
The Return of Sherlock Holmes first published 1905
The Case-Book of Sherlock Holmes first published 1927
This selection first published in the Penguin English Library 2014
This edition published 2016
001

Cover illustration: Coralie Bickford-Smith

Set in 11/13 pt Dante MT Std
Typeset by Jouve (UK), Milton Keynes
Printed in Great Britain by Clays Ltd, St Ives plc

A CIP catalogue record for this book is available from the British Library

ISBN: 978–0–241–30967–4

www.greenpenguin.co.uk

MIX
Paper from
responsible sources
FSC
www.fsc.org
FSC® C018179

Penguin Random House is committed to a sustainable future for our business, our readers and our planet. This book is made from Forest Stewardship Council® certified paper.

Contents

The Man with the Twisted Lip

Isa Whitney, brother of the late Elias Whitney, D. D., Principal of the Theological College of St George's, was much addicted to opium. The habit grew upon him, as I understand, from some foolish freak when he was at college, for having read De Quincey's description of his dreams and sensations, he had drenched his tobacco with laudanum in an attempt to produce the same effects. He found, as so many more have done, that the practice is easier to attain than to get rid of, and for many years he continued to be a slave to the drug, an object of mingled horror and pity to his friends and relatives. I can see him now, with yellow, pasty face, drooping lids and pin-point pupils, all huddled in a chair, the wreck and ruin of a noble man.

One night – it was in June, '89 – there came a ring to my bell, about the hour when a man gives his first yawn, and glances at the clock. I sat up in my chair, and my wife laid her needlework down in her lap and made a little face of disappointment.

'A patient!' said she. 'You'll have to go out.'

I groaned, for I was newly come back from a weary day.

We heard the door open, a few hurried words, and then quick steps upon the linoleum. Our own door flew open, and a lady, clad in some dark-coloured stuff with a black veil, entered the room.

'You will excuse my calling so late,' she began, and then, suddenly losing her self-control, she ran forward, threw her arms about my wife's neck, and sobbed upon her shoulder. 'Oh! I'm in such trouble!' she cried; 'I do so want a little help.'

'Why,' said my wife, pulling up her veil, 'it is Kate Whitney. How you startled me, Kate! I had not an idea who you were when you came in.'

'I didn't know what to do, so I came straight to you.' That was always the way. Folk who were in grief came to my wife like birds to a lighthouse.

'It was very sweet of you to come. Now, you must have some wine and water, and sit here comfortably and tell us all about it. Or should you rather that I sent James off to bed?'

'Oh, no, no. I want the Doctor's advice and help too. It's about Isa. He has not been home for two days. I am so frightened about him!'

It was not the first time that she had spoken to us of her husband's trouble, to me as a doctor, to my wife as an old friend and school companion. We soothed and comforted her by such words as we could find. Did she know where her husband was? Was it possible that we could bring him back to her?

It seemed that it was. She had the surest information that of late he had, when the fit was on him, made use of an opium den in the farthest east of the City. Hitherto his orgies had always been confined to one day, and he had come back, twitching and shattered, in the evening. But now the spell had been upon him eight-and-forty hours, and he lay there, doubtless, among the dregs of the docks, breathing in the poison or sleeping off the effects. There he was to be found, she was sure of it, at the Bar of Gold, in Upper Swandam Lane. But what was she to do? How could she, a young and timid woman, make her way into such a place, and pluck her husband out from among the ruffians who surrounded him?

There was the case, and of course there was but one way out of it. Might I not escort her to this place? And then, as a second thought, why should she come at all? I was Isa Whitney's medical adviser, and as such I had influence over him. I could manage it better if I were alone. I promised her on my word that I would send him home in a cab within two hours if he were indeed at the address which she had given me. And so in ten minutes I had left my armchair and cheery sitting-room behind me, and was speeding eastward in a hansom on a strange errand, as it seemed to me at the time, though the future only could show how strange it was to be.

But there was no great difficulty in the first stage of my adventure. Upper Swandam Lane is a vile alley lurking behind the high wharves which line the north side of the river to the east of London Bridge. Between a slop-shop and a gin-shop, approached by a steep flight of steps leading down to a black gap like the mouth of a cave, I found the den of which I was in search. Ordering my cab to wait, I pressed down the steps, worn hollow in the centre by the ceaseless tread of drunken feet, and by the light of a flickering oil lamp above the door I found the latch and made my way into a long, low room, thick and heavy with the brown opium smoke, and terraced with wooden berths, like the forecastle of an emigrant ship.

Through the gloom one could dimly catch a glimpse of bodies lying in strange fantastic poses, bowed shoulders, bent knees, heads thrown back and chins pointing upwards, with here and there a dark, lack-lustre eye turned upon the newcomer. Out of the black shadows there glimmered little red circles of light, now bright, now faint, as the burning poison waxed or waned in the bowls of the metal pipes. The most lay silent, but some muttered to themselves, and others talked together in a strange, low, monotonous voice, their conversation coming in gushes, and then suddenly tailing off into silence, each mumbling out his own thoughts, and paying little heed to the words of his neighbour. At the farther end was a small brazier of burning charcoal, beside which on a three-legged wooden stool there sat a tall, thin old man, with his jaw resting upon his two fists, and his elbows upon his knees, staring into the fire.

As I entered, a sallow Malay attendant had hurried up with a pipe for me and a supply of the drug, beckoning me to an empty berth.

'Thank you, I have not come to stay,' said I. 'There is a friend of mine here, Mr Isa Whitney, and I wish to speak with him.'

There was a movement and an exclamation from my right, and peering through the gloom, I saw Whitney, pale, haggard, and unkempt, staring out at me.

'My God! It's Watson,' said he. He was in a pitiable state of reaction, with every nerve in a twitter. 'I say, Watson, what o'clock is it?'

'Nearly eleven.'

'Of what day?'

'Of Friday, June 19th.'

'Good heavens! I thought it was Wednesday. It is Wednesday. What d'you want to frighten a chap for?' He sank his face on to his arms, and began to sob in a high treble key.

'I tell you that it is Friday, man. Your wife has been waiting this two days for you. You should be ashamed of yourself!'

'So I am. But you've got mixed, Watson, for I have only been here a few hours, three pipes, four pipes – I forget how many. But I'll go home with you. I wouldn't frighten Kate – poor little Kate. Give me your hand! Have you a cab?'

'Yes. I have one waiting.'

'Then I shall go in it. But I must owe something. Find what I owe, Watson. I am all off colour. I can do nothing for myself.'

I walked down the narrow passage between the double row of sleepers, holding my breath to keep out the vile, stupefying fumes of the drug, and looking about for the manager. As I passed the tall man who sat by the brazier I felt a sudden pluck at my skirt, and a low voice whispered, 'Walk past me, and then look back at me.' The words fell quite distinctly upon my ear. I glanced down. They could only have come from the old man at my side, and yet he sat now as absorbed as ever, very thin, very wrinkled, bent with age, an opium pipe dangling down from between his knees, as though it had dropped in sheer lassitude from his fingers. I took two steps forward and looked back. It took all my self-control to prevent me from breaking out into a cry of astonishment. He had turned his back so that none could see him but I. His form had filled out, his wrinkles were gone, the dull eyes had regained their fire, and there, sitting by the fire, and grinning at my surprise, was none other than Sherlock Holmes. He made a slight motion to me to approach him, and instantly, as he turned his face half round to the company once more, subsided into a doddering, loose-lipped senility.

'Holmes!' I whispered, 'what on earth are you doing in this den?'

'As low as you can,' he answered, 'I have excellent ears. If you would have the great kindness to get rid of that sottish friend of yours, I should be exceedingly glad to have a little talk with you.'

'I have a cab outside.'

'Then pray send him home in it. You may safely trust him, for he appears to be too limp to get into any mischief. I should recommend you also to send a note by the cabman to your wife to

'HOLMES! I WHISPERED.'

say that you have thrown in your lot with me. If you will wait outside, I shall be with you in five minutes.'

It was difficult to refuse any of Sherlock Holmes's requests, for they were always so exceedingly definite, and put forward with such an air of mastery. I felt, however, that when Whitney was once confined in the cab, my mission was practically accomplished; and for the rest, I could not wish anything better than to be associated with my friend in one of those singular adventures which were the normal condition of his existence. In a few minutes I had written my note, paid Whitney's bill, led him out to the cab, and seen him driven through the darkness. In a very short time a decrepit figure had emerged from the opium den, and I was walking down the street with Sherlock Holmes. For two streets he shuffled along with a bent back and an uncertain foot. Then, glancing quickly round, he straightened himself out and burst into a hearty fit of laughter.

'I suppose, Watson,' said he, 'that you imagine that I have added opium-smoking to cocaine injections and all the other little weaknesses on which you have favoured me with your medical views.'

'I was certainly surprised to find you there.'

'But not more so than I to find you.'

'I came to find a friend.'

'And I to find an enemy!'

'An enemy?'

'Yes, one of my natural enemies, or, shall I say, my natural prey. Briefly, Watson, I am in the midst of a very remarkable inquiry, and I have hoped to find a clue in the incoherent ramblings of these sots, as I have done before now. Had I been recognized in that den my life would not have been worth an hour's purchase, for I have used it before now for my own purposes, and the rascally Lascar who runs it has sworn vengeance upon me. There is a trap-door at the back of that building, near the corner of Paul's Wharf, which could tell some strange tales of what has passed through it upon the moonless nights.'

'What! You do not mean bodies?'

'Aye, bodies, Watson. We should be rich men if we had a thousand pounds for every poor devil who has been done to death in that den. It is the vilest murder-trap on the whole riverside, and I fear Neville St Clair has entered it never to leave it more. But our trap should be here!' He put his two forefingers between his teeth and whistled shrilly, a signal which was answered by a similar whistle from the distance, followed shortly by the rattle of wheels and the clink of horses' hoofs. 'Now, Watson,' said Holmes, as a tall dog-cart dashed up through the gloom, throwing out two golden tunnels of yellow light from its side-lanterns, 'you'll come with me, won't you?'

'If I can be of use.'

'Oh, a trusty comrade is always of use. And a chronicler still more so. My room at the Cedars is a double-bedded one.'

'The Cedars?'

'Yes; that is Mr St Clair's house. I am staying there while I conduct the inquiry.'

'Where is it, then?'

'Near Lee, in Kent. We have a seven-mile drive before us.'

'But I am all in the dark.'

'Of course you are. You'll know all about it presently. Jump up here! All right, John, we shall not need you. Here's half a crown. Look out for me tomorrow about eleven. Give her her head! So long, then!'

He flicked the horse with his whip, and we dashed away through the endless succession of sombre and deserted streets, which widened gradually, until we were flying across a broad balustraded bridge, with the murky river flowing sluggishly beneath us. Beyond lay another broad wilderness of bricks and mortar, its silence broken only by the heavy, regular footfall of the policeman, or the songs and shouts of some belated party of revellers. A dull wrack was drifting slowly across the sky, and a star or two twinkled dimly here and there through the rifts of the clouds. Holmes drove in silence, with his head sunk upon his breast, and the air of a man who is lost in thought, whilst I sat beside him curious to learn what this new quest might be which seemed to tax his powers so sorely, and yet afraid to break in upon the current of his thoughts. We had driven several miles, and were beginning to get to the fringe of the belt of suburban villas, when he shook himself, shrugged his shoulders, and lit up his pipe with the air of a man who has satisfied himself that he is acting for the best.

'You have a grand gift of silence, Watson,' said he. 'It makes you quite invaluable as a companion. 'Pon my word, it is a great thing for me to have someone to talk to, for my own thoughts are not over-pleasant. I was wondering what I should say to this dear little woman tonight when she meets me at the door.'

'You forget that I know nothing about it.'

'I shall just have time to tell you the facts of the case before we get to Lee. It seems absurdly simple, and yet, somehow, I can get nothing to go upon. There's plenty of thread, no doubt, but I can't get the end of it in my hand. Now, I'll state the case clearly and concisely to you, Watson, and maybe you may see a spark where all is dark to me.'

'Proceed, then.'

'Some years ago – to be definite, in May, 1884 – there came to Lee a gentleman, Neville St Clair by name, who appeared to have plenty of money. He took a large villa, laid out the grounds very nicely, and lived generally in good style. By degrees he made friends in the neighbourhood, and in 1887 he married the daughter of a local brewer, by whom he has now had two children. He had no occupation, but was interested in several companies, and went into town as a rule in the morning, returning by the 5.14 from Cannon Street every night. Mr St Clair is now thirty-seven years of age, is a man of temperate habits, a good husband, a very affectionate father, and a man who is popular with all who know him. I may add that his whole debts at the present moment, as far as we have been able to ascertain, amount to £88 10s., while he has £220 standing to his credit in the Capital and Counties Bank. There is no reason, therefore, to think that money troubles have been weighing upon his mind.

'Last Monday Mr Neville St Clair went into town rather earlier than usual, remarking before he started that he had two important commissions to perform, and that he would bring his little boy home a box of bricks. Now, by the merest chance his wife received a telegram upon this same Monday, very shortly after his departure, to the effect that a small parcel of considerable value which she had been expecting was waiting for her at the offices of the Aberdeen Shipping Company. Now, if you are well up in your London, you will know that the office of the company is in Fresno Street, which branches out of Upper Swandam Lane, where you found me tonight. Mrs St Clair had her lunch, started for the City, did some shopping, proceeded to the company's office, got her packet, and found herself exactly at 4.35 walking through Swandam Lane on her way back to the station. Have you followed me so far?'

'It is very clear.'

'If you remember, Monday was an exceedingly hot day, and Mrs St Clair walked slowly, glancing about in the hope of seeing a cab, as she did not like the neighbourhood in which she found herself. While she walked in this way down Swandam Lane she suddenly heard an ejaculation or cry, and was struck cold to see her husband looking down at her, and, as it seemed to her, beckoning to her from a second-floor window. The window was open, and she distinctly saw his face, which she describes as being terribly agitated. He waved his hands frantically to her, and then vanished from the window so suddenly that it seemed to her that he had been plucked back by some irresistible force from behind. One singular point which struck her quick feminine eye was that, although he wore some dark coat, such as he had started to town in, he had on neither collar nor necktie.

'Convinced that something was amiss with him, she rushed down the steps – for the house was none other than the opium den in which you found me tonight – and, running through the front room, she attempted to ascend the stairs which led to the first floor. At the foot of the stairs, however, she met this Lascar scoundrel, of whom I have spoken, who thrust her back, and, aided by a Dane, who acts as assistant there, pushed her out into the street. Filled with the most maddening doubts and fears, she rushed down the lane, and, by rare good fortune, met, in Fresno Street, a number of constables with an inspector, all on their way to their beat. The inspector and two men accompanied her back, and, in spite of the continued resistance of the proprietor, they made their way to the room in which Mr St Clair had last been seen. There was no sign of him there. In fact, in the whole of that floor there was no one to be found, save a crippled wretch of hideous aspect, who, it seems, made his home there. Both he and the Lascar stoutly swore that no one else had been in the front room during that afternoon. So determined was their denial that the inspector was staggered, and had almost come to believe that Mrs St Clair had been deluded when, with a cry, she sprang at a small deal box which lay upon the table, and tore the lid from it. Out there fell a cascade of children's bricks. It was the toy which he had promised to bring home.

'This discovery, and the evident confusion which the cripple showed, made the inspector realize that the matter was serious. The rooms were carefully examined, and results all pointed to an abominable crime. The front room was plainly furnished as a sitting-room, and led into a small bedroom, which looked out upon the back of one of the wharves. Between the wharf and the bedroom window is a narrow strip, which is dry at low tide, but is covered at high tide with at least four and a half feet of water. The bedroom window was a broad one, and opened from below. On examination traces of blood were to be seen upon the window-sill, and several scattered drops were visible upon the wooden floor of the bedroom. Thrust away behind a curtain in the front room were all the clothes of Mr Neville St Clair, with the exception of his coat. His boots, his socks, his hat, and his watch – all were there. There were no signs of violence upon any of these garments, and there were no other traces of Mr Neville St Clair. Out of the window he must apparently have gone, for no other exit could be discovered, and the ominous bloodstains upon the sill gave little promise that he could save himself by swimming, for the tide was at its very highest at the moment of the tragedy.

'And now as to the villains who seemed to be immediately implicated in the matter. The Lascar was known to be a man of the vilest antecedents, but as by Mrs St Clair's story he was known to have been at the foot of the stair within a few seconds of her husband's appearance at the window, he could hardly have been more than an accessory to the crime. His defence was one of absolute ignorance, and he protested that he had no knowledge as to the doings of Hugh Boone, his lodger, and that he could not account in any way for the presence of the missing gentleman's clothes.

'So much for the Lascar manager. Now for the sinister cripple who lives upon the second floor of the opium den, and who was certainly the last human being whose eyes rested upon Neville St Clair. His name is Hugh Boone, and his hideous face is one which is familiar to every man who goes much to the City. He is a professional beggar, though in order to avoid the police regulations he pretends to a small trade in wax vestas. Some little distance down Threadneedle Street upon the left-hand side there is, as you may have remarked, a small angle in the wall. Here it is that the creature takes his daily seat, cross-legged, with his tiny stock of matches on his lap, and as he is a piteous spectacle a small rain of charity descends into the greasy leather cap which lies upon the pavement before him. I have watched this fellow more than once, before ever I thought of making his professional acquaintance, and I have been surprised at the harvest which he has reaped in so short a time. His appearance, you see, is so remarkable that no one can pass him without observing him. A shock of orange hair, a pale face disfigured by a horrible scar, which, by its contraction, has turned up the outer edge of his upper lip, a bull-dog chin, and a pair of very penetrating dark eyes, which present a singular contrast to the colour of his hair, all mark him out from amid the common crowd of mendicants, and so, too, does his wit, for he is ever ready with a reply to any piece of chaff which may be thrown at him by the passers-by. This is the man whom we now learn to have been the lodger at the opium den, and to have been the last man to see the gentleman of whom we are in quest.'

'But a cripple!' said I. 'What could he have done single-handed against a man in the prime of life?'

'He is a cripple in the sense that he walks with a limp; but, in other respects, he appears to be a powerful and well-nurtured man. Surely your medical experience would tell you, Watson, that weakness in one limb is often compensated for by exceptional strength in the others.'

'Pray continue your narrative.'

'Mrs St Clair had fainted at the sight of the blood upon the window, and she was escorted home in a cab by the police, as her presence could be of no help to them in their investigations. Inspector Barton, who had charge of the case, made a very careful examination of the premises, but without finding anything which threw any light upon the matter. One mistake had been made in not arresting Boone instantly, as he was allowed some few minutes during which he might have communicated with his friend the Lascar, but this fault was soon remedied, and he was seized and searched, without anything being found which could incriminate him. There were, it is true, some bloodstains upon his right shirt-sleeve, but he pointed to his ring finger, which had been cut near the nail, and explained that the bleeding came from there, adding that he had been to the window not long before, and that the stains which had been observed there came doubtless from the same source. He denied strenuously having ever seen Mr Neville St Clair, and swore that the presence of the clothes in his room was as much a mystery to him as to the police. As to Mrs St Clair's assertion, that she had actually seen her husband at the window, he declared that she must have been either mad or dreaming. He was removed, loudly protesting, to the police-station, while the inspector remained upon the premises in the hope that the ebbing tide might afford some fresh clue.

'And it did, though they hardly found upon the mudbank what they had feared to find. It was Neville St Clair's coat, and not Neville St Clair, which lay uncovered as the tide receded. And what do you think they found in the pockets?'

'I cannot imagine.'

'No, I don't think you will guess. Every pocket stuffed with pennies and halfpennies – four hundred and twenty-one pennies, and two hundred and seventy halfpennies. It was no wonder that it had not been swept away by the tide. But a human body is a different matter. There is a fierce eddy between the wharf and the house. It seemed likely enough that the weighted coat had remained when the stripped body had been sucked away into the river.'

'But I understand that all the other clothes were found in the room. Would the body be dressed in a coat alone?'

'No, sir, but the facts might be met speciously enough. Suppose that this man Boone had thrust Neville St Clair through the window, there is no human eye which could have seen the deed. What would he do then? It would of course instantly strike him that he must get rid of the tell-tale garments. He would seize the coat then, and be in the act of throwing it out when it would occur to him that it would swim and not sink. He has little time, for he has heard the scuffle downstairs when the wife tried to force her way up, and perhaps he has already heard from his Lascar confederate that the police are hurrying up the street. There is not an instant to be lost. He rushes to some secret hoard, where he has accumulated the fruits of his beggary, and he stuffs all the coins upon which he can lay his hands into the pockets to make sure of the coat's sinking. He throws it out, and would have done the same with the other garments had not he heard the rush of steps below, and only just had time to close the window when the police appeared.'

'It certainly sounds feasible.'

'Well, we will take it as a working hypothesis for want of a better. Boone, as I have told you, was arrested and taken to the station, but it could not be shown that there had ever before been anything against him. He had for years been known as a professional beggar, but his life appeared to have been a very quiet and innocent one. There the matter stands at present, and the questions which have to be solved, what Neville St Clair was doing in the opium den, what happened to him when there, where he is now, and what Hugh Boone had to do with his disappearance, are all as far from solution as ever. I confess that I cannot recall any case within my experience which looked at the first glance so simple, and yet which presented such difficulties.'

Whilst Sherlock Holmes had been detailing this singular series of events we had been whirling through the outskirts of the great town until the last straggling houses had been left behind, and we rattled along with a country hedge upon either side of us. Just as he finished, however, we drove through two scattered villages, where a few lights still glimmered in the windows.

'We are on the outskirts of Lee,' said my companion. 'We have touched on three English counties in our short drive, starting in Middlesex, passing over an angle of Surrey, and ending in Kent. See that light among the trees? That is the Cedars, and beside that lamp sits a woman whose anxious ears have already, I have little doubt, caught the clink of our horse's feet.'

'But why are you not conducting the case from Baker Street?' I asked.

'Because there are many inquiries which must be made out here. Mrs St Clair has most kindly put two rooms at my disposal, and you may rest assured that she will have nothing but a welcome for my friend and colleague. I hate to meet her, Watson, when I have no news of her husband. Here we are. Whoa, there, whoa!'

We had pulled up in front of a large villa which stood within its own grounds. A stable-boy had run out to the horse's head, and, springing down, I followed Holmes up the small, winding gravel drive which led to the house. As we approached, the door flew open, and a little blonde woman stood in the opening, clad in some sort of light *mousseline-de-soie*, with a touch of fluffy pink chiffon at her neck and wrists. She stood with her figure outlined against the flood of light, one hand upon the door, one half raised in eagerness, her body slightly bent, her head and face protruded, with eager eyes and parted lips, a standing question.

'Well?' she cried, 'well?' And then, seeing that there were two of us, she gave a cry of hope which sank into a groan as she saw that my companion shook his head and shrugged his shoulders.

'No good news?'

'None.'

'No bad?'

'No.'

'Thank God for that. But come in. You must be weary, for you have had a long day.'

'This is my friend, Dr Watson. He has been of most vital use to me in several of my cases, and a lucky chance has made it possible for me to bring him out and associate him with this investigation.'

'I am delighted to see you,' said she, pressing my hand warmly. 'You will, I am sure, forgive anything which may be wanting in our arrangements, when you consider the blow which has come so suddenly upon us.'

'My dear madam,' said I, 'I am an old campaigner, and if I were not, I can very well see that no apology is needed. If I can be of any assistance, either to you or to my friend here, I shall be indeed happy.'

'Now, Mr Sherlock Holmes,' said the lady as we entered a well-lit dining-room, upon the table of which a cold supper had been laid out, 'I should very much like to ask you one or two plain questions, to which I beg that you will give a plain answer.'

'Certainly, madam.'

'Do not trouble about my feelings. I am not hysterical, nor given to fainting. I simply wish to hear your real, real opinion.'

'Upon what point?'

'In your heart of hearts, do you think that Neville is alive?'

Sherlock Holmes seemed to be embarrassed by the question. 'Frankly now!' she repeated, standing upon the rug, and looking keenly down at him, as he leaned back in a basket chair.

'Frankly, then, madam, I do not.'

'You think that he is dead?'

'I do.'

'Murdered?'

'I don't say that. Perhaps.'

'And on what day did he meet his death?'

'On Monday.'

'Then perhaps, Mr Holmes, you will be good enough to explain how it is that I have received this letter from him today?'

Sherlock Holmes sprang out of his chair as if he had been galvanized.

'What!' he roared.

'Yes, today.' She stood smiling, holding up a little slip of paper in the air.

'May I see it?'

'Certainly.'

He snatched it from her in his eagerness, and smoothing it out upon the table, he drew over the lamp, and examined it intently. I

'"FRANKLY, NOW!" SHE REPEATED.'

had left my chair, and was gazing at it over his shoulder. The envelope was a very coarse one, and was stamped with the Gravesend postmark, and with the date of that very day, or rather of the day before, for it was considerably after midnight.

'Coarse writing!' murmured Holmes. 'Surely this is not your husband's writing, madam.'

'No, but the enclosure is.'

'I perceive also that whoever addressed the envelope had to go and inquire as to the address.'

'How can you tell that?'

'The name, you see, is in perfectly black ink, which has dried itself. The rest is of the greyish colour which shows that blotting-paper has been used. If it had been written straight off, and then blotted, none would be of a deep black shade. This man has written the name, and there has then been a pause before he wrote the address, which can only mean that he was not familiar with it. It is, of course, a trifle, but there is nothing so important as trifles. Let us now see the letter! Ha! there has been an enclosure here!'

'Yes, there was a ring. His signet ring.'

'And you are sure that this is your husband's hand?'

'One of his hands.'

'One?'

'His hand when he wrote hurriedly. It is very unlike his usual writing, and yet I know it well.'

'"Dearest, do not be frightened. All will come well. There is a huge error which it may take some little time to rectify. Wait in patience. – Neville." Written in pencil upon a flyleaf of a book, octavo size, no watermark. Posted today in Gravesend by a man with a dirty thumb. Ha! And the flap has been gummed, if I am not very much in error, by a person who has been chewing tobacco. And you have no doubt that it is your husband's hand, madam?'

'None. Neville wrote those words.'

'And they were posted today at Gravesend. Well, Mrs St Clair, the clouds lighten, though I should not venture to say that the danger is over.'

'But he must be alive, Mr Holmes.'

'Unless this is a clever forgery to put us on the wrong scent. The ring, after all, proves nothing. It may have been taken from him.'

'No, no; it is, it is, it is his very own writing!'

'Very well. It may, however, have been written on Monday, and only posted today.'

'That is possible.'

'If so, much may have happened between.'

'Oh, you must not discourage me, Mr Holmes. I know that all is well with him. There is so keen a sympathy between us that I should know if evil came upon him. On the very day that I saw him last he cut himself in the bedroom, and yet I in the dining-room rushed upstairs instantly with the utmost certainty that something had happened. Do you think that I would respond to such a trifle, and yet be ignorant of his death?'

'I have seen too much not to know that the impression of a woman may be more valuable than the conclusion of an analytical reasoner. And in this letter you certainly have a very strong piece of evidence to corroborate your view. But if your husband is alive and able to write letters, why should he remain away from you?'

'I cannot imagine. It is unthinkable.'

'And on Monday he made no remarks before leaving you?'

'No.'

'And you were surprised to see him in Swandam Lane?'

'Very much so.'

'Was the window open?'

'Yes.'

'Then he might have called to you?'

'He might.'

'He only, as I understand, gave an inarticulate cry?'

'Yes.'

'A call for help, you thought?'

'Yes. He waved his hands.'

'But it might have been a cry of surprise. Astonishment at the unexpected sight of you might cause him to throw up his hands.'

'It is possible.'

'And you thought he was pulled back?'

'He disappeared so suddenly.'

'He might have leaped back. You did not see anyone else in the room?'

'No, but this horrible man confessed to having been there, and the Lascar was at the foot of the stairs.'

'Quite so. Your husband, as far as you could see, had his ordinary clothes on?'

'But without his collar or tie. I distinctly saw his bare throat.'

'Had he ever spoken of Swandam Lane?'

'Never.'

'Had he ever shown any signs of having taken opium?'

'Never.'

'Thank you, Mrs St Clair. Those are the principal points about which I wished to be absolutely clear. We shall now have a little supper and then retire, for we may have a very busy day tomorrow.'

A large and comfortable double-bedded room had been placed at our disposal, and I was quickly between the sheets, for I was weary after my night of adventure. Sherlock Holmes was a man, however, who when he had an unsolved problem upon his mind would go for days, and even for a week, without rest, turning it over, rearranging his facts, looking at it from every point of view, until he had either fathomed it, or convinced himself that his data were insufficient. It was soon evident to me that he was now preparing for an all-night sitting. He took off his coat and waistcoat, put on a large blue dressing-gown, and then wandered about the room collecting pillows from his bed, and cushions from the sofa and armchairs. With these he constructed a sort of Eastern divan, upon which he perched himself cross-legged, with an ounce of shag tobacco and a box of matches laid out in front of him. In the dim light of the lamp I saw him sitting there, an old brier pipe between his lips, his eyes fixed vacantly upon the corner of the ceiling, the blue smoke curling up from him, silent, motionless, with the light shining upon his strong-set aquiline features. So he sat as I dropped off to sleep, and so he sat when a sudden ejaculation caused me to wake up, and I found the summer sun shining into the apartment. The pipe was still between his lips, the smoke still curled upwards, and the room was full of a dense tobacco haze, but nothing remained of the heap of shag which I had seen upon the previous night.

'Awake, Watson?' he asked.

'Yes.'

'Game for a morning drive?'

'Certainly.'

'Then dress. No one is stirring yet, but I know where the stable-boy sleeps, and we shall soon have the trap out.' He chuckled to himself as he spoke, his eyes twinkled, and he seemed a different man to the sombre thinker of the previous night.

As I dressed I glanced at my watch. It was no wonder that no one was stirring. It was twenty-five minutes past four. I had hardly finished when Holmes returned with the news that the boy was putting in the horse.

'I want to test a little theory of mine,' said he, pulling on his boots. 'I think, Watson, that you are now standing in the presence of one of the most absolute fools in Europe. I deserve to be kicked from here to Charing Cross. But I think I have the key of the affair now.'

'And where is it?' I asked, smiling.

'In the bathroom,' he answered. 'Oh, yes, I am not joking,' he continued, seeing my look of incredulity. 'I have just been there, and I have taken it out, and I have got it in this Gladstone bag. Come on, my boy, and we shall see whether it will not fit the lock.'

We made our way downstairs as quietly as possible; and out into the bright morning sunshine. In the road stood our horse and trap, with the half-clad stable-boy waiting at the head. We both sprang in, and away we dashed down the London road. A few country carts were stirring, bearing in vegetables to the metropolis, but the lines of villas on either side were as silent and lifeless as some city in a dream.

'It has been in some points a singular case,' said Holmes, flicking the horse on into a gallop. 'I confess that I have been as blind as a mole, but it is better to learn wisdom late, than never to learn it at all.'

In town, the earliest risers were just beginning to look sleepily from their windows as we drove through the streets of the Surrey side. Passing down the Waterloo Bridge Road we crossed over the river, and dashing up Wellington Street wheeled sharply to the right, and found ourselves in Bow Street. Sherlock Holmes was well known to the force, and the two constables at the door saluted him. One of them held the horse's head while the other led us in.

'Who is on duty?' asked Holmes.

'Inspector Bradstreet, sir.'

'Ah, Bradstreet, how are you?' A tall, stout official had come down the stone-flagged passage, in a peaked cap and frogged jacket. 'I wish to have a word with you, Bradstreet.'

'Certainly, Mr Holmes. Step into my room here.'

It was a small office-like room, with a huge ledger upon the table, and a telephone projecting from the wall. The inspector sat down at his desk.

'What can I do for you, Mr Holmes?'

'I called about that beggar-man, Boone – the one who was charged with being concerned in the disappearance of Mr Neville St Clair, of Lee.'

'Yes. He was brought up and remanded for further inquiries.'

'So I heard. You have him here?'

'In the cells.'

'Is he quiet?'

'Oh, he gives no trouble. But he is a dirty scoundrel.'

'Dirty?'

'Yes, it is all we can do to make him wash his hands, and his face is as black as a tinker's. Well, when once his case has been settled he will have a regular prison bath; and I think, if you saw him you would agree with me that he needed it.'

'I should like to see him very much.'

'Would you? That is easily done. Come this way. You can leave your bag.'

'No, I think I'll take it.'

'Very good. Come this way, if you please.' He led us down a

passage, opened a barred door, passed down a winding stair, and brought us to a whitewashed corridor with a line of doors on each side.

'The third on the right is his,' said the inspector. 'Here it is!' He quietly shot back a panel in the upper part of the door, and glanced through.

'He is asleep,' said he. 'You can see him very well.'

We both put our eyes to the grating. The prisoner lay with his face towards us, in a very deep sleep, breathing slowly and heavily. He was a middle-sized man, coarsely clad as became his calling, with a coloured shirt protruding through the rent in his tattered coat. He was, as the inspector had said, extremely dirty, but the grime which covered his face could not conceal its repulsive ugliness. A broad weal from an old scar ran across it from eye to chin, and by its contraction had turned up one side of the upper lip, so that three teeth were exposed in a perpetual snarl. A shock of very bright red hair grew low over his eyes and forehead.

'He's a beauty, isn't he?' said the inspector.

'He certainly needs a wash,' remarked Holmes. 'I had an idea that he might, and I took the liberty of bringing the tools with me.' He opened his Gladstone bag as he spoke, and took out, to my astonishment, a very large bath sponge.

'He! he! You are a funny one,' chuckled the inspector.

'Now, if you will have the great goodness to open that door very quietly, we will soon make him cut a much more respectable figure.'

'Well, I don't know why not,' said the inspector. 'He doesn't look a credit to the Bow Street cells, does he?' He slipped his key into the lock, and we all very quietly entered the cell. The sleeper half turned, and then settled down once more into a deep slumber. Holmes stooped to the water jug, moistened his sponge, and then rubbed it twice vigorously across and down the prisoner's face.

'Let me introduce you,' he shouted, 'to Mr Neville St Clair, of Lee, in the county of Kent.'

Never in my life have I seen such a sight. The man's face peeled off under the sponge like the bark from a tree. Gone was the coarse brown tint! Gone, too, the horrid scar which had seamed it across, and the twisted lip which had given the repulsive sneer to the face! A twitch brought away the tangled red hair, and there, sitting up in his bed, was a pale, sad-faced, refined-looking man, black-haired and smooth-skinned, rubbing his eyes, and staring about him with sleepy bewilderment. Then suddenly realizing the exposure, he broke into a scream, and threw himself down with his face to the pillow.

'Great heaven!' cried the inspector, 'it is, indeed, the missing man. I know him from the photograph.'

The prisoner turned with the reckless air of a man who abandons himself to his destiny. 'Be it so,' said he. 'And pray what am I charged with?'

'With making away with Mr Neville St – Oh, come, you can't

'HE BROKE INTO A SCREAM.'

be charged with that, unless they make a case of attempted suicide of it,' said the inspector, with a grin. 'Well, I have been twenty-seven years in the Force, but this really takes the cake.'

'If I am Mr Neville St Clair, then it is obvious that no crime has been committed, and that, therefore, I am illegally detained.'

'No crime, but a very great error has been committed,' said Holmes. 'You would have done better to have trusted your wife.'

'It was not the wife, it was the children,' groaned the prisoner. 'God help me, I would not have them ashamed of their father. My God! What an exposure! What can I do?'

Sherlock Holmes sat down beside him on the couch, and patted him kindly on the shoulder.

'If you leave it to a court of law to clear the matter up,' said he, 'of course you can hardly avoid publicity. On the other hand, if you convince the police authorities that there is no possible case against you, I do not know that there is any reason that the details should find their way into the papers. Inspector Bradstreet would, I am sure, make notes upon anything which you might tell us, and submit it to the proper authorities. The case would then never go into court at all.'

'God bless you!' cried the prisoner passionately. 'I would have endured imprisonment, aye, even execution, rather than have left my miserable secret as a family blot to my children.

'You are the first who have ever heard my story. My father was a schoolmaster in Chesterfield, where I received an excellent education. I travelled in my youth, took to the stage, and finally became a reporter on an evening paper in London. One day my editor wished to have a series of articles upon begging in the metropolis, and I volunteered to supply them. There was the point from which all my adventures started. It was only by trying begging as an amateur that I could get the facts upon which to base my articles. When an actor I had, of course, learned all the secrets of making up, and had been famous in the green-room for my skill. I took advantage now of my attainments. I painted my face, and to make myself as pitiable as possible I made a good scar and fixed one side of my lip in a twist by the aid of a small slip of flesh-coloured plaster. Then with a red head of hair, and an appropriate dress, I took my station in the busiest part of the City, ostensibly as a match-seller, but really as a beggar. For seven hours I plied my trade, and when I returned home in the evening I found, to my surprise, that I had received no less than twenty-six shillings and fourpence.

'I wrote my articles, and thought little more of the matter until, some time later, I backed a bill for a friend, and had a writ served upon me for £25. I was at my wits' end where to get the money, but a sudden idea came to me. I begged a fortnight's grace from the creditor, asked for a holiday from my employers, and spent the time in begging in the City under my disguise. In ten days I had the money, and had paid the debt.

'Well, you can imagine how hard it was to settle down to arduous work at two pounds a week, when I knew that I could earn as much in a day by smearing my face with a little paint, laying my cap on the ground, and sitting still. It was a long fight between my pride and the money, but the dollars won at last, and I threw up reporting, and sat day after day in the corner which I had chosen, inspiring pity by my ghastly face and filling my pockets with coppers. Only one man knew my secret. He was the keeper of a low den in which I used to lodge in Swandam Lane, where I could every morning emerge as a squalid beggar and in the evening transform myself into a well-dressed man about town. This fellow, a Lascar, was well paid by me for his rooms, so that I knew that my secret was safe in his possession.

'Well, very soon I found that I was saving considerable sums of money. I do not mean that any beggar in the streets of London could earn seven hundred pounds a year – which is less than my average takings – but I had exceptional advantages in my power of making up, and also in a facility in repartee, which improved by practice, and made me quite a recognized character in the City. All day a stream of pennies, varied by silver, poured in upon me, and it was a very bad day upon which I failed to take two pounds.

'As I grew richer I grew more ambitious, took a house in the country, and eventually married, without anyone having a suspicion as to my real occupation. My dear wife knew that I had business in the City. She little knew what.

'Last Monday I had finished for the day, and was dressing in my room above the opium den, when I looked out of the window, and saw, to my horror and astonishment, that my wife was standing in the street, with her eyes fixed full upon me. I gave a cry of surprise, threw up my arms to cover my face, and rushing to my confidant, the Lascar, entreated him to prevent anyone from coming up to me. I heard her voice downstairs, but I knew that she could not ascend. Swiftly I threw off my clothes, pulled on those of a beggar, and put on my pigments and wig. Even a wife's eyes could not pierce so complete a disguise. But then it occurred to me that there might be a search in the room and that the clothes might betray me. I threw open the window, reopening by my violence a small cut which I had inflicted upon myself in the bedroom that morning. Then I seized my coat, which was weighted by the coppers which I had just transferred to it from the leather bag in which I carried my takings. I hurled it out of the window, and it disappeared into the Thames. The other clothes would have followed, but at that moment there was a rush of constables up the stairs, and a few minutes after I found, rather, I confess, to my relief, that instead of being identified as Mr Neville St Clair, I was arrested as his murderer.

'I do not know that there is anything else for me to explain. I was determined to preserve my disguise as long as possible, and hence my preference for a dirty face. Knowing that my wife would be terribly anxious, I slipped off my ring, and confided it to the Lascar at a moment when no constable was watching me, together with a hurried scrawl, telling her that she had no cause to fear.'

'That note only reached her yesterday,' said Holmes.

'Good God! What a week she must have spent.'

'The police have watched this Lascar,' said Inspector Bradstreet, 'and I can quite understand that he might find it difficult to post a letter unobserved. Probably he handed it to some sailor customer of his, who forgot all about it for some days.'

'That was it,' said Holmes, nodding approvingly, 'I have no doubt of it. But have you never been prosecuted for begging?'

'Many times; but what was a fine to me?'

'It must stop here, however,' said Bradstreet. 'If the police are to hush this thing up, there must be no more of Hugh Boone.'

'I have sworn it by the most solemn oaths which a man can take.'

'In that case I think that it is probable that no further steps may be taken. But if you are found again, then all must come out. I am sure, Mr Holmes, that we are very much indebted to you for having cleared the matter up. I wish I knew how you reach your results.'

'I reached this one,' said my friend, 'by sitting upon five pillows and consuming an ounce of shag. I think, Watson, that if we drive to Baker Street we shall just be in time for breakfast.'

The Adventure of the Yellow Face

In publishing these short sketches, based upon the numerous cases which my companion's singular gifts have made me the listener to, and eventually the actor in, some strange drama, it is only natural that I should dwell rather upon his successes than upon his failures. And this is not so much for the sake of his reputation, for indeed it was when he was at his wits' end that his energy and his versatility were most admirable, but because where he failed it happened too often that no one else succeeded, and that the tale was left for ever without a conclusion. Now and again, however, it chanced that even when he erred the truth was still discovered. I have notes of some half-dozen cases of the kind, of which the affair of the second stain, and that which I am now about to recount, are the two which present the strongest features of interest.

Sherlock Holmes was a man who seldom took exercise for exercise's sake. Few men were capable of greater muscular effort, and he was undoubtedly one of the finest boxers of his weight that I have ever seen; but he looked upon aimless bodily exertion as a waste of energy, and he seldom bestirred himself save where there was some professional object to be served. Then he was absolutely untiring and indefatigable. That he should have kept himself in training under such circumstances is remarkable, but his diet was usually of the sparest, and his habits were simple to the verge of austerity. Save for the occasional use of cocaine he had no vices, and he only turned to the drug as a protest against the monotony of existence when cases were scanty and the papers uninteresting.

One day in early spring he had so far relaxed as to go for a walk with me in the Park, where the first faint shoots of green were breaking out upon the elms, and the sticky spearheads of the chestnuts were just beginning to burst into their fivefold leaves. For two hours we rambled about together, in silence for the most part, as befits two men who know each other intimately. It was nearly five before we were back in Baker Street once more.

'Beg pardon, sir,' said our page-boy, as he opened the door; 'there's been a gentleman here asking for you, sir.'

Holmes glanced reproachfully at me. 'So much for afternoon walks!' said he. 'Has this gentleman gone, then?'

'Yes, sir.'

'Didn't you ask him in?'

'Yes, sir; he came in.'

'How long did he wait?'

'Half an hour, sir. He was a very restless gentleman, sir, a-walkin' and a-stampin' all the time he was here. I was waitin' outside the door, sir, and I could hear him. At last he goes out into the passage and he cries: "Is that man never goin' to come?" Those were his very words, sir. "You'll only need to wait a little longer," says I. "Then I'll wait in the open air, for I feel half choked," says he. "I'll be back before long," and with that he ups and he outs, and all I could say wouldn't hold him back.'

'Well, well, you did your best,' said Holmes, as we walked into our room. 'It's very annoying though, Watson. I was badly in need of a case, and this looks, from the man's impatience, as if it were of importance. Halloa! that's not your pipe on the table! He must have left his behind him. A nice old briar, with a good long stem of what the tobacconists call amber. I wonder how many real amber mouthpieces there are in London. Some people think a fly in it is a sign. Why, it is quite a branch of trade, the putting of sham flies into the sham amber. Well, he must have been disturbed in his mind to leave a pipe behind him which he evidently values highly.'

'How do you know that he values it highly?' I asked.

'Well, I should put the original cost of the pipe at seven-and-sixpence. Now it has, you see, been twice mended: once in the wooden stem and once in the amber. Each of these mends, done, as you observe, with silver bands, must have cost more than the pipe did originally. The man must value the pipe highly when he prefers to patch it up rather than buy a new one with the same money.'

'Anything else?' I asked, for Holmes was turning the pipe about in his hand and staring at it in his peculiar, pensive way.

He held it up and tapped on it with his long, thin forefinger as a professor might who was lecturing on a bone.

'Pipes are occasionally of extraordinary interest,' said he. 'Nothing has more individuality save, perhaps, watches and bootlaces. The indications here, however, are neither very marked nor very important. The owner is obviously a muscular man, left-handed, with an excellent set of teeth, careless in his habits, and with no need to practise economy.'

My friend threw out the information in a very off-hand way, but I saw that he cocked his eye at me to see if I had followed his reasoning.

'You think a man must be well-to-do if he smokes a seven-shilling pipe?' said I.

'This is Grosvenor mixture at eightpence an ounce,' Holmes answered, knocking a little out on his palm. 'As he might get an excellent smoke for half the price, he has no need to practise economy.'

'And the other points?'

'He has been in the habit of lighting his pipe at lamps and gas-jets. You can see that it is quite charred all down one side. Of course, a match could not have done that. Why should a man hold a match to the side of his pipe? But you cannot light it at a lamp without getting the bowl charred. And it is on the right side of the pipe. From that I gather that he is a left-handed man. You hold your own pipe to the lamp, and see how naturally you, being right-handed, hold the left side to the flame. You might do it once the other way, but not as a constancy. This has always been held so. Then he has bitten through his amber. It takes a muscular, energetic fellow, and one with a good set of teeth to do that. But if I am not mistaken I hear him upon the stair, so we shall have something more interesting than his pipe to study.'

An instant later our door opened, and a tall young man entered the room. He was well but quietly dressed in a dark-grey suit, and carried a brown wide-awake in his hand. I should have put him at about thirty, though he was really some years older.

'I beg your pardon,' said he, with some embarrassment; 'I suppose I should have knocked. Yes, of course I should have knocked. The fact is that I am a little upset, and you must put it all down to that.' He passed his hand over his forehead like a man who is half dazed, and then fell, rather than sat, down upon a chair.

'I can see that you have not slept for a night or two,' said Holmes, in his easy, genial way. 'That tries a man's nerves more than work, and more even than pleasure. May I ask how I can help you?'

'I wanted your advice, sir. I don't know what to do, and my whole life seems to have gone to pieces.'

'You wish to employ me as a consulting detective?'

'Not that only. I want your opinion as a judicious man – as a man of the world. I want to know what I ought to do next. I hope to God you'll be able to tell me.'

He spoke in little, sharp, jerky outbursts, and it seemed to me that to speak at all was very painful to him, and that his will all through was overriding his inclinations.

'It's a very delicate thing,' said he. 'One does not like to speak of one's domestic affairs to strangers. It seems dreadful to discuss the conduct of one's wife with two men whom I have never seen before. It's horrible to have to do it. But I've got to the end of my tether, and I must have advice.'

'My dear Mr Grant Munro –' began Holmes.

'OUR VISITOR SPRANG FROM HIS CHAIR.'

Our visitor sprang from his chair. 'What!' he cried. 'You know my name?'

'If you wish to preserve your *incognito*,' said Holmes, smiling, 'I should suggest that you cease to write your name upon the lining of your hat, or else that you turn the crown towards the person whom you are addressing. I was about to say that my friend and I have listened to many strange secrets in this room, and that we have had the good fortune to bring peace to many troubled souls. I trust that we may do as much for you. Might I beg you, as time may prove to be of importance, to furnish me with the facts of your case without further delay?'

Our visitor again passed his hand over his forehead as if he found it bitterly hard. From every gesture and expression I could see that he was a reserved, self-contained man, with a dash of pride in his nature, more likely to hide his wounds than to expose them. Then suddenly, with a fierce gesture of his closed hand, like one who throws reserve to the winds, he began.

'The facts are these, Mr Holmes,' said he. 'I am a married man, and have been so for three years. During that time my wife and I have loved each other as fondly, and lived as happily, as any two that ever were joined. We have not had a difference, not one, in thought, or word, or deed. And now, since last Monday, there has suddenly sprung up a barrier between us, and I find that there is something in her life and in her thoughts of which I know as little as if she were the woman who brushes by me in the street. We are estranged, and I want to know why.

'Now there is one thing I want to impress upon you before I go any further, Mr Holmes: Effie loves me. Don't let there be any mistake about that. She loves me with her whole heart and soul, and never more than now. I know it, I feel it. I don't want to argue about that. A man can tell easily enough when a woman loves him. But there's this secret between us, and we can never be the same until it is cleared.'

'Kindly let me have the facts, Mr Munro,' said Holmes, with some impatience.

'I'll tell you what I know about Effie's history. She was a widow when I first met her, though quite young – only twenty-five. Her name then was Mrs Hebron. She went out to America when she was young and lived in the town of Atlanta, where she married this Hebron, who was a lawyer with a good practice. They had one child, but the yellow fever broke out badly in the place, and both husband and child died of it. I have seen his death certificate. This sickened her of America, and she came back to live with a maiden aunt at Pinner, in Middlesex. I may mention that her husband had left her comfortably off, and that she had a capital of about four thousand five hundred pounds, which had been so well invested by him that it returned an average of 7 per cent. She had only been six months at Pinner when I met her; we fell in love with each other, and we married a few weeks afterwards.

'I am a hop merchant myself, and as I have an income of seven or eight hundred, we found ourselves comfortably off, and took a nice eighty-pound-a-year villa at Norbury. Our little place was very countrified, considering that it is so close to town. We had an inn and two houses a little above us, and a single cottage at the other side of the field which faces us, and except those there were no houses until you get half-way to the station. My business took me into town at certain seasons, but in summer I had less to do, and then in our country home my wife and I were just as happy as could be wished. I tell you that there never was a shadow between us until this accursed affair began.

'There's one thing I ought to tell you before I go further. When we married, my wife made over all her property to me – rather against my will, for I saw how awkward it would be if my business affairs went wrong. However, she would have it so, and it was done. Well, about six weeks ago she came to me.

' "Jack," said she, "when you took my money you said that if ever I wanted any I was to ask you for it."

' "Certainly," said I, "it's all your own."

' "Well," said she, "I want a hundred pounds."

'I was a bit staggered at this, for I had imagined it was simply a new dress or something of the kind that she was after.

' "What on earth for?" I asked.

' "Oh," said she, in her playful way, "you said that you were only my banker, and bankers never ask questions, you know."

' "If you really mean it, of course you shall have the money," said I.

' "Oh, yes, I really mean it."

' "And you won't tell me what you want it for?"

' "Some day, perhaps, but not just at present, Jack."

'So I had to be content with that, though it was the first time that there had ever been any secret between us. I gave her a cheque, and I never thought any more of the matter. It may have nothing to do with what came afterwards, but I thought it only right to mention it.

'Well, I told you just now that there is a cottage not far from our house. There is just a field between us, but to reach it you have to go along the road and then turn down a lane. Just beyond it is a nice little grove of Scotch firs, and I used to be very fond of strolling down there, for trees are always neighbourly kinds of things. The cottage had been standing empty this eight months, and it was a pity, for it was a pretty two-storeyed place, with an old-fashioned porch and honeysuckle about it. I have stood many a time and thought what a neat little homestead it would make.

'Well, last Monday evening I was taking a stroll down that way, when I met an empty van coming up the lane, and saw a pile of carpets and things lying about on the grass-plot beside the porch. It was clear that the cottage had at last been let. I walked past it, and then stopping, as an idle man might, I ran my eye over it, and wondered what sort of folk they were who had come to live so near us. And as I looked I suddenly became aware that a face was watching me out of one of the upper windows.

'I don't know what there was about that face, Mr Holmes, but it seemed to send a chill right down my back. I was some little way off, so that I could not make out the features, but there was something unnatural and inhuman about the face. That was the impression I had, and I moved quickly forwards to get a nearer view of the person who was watching me. But as I did so the face suddenly disappeared, so suddenly that it seemed to have been plucked away into the darkness of the room. I stood for five minutes thinking the business over, and trying to analyse my impressions. I could not tell if the face was that of a man or a woman. But the colour was what impressed me most. It was of a livid dead yellow, and with something set and rigid about it, which was shockingly unnatural. So disturbed was I, that I determined to see a little more of the new inmates of the cottage. I approached and knocked at the door, which was instantly opened by a tall, gaunt woman, with a harsh, forbidding face.

'"What may you be wantin'?" she asked, in a northern accent.

'"I am your neighbour over yonder," said I, nodding towards my house. "I see that you have only just moved in, so I thought that if I could be of any help to you in any –"

'"Aye, we'll just ask ye when we want ye," said she, and shut the door in my face. Annoyed at the churlish rebuff, I turned my back and walked home. All the evening, though I tried to think of other things, my mind would still turn to the apparition at the window and the rudeness of the woman. I determined to say nothing about the former to my wife, for she is a nervous, highly-strung woman, and I had no wish that she should share the unpleasant impression which had been produced upon myself. I remarked to her, however, before I fell asleep that the cottage was now occupied, to which she returned no reply.

'I am usually an extremely sound sleeper. It has been a standing jest in the family that nothing could ever wake me during the night; and yet somehow on that particular night, whether it may have been the slight excitement produced by my little adventure or not, I know not, but I slept much more lightly than usual. Half in my dreams I was dimly conscious that something was going on in the room, and gradually became aware that my wife had dressed herself and was slipping on her mantle and her bonnet. My lips were parted to murmur out some sleepy words of surprise or remonstrance at this untimely preparation, when suddenly my half-opened eyes fell upon her face, illuminated by the candle light, and astonishment held me dumb. She wore an expression such as I had never seen before – such as I should have thought her incapable of assuming. She was deadly pale, and breathing fast, glancing furtively towards the bed, as she fastened her mantle, to see if she had disturbed me. Then, thinking that I was still asleep, she slipped noiselessly from the room, and an instant later I heard a sharp creaking, which could only come from the hinges of the front door. I sat up in bed and rapped my knuckles against the rail to make certain that I was truly awake. Then I took my watch from under the pillow. It was three in the morning. What on earth could my wife be doing out on the country road at three in the morning?

'I had sat for about twenty minutes turning the thing over in my mind and trying to find some possible explanation. The more I thought, the more extraordinary and inexplicable did it appear. I was still puzzling over it when I heard the door gently close again and her footsteps coming up the stairs.

' "Where in the world have you been, Effie?" I asked, as she entered.

'She gave a violent start and a kind of gasping cry when I spoke, and that cry and start troubled me more than all the rest, for there was something indescribably guilty about them. My wife had always been a woman of a frank, open nature, and it gave me a chill to see her slinking into her own room, and crying out and wincing when her own husband spoke to her.

' "You awake, Jack?" she cried, with a nervous laugh. "Why, I thought that nothing could awaken you."

' "Where have you been?" I asked, more sternly.

' "I don't wonder that you are surprised," said she, and I could see that her fingers were trembling as she undid the fastening of her mantle. "Why, I never remember having done such a thing in my life before. The fact is, that I felt as though I were choking, and had a perfect longing for a breath of fresh air. I really think that I should have fainted if I had not gone out. I stood at the door for a few minutes, and now I am quite myself again."

'All the time that she was telling me this story she never once looked in my direction, and her voice was quite unlike her usual tones. It was evident to me that she was saying what was false. I said nothing in reply, but turned my face to the wall, sick at heart, with my mind filled with a thousand venomous doubts and suspicions. What was it that my wife was concealing from me? Where had she been during that strange expedition? I felt that I should have no peace until I knew, and yet I shrank from asking her again after once she had told me what was false. All the rest of the night I tossed and tumbled, framing theory after theory, each more unlikely than the last.

'I should have gone to the City that day, but I was too perturbed in my mind to be able to pay attention to business matters. My wife seemed to be as upset as myself, and I could see from the little questioning glances which she kept shooting at me, that she understood that I disbelieved her statement, and that she was at her wits' end what to do. We hardly exchanged a word during breakfast, and immediately afterwards I went out for a walk, that I might think the matter over in the fresh morning air.

'I went as far as the Crystal Palace, spent an hour in the grounds, and was back in Norbury by one o'clock. It happened that my way took me past the cottage, and I stopped for an instant to look at the windows and to see if I could catch a glimpse of the strange face which had stared out at me on the day before. As I stood there, imagine my surprise, Mr Holmes, when the door suddenly opened and my wife walked out!

'I was struck dumb with astonishment at the sight of her, but my emotions were nothing to those which showed themselves upon her face when our eyes met. She seemed for an instant to wish to shrink back inside the house again, and then, seeing how useless all concealment must be, she came forward with a very white face and frightened eyes which belied the smile upon her lips.

' "Oh, Jack!" she said, "I have just been in to see if I can be of any assistance to our new neighbours. Why do you look at me like that, Jack? You are not angry with me?"

' "So," said I, "this is where you went during the night?"

' "What do you mean?" she cried.

' "You came here. I am sure of it. Who are these people that you should visit them at such an hour?"

'"I have not been here before."

'"How can you tell me what you know is false?" I cried. "Your very voice changes as you speak. When have I ever had a secret from you? I shall enter that cottage, and I shall probe the matter to the bottom."

'"No, no, Jack, for God's sake!" she gasped, in uncontrollable emotion. Then as I approached the door, she seized my sleeve and pulled me back with convulsive strength.

'"I implore you not to do this, Jack," she cried. "I swear that I will tell you everything some day, but nothing but misery can come of it if you enter that cottage." Then, as I tried to shake her off, she clung to me in a frenzy of entreaty.

'"Trust me, Jack!" she cried. "Trust me only this once. You will never have cause to regret it. You know that I would not have a secret from you if it were not for your own sake. Our whole lives are at stake on this. If you come home with me all will be well. If you force your way into that cottage, all is over between us."

'There was such earnestness, such despair in her manner that her words arrested me, and I stood irresolute before the door.

'"I will trust you on one condition, and on one condition only," said I at last. "It is that this mystery comes to an end from now. You are at liberty to preserve your secret, but you must promise me that there shall be no more nightly visits, no more doings which are kept from my knowledge. I am willing to forget those which are past if you will promise that there shall be no more in the future."

'"I was sure that you would trust me," she cried, with a great sigh of relief. "It shall be just as you wish. Come away, oh, come away up to the house!" Still plucking at my sleeve she led me away from the cottage. As we went I glanced back, and there was that yellow, livid face watching us out of the upper window. What link could there be between that creature and my wife? Or how could the coarse, rough woman whom I had seen the day before be connected with her? It was a strange puzzle, and yet I knew that my mind could never know ease again until I had solved it.

'For two days after this I stayed at home, and my wife appeared to abide loyally by our engagement, for, as far as I know, she never stirred out of the house. On the third day, however, I had ample evidence that her solemn promise was not enough to hold her back from this secret influence which drew her away from her husband and her duty.

'I had gone into town on that day, but I returned by the 2.40 instead of the 3.36, which is my usual train. As I entered the house the maid ran into the hall with a startled face.

' "Where is your mistress?" I asked.

' "I think that she has gone out for a walk," she answered.

'My mind was instantly filled with suspicion. I rushed upstairs to make sure that she was not in the house. As I did so I happened to glance out of one of the upper windows, and saw the maid with whom I had just been speaking running across the field in the direction of the cottage. Then, of course, I saw exactly what it all meant. My wife had gone over there and had asked the servant to call her if I should return. Tingling with anger, I rushed down and strode across, determined to end the matter once and for ever. I saw my wife and the maid hurrying back together along the lane, but I did not stop to speak with them. In the cottage lay the secret which was casting a shadow over my life. I vowed that, come what might, it should be a secret no longer. I did not even knock when I reached it, but turned the handle and rushed into the passage.

'It was all still and quiet upon the ground floor. In the kitchen a kettle was singing on the fire, and a large black cat lay coiled up in a basket, but there was no sign of the woman whom I had seen before. I ran into the other room, but it was equally deserted. Then I rushed up the stairs, but only to find two other rooms empty and deserted at the top. There was no one at all in the whole house. The furniture and pictures were of the most common and vulgar description, save in the one chamber at the window of which I had seen the strange face. That was comfortable and elegant, and all my suspicions rose into a fierce, bitter blaze when I saw that on the mantelpiece stood a full-length photograph of my wife, which had been taken at my request only three months ago.

'I stayed long enough to make certain that the house was absolutely empty. Then I left it, feeling a weight at my heart such as I had never had before. My wife came out into the hall as I entered my house, but I was too hurt and angry to speak with her, and pushing past her I made my way into my study. She followed me, however, before I could close the door.

'"I am sorry that I broke my promise, Jack," said she, "but if you knew all the circumstances I am sure you would forgive me."

'"Tell me everything, then," said I.

'"I cannot, Jack, I cannot!" she cried.

'"TELL ME EVERYTHING," SAID I.'

'"Until you tell me who it is that has been living in that cottage, and who it is to whom you have given that photograph, there can never be any confidence between us," said I, and breaking away from her I left the house. That was yesterday, Mr Holmes, and I have not seen her since, nor do I know anything more about this strange business. It is the first shadow that has come between us, and it has so shaken me that I do not know what I should do for the best. Suddenly this morning it occurred to me that you were the man to advise me, so I have hurried to you now, and I place myself unreservedly in your hands. If there is any point which I have not made clear, pray question me about it. But above all tell me quickly what I have to do, for this misery is more than I can bear.'

Holmes and I had listened with the utmost interest to this extraordinary statement, which had been delivered in the jerky, broken fashion of a man who is under the influence of extreme emotion. My companion sat silent now for some time, with his chin upon his hand, lost in thought.

'Tell me,' said he at last, 'could you swear that this was a man's face which you saw at the window?'

'Each time that I saw it I was some distance away from it, so that it is impossible for me to say.'

'You appear, however, to have been disagreeably impressed by it.'

'It seemed to be of an unnatural colour and to have a strange rigidity about the features. When I approached, it vanished with a jerk.'

'How long is it since your wife asked you for a hundred pounds?'

'Nearly two months.'

'Have you ever seen a photograph of her first husband?'

'No; there was a great fire at Atlanta very shortly after his death, and all her papers were destroyed.'

'And yet she had a certificate of death. You say that you saw it?'

'Yes, she got a duplicate after the fire.'

'Did you ever meet anyone who knew her in America?'

'No.'

'Did she ever talk of revisiting the place?'

'No.'

'Or get letters from it?'

'Not to my knowledge.'

'Thank you. I should like to think over the matter a little now. If the cottage is permanently deserted we may have some difficulty; if on the other hand, as I fancy is more likely, the inmates were warned of your coming, and left before you entered yesterday, then they may be back now, and we should clear it all up easily. Let me advise you then, to return to Norbury and to examine the windows of the cottage again. If you have reason to believe that it is inhabited do not force your way in, but send a wire to my friend and me. We shall be with you within an hour of receiving it, and we shall then very soon get to the bottom of the business.'

'And if it is still empty?'

'In that case I shall come out tomorrow and talk it over with you. Good-bye, and above all things do not fret until you know that you really have a cause for it.'

'I am afraid that this is a bad business, Watson,' said my companion, as he returned after accompanying Mr Grant Munro to the door. 'What do you make of it?'

'It had an ugly sound,' I answered.

'Yes. There's blackmail in it, or I am much mistaken.'

'And who is the blackmailer?'

'Well, it must be this creature who lives in the only comfortable room in the place, and has her photograph above his fireplace. Upon my word, Watson, there is something very attractive about that livid face at the window and I would not have missed the case for worlds.'

'You have a theory?'

'Yes, a provisional one. But I shall be surprised if it does not turn out to be correct. This woman's first husband is in that cottage.'

'Why do you think so?'

'How else can we explain her frenzied anxiety that her second one should not enter it? The facts, as I read them, are something like this: This woman was married in America. Her husband developed some hateful qualities, or, shall we say, that he contracted some loathsome disease, and became a leper or an imbecile. She fled from him at last, returned to England, changed her name, and started her life, as she thought, afresh. She had been married three years, and believed that her position was quite secure – having shown her husband the death certificate of some man whose name she had assumed – when suddenly her whereabouts was discovered by her first husband, or, we may suppose, by some unscrupulous woman, who had attached herself to the invalid. They write to the wife and threaten to come and expose her. She asks for a hundred pounds and endeavours to buy them off. They come in spite of it, and when the husband mentions casually to the wife that there are newcomers in the cottage, she knows in some way that they are her pursuers. She waits until her husband is asleep, and then she rushes down to endeavour to persuade them to leave her in peace. Having no success, she goes again next morning, and her husband meets her, as he told us, as she came out. She promises him then not to go there again, but two days afterwards, the hope of getting rid of those dreadful neighbours is too strong for her, and she makes another attempt, taking down with her the photograph which had probably been demanded from her. In the midst of this interview the maid rushes in to say that the master has come home, on which the wife, knowing that he would come straight down to the cottage, hurries the inmates out at the back door, into that grove of fir trees, probably, which was mentioned as standing near. In this way he finds the place deserted. I shall be very much surprised, however, if it is still so when he reconnoitres it this evening. What do you think of my theory?'

'It is all surmise.'

'But at least it covers all the facts. When new facts come to our knowledge which cannot be covered by it, it will be time enough to reconsider it. At present we can do nothing until we have a fresh message from our friend at Norbury.'

But we had not very long to wait. It came just as we had finished our tea. 'The cottage is still tenanted,' it said. 'Have seen the face again at the window. I'll meet the seven o'clock train, and take no steps until you arrive.'

He was waiting on the platform when we stepped out, and we could see in the light of the station lamps that he was very pale, and quivering with agitation.

'They are still there, Mr Holmes,' said he, laying his hand upon my friend's sleeve. 'I saw lights in the cottage as I came down. We shall settle it now, once and for all.'

'What is your plan, then?' asked Holmes, as we walked down the dark, tree-lined road.

'I am going to force my way in and see for myself who is in the house. I wish you both to be there as witnesses.'

'You are quite determined to do this, in spite of your wife's warning that it is better that you should not solve the mystery?'

'Yes, I am determined.'

'Well, I think that you are in the right. Any truth is better than indefinite doubt. We had better go up at once. Of course, legally we are putting ourselves hopelessly in the wrong, but I think that it is worth it.'

It was a very dark night and a thin rain began to fall as we turned from the high-road into a narrow lane, deeply rutted, with hedges on either side. Mr Grant Munro pushed impatiently forward, however, and we stumbled after him as best we could.

'There are the lights of my house,' he murmured, pointing to a glimmer among the trees, 'and here is the cottage which I am going to enter.'

We turned a corner in the lane as he spoke, and there was the building close beside us. A yellow bar falling across the black foreground showed that the door was not quite closed, and one window in the upper storey was brightly illuminated. As we looked we saw a dark blur moving across the blind.

'There is that creature,' cried Grant Munro; 'you can see for yourselves that someone is there. Now follow me, and we shall soon know all.'

We approached the door, but suddenly a woman appeared out of the shadow and stood in the golden track of the lamp-light. I could not see her face in the darkness, but her arms were thrown out in an attitude of entreaty.

'For God's sake, don't, Jack!' she cried. 'I had a presentiment that you would come this evening. Think better of it, dear! Trust me again, and you will never have cause to regret it.'

'I have trusted you too long, Effie!' he cried sternly. 'Leave go of me! I must pass you. My friends and I are going to settle this matter once and for ever.' He pushed her to one side and we followed closely after him. As he threw the door open an elderly woman ran out in front of him and tried to bar his passage, but he thrust her back, and an instant afterwards we were all upon the stairs. Grant Munro rushed into the lighted room at the top, and we entered it at his heels.

It was a cosy, well-furnished apartment, with two candles burning upon the table and two upon the mantelpiece. In the corner, stooping over a desk, there sat what appeared to be a little girl. Her face was turned away as we entered, but we could see that she was dressed in a red frock, and that she had long white gloves on. As she whisked round to us I gave a cry of surprise and horror. The face which she turned towards us was of the strangest livid tint, and the features were absolutely devoid of any expression. An instant later the mystery was explained.

Holmes, with a laugh, passed his hand behind the child's ear, a mask peeled off from her countenance, and there was a little coal-black negress with all her white teeth flashing in amusement at our amazed faces. I burst out laughing out of sympathy with her merriment, but Grant Munro stood staring, with his hand clutching at his throat.

'My God!' he cried, 'what can be the meaning of this?'

'I will tell you the meaning of it,' cried the lady, sweeping into the room with a proud, set face. 'You have forced me against my own judgement to tell you, and now we must both make the best of it. My husband died at Atlanta. My child survived.'

'Your child!'

She drew a large silver locket from her bosom. 'You have never seen this open.'

'I understood that it did not open.'

She touched a spring, and the front hinged back. There was a portrait within of a man, strikingly handsome and intelligent, but bearing unmistakable signs upon his features of his African descent.

'That is John Hebron, of Atlanta,' said the lady, 'and a nobler man never walked the earth. I cut myself off from my race in order to wed him; but never once while he lived did I for one instant regret it. It was our misfortune that our only child took after his people rather than mine. It is often so in such matches, and little Lucy is darker far than ever her father was. But, dark or fair, she is my own dear little girlie, and her mother's pet.' The little creature ran across at the words and nestled up against the lady's dress.

'When I left her in America,' she continued, 'it was only because her health was weak, and the change might have done her harm. She was given to the care of a faithful Scotchwoman who had once been our servant. Never for an instant did I dream of disowning her as my child. But when chance threw you in my way, Jack, and I learned to love you, I feared to tell you about my child. God forgive me, I feared that I should lose you, and I had not the courage to tell you. I had to choose between you, and in my weakness I turned away from my own little girl. For three years I have kept her existence a secret from you, but I heard from the nurse, and I knew that all was well with her. At last, however, there came an overwhelming desire to see the child once more. I struggled against it, but in vain. Though I knew the danger I determined to have the child over, if it were but for a few weeks. I sent a hundred pounds to the nurse, and I gave her instructions about this cottage, so that she might come as a neighbour without my appearing to be in any way connected with her. I pushed my precautions so far as to order her to keep the child in the house during the day-time, and to cover up her little face and hands, so that even those who might see her at the window should not gossip about there being a black child in the neighbourhood. If I had been less cautious I might have been more wise, but I was half crazy with fear lest you should learn the truth.

'It was you who told me first that the cottage was occupied. I should have waited for the morning, but I could not sleep for excitement, and so at last I slipped out, knowing how difficult it is to awaken you. But you saw me go, and that was the beginning of my troubles. Next day you had my secret at your mercy, but you nobly refrained from pursuing your advantage. Three days later, however, the nurse and child only just escaped from the back door as you rushed in at the front one. And now tonight you at last know all, and I ask you what is to become of us, my child and me?' She clasped her hands and waited for an answer.

It was a long two minutes before Grant Munro broke the silence, and when his answer came it was one of which I love to think. He lifted the little child, kissed her, and then, still carrying her, he held his other hand out to his wife, and turned towards the door.

'We can talk it over more comfortably at home,' said he. 'I am

'HE LIFTED THE LITTLE CHILD.'

not a very good man, Effie, but I think that I am a better one than you have given me credit for being.'

Holmes and I followed them down to the lane, and my friend plucked at my sleeve as we came out. 'I think,' said he, 'that we shall be of more use in London than in Norbury.'

Not another word did he say of the case until late that night when he was turning away, with his lighted candle, for his bedroom.

'Watson,' said he, 'if it should ever strike you that I am getting a little over-confident in my powers, or giving less pains to a case than it deserves, kindly whisper "Norbury" in my ear, and I shall be infinitely obliged to you.'

The Adventure of the Resident Patient

In glancing over the somewhat incoherent series of memoirs with which I have endeavoured to illustrate a few of the mental peculiarities of my friend, Mr Sherlock Holmes, I have been struck by the difficulty which I have experienced in picking out examples which shall in every way answer my purpose. For in those cases in which Holmes has performed some *tour de force* of analytical reasoning, and has demonstrated the value of his peculiar methods of investigation, the facts themselves have often been so slight or so commonplace that I could not feel justified in laying them before the public. On the other hand, it has frequently happened that he has been concerned in some research where the facts have been of the most remarkable and dramatic character, but where the share which he has himself taken in determining their causes has been less pronounced than I, as his biographer, could wish. The small matter which I have chronicled under the heading of *A Study in Scarlet*, and that other later one connected with the loss of the *Gloria Scott*, may serve as examples of this Scylla and Charybdis which are forever threatening his historian. It may be that, in the business of which I am now about to write, the part which my friend played is not sufficiently accentuated; and yet the whole train of circumstances is so remarkable that I cannot bring myself to omit it entirely from this series.

It had been a close, rainy day in August. Our blinds were half drawn, and Holmes lay curled upon the sofa, reading and re-reading a letter which he had received by the morning post. For myself, my term of service in India had trained me to stand heat better than cold, and a thermometer of 90 was no hardship. But the paper was uninteresting. Parliament had risen. Everybody was out of town, and I yearned for the glades of the New Forest or the shingle of Southsea. A depleted bank account had caused me to postpone my holiday, and as to my companion, neither the country nor the sea presented the slightest attraction to him. He loved to lie in the very centre of five millions of people, with his filaments stretching out and running through them, responsive to every little rumour or suspicion of unsolved crime. Appreciation of Nature found no place among his many gifts, and his only change was when he turned his mind from the evil-doer of the town to track down his brother of the country.

Finding that Holmes was too absorbed for conversation, I had tossed aside the barren paper, and, leaning back in my chair, I fell into a brown study. Suddenly my companion's voice broke in upon my thoughts.

'You are right, Watson,' said he. 'It does seem a very preposterous way of settling a dispute.'

'Most preposterous!' I exclaimed, and then suddenly realizing how he had echoed the inmost thought of my soul, I sat up in my chair and stared at him in blank amazement.

'What is this, Holmes?' I cried. 'This is beyond anything which I could have imagined.'

He laughed heartily at my perplexity.

'You remember,' said he, 'that some little time ago when I read you a passage in one of Poe's sketches, in which a close reasoner follows the unspoken thoughts of his companion, you were inclined to treat the matter as a mere *tour de force* of the author. On my remarking that I was constantly in the habit of doing the same thing you expressed incredulity.'

'Oh, no!'

'Perhaps not with your tongue, my dear Watson, but certainly with your eyebrows. So when I saw you throw down your paper and enter upon a train of thought, I was very happy to have the opportunity of reading it off, and eventually of breaking into it, as a proof that I had been *en rapport* with you.'

But I was still far from satisfied. 'In the example which you read to me,' said I, 'the reasoner drew his conclusions from the actions of the man whom he observed. If I remember right, he stumbled over a heap of stones, looked up at the stars, and so on. But I have been seated quietly in my chair, and what clues can I have given you?'

'You do yourself an injustice. The features are given to man as the means by which he shall express his emotions, and yours are faithful servants.'

'Do you mean to say that you read my train of thoughts from my features?'

'Your features, and especially your eyes. Perhaps you cannot yourself recall how your reverie commenced?'

'No, I cannot.'

'Then I will tell you. After throwing down your paper, which was the action which drew my attention to you, you sat for half a minute with a vacant expression. Then your eyes fixed themselves upon your newly framed picture of General Gordon, and I saw by the alteration in your face that a train of thought had been started. But it did not lead very far. Your eyes turned across to the unframed portrait of Henry Ward Beecher which stands upon the top of your books. You then glanced up at the wall, and of course your meaning was obvious. You were thinking that if the portrait were framed, it would just cover that bare space and correspond with Gordon's picture over there.'

'You have followed me wonderfully!' I exclaimed.

'So far I could hardly have gone astray. But now your thoughts went back to Beecher, and you looked hard across as if you were studying the character in his features. Then your eyes ceased to pucker, but you continued to look across, and your face was thoughtful. You were recalling the incidents of Beecher's career. I was well aware that you could not do this without thinking of the mission which he undertook on behalf of the North at the time of the Civil War, for I remember your expressing your passionate indignation at the way in which he was received by the more turbulent of our people. You felt so strongly about it, that I knew you could not think of Beecher without thinking of that also. When a moment later I saw your eyes wander away from the picture, I suspected that your mind had now turned to the Civil War, and when I observed that your lips set, your eyes sparkled, and your hands clenched, I was positive that you were indeed thinking of the gallantry which was shown by both sides in that desperate struggle. But then, again, your face grew sadder; you shook your head. You were dwelling upon the sadness and horror and useless waste of life. Your hand stole towards your own old wound and a smile quivered on your lips, which showed me that the ridiculous side of this method of settling international questions had forced itself upon your mind. At this point I agreed with you that it was preposterous, and was glad to find that all my deductions had been correct.'

'Absolutely!' said I. 'And now that you have explained it, I confess that I am as amazed as before.'

'It was very superficial, my dear Watson, I assure you. I should have not intruded it upon your attention had you not shown some incredulity the other day. But the evening has brought a breeze with it. What do you say to a ramble through London?'

I was weary of our little sitting-room, and gladly acquiesced. For three hours we strolled about together, watching the ever-changing kaleidoscope of life as it ebbs and flows through Fleet Street and the Strand. Holmes's characteristic talk, with its keen observance of detail and subtle power of inference, held me amused and enthralled.

It was ten o'clock before we reached Baker Street again. A brougham was waiting at our door.

'Hum! A doctor's – general practitioner, I perceive,' said Holmes. 'Not been long in practice, but has had a good deal to do. Come to consult us, I fancy! Lucky we came back!'

I was sufficiently conversant with Holmes's methods to be able

'WE STROLLED ABOUT TOGETHER.'

to follow his reasoning, and to see that the nature and state of the various medical instruments in the wicker basket which hung in the lamp-light inside the brougham had given him the data for his swift deduction. The light in our window above showed that this late visit was indeed intended for us. With some curiosity as to what could have sent a brother medico to us at such an hour, I followed Holmes into our sanctum.

A pale, taper-faced man with sandy whiskers rose up from a chair by the fire as we entered. His age may not have been more than three- or four-and-thirty, but his haggard expression and unhealthy hue told of a life which had sapped his strength and robbed him of his youth. His manner was nervous and shy, like that of a sensitive gentleman, and the thin white hand which he laid on the mantelpiece as he rose was that of an artist rather than of a surgeon. His dress was quiet and sombre, a black frock-coat, dark trousers, and a touch of colour about his necktie.

'Good evening, doctor,' said Holmes cheerily; 'I am glad to see that you have only been waiting a very few minutes.'

'You spoke to my coachman, then?'

'No, it was the candle on the side table that told me. Pray resume your seat and let me know how I can serve you.'

'My name is Doctor Percy Trevelyan,' said our visitor, 'and I live at 403 Brook Street.'

'Are you not the author of a monograph upon obscure nervous lesions?' I asked.

His pale cheeks flushed with pleasure at hearing that his work was known to me.

'I so seldom hear of the work that I thought it was quite dead,' said he. 'My publishers give me a most discouraging account of its sale. You are yourself, I presume, a medical man?'

'A retired Army surgeon.'

'My own hobby has always been nervous disease. I should wish to make it an absolute speciality, but, of course, a man must take what he can get first. This, however, is beside the question, Mr Sherlock Holmes, and I quite appreciate how valuable your time is. The fact is that a very singular train of events has occurred recently at my house in Brook Street, and tonight they came to such a head that I felt it was quite impossible for me to wait another hour before asking for your advice and assistance.'

Sherlock Holmes sat down and lit his pipe. 'You are very welcome to both,' said he. 'Pray let me have a detailed account of what the circumstances are which have disturbed you.'

'One or two of them are so trivial,' said Dr Trevelyan, 'that really I am almost ashamed to mention them. But the matter is so inexplicable, and the recent turn which it has taken is so elaborate, that I shall lay it all before you, and you shall judge what is essential and what is not.

'I am compelled, to begin with, to say something of my own

college career. I am a London University man, you know, and I am sure you will not think that I am unduly singing my own praises if I say that my student career was considered by my professors to be a very promising one. After I had graduated I continued to devote myself to research, occupying a minor position in King's College Hospital, and I was fortunate enough to excite considerable interest by my research into the pathology of catalepsy, and finally to win the Bruce Pinkerton prize and medal by the monograph on nervous lesions to which your friend has just alluded. I should not go too far if I were to say that there was a general impression at that time that a distinguished career lay before me.

'But the one great stumbling-block lay in my want of capital. As you will readily understand, a specialist who aims high is compelled to start in one of a dozen streets in the Cavendish Square quarter, all of which entail enormous rents and furnishing expenses. Besides this preliminary outlay, he must be prepared to keep himself for some years, and to hire a presentable carriage and horse. To do this was quite beyond my power, and I could only hope that by economy I might in ten years' time save enough to enable me to put up my plate. Suddenly, however, an unexpected incident opened up quite a new prospect to me.

'This was a visit from a gentleman of the name of Blessington, who was a complete stranger to me. He came up into my room one morning, and plunged into business in an instant.

' "You are the same Percy Trevelyan who has had so distinguished a career and won a great prize lately?" said he.

'I bowed.

' "Answer me frankly," he continued, "for you will find it to your interest to do so. You have all the cleverness which makes a successful man. Have you the tact?"

'I could not help but smile at the abruptness of the question.

' "I trust that I have my share," I said.

' "Any bad habits? Not drawn towards drink, eh?"

'"Really, sir!" I cried.

'"Quite right! That's all right! But I was bound to ask. With all these qualities why are you not in practice?"

'I shrugged my shoulders.

'"Come, come!" said he, in his bustling way. "It's the old story. More in your brains than in your pocket, eh? What would you say if I were to start you in Brook Street?"

'I stared at him in astonishment.

'"Oh, it's for my sake, not for yours," he cried. "I'll be perfectly frank with you, and if it suits you it will suit me very well. I have a few thousands to invest, d'ye see, and I think I'll sink them in you."

'"But why?" I gasped.

'"Well, it's just like any other speculation, and safer than most."

'"What am I to do, then?"

'"I'll tell you. I'll take the house, furnish it, pay the maids, and run the whole place. All you have to do is to wear out your chair in the consulting-room. I'll let you have pocket money and everything. Then you hand over to me three-quarters of what you earn, and you keep the other quarter for yourself."

'This was the strange proposal, Mr Holmes, with which the man Blessington approached me. I won't weary you with the account of how we bargained and negotiated. It ended in my moving into the house next Lady Day, and starting in practice on very much the same conditions as he had suggested. He came himself to live with me in the character of a resident patient. His heart was weak, it appears, and he needed constant medical supervision. He turned the two best rooms on the first floor into a sitting-room and bedroom for himself. He was a man of singular habits, shunning company and very seldom going out. His life was irregular, but in one respect he was regularity itself. Every evening at the same hour he walked into the consulting-room, examined the books, put down five and three-pence for every guinea that I had earned, and carried the rest off to the strong-box in his own room.

'I may say with confidence that he never had occasion to regret his speculation. From the first it was a success. A few good cases and the reputation which I had won in the hospital brought me rapidly to the front, and during the last year or two I have made him a rich man.

'So much, Mr Holmes, for my past history and my relations with Mr Blessington. It only remains for me now to tell you what has occurred to bring me here tonight.

'Some weeks ago Mr Blessington came down to me in, as it seemed to me, a state of considerable agitation. He spoke of some burglary which, he said, had been committed in the West End, and he appeared, I remember, to be quite unnecessarily excited about it, declaring that a day should not pass before we should add stronger bolts to our windows and doors. For a week he continued to be in a peculiar state of restlessness, peering continually out of the windows, and ceasing to take the short walk which had usually been the prelude to his dinner. From his manner it struck me that he was in mortal dread of something or somebody, but when I questioned him upon the point he became so offensive that I was compelled to drop the subject. Gradually as time passed his fears appeared to die away, and he had renewed his former habits, when a fresh event reduced him to the pitiable state of prostration in which he now lies.

'What happened was this. Two days ago I received the letter which I now read to you. Neither address nor date is attached to it.

' "A Russian nobleman who is now resident in England," it runs, "would be glad to avail himself of the professional assistance of Dr Percy Trevelyan. He has been for some years a victim to cataleptic attacks, on which, as is well known, Dr Trevelyan is an authority. He proposes to call at about a quarter past six tomorrow evening, if Dr Trevelyan will make it convenient to be at home."

'This letter interested me deeply, because the chief difficulty in the study of catalepsy is the rareness of the disease. You may believe, then, that I was in my consulting-room when, at the appointed hour, the page showed in the patient.

'He was an elderly man, thin, demure, and commonplace – by no means the conception one forms of a Russian nobleman. I was much more struck by the appearance of his companion. This was a tall young man, surprisingly handsome, with a dark, fierce face, and the limbs and chest of a Hercules. He had his hand under the other's arm as they entered, and helped him to a chair with a tenderness which one would hardly have expected from his appearance.

' "You will excuse my coming in, Doctor," said he to me, speaking English with a slight lisp. "This is my father, and his health is a matter of the most overwhelming importance to me."

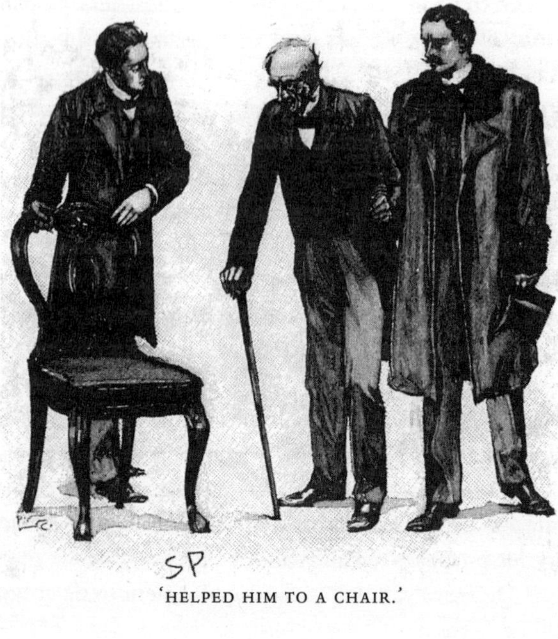

'HELPED HIM TO A CHAIR.'

'I was touched by his filial anxiety. "You would, perhaps, care to remain during the consultation?" said I.

' "Not for the world," he cried, with a gesture of horror. "It is more painful to me that I can express. If I were to see my father in one of those dreadful seizures, I am convinced that I should never survive it. My own nervous system is an exceptionally sensitive one. With your permission I will remain in the waiting-room while you go into my father's case."

'To this, of course, I assented, and the young man withdrew. The patient and I then plunged into a discussion of his case, of which I took exhaustive notes. He was not remarkable for intelligence, and his answers were frequently obscure, which I attributed to his limited acquaintance with our language. Suddenly, however, as I sat writing he ceased to give any answer at all to my inquiries, and on my turning towards him I was shocked to see that he was sitting bolt upright in his chair, staring at me with a perfectly blank and rigid face. He was again in the grip of his mysterious malady.

'My first feeling, as I have just said, was one of pity and horror. My second, I fear, was rather one of professional satisfaction. I made notes of my patient's pulse and temperature, tested the rigidity of his muscles, and examined his reflexes. There was nothing markedly abnormal in any of these conditions, which harmonized with my former experiences. I had obtained good results in such cases by the inhalation of nitrate of amyl, and the present seemed an admirable opportunity of testing its virtues. The bottle was downstairs in my laboratory, so, leaving my patient seated in his chair, I ran down to get it. There was some little delay in finding it – five minutes, let us say – and then I returned. Imagine my amazement to find the room empty and the patient gone!

'Of course, my first act was to run into the waiting-room. The son had gone also. The hall door had been closed, but not shut. My page who admits patients is a new boy, and by no means quick. He waits downstairs, and runs up to show patients out when I ring the consulting-room bell. He had heard nothing, and the affair remained a complete mystery. Mr Blessington came in from his walk shortly afterwards, but I did not say anything to him upon the subject, for to tell the truth, I have got in the way of late of holding as little communication with him as possible.

'Well, I never thought that I should see anything more of the Russian and his son, so you can imagine my amazement when at the very same hour this evening they both came marching into my consulting-room, just as they had done before.

'"I feel that I owe you a great many apologies for my abrupt departure yesterday, Doctor," said my patient.

'"I confess that I was very much surprised at it," said I.

'"Well, the fact is," he remarked, "that when I recover from these attacks my mind is always very clouded as to all that has gone before. I woke up in a strange room, as it seemed to me, and made my way out into the street in a sort of dazed way when you were absent."

'"And I," said the son, "seeing my father pass the door of the waiting-room, naturally thought that the consultation had come to an end. It was not until we had reached home that I began to realize the true state of affairs."

'"Well," said I, laughing, "there is no harm done, except that you puzzled me terribly; so if you, sir, would kindly step into the waiting-room, I shall be happy to continue our consultation, which was brought to so abrupt an ending."

'For half an hour or so I discussed the old gentleman's symptoms with him, and then, having prescribed for him, I saw him go off on the arm of his son.

'I have told you that Mr Blessington generally chose this hour of the day for his exercise. He came in shortly afterwards and passed upstairs. An instant later I heard him running down, and he burst into my consulting-room like a man who is mad with panic.

'"Who has been in my room?" he cried.

'"No one," said I.

'"It's a lie!" he yelled. "Come up and look."

'I passed over the grossness of his language, as he seemed half out of his mind with fear. When I went upstairs with him he pointed to several footprints upon the light carpet.

'"D'you mean to say those are mine?" he cried.

'They were certainly very much larger than any which he could have made, and were evidently quite fresh. It rained hard this afternoon, as you know, and my patients were the only people who called. It must have been the case, then, that the man in the waiting-room had for some unknown reason, while I was busy with the other, ascended to the room of my resident patient. Nothing had been touched or taken, but there were the footprints to prove that the intrusion was an undoubted fact.

'Mr Blessington seemed more excited over the matter than I should have thought possible, though, of course, it was enough to disturb anybody's peace of mind. He actually sat crying in an armchair, and I could hardly get him to speak coherently. It was his suggestion that I should come round to you, and of course I at once saw the propriety of it, for certainly the incident is a very singular one, though he appears to completely overrate its importance. If you would only come back with me in my brougham, you would at least be able to soothe him, though I can hardly hope that you will be able to explain this remarkable occurrence.'

Sherlock Holmes had listened to this long narrative with an intentness which showed me that his interest was keenly aroused. His face was as impassive as ever, but his lids had dropped more heavily over his eyes, and his smoke had curled up more thickly from his pipe to emphasize each curious episode in the doctor's tale. As our visitor concluded Holmes sprang up without a word, handed me my hat, picked up his own from the table, and followed Dr Trevelyan to the door. Within a quarter of an hour we had been dropped at the door of the physician's residence in Brook Street, one of those sombre, flat-faced houses which one associates with a West End practice. A small page admitted us, and we began at once to ascend the broad, well-carpeted stair.

But a singular interruption brought us to a standstill. The light at the top was suddenly whisked out, and from the darkness came a reedy, quavering voice.

'I have a pistol,' it cried; 'I give you my word that I'll fire if you come any nearer.'

'This really grows outrageous, Mr Blessington,' cried Dr Trevelyan.

'Oh, then it is you, Doctor?' said the voice, with a great heave of relief. 'But those other gentlemen, are they what they pretend to be?'

We were conscious of a long scrutiny out of the darkness.

'Yes, yes, it's all right,' said the voice at last. 'You can come up, and I am sorry if my precautions have annoyed you.'

He re-lit the stair gas as he spoke, and we saw before us a singular-looking man, whose appearance, as well as his voice, testified to his jangled nerves. He was very fat, but had apparently at some time been much fatter, so that the skin hung about his face in loose pouches, like the cheeks of a bloodhound. He was of a sickly colour, and his thin, sandy hair seemed to bristle up with the intensity of his emotion. In his hand he held a pistol, but he thrust it into his pocket as we advanced.

'Good evening, Mr Holmes,' said he; 'I am sure I am very much obliged to you for coming round. No one ever needed your advice more than I do. I suppose that Dr Trevelyan has told you of this most unwarrantable intrusion into my rooms?'

'Quite so,' said Holmes. 'Who are these two men, Mr Blessington, and why do they wish to molest you?'

'Well, well,' said the resident patient, in a nervous fashion, 'of course it is hard to say that. You can hardly expect me to answer that, Mr Holmes.'

'Do you mean that you don't know?'

'Come in here, if you please. Just have the kindness to step in here.'

He led the way into his bedroom, which was large and comfortably furnished.

'You see that?' said he, pointing to a big black box at the end of his bed. 'I have never been a very rich man, Mr Holmes – never made but one investment in my life, as Dr Trevelyan would tell you. But I don't believe in bankers. I would never trust a banker, Mr Holmes. Between ourselves, what little I have is in that box, so you can understand what it means to me when unknown people force themselves into my rooms.'

Holmes looked at Blessington in his questioning way, and shook his head.

'I cannot possibly advise you if you try to deceive me,' said he.

'But I have told you everything.'

Holmes turned on his heel with a gesture of disgust. 'Good night, Dr Trevelyan,' said he.

'And no advice for me?' cried Blessington, in a breaking voice.

'My advice to you, sir, is to speak the truth.'

A minute later we were in the street and walking for home. We had crossed Oxford Street, and were half-way down Harley Street before I could get a word from my companion.

'Sorry to bring you out on such a fool's errand, Watson,' he said, at last. 'It is an interesting case, too, at the bottom of it.'

'I can make little of it,' I confessed.

'Well, it is quite evident that there are two men – more, perhaps, but at least two – who are determined for some reason to get at this fellow, Blessington. I have no doubt in my mind that both on the first and on the second occasion that young man penetrated to Blessington's room, while his confederate, by an ingenious device, kept the doctor from interfering.'

'And the catalepsy!'

'A fraudulent imitation, Watson, though I should hardly dare to hint as much to our specialist. It is a very easy complaint to imitate. I have done it myself.'

'And then?'

'By the purest chance Blessington was out on each occasion. Their reason for choosing so unusual an hour for a consultation was obviously to ensure that there should be no other patient in the waiting-room. It just happened, however, that this hour coincided with Blessington's constitutional, which seems to show that they were not very well acquainted with his daily routine. Of course, if they had been merely after plunder they would at least have made some attempt to search for it. Besides, I can read in a man's eye when it is his own skin that he is frightened for. It is inconceivable that this fellow could have made two such vindictive enemies as these appear to be without knowing of it. I hold it, therefore, to be certain that he does know who these men are, and that for reasons of his own he suppresses it. It is just possible that tomorrow may find him in a more communicative mood.'

'Is there not one alternative,' I suggested, 'grotesquely improbable, no doubt, but still just conceivable? Might the whole story of the cataleptic Russian and his son be a concoction of Dr Trevelyan's, who has, for his own purposes, been in Blessington's rooms?'

I saw in the gaslight that Holmes wore an amused smile at this brilliant departure of mine.

'My dear fellow,' said he, 'it was one of the first solutions which occurred to me, but I was soon able to corroborate the doctor's tale. This young man has left prints upon the stair carpet which made it quite superfluous for me to ask to see those which he had made in the room. When I tell you that his shoes were square-toed, instead of being pointed like Blessington's, and were quite an inch and a third longer than the doctor's, you will acknowledge that there can be no doubt as to his individuality. But we may sleep on it now, for I shall be surprised if we do not hear something further from Brook Street in the morning.'

Sherlock Holmes's prophecy was soon fulfilled, and in a dramatic fashion. At half-past seven next morning, in the first glimmer of daylight, I found him standing by my bedside in his dressing-gown.

'There's a brougham waiting for us, Watson,' said he.

'What's the matter, then?'

'The Brook Street business.'

'Any fresh news?'

'Tragic, but ambiguous,' said he, pulling up the blind. 'Look at this – a sheet from a notebook with "For God's sake, come at once – P. T." scrawled upon it in pencil. Our friend the doctor was hard put to it when he wrote this. Come along, my dear fellow, for it's an urgent call.'

In a quarter of an hour or so we were back at the physician's house. He came running out to meet us with a face of horror.

'Oh, such a business!' he cried, with his hands to his temples.

'What, then?'

'Blessington has committed suicide!'

Holmes whistled.

'Yes, he hanged himself during the night!'

We had entered, and the doctor had preceded us into what was evidently his waiting-room.

'I really hardly know what I am doing,' he cried. 'The police are already upstairs. It has shaken me most dreadfully.'

'When did you find it out?'

'He has a cup of tea taken to him early every morning. When the maid entered about seven, there the unfortunate fellow was hanging in the middle of the room. He had tied his cord to the hook on which the heavy lamp used to hang, and he had jumped off from the top of the very box that he showed us yesterday.'

Holmes stood for a moment in deep thought.

'With your permission,' said he at last, 'I should like to go upstairs and look into the matter.' We both ascended, followed by the doctor.

It was a dreadful sight which met us as we entered the bedroom door. I have spoken of the impression of flabbiness which this man Blessington conveyed. As he dangled from the hook it was exaggerated and intensified until he was scarce human in his appearance. The neck was drawn out like a plucked chicken's, making the rest of him seem the more obese and unnatural by the contrast. He was clad only in his long night-dress, and his swollen ankles and ungainly feet protruded starkly from beneath it. Beside him stood a smart-looking police inspector, who was taking notes in a pocket-book.

'Ah, Mr Holmes,' said he, as my friend entered. 'I am delighted to see you.'

'Good morning, Lanner,' answered Holmes. 'You won't think me an intruder, I am sure. Have you heard of the events which led up to this affair?'

'Yes, I heard something of them.'

'Have you formed any opinion?'

'As far as I can see, the man has been driven out of his senses by fright. The bed has been well slept in, you see. There's his impression deep enough. It's about five in the morning, you know, that suicides are most common. That would be about his time for hanging himself. It seems to have been a very deliberate affair.'

'I should say that he has been dead about three hours, judging by the rigidity of the muscles,' said I.

'Noticed anything peculiar about the room?' asked Holmes.

'Found a screwdriver and some screws on the wash-hand stand. Seems to have smoked heavily during the night, too. Here are four cigar ends that I picked out of the fireplace.'

'Hum!' said Holmes. 'Have you got his cigar-holder?'

'No, I have seen none.'

'His cigar-case, then?'

'Yes, it was in his coat-pocket.'

Holmes opened it and smelled the single cigar which it contained.

'Oh, this is a Havana, and these others are cigars of the peculiar sort which are imported by the Dutch from their East Indian colonies. They are usually wrapped in straw, you know, and are thinner for their length than any other brand.' He picked up the four ends and examined them with his pocket-lens.

'Two of these have been smoked from a holder and two without,' said he. 'Two have been cut by a not very sharp knife, and two have had the ends bitten off by a set of excellent teeth. This is no suicide, Mr Lanner. It is a very deeply planned and cold-blooded murder.'

'Impossible!' cried the inspector.

'And why?'

'Why should anyone murder a man in so clumsy a fashion as by hanging him?'

'HOLMES OPENED IT AND SMELLED THE SINGLE CIGAR WHICH IT CONTAINED.'

'That is what we have to find out.'

'How could they get in?'

'Through the front door.'

'It was barred in the morning.'

'Then it was barred after them.'

'How do you know?'

'I saw their traces. Excuse me a moment, and I may be able to give you some further information about it.'

He went over to the door, and turning the lock he examined it in his methodical fashion. Then he took out the key, which was on the inside, and inspected that also. The bed, the carpet, the chairs, the mantelpiece, the dead body, and the rope were each in turn examined, until at last he professed himself satisfied, and with my aid and that of the inspector cut down the wretched object, and laid it reverently under a sheet.

'How about this rope?' he asked.

'It is cut off this,' said Dr Trevelyan, drawing a large coil from under the bed. 'He was morbidly nervous of fire, and always kept this beside him, so that he might escape by the window in case the stairs were burning.'

'That must have saved them trouble,' said Holmes thoughtfully. 'Yes, the actual facts are very plain, and I shall be surprised if by the afternoon I cannot give you the reasons for them as well. I will take this photograph of Blessington which I see upon the mantelpiece, as it may help me in my inquiries.'

'But you have told us nothing,' cried the doctor.

'Oh, there can be no doubt as to the sequence of events,' said Holmes. 'There were three of them in it: the young man, the old man, and a third to whose identity I have no clue. The first two, I need hardly remark, are the same who masqueraded as the Russian Count and his son, so we can give a very full description of them. They were admitted by a confederate inside the house. If I might offer you a word of advice, Inspector, it would be to arrest the page, who, as I understand, has only recently come into your service, Doctor.'

'The young imp cannot be found,' said Dr Trevelyan; 'the maid and the cook have just been searching for him.'

Holmes shrugged his shoulders.

'He has played a not unimportant part in this drama,' said he. 'The three men having ascended the stair, which they did on tip-toe, the elder man first, the younger man second, and the unknown man in the rear – '

'My dear Holmes!' I ejaculated.

'Oh, there could be no question as to the superimposing of the footmarks. I had the advantage of learning which was which last night. They ascended then to Mr Blessington's room, the door of which they found to be locked. With the help of a wire, however, they forced round the key. Even without the lens, you will perceive, by the scratches on this ward, where the pressure was applied.

'On entering the room, their first proceeding must have been to gag Mr Blessington. He may have been asleep, or he may have been so paralysed with terror as to have been unable to cry out. These walls are thick, and it is conceivable that his shriek, if he had time to utter one, was unheard.

'Having secured him, it is evident to me that a consultation of some sort was held. Probably it was something in the nature of a judicial proceeding. It must have lasted for some time, for it was then that these cigars were smoked. The older man sat in that wicker chair: it was he who used the cigar-holder. The younger man sat over yonder; he knocked his ash off against the chest of drawers. The third fellow paced up and down. Blessington, I think, sat upright in the bed, but of that I cannot be absolutely certain.

'Well, it ended by their taking Blessington and hanging him. The matter was so pre-arranged that it is my belief that they brought with them some sort of block or pulley which might serve as a gallows. That screwdriver and those screws were, as I conceive, for fixing it up. Seeing the hook, however, they naturally saved themselves the trouble. Having finished their work they made off, and the door was barred behind them by their confederate.'

We had all listened with the deepest interest to this sketch of the night's doings, which Holmes had deduced from signs so subtle and minute, that even when he had pointed them out to us, we could scarcely follow him in his reasonings. The inspector hurried away on the instant to make inquiries about the page, while Holmes and I returned to Baker Street for breakfast.

'I'll be back by three,' said he when we had finished our meal. 'Both the inspector and the doctor will meet me here at that hour, and I hope by that time to have cleared up any little obscurity which the case may still present.'

Our visitors arrived at the appointed time, but it was a quarter to four before my friend put in an appearance. From his expression as he entered, however, I could see that all had gone well with him.

'Any news, Inspector?'

'We have got the boy, sir.'

'Excellent, and I have got the men.'

'You have got them!' we cried all three.

'Well, at least I have got their identity. This so-called Blessington is, as I expected, well known at headquarters, and so are his assailants. Their names are Biddle, Hayward, and Moffat.'

'The Worthingdon bank gang,' cried the inspector.

'Precisely,' said Holmes.

'Then Blessington must have been Sutton?'

'Exactly,' said Holmes.

'Why, that makes it as clear as crystal,' said the inspector.

But Trevelyan and I looked at each other in bewilderment.

'You must surely remember the great Worthingdon bank business,' said Holmes; 'five men were in it, these four and a fifth called Cartwright. Tobin, the caretaker, was murdered, and the thieves got away with seven thousand pounds. This was in 1875.

They were all five arrested, but the evidence against them was by no means conclusive. This Blessington or Sutton, who was the worst of the gang, turned informer. On his evidence Cartwright was hanged, and the other three got fifteen years apiece. When they got out the other day, which was some years before their full term, they set themselves, as you perceive, to hunt down the traitor and to avenge the death of their comrade upon him. Twice they tried to get at him and failed; a third time, you see, it came off. Is there anything further which I can explain, Dr Trevelyan?'

'I think you have made it all remarkably clear,' said the doctor. 'No doubt the day on which he was so perturbed was the day when he read of their release in the newspapers.'

'Quite so. His talk about a burglary was the merest blind.'

'But why could he not tell you this?'

'Well, my dear sir, knowing the vindictive character of his old associates, he was trying to hide his own identity from everybody as long as he could. His secret was a shameful one, and he could not bring himself to divulge it. However, wretch as he was, he was still living under the shield of British law, and I have no doubt, Inspector, that you will see that, though that shield may fail to guard, the sword of justice is still there to avenge.'

Such were the singular circumstances in connection with the resident patient and the Brook Street doctor. From that night nothing has been seen of the three murderers by the police, and it is surmised at Scotland Yard that they were among the passengers of the ill-fated steamer *Norah Creina*, which was lost some years ago with all hands upon the Portuguese coast, some leagues to the north of Oporto. The proceedings against the page broke down for want of evidence, and the 'Brook Street Mystery', as it was called, has never, until now, been fully dealt with in any public print.

The Problem of Thor Bridge

Somewhere in the vaults of the bank of Cox and Co., at Charing Cross, there is a travel-worn and battered tin dispatch-box with my name, John H. Watson, M. D., Late Indian Army, painted upon the lid. It is crammed with papers, nearly all of which are records of cases to illustrate the curious problems which Mr Sherlock Holmes had at various times to examine. Some, and not the least interesting, were complete failures, and as such will hardly bear narrating, since no final explanation is forthcoming. A problem without a solution may interest the student, but can hardly fail to annoy the casual reader. Among these unfinished tales is that of Mr James Phillimore, who, stepping back into his own house to get his umbrella, was never more seen in this world. No less remarkable is that of the cutter *Alicia*, which sailed one spring morning into a small patch of mist from where she never again emerged, nor was anything further ever heard of herself and her crew. A third case worthy of note is that of Isadora Persano, the well-known journalist and duellist, who was found stark staring mad with a matchbox in front of him which contained a remarkable worm, said to be unknown to science. Apart from these unfathomed cases, there are some which involve the secrets of private families to an extent which would mean consternation in many exalted quarters if it were thought possible that they might find their way into print. I need not say that such a breach of confidence is unthinkable, and that these records will be separated and destroyed now that my friend has time to turn his energies to the matter. There remain a considerable residue of cases of greater or less interest which I might have edited before had I not feared to give the public a surfeit which might react upon the reputation of the man whom above all others I revere. In some I was myself concerned and can speak as an eye-witness, while in others I was either not present or played so small a part that they could only be told as by a third person. The following narrative is drawn from my own experience.

It was a wild morning in October, and I observed as I was dressing how the last remaining leaves were being whirled from the solitary plane tree which graces the yard behind our house. I descended to breakfast prepared to find my companion in depressed spirits, for, like all great artists, he was easily impressed by his surroundings. On the contrary, I found that he had nearly finished his meal, and that his mood was particularly bright and joyous, with that somewhat sinister cheerfulness which was characteristic of his lighter moments.

'You have a case, Holmes?' I remarked.

'The faculty of deduction is certainly contagious, Watson,' he answered. 'It has enabled you to probe my secret. Yes, I have a case. After a month of trivialities and stagnation the wheels move once more.'

'Might I share it?'

'There is little to share, but we may discuss it when you have consumed the two hard-boiled eggs with which our new cook has favoured us. Their condition may not be unconnected with the copy of the *Family Herald* which I observed yesterday upon the hall-table. Even so trivial a matter as cooking an egg demands an attention which is conscious of the passage of time, and incompatible with the love romance in that excellent periodical.'

A quarter of an hour later the table had been cleared and we were face to face. He had drawn a letter from his pocket.

'You have heard of Neil Gibson, the Gold King?' he said.

'You mean the American Senator?'

'Well, he was once Senator for some Western State, but is better known as the greatest gold-mining magnate in the world.'

'Yes, I know of him. He has surely lived in England for some time. His name is very familiar.'

'Yes, he bought a considerable estate in Hampshire some five years ago. Possibly you have already heard of the tragic end of his wife?'

'Of course. I remember it now. That is why the name is familiar. But I really know nothing of the details.'

Holmes waved his hand towards some papers on a chair. 'I had no idea that the case was coming my way or I should have had my extracts ready,' said he. 'The fact is that the problem, though exceedingly sensational, appeared to present no difficulty. The interesting personality of the accused does not obscure the clearness of the evidence. That was the view taken by the coroner's jury and also in the police-court proceedings. It is now referred to the Assizes at Winchester. I fear it is a thankless business. I can discover facts, Watson, but I cannot change them. Unless some entirely new and unexpected ones come to light I do not see what my client can hope for.'

'Your client?'

'Ah, I forgot I had not told you. I am getting into your involved habit, Watson, of telling a story backwards. You had best read this first.'

The letter which he handed to me, written in a bold, masterful hand, ran as follows:

CLARIDGE'S HOTEL, October 3rd.

DEAR MR SHERLOCK HOLMES,

I can't see the best woman God ever made go to her death without doing all that is possible to save her. I can't explain things – I can't even try to explain them, but I know beyond all doubt that Miss Dunbar is innocent. You know the facts – who doesn't? It has been the gossip of the country. And never a voice raised for her! It's the damned injustice of it all that makes me crazy. That woman has a heart that wouldn't let her kill a fly. Well, I'll come at eleven tomorrow and see if you can get some ray of light in the dark. Maybe I have a clue and don't know it. Anyhow, all I know and all I have and all I am are for your use if only you can save her. If ever in your life you showed your powers, put them now into this case.

Yours faithfully,
J. NEIL GIBSON

'There you have it,' said Sherlock Holmes, knocking out the ashes of his after-breakfast pipe and slowly refilling it. 'That is the gentleman I await. As to the story, you have hardly time to master all these papers, so I must give it to you in a nutshell if you are to take an intellectual interest in the proceedings. This man is the greatest financial power in the world, and a man, as I understand, of most violent and formidable character. He married a wife, the victim of this tragedy, of whom I know nothing save that she was past her prime, which was the more unfortunate as a very attractive governess superintended the education of two young children. These are the three people concerned, and the scene is a grand old manor-house, the centre of an historical English estate. Then as to the tragedy. The wife was found in the grounds nearly half a mile from the house, late at night, clad in her dinner dress, with a shawl over her shoulders and a revolver bullet through her brain. No weapon was found near her and there was no local clue as to the murder. No weapon near her, Watson – mark that! The crime seems to have been committed late in the evening, and the body was found by a gamekeeper about eleven o'clock, when it was examined by the police and by a doctor before being carried up to the house. Is this too condensed, or can you follow it clearly?'

'It is all very clear. But why suspect the governess?'

'Well, in the first place there is some very direct evidence. A

revolver with one discharged chamber and a calibre which corresponded with the bullet was found on the floor of her wardrobe.' His eyes fixed and he repeated in broken words, 'On – the – floor – of – her – wardrobe.' Then he sank into silence, and I saw that some train of thought had been set moving which I should be foolish to interrupt. Suddenly with a start he emerged into brisk life once more. 'Yes, Watson, it was found. Pretty damning, eh? So the two juries thought. Then the dead woman had a note upon her making an appointment at that very place and signed by the governess. How's that? Finally, there is the motive. Senator Gibson is an attractive person. If his wife dies, who more likely to succeed her than the young lady who had already by all accounts received pressing attentions from her employer. Love, fortune, power, all depending upon one middle-aged life. Ugly, Watson – very ugly!'

'Yes, indeed, Holmes.'

'Nor could she prove an alibi. On the contrary, she had to admit that she was down near Thor Bridge – that was the scene of the tragedy – about that hour. She couldn't deny it, for some passing villager had seen her there.'

'That really seems final.'

'And yet, Watson – and yet! This bridge – a single broad span of stone with balustraded sides – carried the drive over the narrowest part of a long, deep, reed-girt sheet of water. Thor Mere it is called. In the mouth of the bridge lay the dead woman. Such are the main facts. But here, if I mistake not, is our client, considerably before his time.'

Billy had opened the door, but the name he announced was an unexpected one. Mr Marlow Bates was a stranger to both of us. He was a thin, nervous wisp of a man with frightened eyes, and a twitching, hesitating manner – a man whom my own professional eye would judge to be on the brink of an absolute nervous breakdown.

'You seem agitated, Mr Bates,' said Holmes. 'Pray sit down. I fear I can only give you a short time, for I have an appointment at eleven.'

'I know you have,' our visitor gasped, shooting out short sentences like a man who is out of breath. 'Mr Gibson is coming. Mr Gibson is my employer. I am manager of his estate. Mr Holmes, he is a villain – an infernal villain.'

'Strong language, Mr Bates.'

'I have to be emphatic, Mr Holmes, for the time is so limited. I would not have him find me here for the world. He is almost due now. But I was so situated that I could not come earlier. His secretary, Mr Ferguson, only told me this morning of his appointment with you.'

'And you are his manager?'

'I have given him notice. In a couple of weeks I shall have shaken off his accursed slavery. A hard man, Mr Holmes, hard to all about him. Those public charities are a screen to cover his private iniquities. But his wife was his chief victim. He was brutal to her – yes, sir, brutal! How she came by her death I do not know, but I am sure that he had made her life a misery to her. She was a creature of the Tropics, a Brazilian by birth, as no doubt you know?'

'No; it had escaped me.'

'Tropical by birth and tropical by nature. A child of the sun and of passion. She had loved him as such women can love, but when her own physical charms had faded – I am told that they once were great – there was nothing to hold him. We all liked her and felt for her and hated him for the way that he treated her. But he is plausible and cunning. That is all I have to say to you. Don't take him at his face value. There is more behind. Now I'll go. No no, don't detain me! He is almost due.'

With a frightened look at the clock our strange visitor literally ran to the door and disappeared.

'Well! Well!' said Holmes, after an interval of silence. 'Mr Gibson seems to have a nice loyal household. But the warning is a useful one, and now we can only wait till the man himself appears.'

Sharp at the hour we heard a heavy step upon the stairs, and the famous millionaire was shown into the room. As I looked upon him I understood not only the fears and dislike of his manager, but also the execrations which so many business rivals have heaped upon his head. If I were a sculptor and desired to idealize the successful man of affairs, iron of nerve and leathery of conscience, I should choose Mr Neil Gibson as my model. His tall, gaunt craggy figure had a suggestion of hunger and rapacity. An Abraham Lincoln keyed to base uses instead of high ones would give some idea of the man. His face might have been chiselled in granite, hard-set, craggy, remorseless, with deep lines upon it, the scars of many a crisis. Cold grey eyes, looking shrewdly out from under bristling brows, surveyed us each in turn. He bowed in perfunctory fashion as Holmes mentioned my name, and then with a masterful air of possession he drew a chair up to my companion and seated himself with his bony knees almost touching him.

'Let me say right here, Mr Holmes,' he began, 'that money is nothing to me in this case. You can burn it if it's any use in lighting you to the truth. This woman is innocent and this woman has to be cleared, and it's up to you to do it. Name your figure!'

'My professional charges are upon a fixed scale,' said Holmes coldly. 'I do not vary them, save when I remit them altogether.'

'Well, if dollars make no difference to you, think of the reputation. If you pull this off every paper in England and America will be booming you. You'll be the talk of two continents.'

'Thank you, Mr Gibson, I do not think that I am in need of booming. It may surprise you to know that I prefer to work anonymously, and that it is the problem itself which attracts me. But we are wasting time. Let us get down to the facts.'

'I think that you will find all the main ones in the Press reports. I don't know that I can add anything which will help you. But if there is anything you would wish more light upon – well, I am here to give it.'

'Well, there is just one point.'

'What is it?'

'What were the exact relations between you and Miss Dunbar?'

The Gold King gave a violent start, and half rose from his chair. Then his massive calm came back to him.

'I suppose you are within your rights – and maybe doing your duty – in asking such a question, Mr Holmes.'

'We will agree to suppose so,' said Holmes.

'Then I can assure you that our relations were entirely and always those of an employer towards a young lady whom he never conversed with, or ever saw, save when she was in the company of his children.'

Holmes rose from his chair.

'I am a rather busy man, Mr Gibson,' said he, 'and I have no time or taste for aimless conversations. I wish you good morning.'

Our visitor had risen also and his great loose figure towered above Holmes. There was an angry gleam from under those bristling brows and a tinge of colour in the sallow cheeks.

'What the devil do you mean by this, Mr Holmes? Do you dismiss my case?'

'Well, Mr Gibson, at least I dismiss you. I should have thought my words were plain.'

'Plain enough, but what's at the back of it? Raising the price on me, or afraid to tackle it, or what? I've a right to a plain answer.'

'Well, perhaps you have,' said Holmes. 'I'll give you one. This case is quite sufficiently complicated to start with, without the further difficulty of false information.'

'Meaning that I lie.'

'Well, I was trying to express it as delicately as I could, but if you insist upon the word I will not contradict you.'

I sprang to my feet, for the expression upon the millionaire's face was fiendish in its intensity, and he had raised his great knotted fist. Holmes smiled languidly and reached his hand out for his pipe.

'Don't be noisy, Mr Gibson. I find that after breakfast even the smallest argument is unsettling. I suggest that a stroll in the morning air and a little quiet thought will be greatly to your advantage.'

With an effort the Gold King mastered his fury. I could not but admire him, for by a supreme self-command he had turned in a minute from a hot flame of anger to a frigid and contemptuous indifference.

'Well, it's your choice. I guess you know how to run your own business. I can't make you touch the case against your will. You've done yourself no good this morning, Mr Holmes, for I have broken stronger men than you. No man ever crossed me and was the better for it.'

'So many have said so, and yet here I am,' said Holmes, smiling. 'Well, good morning, Mr Gibson. You have a good deal yet to learn.'

Our visitor made a noisy exit, but Holmes smoked in imperturbable silence with dreamy eyes fixed upon the ceiling.

'Any views, Watson?' he asked at last.

'Well, Holmes, I must confess that when I consider that this is a man who would certainly brush any obstacle from his path, and when I remember that his wife may have been an obstacle and an object of dislike, as that man Bates plainly told us, it seems to me –'

'Exactly. And to me also.'

'But what were his relations with the governess and how did you discover them?'

'Bluff, Watson, bluff! When I considered the passionate, unconventional, unbusinesslike tone of his letter, and contrasted it with his self-contained manner and appearance, it was pretty clear that there was some deep emotion which centred upon the accused woman rather than upon the victim. We've got to understand the exact relations of those three people if we are to reach the truth. You saw the frontal attack which I made upon him and how imperturbably he received it. Then I bluffed him by giving him the impression that I was absolutely certain, when in reality I was only suspicious.'

'Perhaps he will come back?'

'He is sure to come back. He *must* come back. He can't leave it where it is. Ha! isn't that a ring? Yes, there is his footstep. Well, Mr Gibson, I was just saying to Dr Watson that you were somewhat overdue.'

The Gold King had re-entered the room in a more chastened mood than he had left it. His wounded pride still showed in his resentful eyes, but his common sense had shown him that he must yield if he would attain his end.

'I've been thinking it over, Mr Holmes, and I feel that I have been hasty in taking your remarks amiss. You are justified in getting down to the facts, whatever they may be, and I think the more of you for it. I can assure you, however, that the relations between Miss Dunbar and me don't really touch this case.'

'That is for me to decide, is it not?'

'Yes, I guess that is so. You're like a surgeon who wants every symptom before he can give his diagnosis.'

'Exactly. That expresses it. And it is only a patient who has an object in deceiving his surgeon who would conceal the facts of his case.'

'That may be so, but you will admit, Mr Holmes, that most men would shy off a bit when they are asked point-blank what their relations with a woman may be – if there is really some serious feeling in the case. I guess most men have a little private reserve of their own in some corner of their souls where they don't welcome intruders. And you burst suddenly into it. But the object excuses you, since it was to try and save her. Well, the stakes are down and the reserve open and you can explore where you will. What is it you want?'

'The truth.'

The Gold King paused for a moment as one who marshals his thoughts. His grim, deep-lined face had become even sadder and more grave.

'I can give it to you in a very few words, Mr Holmes,' said he at last. 'There are some things that are painful as well as difficult to say, so I won't go deeper than is needful. I met my wife when I was gold-hunting in Brazil. Maria Pinto was the daughter of a Government official at Manáos, and she was very beautiful. I was young and ardent in those days, but even now, as I look back with colder blood and a more critical eye, I can see that she was rare and wonderful in her beauty. It was a deep rich nature, too, passionate, whole-hearted, tropical, ill-balanced, very different from the American women whom I had known. Well, to make a long story short, I loved her and I married her. It was only when the romance had passed – and it lingered for years – that I realized that we had nothing – absolutely nothing – in common. My love faded. If hers had faded also it might have been easier. But you know the wonderful way of women! Do what I might nothing could turn her from me. If I have been harsh to her, even brutal as some have said, it has been because I knew that if I could kill her love, or if it turned to hate, it would be easier for both of us. But nothing changed her. She adored me in those English woods as she had adored me twenty years ago on the banks of the Amazon. Do what I might, she was devoted as ever.

'Then came Miss Grace Dunbar. She answered our advertisement and became governess to our two children. Perhaps you have seen her portrait in the papers. The whole world has proclaimed that she also is a very beautiful woman. Now, I make no pretence to be more moral than my neighbours, and I will admit to you that I could not live under the same roof with such a woman and in daily contact with her without feeling a passionate regard for her. Do you blame me, Mr Holmes?'

'I do not blame you for feeling it. I should blame you if you expressed it, since this young lady was in a sense under your protection.'

'Well, maybe so,' said the millionaire, though for a moment the reproof had brought the old angry gleam into his eyes. 'I'm not pretending to be any better than I am. I guess all my life I've been a man that reached out his hand for what he wanted and I never wanted anything more than the love and possession of that woman. I told her so.'

'Oh, you did, did you?'

Holmes could look very formidable when he was moved.

'I said to her that if I could marry her I would, but that it was out of my power. I said that money was no object and that all I could do to make her happy and comfortable would be done.'

'Very generous, I am sure,' said Holmes, with a sneer.

'See here, Mr Holmes. I came to you on a question of evidence, not on a question of morals. I'm not asking for your criticism.'

'It is only for the young lady's sake that I touch your case at all,' said Holmes sternly. 'I don't know that anything she is accused of is really worse than what you have yourself admitted, that you have tried to ruin a defenceless girl who was under your roof. Some of you rich men have to be taught that all the world cannot be bribed into condoning your offences.'

To my surprise the Gold King took the reproof with equanimity.

'That's how I feel myself about it now. I thank God that my plans did not work out as I intended. She would have none of it, and she wanted to leave the house instantly.'

'Why did she not?'

'Well, in the first place, others were dependent upon her, and it was no light matter for her to let them all down by sacrificing her living. When I had sworn – as I did – that she should never be molested again, she consented to remain. But there was another reason. She knew the influence she had over me, and that it was stronger than any other influence in the world. She wanted to use it for good.'

'How?'

'Well, she knew something of my affairs. They are large, Mr Holmes – large beyond the belief of an ordinary man. I can make or break – and it is usually break. It wasn't individuals only. It was communities, cities, even nations. Business is a hard game, and the weak go to the wall. I played the game for all it was worth. I never squealed myself and I never cared if the other fellow squealed. But she saw it different. I guess she was right. She believed and said that a fortune for one man that was more than he needed should not be built on ten thousand ruined men who were left without the means of life. That was how she saw it, and I guess she could see past the dollars to something that was more lasting. She found that I listened to what she said, and she believed she was serving the world by influencing my actions. So she stayed – and then this came along.'

'Can you throw any light upon that?'

The Gold King paused for a minute or more, his head sunk in his hands, lost in deep thought.

'It's very black against her. I can't deny that. And women lead an inward life and may do things beyond the judgement of a man. At first I was so rattled and taken aback that I was ready to think she had been led away in some extraordinary fashion that was clean against her usual nature. One explanation came into my head. I give it to you, Mr Holmes, for what it is worth. There is no doubt that my wife was bitterly jealous. There is a soul-jealousy that can be as frantic as any body-jealousy, and though my wife had no cause – and I think she understood this – for the latter, she was aware that this English girl exerted an influence upon my mind and my acts that she herself never had. It was an influence for good, but that did not mend the matter. She was crazy with hatred, and the heat of the Amazon was always in her blood. She might have planned to murder Miss Dunbar – or we will say to threaten her with a gun and so frighten her into leaving us. Then there might have been a scuffle and the gun gone off and shot the woman who held it.'

'That possibility had already occurred to me,' said Holmes. 'Indeed, it is the only obvious alternative to deliberate murder.'

'But she utterly denies it.'

'Well, that is not final – is it? One can understand that a woman placed in so awful a position might hurry home still in her bewilderment holding the revolver. She might even throw it down among her clothes, hardly knowing what she is doing, and when it was found she might try to lie her way out by a total denial, since all explanation was impossible. What is against such a supposition?'

'Miss Dunbar herself.'

'Well, perhaps.'

Holmes looked at his watch. 'I have no doubt we can get the necessary permits this morning and reach Winchester by the evening train. When I have seen this young lady, it is very possible that I may be of more use to you in the matter, though I cannot promise that my conclusions will necessarily be such as you desire.'

There was some delay in the official pass, and instead of reaching Winchester that day we went down to Thor Place, the Hampshire estate of Mr Neil Gibson. He did not accompany us himself, but we had the address of Sergeant Coventry, of the local police, who had first examined into the affair. He was a tall, thin, cadaverous man, with a secretive and mysterious manner, which conveyed the idea that he knew or suspected a very great deal more than he dared to say. He had a trick, too, of suddenly sinking his voice to a whisper as if he had come upon something of vital importance, though the information was usually commonplace enough. Behind these tricks of manner he soon showed himself to be a decent, honest fellow who was not too proud to admit that he was out of his depth and would welcome any help.

'Anyhow, I'd rather have you than Scotland Yard, Mr Holmes,' said he. 'If the Yard gets called into a case, then the local loses all credit for success and may be blamed for failure. Now, you play straight, so I've heard.'

'I need not appear in the matter at all,' said Holmes, to the evident relief of our melancholy acquaintance. 'If I can clear it up I don't ask to have my name mentioned.'

'Well, it's very handsome of you, I am sure. And your friend, Dr Watson, can be trusted, I know. Now, Mr Holmes, as we walk down to the place there is one question I should like to ask you. I'd breathe it to no soul but you.' He looked round as though he hardly dare utter the words. 'Don't you think there might be a case against Mr Neil Gibson himself?'

'I have been considering that.'

'You've not seen Miss Dunbar. She is a wonderful fine woman in every way. He may well have wished his wife out of the road. And these Americans are readier with pistols than our folk are. It was *his* pistol, you know.'

'Was that clearly made out?'

'Yes, sir. It was one of a pair that he had.'

'One of a pair? Where is the other?'

'Well, the gentleman has a lot of fire-arms of one sort and another. We never quite matched that particular pistol – but the box was made for two.'

'If it was one of a pair you should surely be able to match it.'

'Well, we have them all laid out at the house if you would care to look them over.'

'Later, perhaps. I think we will walk down together and have a look at the scene of the tragedy.'

The conversation had taken place in the little front room of Sergeant Coventry's humble cottage which served as the local police-station. A walk of half a mile or so across a wind-swept heath, all gold and bronze with the fading ferns, brought us to a side-gate opening into the grounds of the Thor Place estate. A path led us through the pleasant preserves, and then from a clearing we saw the wide-spread, half-timbered house, half Tudor and half Georgian, upon the crest of the hill. Beside us there was a long, reedy pool, constricted in the centre where the main carriage drive passed over a stone bridge, but swelling into small lakes on either side. Our guide paused at the mouth of this bridge, and he pointed to the ground.

'That was where Mrs Gibson's body lay. I marked it by that stone.'

'I understand that you were there before it was moved?'

'Yes; they sent for me at once.'

'Who did?'

'Mr Gibson himself. The moment the alarm was given and he had rushed down with others from the house, he insisted that nothing should be moved until the police should arrive.'

'That was sensible. I gathered from the newspaper report that the shot was fired from close quarters.'

'Yes, sir, very close.'

'Near the right temple?'

'Just behind it, sir.'

'How did the body lie?'

'On the back, sir. No trace of a struggle. No marks. No weapon. The short note from Miss Dunbar was clutched in her left hand.'

'Clutched, you say?'

'Yes, sir; we could hardly open the fingers.'

'That is of great importance. It excludes the idea that anyone could have placed the note there after death in order to furnish a false clue. Dear me! The note, as I remember, was quite short. "I will be at Thor Bridge at nine o'clock. – G. Dunbar." Was that not so?'

'Yes, sir.'

'Did Miss Dunbar admit writing it?'

'Yes, sir.'

'What was her explanation?'

'Her defence was reserved for the Assizes. She would say nothing.'

'The problem is certainly a very interesting one. The point of the letter is very obscure, is it not?'

'Well, sir,' said the guide, 'it seemed, if I may be so bold as to say so, the only really clear point in the whole case.'

Holmes shook his head.

'Granting that the letter is genuine and was really written, it was certainly received some time before – say one hour or two. Why, then, was this lady still clasping it in her left hand? Why should she carry it so carefully? She did not need to refer to it in the interview. Does it not seem remarkable?'

'Well, sir, as you put it, perhaps it does.'

'I think I should like to sit quietly for a few minutes and think it out.' He seated himself upon the stone ledge of the bridge, and I could see his quick grey eyes darting their questioning glances in every direction. Suddenly he sprang up again and ran across to the opposite parapet, whipped his lens from his pocket, and began to examine the stonework.

'This is curious,' said he.

'Yes, sir; we saw the chip on the ledge. I expect it's been done by some passer-by.'

The stonework was grey, but at this one point it showed white for a space not larger than a sixpence. When examined closely one could see that the surface was chipped as by a sharp blow.

'It took some violence to do that,' said Holmes thoughtfully. With his cane he struck the ledge several times without leaving a mark. 'Yes, it was a hard knock. In a curious place, too. It was not from above but from below, for you see that it is on the *lower* edge of the parapet.'

'But it is at least fifteen feet from the body.'

'Yes, it is fifteen feet from the body. It may have nothing to do with the matter, but it is a point worth nothing. I do not think we have anything more to learn here. There were no footsteps, you say?'

'The ground was iron hard, sir. There were no traces at all.'

'Then we can go. We will go up to the house first and look over these weapons of which you speak. Then we shall get on to Winchester, for I should desire to see Miss Dunbar before we go farther.'

Mr Neil Gibson had not returned from town, but we saw in the house the neurotic Mr Bates who had called upon us in the morning. He showed us with a sinister relish the formidable array of firearms of various shapes and sizes which his employer had accumulated in the course of an adventurous life.

'Mr Gibson has his enemies, as anyone would expect who knew him and his methods,' said he. 'He sleeps with a loaded revolver in the drawer beside his bed. He is a man of violence, sir, and there are times when all of us are afraid of him. I am sure that the poor lady who has passed was often terrified.'

'Did you ever witness physical violence towards her?'

'No, I cannot say that. But I have heard words which were nearly as bad – words of cold, cutting contempt, even before the servants.'

'Our millionaire does not seem to shine in private life,' remarked Holmes, as we made our way to the station. 'Well, Watson, we have come on a good many facts, some of them new ones, and yet I seem some way from my conclusion. In spite of the very evident dislike which Mr Bates has to his employer, I gather from him that when the alarm came he was undoubtedly in his library. Dinner was over at eight-thirty and all was normal up to then. It is true that the alarm was somewhat late in the evening, but the tragedy certainly occurred about the hour named in the note. There is no evidence at all that Mr Gibson had been out of doors since his return from town at five o'clock. On the other hand, Miss Dunbar, as I understand it, admits that she had made an appointment to meet Mrs Gibson at the bridge. Beyond this she would say nothing, as her lawyer had advised her to reserve her defence. We have several very vital questions to ask that young lady, and my mind will not be easy until we have seen her. I must confess that the case would seem to me to be very black against her if it were not for one thing.'

'And what is that, Holmes?'

'The finding of the pistol in her wardrobe.'

'Dear me, Holmes!' I cried, 'that seemed to me to be the most damning incident of all.'

'Not so, Watson. It had struck me even at my first perfunctory reading as very strange, and now that I am in closer touch with the case it is my only firm ground for hope. We must look for consistency. Where there is a want of it we must suspect deception.'

'I hardly follow you.'

'Well, now, Watson, suppose for a moment that we visualize you in the character of a woman who, in a cold, premeditated fashion, is about to get rid of a rival. You have planned it. A note has been written. The victim has come. You have your weapon. The crime is done. It has been workmanlike and complete. Do you tell me that after carrying out so crafty a crime you would now ruin your reputation as a criminal by forgetting to fling your weapon into those adjacent reed-beds which would for ever cover it, but you must needs carry it carefully home and put it in your own wardrobe, the very first place that would be searched? Your best friends would hardly call you a schemer, Watson, and yet I could not picture you doing anything so crude as that.'

'In the excitement of the moment –'

'No, no, Watson, I will not admit that it is possible. Where a crime is coolly premeditated, then the means of covering it are coolly premeditated also. I hope, therefore, that we are in the presence of a serious misconception.'

'But there is so much to explain.'

'Well, we shall set about explaining it. When once your point of view is changed, the very thing which was so damning becomes a clue to the truth. For example, there is the revolver. Miss Dunbar disclaims all knowledge of it. On our new theory she is speaking truth when she says so. Therefore, it was placed in her wardrobe. Who placed it there? Someone who wished to incriminate her. Was not that person the actual criminal? You see how we come at once upon a most fruitful line of inquiry.'

We were compelled to spend the night at Winchester, as the formalities had not yet been completed, but next morning, in the company of Mr Joyce Cummings, the rising barrister who was entrusted with the defence, we were allowed to see the young lady in her cell. I had expected from all that we had heard to see a beautiful woman, but I can never forget the effect which Miss Dunbar produced upon me. It was no wonder that even the masterful millionaire had found in her something more powerful than himself – something which could control and guide him. One felt, too, as one looked at that strong, clear-cut and yet sensitive face, that even should she be capable of some impetuous deed, none the less there was an innate nobility of character which would make her influence always for the good. She was a brunette, tall, with a noble figure and commanding presence, but her dark eyes had in them this appealing, helpless expression of the hunted creature who feels the nets around it, but can see no way out from the toils. Now, as she realized the presence and the help of my famous friend, there came a touch of colour in her wan cheeks and a light of hope began to glimmer in the glance which she turned upon us.

'Perhaps Mr Neil Gibson has told you something of what occurred between us?' she asked, in a low, agitated voice.

'Yes,' Holmes answered; 'you need not pain yourself by entering into that part of the story. After seeing you, I am prepared to accept Mr Gibson's statement both as to the influence which you had over him and as to the innocence of your relations with him. But why was the whole situation not brought out in court?'

'It seemed to me incredible that such a charge could be sustained. I thought that if we waited the whole thing must clear itself up without our being compelled to enter into painful details of the inner life of the family. But I understand that far from clearing it has become even more serious.'

'My dear young lady,' cried Holmes earnestly, 'I beg you to have no illusions upon the point. Mr Cummings here would assure you that all the cards are at present against us, and that we must do everything that is possible if we are to win clear. It would be a cruel deception to pretend that you are not in very great danger. Give me all the help you can, then, to get at the truth.'

'I will conceal nothing.'

'Tell us, then, of your true relations with Mr Gibson's wife.'

'She hated me, Mr Holmes. She hated me with all the fervour of her tropical nature. She was a woman who would do nothing by halves, and the measure of her love for her husband was the measure also of her hatred for me. It is probable that she misunderstood our relations. I would not wish to wrong her, but she loved so vividly in a physical sense that she could hardly understand the mental, and even spiritual, tie which held her husband to me, or imagine that it was only my desire to influence his power to good ends which kept me under his roof. I can see now that I was wrong. Nothing could justify me in remaining where I was a cause of unhappiness, and yet it is certain that the unhappiness would have remained even if I had left the house.'

'Now, Miss Dunbar,' said Holmes, 'I beg you to tell us exactly what occurred that evening.'

'I can tell you the truth so far as I know it, Mr Holmes, but I am in a position to prove nothing, and there are points – the most vital points – which I can neither explain nor can I imagine any explanation.'

'If you will find the facts, perhaps others may find the explanation.'

'With regard, then, to my presence at Thor Bridge that night, I received a note from Mrs Gibson in the morning. It lay on the table of the schoolroom, and it may have been left there by her own hand. It implored me to see her there after dinner, said she had something important to say to me, and asked me to leave an answer on the sundial in the garden, as she desired no one to be in our confidence. I saw no reason for such secrecy, but I did as she asked, accepting the appointment. She asked me to destroy her note and I burned it in the schoolroom grate. She was very much afraid of her husband, who treated her with a harshness for which I frequently reproached him, and I could only imagine that she acted in this way because she did not wish him to know of our interview.'

'Yet she kept your reply very carefully?'

'Yes. I was surprised to hear that she had it in her hand when she died.'

'Well, what happened then?'

'I went down as I had promised. When I reached the bridge she was waiting for me. Never did I realize till that moment how this poor creature hated me. She was like a mad woman – indeed, I think she *was* a mad woman, subtly mad with the deep power of deception which insane people may have. How else could she have met me with unconcern every day and yet had so raging a hatred of me in her heart? I will not say what she said. She poured

her whole wild fury out in burning and horrible words. I did not even answer – I could not. It was dreadful to see her. I put my hands to my ears and rushed away. When I left her she was standing still shrieking out her curses at me, in the mouth of the bridge.'

'Where she was afterwards found?'

'Within a few yards from the spot.'

'And yet, presuming that she met her death shortly after you left her, you heard no shot?'

'No, I heard nothing. But, indeed, Mr Holmes, I was so agitated and horrified by this terrible outbreak that I rushed to get back to the peace of my own room, and I was incapable of noticing anything which happened.'

'You say that you returned to your room. Did you leave it again before next morning?'

'Yes; when the alarm came that the poor creature had met her death I ran out with the others.'

'Did you see Mr Gibson?'

'Yes; he had just returned from the bridge when I saw him. He had sent for the doctor and the police.'

'Did he seem to you much perturbed?'

'Mr Gibson is a very strong, self-contained man. I do not think that he would ever show his emotions on the surface. But I, who knew him so well, could see that he was deeply concerned.'

'Then we come to the all-important point. This pistol that was found in your room. Had you ever seen it before?'

'Never, I swear it.'

'When was it found?'

'Next morning, when the police made their search.'

'Among your clothes?'

'Yes; on the floor of my wardrobe under my dresses.'

'You could not guess how long it had been there?'

'It had not been there the morning before.'

'How do you know?'

'Because I tidied out the wardrobe.'

'That is final. Then someone came into your room and placed the pistol there in order to inculpate you.'

'It must have been so.'

'And when?'

'It could only have been at meal-time, or else at the hours when I would be in the schoolroom with the children.'

'As you were when you got the note?'

'Yes; from that time onwards for the whole morning.'

'Thank you, Miss Dunbar. Is there any other point which could help me in the investigation?'

'I can think of none.'

'There was some sign of violence on the stonework of the bridge – a perfectly fresh chip just opposite the body. Could you suggest any possible explanation of that?'

'Surely it must be a mere coincidence.'

'Curious, Miss Dunbar, very curious. Why should it appear at the very time of the tragedy and why at the very place?'

'But what could have caused it? Only great violence could have such an effect.'

Holmes did not answer. His pale, eager face had suddenly assumed that tense, far-away expression which I had learned to associate with the supreme manifestations of his genius. So evident was the crisis in his mind that none of us dared to speak, and we sat, barrister, prisoner, and myself, watching him in a concentrated and absorbed silence. Suddenly he sprang from his chair, vibrating with nervous energy and the pressing need for action.

'Come, Watson, come!' he cried.

'What is it, Mr Holmes?'

'Never mind, my dear lady. You will hear from me, Mr Cummings. With the help of the God of justice I will give you a case which will make England ring. You will get news by tomorrow, Miss Dunbar, and meanwhile take my assurance that the clouds are lifting and that I have every hope that the light of truth is breaking through.'

It was not a long journey from Winchester to Thor Place, but it was long to me in my impatience, while for Holmes it was evident that it seemed endless; for, in his nervous restlessness, he could not sit still, but paced the carriage or drummed with his long, sensitive fingers upon the cushions beside him. Suddenly, however, as we neared our destination he seated himself opposite to me – we had a first-class carriage to ourselves – and laying a hand upon each of my knees he looked into my eyes with the peculiarly mischievous gaze which was characteristic of his more imp-like moods.

'Watson,' said he, 'I have some recollection that you go armed upon these excursions of ours.'

It was as well for him that I did so, for he took little care for his own safety when his mind was once absorbed by a problem, so that more than once my revolver had been a good friend in need. I reminded him of the fact.

'Yes, yes, I am a little absent-minded in such matters. But have you your revolver on you?'

I produced it from my hip-pocket, a short, handy, but very serviceable little weapon. He undid the catch, shook out the cartridges, and examined it with care.

'It's heavy – remarkably heavy,' said he.

'Yes, it is a solid bit of work.'

He mused over it for a minute.

'Do you know, Watson,' said he, 'I believe your revolver is going to have a very intimate connection with the mystery which we are investigating.'

'My dear Holmes, you are joking.'

'No, Watson, I am very serious. There is a test before us. If the test comes off, all will be clear. And the test will depend upon the conduct of this little weapon. One cartridge out. Now we will replace the other five and put on the safety-catch. So! That increases the weight and makes it a better reproduction.'

I had no glimmer of what was in his mind nor did he enlighten me, but sat lost in thought until we pulled up in the little Hampshire station. We secured a ramshackle trap, and in a quarter of an hour were at the house of our confidential friend, the sergeant.

'A clue, Mr Holmes? What is it?'

'It all depends upon the behaviour of Dr Watson's revolver,' said my friend. 'Here it is. Now, officer, can you give me ten yards of string?'

The village shop provided a ball of stout twine.

'I think that this is all we will need,' said Holmes. 'Now, if you please, we will get off on what I hope is the last stage of our journey.'

The sun was setting and turning the rolling Hampshire moor into a wonderful autumnal panorama. The sergeant, with many critical and incredulous glances, which showed his deep doubts of the sanity of my companion, lurched along beside us. As we approached the scene of the crime I could see that my friend under all his habitual coolness was in truth deeply agitated.

'Yes,' he said, in answer to my remark, 'you have seen me miss my mark before, Watson. I have an instinct for such things, and yet it has sometimes played me false. It seemed a certainty when first it flashed across my mind in the cell at Winchester, but one drawback of an active mind is that one can always conceive alternative explanations which would make our scent a false one. And yet – and yet – Well, Watson, we can but try.'

As he walked he had firmly tied one end of the string to the handle of the revolver. We had now reached the scene of the tragedy. With great care he marked out under the guidance of the policeman the exact spot where the body had been stretched. He then hunted among the heather and the ferns until he found a considerable stone. This he secured to the other end of his line of string, and he hung it over the parapet of the bridge so that it swung clear above the water. He then stood on the fatal spot, some distance from the edge of the bridge, with my revolver in his hand, the string being taut between the weapon and the heavy stone on the farther side.

'Now for it!' he cried.

At the words he raised the pistol to his head, and then let go his

'HOLMES WAS KNEELING BESIDE THE STONEWORK, AND A JOYOUS CRY SHOWED THAT HE HAD FOUND WHAT HE EXPECTED.'

grip. In an instant it had been whisked away by the weight of the stone, had struck with a sharp crack against the parapet, and had vanished over the side into the water. It had hardly gone before Holmes was kneeling beside the stonework, and a joyous cry showed that he had found what he expected.

'Was there ever a more exact demonstration?' he cried. 'See, Watson, your revolver has solved the problem!' As he spoke he pointed to a second chip of the exact size and shape of the first which had appeared on the under edge of the stone balustrade.

'We'll stay at the inn tonight,' he continued, as he rose and faced the astonished sergeant. 'You will, of course, get a grappling-hook and you will easily restore my friend's revolver. You will also find beside it the revolver, string and weight with which this vindictive woman attempted to disguise her own crime and to fasten a charge of murder upon an innocent victim. You can let Mr Gibson know that I will see him in the morning, when steps can be taken for Miss Dunbar's vindication.'

Late that evening, as we sat together smoking our pipes in the village inn, Holmes gave me a brief review of what had passed.

'I fear, Watson,' said he, 'that you will not improve any reputation which I may have acquired by adding the Case of the Thor Bridge Mystery to your annals. I have been sluggish in mind and wanting in that mixture of imagination and reality which is the basis of my art. I confess that the chip in the stonework was a sufficient clue to suggest the true solution, and that I blame myself for not having attained it sooner.

'It must be admitted that the workings of this unhappy woman's mind were deep and subtle, so that it was no very simple matter to unravel her plot. I do not think that in our adventures we have ever come across a stranger example of what perverted love can bring about. Whether Miss Dunbar was her rival in a physical or in a merely mental sense seems to have been equally unforgivable in her eyes. No doubt she blamed this innocent lady for all those harsh dealings and unkind words with which her husband tried to repel her too demonstrative affection. Her first resolution was to end her own life. Her second was to do it in such a way as to involve her victim in a fate which was worse far than any sudden death could be.

'We can follow the various steps quite clearly, and they show a remarkable subtlety of mind. A note was extracted very cleverly from Miss Dunbar which would make it appear that she had chosen the scene of the crime. In her anxiety that it should be discovered she somewhat overdid it, by holding it in her hand to the last. This alone should have excited any suspicions earlier than it did.

'Then she took one of her husband's revolvers – there was, as you saw, an arsenal in the house – and kept it for her own use. A similar one she concealed that morning in Miss Dunbar's wardrobe after discharging one barrel, which she could easily do in the woods without attracting attention. She then went down to the bridge where she had contrived this exceedingly ingenious method for getting rid of her weapon. When Miss Dunbar appeared she used her last breath in pouring out her hatred, and then, when she was out of hearing, carried out her terrible purpose. Every link is now in its place and the chain is complete. The papers may ask why the mere was not dragged in the first instance, but it is easy to be wise after the event, and in any case the expanse of a reed-filled lake is no easy matter to drag unless you have a clear perception of what you are looking for and where. Well, Watson, we have helped a remarkable woman, and also a formidable man. Should they in the future join their forces, as seems not unlikely, the financial world may find that Mr Neil Gibson has learned something in that schoolroom of Sorrow where our earthly lessons are taught.'

The Adventure of the Gloria Scott

'I have some papers here,' said my friend, Sherlock Holmes, as we sat one winter's night on either side of the fire, 'which I really think, Watson, it would be worth your while to glance over. These are the documents in the extraordinary case of the *Gloria Scott*, and this is the message which struck Justice of the Peace Trevor dead with horror when he read it.'

He had picked from a drawer a little tarnished cylinder, and, undoing the tape, he handed me a short note scrawled upon a half-sheet of slate-grey paper.

'The supply of game for London is going steadily up,' it ran. 'Head-keeper Hudson, we believe, has been now told to receive all orders for fly-paper, and for preservation of your hen pheasant's life.'

As I glanced up from reading this enigmatical message I saw Holmes chuckling at the expression upon my face.

'You look a little bewildered,' said he.

'I cannot see how such a message as this could inspire horror. It seems to me to be rather grotesque than otherwise.'

'Very likely. Yet the fact remains that the reader, who was a fine, robust old man, was knocked clean down by it, as if it had been the butt-end of a pistol.'

'You arouse my curiosity,' said I. 'But why did you say just now that there were very particular reasons why I should study this case?'

'Because it was the first in which I was ever engaged.'

I had often endeavoured to elicit from my companion what had first turned his mind in the direction of criminal research, but I had never caught him before in a communicative humour.

Now he sat forward in his armchair, and spread out the documents upon his knees. Then he lit his pipe and sat for some time smoking and turning them over.

'You never heard me talk of Victor Trevor?' he asked. 'He was the only friend I made during the two years that I was at college. I was never a very sociable fellow, Watson, always rather fond of moping in my rooms and working out my own little methods of thought, so that I never mixed much with the men of my year. Bar fencing and boxing I had few athletic tastes, and then my line of study was quite distinct from that of the other fellows, so that we had no points of contact at all. Trevor was the only man I knew, and that only through the accident of his bull-terrier freezing on to my ankle one morning as I went down to chapel.

'It was a prosaic way of forming a friendship, but it was effective. I was laid by the heels for ten days, and Trevor used to come in to inquire after me. At first it was only a minute's chat, but soon his visits lengthened, and before the end of the term we

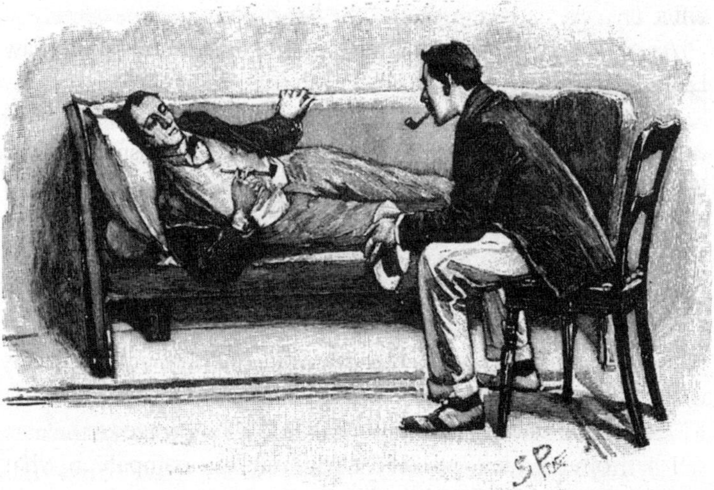

'TREVOR USED TO COME IN TO INQUIRE AFTER ME.'

were close friends. He was a hearty, full-blooded fellow, full of spirit and energy, the very opposite to me in most respects; but we found we had some subjects in common, and it was a bond of union when I learned that he was as friendless as I. Finally, he invited me down to his father's place at Donnithorpe, in Norfolk, and I accepted his hospitality for a month of the long vacation.

'Old Trevor was evidently a man of some wealth and consideration, a J. P. and a landed proprietor. Donnithorpe is a little hamlet just to the north of Langmere, in the country of the Broads. The house was an old-fashioned, wide-spread, oak-beamed, brick building, with a fine lime-lined avenue leading up to it. There was excellent wild-duck shooting in the fens, remarkably good fishing, a small but select library, taken over, as I understood, from a former occupant, and a tolerable cook, so that it would be a fastidious man who could not put in a pleasant month there.

'Trevor senior was a widower, and my friend was his only son. There had been a daughter, I heard, but she had died of diphtheria while on a visit to Birmingham. The father interested me extremely. He was a man of little culture, but with a considerable amount of rude strength both physically and mentally. He knew hardly any books, but he had travelled far, had seen much of the world, and had remembered all that he had learned. In person he was a thick-set, burly man with a shock of grizzled hair, a brown, weather-beaten face, and blue eyes which were keen to the verge of fierceness. Yet he had a reputation for kindness and charity in the countryside, and was noted for the leniency of his sentences from the bench.

'One evening, shortly after my arrival, we were sitting over a glass of port after dinner, when young Trevor began to talk about those habits of observation and inference which I had already formed into a system, although I had not yet appreciated the part which they were to play in my life. The old man evidently thought that his son was exaggerating in his description of one or two trivial feats which I had performed.

'"Come now, Mr Holmes," said he, laughing good-humouredly, "I'm an excellent subject, if you can deduce anything from me."

'"I fear there is not very much," I answered. "I might suggest that you have gone about in fear of some personal attack within the last twelve months."

'The laugh faded from his lips, and he stared at me in great surprise.

'"Well, that's true enough," said he. "You know, Victor," turning to his son, "when we broke up that poaching gang, they swore to knife us; and Sir Edward Hoby has actually been attacked. I've always been on my guard since then, though I have no idea how you know it."

'"You have a very handsome stick," I answered. "By the inscription, I observed that you had not had it more than a year. But you have taken some pains to bore the head of it and pour melted lead into the hole, so as to make it a formidable weapon. I argued that you would not take such precautions unless you had some danger to fear."

'"Anything else?" he asked, smiling.

'"You have boxed a good deal in your youth."

'"Right again. How did you know it? Is my nose knocked a little out of the straight?"

'"No," said I. "It is your ears. They have the peculiar flattening and thickening which marks the boxing man."

'"Anything else?"

'"You have done a great deal of digging, by your callosities."

'"Made all my money at the gold-fields."

'"You have been in New Zealand."

'"Right again."

'"You have visited Japan."

'"Quite true."

'"And you have been most intimately associated with someone whose initials were J. A., and whom you afterwards were eager to entirely forget."

'Mr Trevor stood slowly up, fixed his large blue eyes on me with a strange, wild stare, and then pitched forward on his face among the nutshells which strewed the cloth, in a dead faint.

'You can imagine, Watson, how shocked both his son and I were. His attack did not last long, however, for when we undid his collar and sprinkled the water from one of the finger glasses over his face, he gave a gasp or two and sat up.

' "Ah, boys!" said he, forcing a smile. "I hope I haven't frightened you. Strong as I look, there is a weak place in my heart, and it does not take much to knock me over. I don't know how you manage this, Mr Holmes, but it seems to me that all the detectives of fact and of fancy would be children in your hands. That's your line of life, sir, and you may take the word of a man who has seen something of the world."

'And that recommendation, with the exaggerated estimate of my ability with which he prefaced it, was, if you will believe me, Watson, the very first thing which ever made me feel that a profession might be made out of what had up to that time been the merest hobby. At the moment, however, I was too much concerned at the sudden illness of my host to think of anything else.

' "I hope that I have said nothing to pain you," said I.

' "Well, you certainly touched upon rather a tender point. Might I ask how you know and how much you know?" He spoke now in a half-jesting fashion, but a look of terror still lurked at the back of his eyes.

' "It is simplicity itself," said I. "When you bared your arm to draw that fish into the boat, I saw that 'J. A.' had been tattooed in the bend of the elbow. The letters were still legible, but it was perfectly clear from their blurred appearance, and from the staining of the skin round them, that efforts had been made to obliterate them. It was obvious, then, that those initials had once been very familiar to you, and that you had afterwards wished to forget them."

' "What an eye you have!" he cried, with a sigh of relief. "It is just as you say. But we won't talk of it. Of all ghosts the ghosts of our old loves are the worst. Come into the billiard-room and have a quiet cigar."

'From that day, amid all his cordiality, there was always a touch of suspicion in Mr Trevor's manner towards me. Even his son remarked it. "You've given the governor such a turn," said he, "that he'll never be sure again of what you know and what you don't know." He did not mean to show it, I am sure, but it was so strongly in his mind that it peeped out at every action. At last I became so convinced that I was causing him uneasiness, that I drew my visit to a close. On the very day, however, before I left, an incident occurred which proved in the sequel to be of importance.

'We were sitting upon the lawn on garden chairs, the three of us, basking in the sun and admiring the view across the Broads, when the maid came out to say that there was a man at the door who wanted to see Mr Trevor.

' "What is his name?" asked my host.

' "He would not give any."

' "What does he want, then?"

' "He says that you know him, and that he only wants a moment's conversation."

' "Show him round here." An instant afterwards there appeared a little weazened fellow, with a cringing manner and a shambling style of walking. He wore an open jacket, with a splotch of tar on the sleeve, a red and black check shirt, dungaree trousers, and heavy boots badly worn. His face was thin and brown and crafty, with a perpetual smile upon it, which showed an irregular line of yellow teeth, and his crinkled hands were half closed in a way that is distinctive of sailors. As he came slouching across the lawn I heard Mr Trevor make a sort of hiccuping noise in his throat, and, jumping out of his chair, he ran into the house. He was back in a moment, and I smelt a strong reek of brandy as he passed me.

' "Well, my man," said he, "what can I do for you?"

'The sailor stood looking at him with puckered eyes, and with the same loose-lipped smile upon his face.

'"You don't know me?" he asked.

'"Why, dear me, it is surely Hudson!" said Mr Trevor, in a tone of surprise.

'"Hudson it is, sir," said the seaman. "Why, it's thirty year and more since I saw you last. Here you are in your house, and me still picking my salt meat out of the harness cask."

'"Tut, you will find that I have not forgotten old times," cried Mr Trevor, and, walking towards the sailor, he said something in a low voice. "Go into the kitchen," he continued out loud, "and you will get food and drink. I have no doubt that I shall find you a situation."

'"Thank you, sir," said the seaman, touching his forelock. "I'm just off a two-yearer in an eight-knot tramp, short-handed at that, and I wants a rest. I thought I'd get it either with Mr Beddoes or with you."

'"HUDSON IT IS, SIR," SAID THE SEAMAN.'

'"Ah!" cried Mr Trevor, "you know where Mr Beddoes is?"

'"Bless you, sir, I know where all my old friends are," said the fellow, with a sinister smile, and slouched off after the maid to the kitchen. Mr Trevor mumbled something to us about having been shipmates with the man when he was going back to the diggings, and then, leaving us on the lawn, he went indoors. An hour later, when we entered the house we found him stretched dead drunk upon the dining-room sofa. The whole incident left a most ugly impression upon my mind, and I was not sorry next day to leave Donnithorpe behind me, for I felt that my presence must be a source of embarrassment to my friend.

'All this occurred during the first month of the long vacation. I went up to my London rooms, where I spent seven weeks working out a few experiments in organic chemistry. One day, however, when the autumn was far advanced and the vacation drawing to a close, I received a telegram from my friend imploring me to return to Donnithorpe, and saying that he was in great need of my advice and assistance. Of course I dropped everything and set out for the north once more.

'He met me with the dog-cart at the station, and I saw at a glance that the last two months had been very trying ones for him. He had grown thin and careworn, and had lost the loud, cheery manner for which he had been remarkable.

'"The governor is dying," were the first words he said.

'"Impossible!" I cried. "What is the matter?"

'"Apoplexy. Nervous shock. He's been on the verge all day. I doubt if we shall find him alive."

'I was, as you may think, Watson, horrified at this unexpected news.

'"What has caused it?" I said.

'"Ah, that is the point. Jump in, and we can talk it over while we drive. You remember that fellow who came upon the evening before you left us?"

'"Perfectly."

'"Do you know who it was that we let into the house that day?"

'"I have no idea."

'"It was the Devil, Holmes!" he cried.

'I stared at him in astonishment.

'"Yes; it was the Devil himself. We have not had a peaceful hour since – not one. The governor has never held up his head from that evening, and now the life has been crushed out of him, and his heart broken, all through this accursed Hudson."

'"What power had he, then?"

'"Ah, that is what I would give so much to know. The kindly, charitable, good old governor! How could he have fallen into the clutches of such a ruffian? But I am so glad that you have come, Holmes. I trust very much to your judgement and discretion, and I know that you will advise me for the best."

'We were dashing along the smooth, white country road, with a long stretch of Broads in front of us glimmering in the red light of the setting sun. From a grove upon our left I could already see the high chimneys and the flagstaff which marked the squire's dwelling.

'"My father made the fellow gardener," said my companion, "and then, as that did not satisfy him, he was promoted to be butler. The house seemed to be at his mercy, and he wandered about and did what he chose in it. The maids complained of his drunken habits and his vile language. The dad raised their wages all round to recompense them for the annoyance. The fellow would take the boat and my father's best gun and treat himself to little shooting parties. And all this with such a sneering, leering, insolent face, that I would have knocked him down twenty times over if he had been a man of my own age. I tell you, Holmes, I have had to keep a tight hold upon myself all this time, and now I am asking myself whether, if I had let myself go a little more, I might not have been a wiser man.

'"Well, matters went from bad to worse with us, and this animal, Hudson, became more and more intrusive, until at last, on his making some insolent reply to my father in my presence one day, I took him by the shoulder and turned him out of the room. He slunk away with a livid face, and two venomous eyes which uttered more threats than his tongue could do. I don't know what passed between the poor dad and him after that, but the dad came to me next day and asked me whether I would mind apologizing to Hudson. I refused, as you can imagine, and asked my father how he could allow such a wretch to take such liberties with himself and his household.

'"'Ah, my boy,' said he, 'it is all very well to talk, but you don't know how I am placed. But you shall know, Victor. I'll see that you shall know, come what may! You wouldn't believe harm of your poor old father, would you, lad?' He was very much moved, and shut himself up in the study all day, where I could see through the window that he was writing busily.

'"That evening there came what seemed to be a grand release, for Hudson told us that he was going to leave us. He walked into the dining-room as we sat after dinner and announced his intention in the thick voice of a half-drunken man.

'"'I've had enough of Norfolk,' said he, 'I'll run down to Mr Beddoes, in Hampshire. He'll be as glad to see me as you were, I dare say.'

'"'You're not going away in an unkind spirit, Hudson, I hope?' said my father, with a tameness which made my blood boil.

'"'I've not had my 'pology,' said he sulkily, glancing in my direction.

'"'Victor, you will acknowledge that you have used this worthy fellow rather roughly?' said the dad, turning to me.

'"'On the contrary, I think that we have both shown extraordinary patience towards him,' I answered.

'"'Oh, you do, do you?' he snarled. 'Very good, mate. We'll see about that!' He slouched out of the room, and half an hour afterwards left the house, leaving my father in a state of pitiable nervousness. Night after night I heard him pacing his room, and it was just as he was recovering his confidence that the blow did at last fall.

' "And how?" I asked eagerly.

' "In a most extraordinary fashion. A letter arrived for my father yesterday evening, bearing the Fordingbridge postmark. My father read it, clapped both his hands to his head, and began running round the room in little circles like a man who has been driven out of his senses. When I at last drew him down on to the sofa, his mouth and eyelids were all puckered on one side, and I saw that he had had a stroke. Dr Fordham came over at once, and we put him to bed; but the paralysis has spread, he has shown no sign of returning consciousness, and I think that we shall hardly find him alive."

' "You horrify me, Trevor!" I cried. "What, then, could have been in this letter to cause so dreadful a result?"

' "Nothing. There lies the inexplicable part of it. The message was absurd and trivial. Ah, my God, it is as I feared!"

'As he spoke we came round the curve of the avenue, and saw in the fading light that every blind in the house had been drawn down. As we dashed up to the door, my friend's face convulsed with grief, a gentleman in black emerged from it.

' "When did it happen, Doctor?" asked Trevor.

' "Almost immediately after you left."

' "Did he recover consciousness?"

' "For an instant before the end."

' "Any message for me?"

' "Only that the papers were in the back drawer of the Japanese cabinet."

'My friend ascended with the doctor to the chamber of death, while I remained in the study, turning the whole matter over and over in my head, and feeling as sombre as ever I had done in my life. What was the past of this Trevor: pugilist, traveller, and gold-digger; and how had he placed himself in the power of this acid-faced seaman? Why, too, should he faint at an allusion to the half-effaced initials upon his arm, and die of fright when he had a letter from Fordingbridge? Then I remembered that Fordingbridge was in Hampshire, and that this Mr Beddoes, whom the seaman had gone to visit, and presumably to blackmail, had also been mentioned as living in Hampshire. The letter, then, might either come from Hudson, the seaman, saying that he had betrayed the guilty secret which appeared to exist, or it might come from Beddoes, warning an old confederate that such a betrayal was imminent. So far it seemed clear enough. But, then, how could the letter be trivial and grotesque as described by the son? He must have misread it. If so, it must have been one of those ingenious secret codes which mean one thing while they seem to mean another. I must see this letter. If there were a hidden meaning in it, I was confident that I could pluck it forth. For an hour I sat pondering over it in the gloom, until at last a weeping maid brought in a lamp, and close at her heels came my friend Trevor, pale and composed, with these very papers, which lie upon my knee, held in his grasp. He sat down opposite to me, drew the lamp to the edge of the table, and handed me a short note scribbled, as you see, upon a single sheet of grey paper. "The supply of game for London is going steadily up," it ran. "Head-keeper Hudson, we believe, has been now told to receive all orders for fly-paper and for preservation of your hen pheasant's life."

'I dare say my face looked as bewildered as yours did just now when first I read this message. Then I re-read it very carefully. It was evidently as I had thought, and some second meaning must be buried in this strange combination of words. Or could it be that there was a pre-arranged significance to such phrases as "fly-paper" and "hen pheasant"? Such a meaning would be arbitrary, and could not be deduced in any way. And yet I was loath to believe that this was the case, and the presence of the word "Hudson" seemed to show that the subject of the message was as I had guessed, and that it was from Beddoes rather than the sailor. I tried it backwards, but the combination, "life pheasant's hen," was not encouraging. Then I tried alternate words, but neither "The of for" nor "supply game London" promised to throw any light upon it. Then in an instant the key of the riddle was in my hands, and I saw that every third word beginning with the first would give a message which might well drive old Trevor to despair.

'It was short and terse, the warning, as I now read it to my companion: "The game is up. Hudson has told all. Fly for your life."

'Victor Trevor sank his face into his shaking hands. "It must be that, I suppose," said he. "This is worse than death, for it means disgrace as well. But what is the meaning of these 'head-keepers' and 'hen pheasants'?"

'"It means nothing to the message, but it might mean a good deal to us if we had no other means of discovering the sender. You see that he has begun by writing, 'The . . . game . . . is,' and

'THE KEY OF THE RIDDLE WAS IN MY HANDS.'

so on. Afterwards he had, to fulfil the pre-arranged cipher, to fill in any two words in each space. He would naturally use the first words which came to his mind, and if there were so many which referred to sport among them, you may be tolerably sure that he is either an ardent shot or interested in breeding. Do you know anything of this Beddoes?"

'"Why, now that you mention it," said he, "I remember that my poor father used to have an invitation from him to shoot over his preserves every autumn."

'"Then it is undoubtedly from him that the note comes," said I. "It only remains for us to find out what this secret was which the sailor Hudson seems to have held over the heads of these two wealthy and respected men."

'"Alas, Holmes, I fear that it is one of sin and shame!" cried my friend. "But from you I shall have no secrets. Here is the statement which was drawn up by my father when he knew that the danger from Hudson had become imminent. I found it in the Japanese cabinet, as he told the doctor. Take it and read it to me, for I have neither the strength nor the courage to do it myself."

'These are the very papers, Watson, which he handed to me, and I will read them to you as I read them in the old study that night to him. They are endorsed outside as you see: "Some particulars of the voyage of the barque *Gloria Scott*, from her leaving Falmouth on the 8th October, 1855, to her destruction in N. lat. 15° 29', W. long. 25° 14', on November 6th." It is in the form of a letter, and runs in this way:

My dear, dear son, –

Now that approaching disgrace begins to darken the closing years of my life, I can write with all truth and honesty that it is not the terror of the law, it is not the loss of my position in the county, nor is it my fall in the eyes of all who have known me, which cuts me to the heart; but it is the thought that you should come to blush for me – you who love me, and who have seldom, I hope, had reason to do other than respect me. But if the blow falls which is forever hanging over me, then I should wish you to read this that you may know straight from me how far I have been to blame. On the other hand, if all should go well (which may kind God Almighty grant!), then if by any chance this paper should be still undestroyed, and should fall into your hands, I conjure you by all you hold sacred, by the memory of your dear mother, and by the love which has been between us, to hurl it into the fire, and to never give one thought to it again.

If, then, your eye goes on to read this line, I know that I shall already have been exposed and dragged from my home, or, as is more likely – for you know that my heart is weak – be lying with my tongue sealed for ever in death. In either case the time for suppression is past, and every word which I tell you is the naked truth; and this I swear as I hope for mercy.

My name, dear lad, is not Trevor. I was James Armitage in my younger days, and you can understand now the shock that it was to me a few weeks ago when your college friend addressed me in words which seemed to imply that he had surmised my secret. As Armitage it was that I entered a London banking house, and as Armitage I was convicted of breaking my country's laws, and was sentenced to transportation. Do not think very harshly of me, laddie. It was a debt of honour, so-called, which I had to pay, and I used money which was not my own to do it, in the certainty that I could replace it before there could be any possibility of its being missed. But the most dreadful ill-luck pursued me. The money which I had reckoned upon never came to hand, and a premature examination of accounts exposed my deficit. The case might have been dealt leniently with, but the laws were more harshly administered thirty years ago than now, and on my twenty-third birthday I found myself chained as a felon with thirty-seven other convicts in the 'tween decks of the barque *Gloria Scott*, bound for Australia.

It was the year '55, when the Crimean War was at its height, and the old convict ships had been largely used as transports in the Black Sea. The Government was compelled therefore to use smaller and less suitable vessels for sending out their prisoners. The *Gloria Scott* had been in the Chinese tea trade, but she was an old-fashioned, heavy-bowed, broad-beamed craft, and the new clippers had cut her out. She was a 500-ton boat, and besides her thirty-eight gaol-birds, she carried twenty-six of a crew, eighteen soldiers, a captain, three mates, a doctor, a chaplain, and four warders. Nearly a hundred souls were in her, all told, when we set sail from Falmouth.

The partitions between the cells of the convicts, instead of being of thick oak, as is usual to convict ships, were quite thin and frail. The man next to me upon the aft side was one whom I had particularly noticed when we were led down to the quay. He was a young man with a clear, hairless face, a long thin nose, and rather nutcracker jaws. He carried his head very jauntily in the air, had a swaggering style of walking, and was above all else remarkable for his extraordinary height. I don't think any of our heads would come up to his shoulder, and I am sure that he could not have measured less than six and a half feet. It was strange among so many sad and weary faces to see one which was full of energy and resolution. The sight of it was to me like a fire in a snowstorm. I was glad then to find that he was my neighbour, and gladder still when, in the dead of the night, I heard a whisper close to my ear, and found that he had managed to cut an opening in the board which separated us.

'Halloa, chummy!' said he, 'what's your name, and what are you here for?'

I answered him, and asked in turn who I was talking with.

'I'm Jack Prendergast,' said he, 'and, by God, you'll learn to bless my name before you've done with me!'

I remembered hearing of his case, for it was one which had made an immense sensation throughout the country, some time before my own arrest. He was a man of good family and of great ability, but of incurably vicious habits, who had, by an ingenious system of fraud, obtained huge sums of money from the leading London merchants.

'Ah, ah! You remember my case?' said he, proudly.

'Very well indeed.'

'Then maybe you remember something queer about it?'

'What was that, then?'

'I had nearly a quarter of a million, hadn't I?'

'So it was said.'

'But none was recovered, eh?'

'No.'

'Well, where d'ye suppose the balance is?' he asked.

'I have no idea,' said I.

'Right between my finger and thumb,' he cried. 'By God, I've got more pounds to my name than you have hairs on your head. And if you've money, my son, and know how to handle it and spread it, you can do *anything*! Now, you don't think it likely that a man who could do anything is going to wear his breeches out sitting in the stinking hold of a rat-gutted, beetle-ridden, mouldy old coffin of a China coaster? No, sir, such a man will look after himself, and will look after his chums. You may lay to that! You hold on to him, and you may kiss the Book that he'll haul you through.'

That was his style of talk, and at first I thought it meant nothing, but after a while, when he had tested me and sworn me in with all possible solemnity, he let me understand that there really was a plot to gain command of the vessel. A dozen of the prisoners had hatched it before they came aboard: Prendergast was the leader, and his money was the motive power.

'I'd a partner,' said he, 'a rare good man, as true as a stock to a barrel. He's got the dibs, he has, and where do you think he is at this moment? Why, he's the chaplain of this ship – the chaplain, no less! He came aboard with a black coat and his papers right, and money enough in his box to buy the thing right from keel to maintruck. The crew are his, body and soul. He could buy 'em at so much a gross with a cash discount, and he did it before ever they signed on. He's got two of the warders and Mercer the second mate, and he'd get the captain himself if he thought him worth it.'

'What are we to do, then?' I asked.

'What do you think?' said he. 'We'll make the coats of some of these soldiers redder than ever the tailor did.'

'But they are armed,' said I.

'And so shall we be, my boy. There's a brace of pistols for every mother's son of us, and if we can't carry this ship, with the crew at our back, it's time we were all sent to a young misses' boarding-school. You speak to your mate on the left tonight, and see if he is to be trusted.'

I did so, and found my other neighbour to be a young fellow in much the same position as myself, whose crime had been forgery. His name was Evans but he afterwards changed it, like myself, and he is now a rich and prosperous man in the South of England. He was ready enough to join the conspiracy, as the only means of saving ourselves, and before we had crossed the Bay there were only two of the prisoners who were not in the secret. One of these was of weak mind, and we did not dare to trust him, and the other was suffering from jaundice, and could not be of any use to us.

From the beginning there was really nothing to prevent us taking possession of the ship. The crew were a set of ruffians, specially picked for the job. The sham chaplain came into our cells to exhort us, carrying a black bag, supposed to be full of tracts; and so often did he come that by the third day we had each stowed away at the foot of our beds a file, a brace of pistols, a pound of powder, and twenty slugs. Two of the warders were agents of Prendergast, and the second mate was his right-hand man. The captain, the two mates, two warders,

Lieutenant Martin, his eighteen soldiers, and the doctor were all that we had against us. Yet, safe as it was, we determined to neglect no precaution, and to make our attack suddenly at night. It came, however, more quickly than we expected, and in this way:

One evening, about the third week after our start, the doctor had come down to see one of the prisoners, who was ill, and, putting his hand down the bottom of his bunk, he felt the outline of the pistols. If he had been silent he might have blown the whole thing; but he was a nervous little chap, so he gave a cry of surprise and turned so pale, that the man knew what was up in an instant and seized him. He was gagged before he could give the alarm, and tied down upon the bed. He had unlocked the door that led to the deck, and we were through it in a rush. The two sentries were shot down, and so was a corporal who came running to see what was the matter. There were two more soldiers at the door of the state-room, and their muskets seemed not to be loaded, for they never fired upon us, and they were shot while trying to fix their bayonets. Then we rushed on into the captain's cabin, but as we pushed open the door there was an explosion from within, and there he lay with his head on the chart of the Atlantic, which was pinned upon the table, while the chaplain stood, with a smoking pistol in his hand, at his elbow. The two mates had both been seized by the crew, and the whole business seemed to be settled.

The state-room was next the cabin, and we flocked in there and flopped down on the settees, all speaking together, for we were just mad with the feeling that we were free once more. There were lockers all round, and Wilson, the sham chaplain, knocked one of them in, and pulled out a dozen of brown sherry. We cracked off the necks of the bottles, poured the stuff out into tumblers, and were just tossing them off, when in an instant, without warning, there came a roar of muskets in our ears, and the saloon was so full of smoke that we could not see across the table. When it cleared away again the place was a shambles. Wilson and eight others were wriggling on the top of each other on the floor, and the blood and brown sherry on that table turn me sick now when I think of it. We were so cowed by the sight that I think we should have given the job up if it had not been for Prendergast. He bellowed like a bull and rushed for the door with all that were left alive at his heels. Out we ran, and there on the poop were the lieutenant and ten of his men. The swing skylights above the saloon table had been a bit open, and they had fired on us through the slit. We got on them before they could load, and they stood to it like men, but we had the upper hand of them, and in five minutes it was all over. My God! was there ever a slaughter-house like that ship? Prendergast was like a raging devil, and he picked the soldiers up as if they had been children and threw them overboard, alive or dead. There was one sergeant that was horribly wounded, and yet kept on swimming for a surprising time, until someone in mercy blew out his brains. When the fighting was over there was no one left of our enemies except just the warders, the mates, and the doctor.

It was over them that the great quarrel arose. There were many of us who were glad enough to win back our freedom, and yet who had no wish to have murder on our souls. It was one thing to knock the soldiers over with their muskets in their hands, and it was another to stand by while men were being killed in cold blood. Eight of us, five convicts and three sailors, said that we would not see it done. But there was no moving Prendergast and those who were with him. Our only chance of safety lay in making a clean job of it, said he, and he would not leave a tongue with power to wag in a witness-box. It nearly came to our sharing the fate of the prisoners, but at last he said that if we wished we might take a boat and go. We jumped at the offer, for we were already sick of these bloodthirsty doings, and we saw that there would be worse before it was done. We were given a suit of sailor's togs each, a barrel of water, two casks, one of junk and one of biscuits, and a compass. Prendergast threw us over a chart, told us that we were shipwrecked mariners whose ship had foundered in lat. 15° N. and long. 25° W., and then cut the painter and let us go.

And now I come to the most surprising part of my story, my dear son. The seamen had hauled the foreyard aback during the rising, but now as we left them they brought it square again, and, as there was a light wind from the north and east, the barque began to draw slowly away from us. Our boat lay, rising and falling, upon the long, smooth rollers, and Evans and I, who were the most educated of the party, were sitting in the sheets working out our position and planning what coast we should make for. It was a nice question, for the Cape of Verde was about 500 miles to the north of us, and the African coast about 700 miles to the east. On the whole, as the wind was coming round to north, we thought that Sierra Leone might be best, and turned our head in that direction, the barque being at that time nearly hull down on our starboard quarter. Suddenly as we looked at her we saw a dense black cloud of smoke shoot up from her, which hung like a monstrous tree upon the skyline. A few seconds later a roar like thunder burst upon our ears, and as the smoke thinned away there was no sign left of the *Gloria Scott*. In an instant we swept the boat's head round again, and pulled with all our strength for the place where the haze, still trailing over the water, marked the scene of this catastrophe.

It was a long hour before we reached it, and at first we feared we had come too late to save anyone. A splintered boat and a number of crates and fragments of spars rising and falling on the waves showed us where the vessel had foundered, but there was no sign of life, and we had turned away in despair when we heard a cry for help, and saw at some distance a piece of wreckage with a man lying stretched across it. When we pulled him aboard the boat he proved to be a young seaman of the name of Hudson, who was so burned and exhausted that he could give us no account of what had happened until the following morning.

It seemed that after we had left, Prendergast and his gang had proceeded to put to death the five remaining prisoners: the two warders had been shot and thrown overboard, and so also had the third mate. Prendergast then descended into the 'tween decks, and with his own hands cut the throat of the unfortunate surgeon. There only remained the first mate, who was a bold and active man. When he saw the convict approaching him with the bloody knife in his hand, he kicked off his bonds, which he had somehow contrived to loosen, and rushing down the deck he plunged into the afterhold.

A dozen convicts who descended with their pistols in search of him found him with a match-box in his hand seated beside an open powder barrel, which was one of a hundred carried on board, and swearing that he would blow all hands up if he were in any way molested. An instant later the explosion occurred, though Hudson thought it was caused by the misdirected bullet of one of the convicts rather than the mate's match. Be the cause what it may, it was the end of the *Gloria Scott*, and of the rabble who held command of her.

Such, in a few words, my dear boy, is the history of this terrible business in which I was involved. Next day we were picked up by the brig *Hotspur*, bound for Australia, whose captain found no difficulty in believing that we were the survivors of a passenger ship which had foundered. The transport ship, *Gloria Scott*, was set down by the Admiralty as being lost at sea, and no word has ever leaked out as to her true fate. After an excellent voyage the *Hotspur* landed us at Sydney, where Evans and I changed our names and made our way to the diggings, where among the crowds who were gathered from all nations, we had no difficulty in losing our former identities.

The rest I need not relate. We prospered, we travelled, we came back as rich colonials to England, and we bought country estates. For more than twenty years we have led peaceful and useful lives, and we hoped that our past was for ever buried. Imagine, then, my feelings when in the seaman who came to us I recognized instantly the man who had been picked off the wreck! He had tracked us down somehow, and had set himself to live upon our fears. You will understand now how it was that I strove to keep peace with him, and you will in some measure sympathize with me in the fears which fill me, now that he has gone from me to his other victim with threats upon his tongue.

'Underneath is written, in a hand so shaky as to be hardly legible, "Beddoes writes in cipher to say that H. has told all. Sweet Lord, have mercy on our souls!"

'That was the narrative which I read that night to young Trevor, and I think, Watson, that under the circumstances it was a dramatic one. The good fellow was heartbroken at it, and went out to the Terai tea planting, where I hear that he is doing well. As to the sailor and Beddoes, neither of them was ever heard of again after that day on which the letter of warning was written. They both disappeared utterly and completely. No complaint had been lodged with the police, so that Beddoes had mistaken a threat for a deed. Hudson had been seen lurking about, and it was believed by the police that he had done away with Beddoes, and had fled. For myself, I believe that the truth was exactly the opposite. I think it is most probable that Beddoes, pushed to desperation, and believing himself to have been already betrayed, had revenged himself upon Hudson, and had fled from the country with as much money as he could lay his hands on. Those are the facts of the case, Doctor, and if they are of any use to your collection, I am sure that they are very heartily at your service.'

The Adventure of the Six Napoleons

It was no very unusual thing for Mr Lestrade, of Scotland Yard, to look in upon us of an evening, and his visits were welcome to Sherlock Holmes, for they enabled him to keep in touch with all that was going on at the police headquarters. In return for the news which Lestrade would bring, Holmes was always ready to listen with attention to the details of any case upon which the detective was engaged, and was able occasionally, without any active interference, to give some hint or suggestion drawn from his own vast knowledge and experience.

On this particular evening Lestrade had spoken of the weather and the newspapers. Then he had fallen silent, puffing thoughtfully at his cigar. Holmes looked keenly at him.

'Anything remarkable on hand?' he asked.

'Oh, no, Mr Holmes, nothing very particular.'

'Then tell me all about it.'

Lestrade laughed.

'Well, Mr Holmes, there is no use denying that there *is* something on my mind. And yet it is such an absurd business that I hesitated to bother you about it. On the other hand, although it is trivial, it is undoubtedly queer, and I know that you have a taste for all that is out of the common. But in my opinion it comes more in Dr Watson's line than ours.'

'Disease?' said I.

'Madness, anyhow. And a queer madness too! You wouldn't think there was anyone living at this time of day who had such a hatred of Napoleon the First that he would break any image of him that he could see.'

Holmes sank back in his chair.

'That's no business of mine,' said he.

'Exactly. That's what I said. But then, when the man commits burglary in order to break images which are not his own, that brings it away from the doctor and on to the policeman.'

Holmes sat up again.

'Burglary! This is more interesting. Let me hear the details.'

Lestrade took out his official notebook and refreshed his memory from its pages.

'The first case reported was four days ago,' said he. 'It was at the shop of Morse Hudson, who has a place for the sale of pictures and statues in the Kennington Road. The assistant had left the front shop for an instant, when he heard a crash, and, hurrying in, found a plaster bust of Napoleon, which stood with several other works of art upon the counter, lying shivered into fragments. He rushed out into the road, but, although several

'LESTRADE TOOK OUT HIS OFFICIAL NOTE-BOOK.'

passers-by declared that they had noticed a man run out of the shop, he could neither see anyone nor could he find any means of identifying the rascal. It seemed to be one of those senseless acts of hooliganism which occur from time to time, and it was reported to the constable on the beat as such. The plaster cast was not worth more than a few shillings, and the whole affair appeared to be too childish for any particular investigation.

'The second case, however, was more serious and also more singular. It occurred only last night.

'In Kennington Road, and within a few hundred yards of Morse Hudson's shop, there lives a well-known medical practitioner, named Dr Barnicot, who has one of the largest practices upon the south side of the Thames. His residence and principal consulting-room is at Kennington Road, but he has a branch surgery and dispensary at Lower Brixton Road, two miles away. This Dr Barnicot is an enthusiastic admirer of Napoleon, and his house is full of books, pictures, and relics of the French Emperor. Some little time ago he purchased from Morse Hudson two duplicate plaster casts of the famous head of Napoleon by the French sculptor Devine. One of these he placed in his hall in the house at Kennington Road, and the other on the mantelpiece of the surgery at Lower Brixton. Well, when Dr Barnicot came down this morning he was astonished to find that his house had been burgled during the night, but that nothing had been taken save the plaster head from the hall. It had been carried out, and had been dashed savagely against the garden wall, under which its splintered fragments were discovered.'

Holmes rubbed his hands.

'This is certainly very novel,' said he.

'I thought it would please you. But I have not got to the end yet. Dr Barnicot was due at his surgery at twelve o'clock, and you can imagine his amazement when, on arriving there, he found that the window had been opened in the night, and that the broken pieces of his second bust were strewn all over the room.

It had been smashed to atoms where it stood. In neither case were there any signs which could give us a clue as to the criminal or lunatic who had done the mischief. Now, Mr Holmes, you have got the facts.'

'They are singular, not to say grotesque,' said Holmes. 'May I ask whether the two busts smashed in Dr Barnicot's rooms were the exact duplicates of the one which was destroyed in Morse Hudson's shop?'

'They were taken from the same mould.'

'Such a fact must tell against the theory that the man who breaks them is influenced by any general hatred of Napoleon. Considering how many hundreds of statues of the great Emperor must exist in London, it is too much to suppose such a coincidence as that a promiscuous iconoclast should chance to begin upon three specimens of the same bust.'

'Well, I thought as you do,' said Lestrade. 'On the other hand, this Morse Hudson is the purveyor of busts in that part of London, and these three were the only ones which had been in his shop for years. So although, as you say, there are many hundreds of statues in London, it is very probable that these three were the only ones in that district. Therefore a local fanatic would begin with them. What do you think, Dr Watson?'

'There are no limits to the possibilities of monomania,' I answered. 'There is the condition which the modern French psychologists have called the "*idée fixe*", which may be trifling in character, and accompanied by complete sanity in every other way. A man who had read deeply about Napoleon, or who had possibly received some hereditary family injury through the great war, might conceivably form such an "*idée fixe*", and under its influence be capable of any fantastic outrage.'

'That won't do, my dear Watson,' said Holmes, shaking his head; 'for no amount of "*idée fixe*" would enable your interesting monomaniac to find out where these busts were situated.'

'Well, how do *you* explain it?'

'I don't attempt to do so. I would only observe that there is a certain method in the gentleman's eccentric proceedings. For example, in Dr Barnicot's hall, where a sound might arouse the family, the bust was taken outside before being broken, whereas in the surgery, where there was less danger of an alarm, it was smashed where it stood. The affair seems absurdly trifling, and yet I dare call nothing trivial when I reflect that some of my most classic cases have had the least promising commencement. You will remember, Watson, how the dreadful business of the Abernetty family was first brought to my notice by the depth which the parsley had sunk into the butter upon a hot day. I can't afford, therefore, to smile at your three broken busts, Lestrade, and I shall be very much obliged to you if you will let me hear of any fresh developments of so singular a chain of events.'

The development for which my friend had asked came in a quicker and an infinitely more tragic form than he could have imagined. I was still dressing in my bedroom next morning, when there was a tap at the door, and Holmes entered, a telegram in his hand. He read it aloud:

Come instantly, 131 Pitt Street, Kensington, LESTRADE

'What is it, then?' I asked.

'Don't know – may be anything. But I suspect it is the sequel of the story of the statues. In that case our friend the image-breaker has begun operations in another quarter of London. There's coffee on the table, Watson, and I have a cab at the door.'

In half an hour we had reached Pitt Street, a quiet little backwater just beside one of the briskest currents of London life. No. 131 was one of a row, all flat-chested, respectable, and most unromantic dwellings. As we drove up we found the railings in front of the house lined by a curious crowd. Holmes whistled.

'By George! it's attempted murder at the least. Nothing less will hold the London message boy. There's a deed of violence indicated in that fellow's round shoulders and outstretched neck. What's this, Watson? The top step swilled down and the other ones dry. Footsteps enough, anyhow! Well, well, there's Lestrade at the front window, and we shall soon know all about it.'

The official received us with a very grave face and showed us into a sitting-room, where an exceedingly unkempt and agitated elderly man, clad in a flannel dressing-gown, was pacing up and down. He was introduced to us as the owner of the house – Mr Horace Harker, of the Central Press Syndicate.

'It's the Napoleon bust business again,' said Lestrade. 'You seemed interested last night, Mr Holmes, so I thought perhaps you would be glad to be present now that the affair has taken a very much graver turn.'

'What has it turned to, then?'

'To murder. Mr Harker, will you tell these gentlemen exactly what has occurred?'

The man in the dressing-gown turned upon us with a most melancholy face.

'It's an extraordinary thing,' said he, 'that all my life I have been collecting other people's news, and now that a real piece of news has come my own way I am so confused and bothered that I can't put two words together. If I had come in here as a journalist I should have interviewed myself and had two columns in every evening paper. As it is, I am giving away valuable copy by telling my story over and over to a string of different people, and I can make no use of it myself. However, I've heard your name, Mr Sherlock Holmes, and if you'll only explain this queer business I shall be paid for my trouble in telling you the story.'

Holmes sat down and listened.

'It all seems to centre round that bust of Napoleon which I bought for this very room about four months ago. I picked it up cheap from Harding Brothers, two doors from the High Street Station. A great deal of my journalistic work is done at night, and

I often write until the early morning. So it was today. I was sitting in my den, which is at the back of the top of the house, about three o'clock, when I was convinced that I heard some sounds downstairs. I listened, but they were not repeated, and I concluded that they came from outside. Then suddenly, about five minutes later, there came a most horrible yell – the most dreadful sound, Mr Holmes, that ever I heard. It will ring in my ears as long as I live. I sat frozen with horror for a minute or two. Then I seized the poker and went downstairs. When I entered this room I found the window wide open, and I at once observed that the bust was gone from the mantelpiece. Why any burglar should take such a thing passes my understanding, for it was only a plaster cast, and of no real value whatever.

'You can see for yourself that anyone going out through that open window could reach the front door step by taking a long stride. This was clearly what the burglar had done, so I went round and opened the door. Stepping out into the dark I nearly fell over a dead man who was lying there. I ran back for a light, and there was the poor fellow, a great gash in his throat and the whole place swimming in blood. He lay on his back, his knees drawn up, and his mouth horribly open. I shall see him in my dreams. I had just time to blow on my police whistle, and then I must have fainted, for I knew nothing more until I found the policeman standing over me in the hall.'

'Well, who was the murdered man?' asked Holmes.

'There's nothing to show who he was,' said Lestrade. 'You shall see the body at the mortuary, but we have made nothing of it up to now. He is a tall man, sunburnt, very powerful, not more than thirty. He is poorly dressed, and yet does not appear to be a labourer. A horn-handled clasp-knife was lying in a pool of blood beside him. Whether it was the weapon which did the deed, or whether it belonged to the dead man, I do not know. There was no name on his clothing, and nothing in his pockets save an apple, some string, a shilling map of London, and a photograph. Here it is.'

It was evidently taken by a snap-shot from a small camera. It represented an alert, sharp-featured simian man with thick eyebrows, and a very peculiar projection of the lower part of the face like the muzzle of a baboon.

'And what became of the bust?' asked Holmes, after a careful study of this picture.

'We had news of it just before you came. It has been found in the front garden of an empty house in Campden House Road. It was broken into fragments. I am going round now to see it. Will you come?'

'Certainly. I must just take one look round.' He examined the carpet and the window. 'The fellow had either very long legs or was a most active man,' said he. 'With an area beneath it was no mean feat to reach that window-ledge and open that window. Getting back was comparatively simple. Are you coming with us to see the remains of your bust, Mr Harker?'

The disconsolate journalist had seated himself at a writing-table.

'I must try and make something of it,' said he, 'though I have no doubt that the first editions of the evening papers are out already with full details. It's like my luck! You remember when the stand fell at Doncaster? Well, I was the only journalist in the stand, and my journal the only one that had no account of it, for I was too shaken to write it. And now I'll be too late with a murder done on my own doorstep.'

As we left the room we heard his pen travelling shrilly over the foolscap.

The spot where the fragments of the bust had been found was only a few hundred yards away. For the first time our eyes rested upon this presentment of the great Emperor, which seemed to raise such frantic and destructive hatred in the mind of the unknown. It lay scattered in splintered shards upon the grass. Holmes picked up several of them and examined them carefully.

I was convinced from his intent face and purposeful manner that at last he was upon a clue.

'Well?' asked Lestrade.

Holmes shrugged his shoulders.

'We have a long way to go yet,' said he. 'And yet – and yet – well, we have some suggestive facts to act upon. The possession of this trifling bust was worth more in the eyes of this strange criminal than a human life. That is one point. Then there is the singular fact that he did not break it in the house, or immediately outside the house, if to break it was his sole object.'

'He was rattled and bustled by meeting this other fellow. He hardly knew what he was doing.'

'Well, that's likely enough. But I wish to call your attention very particularly to the position of this house in the garden of which the bust was destroyed.'

Lestrade looked about him.

'It was an empty house, and so he knew that he would not be disturbed in the garden.'

'Yes, but there is another empty house farther up the street which he must have passed before he came to this one. Why did he not break it there, since it is evident that every yard that he carried it increased the risk of someone meeting him?'

'I give it up,' said Lestrade.

Holmes pointed to the street lamp above our heads.

'He could see what he was doing here, and he could not there. That was the reason.'

'By Jove! that's true,' said the detective. 'Now that I come to think of it, Dr Barnicot's bust was broken not far from his red lamp. Well, Mr Holmes, what are we to do with that fact?'

'To remember it – to docket it. We may come on something later which will bear upon it. What steps do you propose to take now, Lestrade?'

'The most practical way of getting at it, in my opinion, is to

'HOLMES POINTED TO THE STREET LAMP ABOVE OUR HEADS.'

identify the dead man. There should be no difficulty about that. When we have found who he is and who his associates are, we should have a good start in learning what he was doing in Pitt Street last night, and who it was who met him and killed him on the doorstep of Mr Horace Harker. Don't you think so?'

'No doubt; and yet it is not quite the way in which I should approach the case.'

'What would you do then?'

'Oh, you must not let me influence you in any way. I suggest that you go on your line and I on mine. We can compare notes afterwards, and each will supplement the other.'

'Very good,' said Lestrade.

'If you are going back to Pitt Street, you might see Mr Horace Harker. Tell him from me that I have quite made up my mind, and that it is certain that a dangerous homicidal lunatic with

Napoleonic delusions was in his house last night. It will be useful for his article.'

Lestrade stared.

'You don't seriously believe that?'

Holmes smiled.

'Don't I? Well, perhaps I don't. But I am sure that it will interest Mr Horace Harker and the subscribers of the Central Press Syndicate. Now, Watson, I think that we shall find that we have a long and rather complex day's work before us. I should be glad, Lestrade, if you could make it convenient to meet us at Baker Street at six o'clock this evening. Until then I should like to keep this photograph found in the dead man's pocket. It is possible that I may have to ask your company and assistance upon a small expedition which will have to be undertaken tonight, if my chain of reasoning should prove to be correct. Until then, goodbye, and good luck.'

Sherlock Holmes and I walked together to the High Street, where he stopped at the shop of Harding Brothers, whence the bust had been purchased. A young assistant informed us that Mr Harding would be absent until afternoon, and that he was himself a newcomer, who could give us no information. Holmes's face showed his disappointment and annoyance.

'Well, well, we can't expect to have it all our own way, Watson,' he said at last. 'We must come back in the afternoon, if Mr Harding will not be here until then. I am, as you have no doubt surmised, endeavouring to trace these busts to their source, in order to find if there is not something peculiar which may account for their remarkable fate. Let us make for Mr Morse Hudson, of the Kennington Road, and see if he can throw any light upon the problem.'

A drive of an hour brought us to the picture-dealer's establishment. He was a small, stout man with a red face and a peppery manner.

'Yes, sir. On my very counter, sir,' said he. 'What we pay rates and taxes for I don't know, when any ruffian can come in and break one's goods. Yes, sir, it was I who sold Dr Barnicot his two statues. Disgraceful, sir! A Nihilist plot, that's what I make it. No one but an Anarchist would go about breaking statues. Red republicans, that's what I call 'em. Who did I get the statues from? I don't see what that has to do with it. Well, if you really want to know, I got them from Gelder & Co., in Church Street, Stepney. They are a well-known house in the trade, and have been this twenty years. How many had I? Three – two and one are three – two of Dr Barnicot's and one smashed in broad daylight on my own counter. Do I know that photograph? No, I don't. Yes, I do though. Why, it's Beppo! He was a kind of Italian piecework man, who made himself useful in the shop. He could carve a bit, and gild a frame, and do odd jobs. The fellow left me last week, and I've heard nothing of him since. No, I don't know where he came from nor where he went to. I had nothing against him while he was here. He was gone two days before the bust was smashed.'

'Well, that's all we could reasonably expect to get from Morse Hudson,' said Holmes, as we emerged from the shop. 'We have this Beppo as a common factor, both in Kennington and in Kensington, so that is worth a ten-mile drive. Now, Watson, let us make for Gelder & Co., of Stepney, the source and origin of busts. I shall be surprised if we don't get some help down there.'

In rapid succession we passed through the fringe of fashionable London, hotel London, theatrical London, literary London, commercial London, and, finally, maritime London, till we came to a riverside city of a hundred thousand souls, where the tenement houses swelter and reek with the outcasts of Europe. Here, in a broad thoroughfare, once the abode of wealthy city merchants, we found the sculpture works for which we searched. Outside was a considerable yard full of monumental masonry. Inside was a large room in which fifty workers were carving or moulding. The manager, a big blond German, received us civilly, and gave a clear answer to all Holmes's questions. A reference to his books showed that hundreds of casts had been taken from a marble copy of Devine's head of Napoleon, but that the three which had been sent to Morse Hudson a year or so before had been half of a batch of six, the other three being sent to Harding Brothers, of Kensington. There was no reason why those six should be different to any of the other casts. He could suggest no possible cause why anyone should wish to destroy them – in fact, he laughed at the idea. Their wholesale price was six shillings, but the retailer would get twelve or more. The cast was taken in two moulds from each side of the face, and then these two profiles of plaster of Paris were joined together to make the complete bust. The work was usually done by Italians in the room we were in. When finished the busts were put on a table in the passage to dry, and afterwards stored. That was all he could tell us.

But the production of the photograph had a remarkable effect upon the manager. His face flushed with anger, and his brows knotted over his blue Teutonic eyes.

'Ah, the rascal!' he cried. 'Yes, indeed, I know him very well. This has always been a respectable establishment, and the only time that we have ever had the police in it was over this very fellow. It was more than a year ago now. He knifed another Italian in the street, and then he came to the works with the police on his heels, and he was taken here. Beppo was his name – his second name I never knew. Serve me right for engaging a man with such a face. But he was a good workman – one of the best.'

'What did he get?'

'The man lived, and he got off with a year. I have no doubt he is out now; but he has not dared to show his nose here. We have a cousin of his here, and I dare say he could tell you where he is.'

'No, no,' cried Holmes, 'not a word to the cousin, not a word, I beg you. The matter is very important, and the farther I go with it the more important it seems to grow. When you referred in your ledger to the sale of those casts I observed that the date was

3rd June of last year. Could you give me the date when Beppo was arrested?'

'I could tell you roughly by the pay-list,' the manager answered. 'Yes,' he continued, after some turning over of pages, 'he was paid last on May 20th.'

'Thank you,' said Holmes. 'I don't think that I need intrude upon your time and patience any more.' With a last word of caution that he should say nothing as to our researches we turned our faces westward once more.

The afternoon was far advanced before we were able to snatch a hasty luncheon at a restaurant. A news-bill at the entrance announced 'Kensington Outrage. Murder by a Madman', and the contents of the paper showed that Mr Horace Harker had got his account into print after all. Two columns were occupied with a highly sensational and flowery rendering of the whole incident. Holmes propped it against the cruet stand and read it while he ate. Once or twice he chuckled.

'This is all right, Watson,' said he. 'Listen to this: "It is satisfactory to know that there can be no difference of opinion upon this case, since Mr Lestrade, one of the most experienced members of the official force, and Mr Sherlock Holmes, the well-known consulting expert, have each come to the conclusion that the grotesque series of incidents, which have ended in so tragic a fashion, arise from lunacy rather than from deliberate crime. No explanation save mental aberration can cover the facts." The Press, Watson, is a most valuable institution, if you only know how to use it. And now, if you have quite finished, we will hark back to Kensington, and see what the manager of Harding Brothers has to say to the matter.'

The founder of that great emporium proved to be a brisk, crisp little person, very dapper and quick, with a clear head and a ready tongue.

'Yes, sir, I have already read the account in the evening papers. Mr Horace Harker is a customer of ours. We supplied him with the bust some months ago. We ordered three busts of that sort from Gelder & Co., of Stepney. They are all sold now. To whom? Oh, I dare say by consulting our sales book we could very easily tell you. Yes, we have the entries here. One to Mr Harker, you see, and one to Mr Josiah Brown, of Laburnum Lodge, Laburnum Vale, Chiswick, and one to Mr Sandeford, of Lower Grove Road, Reading. No, I have never seen this face which you show me in the photograph. You would hardly forget it – would you, sir? – for I've seldom seen an uglier. Have we any Italians on the staff? Yes, sir, we have several among our workpeople and cleaners. I dare say they might get a peep at that sales book if they wanted to. There is no particular reason for keeping a watch upon that book. Well, well, it's a very strange business, and I hope that you'll let me know if anything comes of your inquiries.'

Holmes had taken several notes during Mr Harding's evidence, and I could see that he was thoroughly satisfied by the turn which affairs were taking. He made no remark, however, save that, unless we hurried, we should be late for our appointment with Lestrade. Sure enough, when we reached Baker Street the detective was already there, and we found him pacing up and down in a fever of impatience. His look of importance showed that his day's work had not been in vain.

'Well?' he asked. 'What luck, Mr Holmes?'

'We have had a very busy day, and not entirely a wasted one,' my friend explained. 'We have seen both the retailers and also the wholesale manufacturers. I can trace each of the busts now from the beginning.'

'The busts!' cried Lestrade. 'Well, well, you have your own methods, Mr Sherlock Holmes, and it is not for me to say a word against them, but I think I have done a better day's work than you. I have identified the dead man.'

'You don't say so!'

'And found a cause for the crime.'

'Splendid!'

'We have an inspector who makes a speciality of Saffron Hill and the Italian quarter. Well, this dead man had some Catholic emblem round his neck, and that, along with his colour, made me think he was from the South. Inspector Hill knew him the moment he caught sight of him. His name is Pietro Venucci, from Naples, and he is one of the greatest cut-throats in London. He is connected with the Mafia, which, as you know, is a secret political society, enforcing its decrees by murder. Now you see how the affair begins to clear up. The other fellow is probably an Italian also, and a member of the Mafia. He has broken the rules in some fashion. Pietro is set upon his track. Probably the photograph we found in his pocket is the man himself, so that he may not knife the wrong person. He dogs the fellow, he sees him enter a house, he waits outside for him, and in the scuffle receives his own death-wound. How is that, Mr Sherlock Holmes?'

Holmes clapped his hands approvingly.

'Excellent, Lestrade, excellent!' he cried. 'But I didn't quite follow your explanation of the destruction of the busts.'

'The busts! You never can get those busts out of your head. After all, that is nothing; petty larceny, six months at the most. It is the murder that we are really investigating, and I tell you that I am gathering all the threads into my hands.'

'And the next stage?'

'Is a very simple one. I shall go down with Hill to the Italian quarter, find the man whose photograph we have got, and arrest him on the charge of murder. Will you come with us?'

'I think not. I fancy we can attain our end in a simpler way. I can't say for certain, because it all depends – well, it all depends upon a factor which is completely outside our control. But I have great hopes – in fact, the betting is exactly two to one – that if you will come with us tonight I shall be able to help you to lay him by the heels.'

'In the Italian quarter?'

'No; I fancy Chiswick is an address which is more likely to find him. If you will come with me to Chiswick tonight, Lestrade, I'll promise to go to the Italian quarter with you tomorrow, and no harm will be done by the delay. And now I think that a few hours' sleep would do us all good, for I do not propose to leave before eleven o'clock, and it is unlikely that we shall be back before morning. You'll dine with us, Lestrade, and then you are welcome to the sofa until it is time for us to start. In the meantime, Watson, I should be glad if you would ring for an express messenger, for I have a letter to send, and it is important that it should go at once.'

Holmes spent the evening in rummaging among the files of the old daily papers with which one of our lumber-rooms was packed. When at last he descended it was with triumph in his eyes, but he said nothing to either of us as to the result of his researches. For my own part, I had followed step by step the methods by which he had traced the various windings of this complex case, and, though I could not yet perceive the goal which we would reach, I understood clearly that Holmes expected this grotesque criminal to make an attempt upon the two remaining busts, one of which, I remembered, was at Chiswick. No doubt the object of our journey was to catch him in the very act, and I could not but admire the cunning with which my friend had inserted the wrong clue in the evening paper so as to give the fellow the idea that he could continue his scheme with impunity. I was not surprised when Holmes suggested that I should take my revolver with me. He had himself picked up the loaded hunting-crop which was his favourite weapon.

A four-wheeler was at the door at eleven, and in it we drove to a spot at the other side of Hammersmith Bridge. Here the cabman was directed to wait. A short walk brought us to a secluded road fringed with pleasant houses, each standing in its own grounds. In the light of a street lamp we read 'Laburnum Villa' upon the gatepost of one of them. The occupants had evidently retired to rest, for all was dark save for a fanlight over the hall door, which shed a single blurred circle on to the garden path. The wooden fence which separated the grounds from the road threw a dense black shadow upon the inner side, and here it was that we crouched.

'I fear that you'll have a long time to wait,' Holmes whispered. 'We may thank our stars that it is not raining. I don't think we can even venture to smoke to pass the time. However, it's a two to one chance that we get something to pay us for our trouble.'

It proved, however, that our vigil was not to be so long as Holmes had led us to fear, and it ended in a very sudden and singular fashion. In an instant, without the least sound to warn us of his coming, the garden gate swung open, and a lithe, dark figure, as swift and active as an ape, rushed up the garden path. We saw it whisk past the light thrown from over the door and disappear against the black shadow of the house. There was a long pause, during which we held our breath, and then a very gentle creaking sound came to our ears. The window was being opened. The noise ceased, and again there was a long silence. The fellow was making his way into the house. We saw the sudden flash of a dark lantern inside the room. What he sought was evidently not there, for again we saw the flash through another blind, and then through another.

'Let us get to the open window. We will nab him as he climbs out,' Lestrade whispered.

But before we could move the man had emerged again. As he came out into the glimmering patch of light we saw that he carried something white under his arm. He looked stealthily all round him. The silence of the deserted street reassured him. Turning his back upon us, he laid down his burden, and the next instant there was the sound of a sharp tap, followed by a clatter and rattle. The man was so intent upon what he was doing that he never heard our steps as we stole across the grass plot. With the bound of a tiger Holmes was on his back, and an instant later

Lestrade and I had him by either wrist, and the handcuffs had been fastened. As we turned him over I saw his hideous, sallow face, with writhing, furious features glaring up at us, and I knew that it was indeed the man of the photograph whom we had secured.

But it was not our prisoner to whom Holmes was giving his attention. Squatted on the doorstep, he was engaged in most carefully examining that which the man had brought from the house. It was a bust of Napoleon like the one which we had seen that morning, and it had been broken into similar fragments. Carefully Holmes held each separate shard to the light, but in no way did it differ from any other shattered piece of plaster. He had just completed his examination, when the hall lights flew up, the door opened and the owner of the house, a jovial, rotund figure in shirt and trousers, presented himself.

'Mr Josiah Brown, I suppose?' said Holmes.

'Yes, sir; and you no doubt are Mr Sherlock Holmes? I had the note which you sent by the express messenger, and I did exactly what you told me. We locked every door in the inside and awaited developments. Well, I'm very glad to see that you have got the rascal. I hope, gentlemen, that you will come in and have some refreshment.'

However, Lestrade was anxious to get his man into safe quarters, so within a few minutes our cab had been summoned and we were all four upon our way to London. Not a word would our captive say; but he glared at us from the shadow of his matted hair, and once, when my hand seemed within his reach, he snapped at it like a hungry wolf. We stayed long enough at the police-station to learn that a search of his clothing revealed nothing save shillings and a long sheath knife, the handle of which bore copious traces of recent blood.

'That's all right,' said Lestrade, as we parted. 'Hill knows all these gentry, and he will give a name to him. You'll find that my theory of the Mafia will work out all right. But I'm sure I am exceedingly obliged to you, Mr Holmes, for the workmanlike way in which you laid hands upon him. I don't quite understand it all yet.'

'I fear it is rather too late an hour for explanations,' said Holmes. 'Besides, there are one or two details which are not finished off, and it is one of those cases which are worth working out to the very end. If you will come round once more to my rooms at six o'clock tomorrow I think I shall be able to show you that even now you have not grasped the entire meaning of this business, which presents some features which make it absolutely original in the history of crime. If ever I permit you to chronicle any more of my little problems, Watson, I foresee that you will enliven your pages by an account of the singular adventure of the Napoleonic busts.'

When we met again next evening, Lestrade was furnished with much information concerning our prisoner. His name, it appeared, was Beppo, second name unknown. He was a well-known ne'er-do-well among the Italian colony. He had once been a skilful sculptor and had earned an honest living, but he had taken to evil courses, and had twice already been in gaol – once for a petty theft and once, as we had already heard, for stabbing a fellow-countryman. He could talk English perfectly well. His reasons for destroying the busts were still unknown, and he refused to answer any questions upon the subject; but the police had discovered that these same busts might very well have been made by his own hands, since he was engaged in this class of work at the establishment of Gelder & Co. To all this information, much of which we already knew, Holmes listened with polite attention; but I, who knew him so well, could clearly see that his thoughts were elsewhere, and I detected a mixture of mingled uneasiness and expectation beneath that mask which he was wont to assume. At last he started in his chair and his eyes brightened. There had been a ring at the bell. A minute later we heard steps upon the stairs, and an elderly, red-faced man with grizzled side-whiskers was ushered in. In his right hand he carried an old-fashioned carpet-bag, which he placed upon the table.

'Is Mr Sherlock Holmes here?'

My friend bowed and smiled. 'Mr Sandeford, of Reading, I suppose?' said he.

'Yes, sir. I fear that I am a little late; but the trains were awkward. You wrote to me about a bust that is in my possession.'

'Exactly.'

'I have your letter here. You said, "I desire to possess a copy of Devine's Napoleon and am prepared to pay you ten pounds for the one which is in your possession." Is that right?'

'Certainly.'

'I was very much surprised at your letter, for I could not imagine how you knew that I owned such a thing.'

'Of course you must have been surprised, but the explanation is very simple. Mr Harding, of Harding Brothers, said that they had sold you their last copy, and he gave me your address.'

'Oh, that was it, was it? Did he tell you what I paid for it?'

'No, he did not.'

'Well, I am an honest man, though not a very rich one. I only gave fifteen shillings for the bust, and I think you ought to know that before I take ten pounds from you.'

'I am sure the scruple does you honour, Mr Sandeford. But I have named that price, so I intend to stick to it.'

'Well, it is very handsome of you, Mr Holmes. I brought the bust up with me, as you asked me to do. Here it is!'

He opened his bag, and at last we saw placed upon our table a complete specimen of that bust which we had already seen more than once in fragments.

Holmes took a paper from his pocket and laid a ten-pound note upon the table.

'You will kindly sign that paper, Mr Sandeford, in the presence of these witnesses. It is simply to say that you transfer every

'I BROUGHT THE BUST UP WITH ME, AS YOU ASKED ME TO DO.'

possible right that you ever had in the bust to me. I am a methodical man, you see, and you never know what turn events might take afterwards. Thank you, Mr Sandeford; here is your money, and I wish you a very good evening.'

When our visitor had disappeared Sherlock Holmes's movements were such as to rivet our attention. He began by taking a clean white cloth from a drawer and laying it over the table. Then he placed his newly acquired bust in the centre of the cloth. Finally he picked up his hunting-crop and struck Napoleon a sharp blow on the top of the head. The figure broke into fragments, and Holmes bent eagerly over the shattered remains. Next instant, with a loud shout of triumph, he held up one splinter, in which a round, dark object was fixed like a plum in a pudding.

'Gentlemen,' he cried, 'let me introduce you to the famous black pearl of the Borgias!'

Lestrade and I sat silent for a moment, and then, with a spontaneous impulse, we both broke out clapping as at the well-wrought crisis of a play. A flush of colour sprang to Holmes's pale cheeks, and he bowed to us like the master dramatist who receives the homage of his audience. It was at such moments that for an instant he ceased to be a reasoning machine and betrayed his human love for admiration and applause. The same singularly proud and reserved nature which turned away with disdain from popular notoriety was capable of being moved to its depth by spontaneous wonder and praise from a friend.

'Yes, gentlemen,' said he, 'it is the most famous pearl now existing in the world, and it has been my good fortune, by a connected chain of inductive reasoning, to trace it from the Prince of Calonna's bedroom at the Dacre Hotel, where it was lost, to the interior of this, the last of the six busts of Napoleon which were manufactured by Gelder & Co., of Stepney. You will remember, Lestrade, the sensation caused by the disappearance of this valuable jewel, and the vain efforts of the London police to recover it. I was myself consulted upon the case; but I was unable to throw any light upon it. Suspicion fell upon the maid of the Princess, who was an Italian, and it was proved that she had a brother in London, but we failed to trace any connection between them. The maid's name was Lucretia Venucci, and there is no doubt in my mind that this Pietro who was murdered two nights ago was the brother. I have been looking up the dates in the old files of the paper, and I find that the disappearance of the pearl was exactly two days before the arrest of Beppo for some crime of violence – an event which took place in the factory of Gelder & Co., at the very moment when these busts were being made. Now you clearly see the sequence of events, though you see them, of course, in the inverse order to the way in which they presented themsleves to me. Beppo had the pearl in his possession. He may have stolen it from Pietro, he may have been Pietro's confederate, he may have been the go-between of Pietro and his sister. It is of no consequence to us which is the correct solution.

'The main fact is that he *had* the pearl, and at that moment, when it was on his person, he was pursued by the police. He made for the factory in which he worked, and he knew that he had only a few minutes in which to conceal this enormously valuable prize, which would otherwise be found on him when he was searched. Six plaster casts of Napoleon were drying in the passage. One of them was still soft. In an instant Beppo, a skilful workman, made a small hole in the wet plaster, dropped in the pearl, and with a few touches covered over the aperture once more. It was an admirable hiding-place. No one could possibly find it. But Beppo was condemned to a year's imprisonment, and in the meanwhile his six busts were scattered over London. He could not tell which contained his treasure. Only by breaking them could he see. Even shaking would tell him nothing for as the plaster was wet it was probable that the pearl would adhere to it – as, in fact, it has done. Beppo did not despair, and he conducted his search with considerable ingenuity and perseverance. Through a cousin who works with Gelder he found out the retail firms who had bought the busts. He managed to find employment with Morse Hudson, and in that way tracked down three of them. The pearl was not there. Then with the help of some Italian employee, he succeeded in finding out where the other three busts had gone. The first was at Harker's. There he was dogged by his confederate, who held Beppo responsible for the loss of the pearl, and he stabbed him in the scuffle which followed.'

'If he was his confederate, why should he carry his photograph?' I asked.

'As a means of tracing him if he wished to inquire about him from any third person. That was the obvious reason. Well, after the murder I calculated that Beppo would probably hurry rather than delay his movements. He would fear that the police would read his secret, and so hastened on before they should get ahead of him. Of course, I could not say that he had not found the pearl in Harker's bust. I had not even concluded for certain that it was the pearl; but it was evident to me that he was looking for something, since he carried the bust past the other houses in order to break it in the garden which had a lamp overlooking it. Since Harker's bust was one in three, the chances were exactly as I told you – two to one against the pearl being inside it. There remained two busts, and it was obvious that he would go for the London one first. I warned the inmates of the house, so as to avoid a second tragedy, and we went down, with the happiest results. By that time, of course, I knew for certain that it was the Borgia pearl that we were after. The name of the murdered man linked the one event with the other. There only remained a single bust – the Reading one – and the pearl must be there. I bought it in your presence from the owner – and there it lies.'

We sat in silence for a moment.

'Well,' said Lestrade, 'I've seen you handle a good many cases, Mr Holmes, but I don't know that I ever knew a more workmanlike one than that. We're not jealous of you at Scotland Yard. No, sir, we are very proud of you, and if you come down tomorrow there's not a man, from the oldest inspector to the youngest constable, who wouldn't be glad to shake you by the hand.'

'Thank you!' said Holmes. 'Thank you!' and as he turned away it seemed to me that he was more nearly moved by the softer human emotions than I had ever seen him. A moment later he was the cold and practical thinker once more. 'Put the pearl in the safe, Watson,' said he, 'and get out the papers of the Conk–Singleton forgery case. Goodbye, Lestrade. If any little problem comes your way I shall be happy, if I can, to give you a hint or two as to its solution.'

The Adventure of the Stockbroker's Clerk

Shortly after my marriage I had bought a connection in the Paddington district. Old Mr Farquhar, from whom I purchased it, had at one time an excellent general practice, but his age, and an affliction of the nature of St Vitus's Dance from which he suffered, had very much thinned it. The public, not unnaturally, goes upon the principle that he who would heal others must himself be whole, and looks askance at the curative powers of the man whose own case is beyond the reach of his drugs. Thus, as my predecessor weakened, his practice declined, until when I purchased it from him it had sunk from twelve hundred to little more than three hundred a year. I had confidence, however, in my own youth and energy, and was convinced that in a very few years the concern would be as flourishing as ever.

For three months after taking over the practice I was kept very closely at work, and saw little of my friend Sherlock Holmes, for I was too busy to visit Baker Street, and he seldom went anywhere himself save upon professional business. I was surprised, therefore, when one morning in June, as I sat reading the *British Medical Journal* after breakfast, I heard a ring at the bell followed by the high, somewhat strident, tones of my old companion's voice.

'Ah, my dear Watson,' said he, striding into the room, 'I am very delighted to see you. I trust that Mrs Watson has entirely recovered from all the little excitements connected with our adventure of the "Sign of Four"?

'Thank you, we are both very well,' said I, shaking him warmly by the hand.

'And I hope also,' he continued, sitting down in the rocking-chair, 'that the cares of medical practice have not entirely obliterated the interest which you used to take in our little deductive problems.'

'On the contrary,' I answered; 'it was only last night that I was looking over my old notes and classifying some of our past results.'

'I trust that you don't consider your collection closed?'

'Not at all. I should wish nothing better than to have some more of such experiences.'

'Today, for example?'

'Yes; today, if you like.'

'And as far off as Birmingham?'

'Certainly, if you wish it.'

'And the practice?'

'I do my neighbour's when he goes. He is always ready to work off the debt.'

'Ha! Nothing could be better!' said Holmes, leaning back in his

'"NOTHING COULD BE BETTER," SAID HOLMES.'

chair and looking keenly at me from under his half-closed lids. 'I perceive that you have been unwell lately. Summer colds are always a little trying.'

'I was confined to the house by a severe chill for three days last week. I thought, however, that I had cast off every trace of it.'

'So you have. You look remarkably robust.'

'How, then, did you know of it?'

'My dear fellow, you know my methods.'

'You deduced it, then?'

'Certainly.'

'And from what?'

'From your slippers.'

I glanced down at the new patent leathers which I was wearing. 'How on earth – ?' I began, but Holmes answered my question before it was asked.

'Your slippers are new,' he said. 'You could not have had them more than a few weeks. The soles which you are at this moment presenting to me are slightly scorched. For a moment I thought they might have got wet and been burned in the drying. But near the instep there is a small circular wafer of paper with the shopman's hieroglyphics upon it. Damp would of course have removed this. You had then been sitting with your feet outstretched to the fire, which a man would hardly do even in so wet a June as this if he were in his full health.'

Like all Holmes's reasoning the thing seemed simplicity itself when it was once explained. He read the thought upon my features, and his smile had a tinge of bitterness.

'I am afraid that I rather give myself away when I explain,' said he. 'Results without causes are much more impressive. You are ready to come to Birmingham, then?'

'Certainly. What is the case?'

'You shall hear it all in the train. My client is outside in a four-wheeler. Can you come at once?'

'In an instant.' I scribbled a note to my neighbour, rushed

upstairs to explain the matter to my wife, and joined Holmes upon the doorstep.

'Your neighbour is a doctor?' said he, nodding at the brass plate.

'Yes. He bought a practice as I did.'

'An old-established one?'

'Just the same as mine. Both have been ever since the houses were built.'

'Ah, then you got hold of the better of the two.'

'I think I did. But how do you know?'

'By the steps, my boy. Yours are worn three inches deeper than his. But this gentleman in the cab is my client, Mr Hall Pycroft. Allow me to introduce you to him. Whip your horse up, cabby, for we have only just time to catch our train.'

The man whom I found myself facing was a well-built, fresh-complexioned young fellow with a frank, honest face and a slight, crisp, yellow moustache. He wore a very shiny top-hat and a neat suit of sober black, which made him look what he was – a smart young City man, of the class who have been labelled Cockneys, but who give us our crack Volunteer regiments, and who turn out more fine athletes and sportsmen than any body of men in these islands. His round, ruddy face was naturally full of cheeriness, but the corners of his mouth seemed to me to be pulled down in a half-comical distress. It was not, however, until we were all in a first-class carriage and well started upon our journey to Birmingham, that I was able to learn what the trouble was which had driven him to Sherlock Holmes.

'We have a clear run here of seventy minutes,' Holmes remarked. 'I want you, Mr Hall Pycroft, to tell my friend your very interesting experience exactly as you have told it to me, or with more detail if possible. It will be of use to me to hear the succession of events again. It is a case, Watson, which may prove to have something in it, or may prove to have nothing, but which at least presents those unusual and *outré* features which are as dear to you as they are to me. Now, Mr Pycroft, I shall not interrupt you again.'

Our young companion looked at me with a twinkle in his eye.

'The worst of the story is,' said he, 'that I show myself up as such a confounded fool. Of course, it may work out all right, and I don't see that I could have done otherwise; but if I have lost my crib and get nothing in exchange, I shall feel what a soft Johnny I have been. I'm not very good at telling a story, Dr Watson, but it is like this with me.

'I used to have a billet at Coxon and Woodhouse, of Drapers' Garden, but they were let in early in the spring through the Venezuelan loan, as no doubt you remember, and came a nasty cropper. I had been with them five years, and old Coxon gave me a ripping good testimonial when the smash came: but, of course, we clerks were all turned adrift, the twenty-seven of us. I tried here and tried there, but there were lots of other chaps on the same lay as myself, and it was a perfect frost for a long time. I had been taking three pounds a week at Coxon's, and I had saved about seventy of them, but I soon worked my way through that and out at the other end. I was fairly at the end of my tether at last, and could hardly find the stamps to answer the advertisements or the envelopes to stick them to. I had worn out my boots padding up office stairs, and I seemed just as far from getting a billet as ever.

'At last I saw a vacancy at Mawson and Williams', the great stockbroking firm in Lombard Street. I dare say E. C. is not much in your line, but I can tell you that this is about the richest house in London. The advertisement was to be answered by letter only. I sent in my testimonial and application, but without the least hope of getting it. Back came an answer by return saying that if I would appear next Monday I might take over my new duties at once, provided that my appearance was satisfactory. No one knows how these things are worked. Some people say the manager just plunges his hand into the heap and takes the first that comes. Anyhow, it was my innings that time, and I don't ever wish to feel better pleased. The screw was a pound a week rise, and the duties just about the same as at Coxon's.

'And now I come to the queer part of the business. I was in diggings out Hampstead way – 17 Potter's Terrace, was the address. Well, I was sitting doing a smoke that very evening after I had been promised the appointment, when up came my landlady with a card which had "Arthur Pinner, financial agent," printed upon it. I had never heard the name before, and could not imagine what he wanted with me, but of course I asked her to show him up. In he walked – a middle-sized, dark-haired, dark-eyed, black-bearded man, with a touch of the sheeny about his nose. He had a brisk kind of way with him and spoke sharply, like a man that knew the value of time.

' "Mr Hall Pycroft, I believe?" said he.

' "Yes, sir," I answered, and pushed a chair towards him.

' "Lately engaged at Coxon and Woodhouse's?"

' "Yes, sir."

' "And now on the staff of Mawson's?"

' "Quite so."

' "Well," said he. "The fact is that I have heard some really extraordinary stories about your financial ability. You remember Parker who used to be Coxon's manager? He can never say enough about it."

'Of course I was pleased to hear this. I had always been pretty smart in the office, but I had never dreamed that I was talked about in the City in this fashion.

' "You have a good memory?" said he.

' "Pretty fair," I answered, modestly.

' "Have you kept in touch with the market while you have been out of work?" he asked.

' "Yes; I read the Stock Exchange List every morning."

‘“Now, that shows real application!” he cried. “That is the way to prosper! You won’t mind my testing you, will you? Let me see! How are Ayrshires?”

‘“One hundred and five, to one hundred and five and a quarter.”

‘“And New Zealand Consolidated?”

‘“A hundred and four.”

‘“And British Broken Hills?”

‘“Seven to seven and six.”

‘“Wonderful!” he cried, with his hands up. “This quite fits in with all that I had heard. My boy, my boy, you are very much too good to be a clerk at Mawson’s!”

‘This outburst rather astonished me, as you can think. “Well,” said I, “other people don’t think quite so much of me as you seem to do, Mr Pinner. I had a hard enough fight to get this berth, and I am very glad to have it.”

‘“Pooh, man, you should soar above it. You are not in your true sphere. Now I’ll tell you how it stands with me. What I have to offer is little enough when measured by your ability, but when compared with Mawson’s it is light to dark. Let me see! When do you go to Mawson’s?”

‘“On Monday.”

‘“Ha! ha! I think I would risk a little sporting flutter that you don’t go there at all.”

‘“Not go to Mawson’s?”

‘“No, sir. By that day you will be business manager of the Franco-Midland Hardware Company, Limited, with one hundred and thirty-four branches in the towns and villages of France, not counting one in Brussels and one in San Remo.”

‘This took my breath away. “I never heard of it,” said I.

‘“Very likely not. It has been kept very quiet, for the capital was all privately subscribed, and it is too good a thing to let the public into. My brother, Harry Pinner, is promoter, and joins the board after allotment as managing director. He knew that I was in the swim down here, and he asked me to pick up a good man cheap – a young pushing man, with plenty of snap about him. Parker spoke of you, and that brought me here tonight. We can only offer you a beggarly five hundred to start with – "

'"Five hundred a year!" I shouted.

'"Only that at the beginning, but you are to have an over-riding commission of one per cent on all business done by your agents, and you may take my word for it that this will come to more than your salary."

'"But I know nothing about hardware."

'"Tut, my boy, you know about figures."

'My head buzzed, and I could hardly sit still in the chair. But suddenly a little chill of doubt came over me.

'"I must be frank with you," said I. "Mawson only gives me two hundred, but Mawson is safe. Now, really, I know so little about your company that – "

'"Ah, smart, smart!" he cried, in a kind of ecstasy of delight. "You are the very man for us! You are not to be talked over, and quite right too. Now here's a note for a hundred pounds; and if you think that we can do business you may just slip it into your pocket as an advance upon your salary."

'"That is very handsome," said I. "When shall I take over my new duties?"

'"Be in Birmingham tomorrow at one," said he. "I have a note in my pocket here which you will take to my brother. You will find him at 126B, Corporation Street, where the temporary offices of the company are situated. Of course he must confirm your engagement, but between ourselves it will be all right."

'"Really, I hardly know how to express my gratitude, Mr Pinner," said I.

'"Not at all, my boy. You have only got your deserts. There are one or two small things – mere formalities – which I must arrange with you. You have a bit of paper beside you there. Kindly write upon it, 'I am perfectly willing to act as business manager to the Franco-Midland Hardware Company, Limited, at a minimum salary of £500.'"

'I did as he asked, and he put the paper in his pocket.

'"There is one other detail," said he. "What do you intend to do about Mawson's?"

'I had forgotten all about Mawson's in my joy.

'"I'll write and resign," said I.

'"Precisely what I don't want you to do. I had a row over you with Mawson's manager. I had gone up to ask him about you, and he was very offensive – accused me of coaxing you away from the service of the firm, and that sort of thing. At last I fairly lost my temper. 'If you want good men you should pay them a good price,' said I. 'He would rather have our small price than your big one,' said he. 'I'll lay you a fiver,' said I, 'that when he has my offer you will never so much as hear from him again.' 'Done!' said he. 'We picked him out of the gutter, and he won't leave us so easily.' Those were his very words."

'"The impudent scoundrel!" I cried. "I've never so much as seen him in my life. Why should I consider him in any way? I shall certainly not write if you would rather that I didn't."

'"Good! That's a promise!" said he, rising from his chair. "Well, I am delighted to have got so good a man for my brother. Here is your advance of a hundred pounds, and here is the letter. Make a note of the address, 126B, Corporation Street, and remember that one o'clock tomorrow is your appointment. Good night, and may you have all the fortune that you deserve."

'That's just about all that passed between us as near as I can remember it. You can imagine, Dr Watson, how pleased I was at such an extraordinary piece of good fortune. I sat up half the night hugging myself over it, and next day I was off to Birmingham in a train that would take me in plenty of time for my appointment. I took my things to an hotel in New Street, and then I made my way to the address which had been given me.

'It was a quarter of an hour before my time, but I thought that would make no difference. 126B was a passage between two large shops which led to a winding stone stair, from which there were many flats, let as offices to companies or professional men. The names of the occupants were painted up at the bottom on the wall, but there was no such name as the Franco-Midland Hardware Company, Limited. I stood for a few minutes with my heart in my boots, wondering whether the whole thing was an elaborate hoax or not, when up came a man and addressed me. He was very like the chap that I had seen the night before, the same figure and voice, but he was clean shaven and his hair was lighter.

'"Are you Mr Hall Pycroft?" he asked.

'"Yes," said I.

'"Ah! I was expecting you, but you are a trifle before your time. I had a note from my brother this morning, in which he sang your praises very loudly."

'"I was just looking for the offices when you came."

'"We have not got our name up yet, for we only secured these temporary premises last week. Come up with me and we will talk the matter over."

'I followed him to the top of a very lofty stair, and there right under the slates were a couple of empty and dusty little rooms, uncarpeted and uncurtained, into which he led me. I had thought of a great office with shining tables and rows of clerks such as I was used to, and I dare say I stared rather straight at the two deal chairs and one little table, which, with a ledger and a waste-paper basket, made up the whole furniture.

'"Don't be disheartened, Mr Pycroft," said my new acquaintance, seeing the length of my face. "Rome was not built in a day, and we have lots of money at our backs, though we don't cut much dash yet in offices. Pray sit down and let me have your letter."

'I gave it to him, and he read it over very carefully.

'"You seem to have made a vast impression upon my brother Arthur," said he, "and I know that he is a pretty shrewd judge. He swears by London, you know, and I by Birmingham, but this time I shall follow his advice. Pray consider yourself definitely engaged."

'"What are my duties?" I asked.

'"You will eventually manage the great depot in Paris, which will pour a flood of English crockery into the shops of one hundred and thirty-four agents in France. The purchase will be completed in a week, and meanwhile you will remain in Birmingham and make yourself useful."

'"How?"

'For answer he took a big red book out of a drawer. "This is a directory of Paris," said he, "with the trades after the names of the people. I want you to take it home with you, and to mark off all the hardware sellers with their addresses. It would be of the greatest use to me to have them."

'"Surely there are classified lists?" I suggested.

'"Not reliable ones. Their system is different to ours. Stick at it and let me have the lists by Monday, at twelve. Good day, Mr Pycroft; if you continue to show zeal and intelligence, you will find the company a good master."

'I went back to the hotel with the big book under my arm, and with very conflicting feelings in my breast. On the one hand I was definitely engaged, and had a hundred pounds in my pocket. On the other, the look of the offices, the absence of name on the wall, and other of the points which would strike a business man had left a bad impression as to the position of my employers. However, come what might, I had my money, so I settled down to my task. All Sunday I was kept hard at work, and yet by Monday I had only got as far as H. I went round to my employer, found him in the same dismantled kind of room, and was told to keep at it until Wednesday, and then come again. On Wednesday it was still unfinished, so I hammered away until Friday – that is, yesterday. Then I brought it round to Mr Harry Pinner.

'"Thank you very much," said he. "I fear that I underrated the difficulty of the task. This list will be of very material assistance to me."

'"It took some time," said I.

'"And now," said he, "I want you to make a list of the furniture shops, for they all sell crockery."

'"Very good."

'"And you can come up tomorrow evening at seven, and let me know how you are getting on. Don't overwork yourself. A couple of hours at Day's Music-Hall in the evening would do you no harm after your labours." He laughed as he spoke, and I saw with a thrill that his second tooth upon the left-hand side had been very badly stuffed with gold.'

Sherlock Holmes rubbed his hands with delight, and I stared in astonishment at our client.

'You may well look surprised, Dr Watson, but it is this way,' said he. 'When I was speaking to the other chap in London at the time that he laughed at my not going to Mawson's, I happened to notice that his tooth was stuffed in this very identical fashion. The glint of the gold in each case caught my eye, you see. When I put that with the voice and figure being the same, and only those things altered which might be changed by a razor or a wig, I could not doubt that it was the same man. Of course, you expect two brothers to be alike, but not that they should have the same tooth stuffed in the same way. He bowed me out and I found myself in the street, hardly knowing whether I was on my head or my heels. Back I went to my hotel, put my head in a basin of cold water, and tried to think it out. Why had he sent me from London to Birmingham; why had he got there before me; and why had he written a letter from himself to himself? It was altogether too much for me, and I could make no sense of it. And then suddenly it struck me that what was dark to me might be very light to Mr Sherlock Holmes. I had just time to get up to town by the night train, to see him this morning, and to bring you both back with me to Birmingham.'

There was a pause after the stockbroker's clerk had concluded his surprising experience. Then Sherlock Holmes cocked his eye at me, leaning back on the cushions with a pleased and yet critical face, like a connoisseur who had just taken his first sip of a comet vintage.

'Rather fine, Watson, is it not?' said he. 'There are points in it which please me. I think you will agree with me that an interview with Mr Arthur Harry Pinner in the temporary offices of the Franco-Midland Hardware Company, Limited, would be a rather interesting experience for both of us.'

'But how can we do it?' I asked.

'Oh, easily enough,' said Hall Pycroft cheerily. 'You are two friends of mine who are in want of a billet, and what could be more natural than that I should bring you both round to the managing director?'

'Quite so! Of course!' said Holmes. 'I should like to have a look at the gentleman and see if I can make anything of his little game. What qualities have you, my friend, which would make your services so valuable? or is it possible that – ' He began biting his nails and staring blankly out of the window, and we hardly drew another word from him until we were in New Street.

At seven o'clock that evening we were walking, the three of us, down Corporation Street to the company's offices.

'It is of no use our being at all before our time,' said our client. 'He only comes there to see me apparently, for the place is deserted up to the very hour he names.'

'That is suggestive,' remarked Holmes.

'By Jove, I told you so!' cried the clerk. 'That's he walking ahead of us there.'

He pointed to a smallish, blond, well-dressed man, who was bustling along the other side of the road. As we watched him he looked across at a boy who was bawling out the latest edition of the evening paper, and, running over among the cabs and buses, he bought one from him. Then clutching it in his hand he vanished through a doorway.

'There he goes!' cried Hall Pycroft. 'Those are the company's offices into which he has gone. Come with me and I'll fix it up as easily as possible.'

Following his lead we ascended five storeys, until we found ourselves outside a half-opened door, at which our client tapped. A voice within bade us 'come in,' and we entered a bare, unfurnished room, such as Hall Pycroft had described. At the single table sat the man whom we had seen in the street, with his evening paper spread out in front of him, and as he looked up at us it seemed to me that I had never looked upon a face which bore such marks of grief, and of something beyond grief – of a horror such as comes to few men in a lifetime. His brow glistened with perspiration, his cheeks were of the dull dead white of a fish's belly, and his eyes were wild and staring. He looked at his clerk as though he failed to recognize him, and I could see, by the

'HE LOOKED UP AT US.'

astonishment depicted upon our conductor's face, that this was by no means the usual appearance of his employer.

'You look ill, Mr Pinner,' he exclaimed.

'Yes, I am not very well,' answered the other, making obvious efforts to pull himself together, and licking his dry lips before he spoke. 'Who are these gentlemen whom you have brought with you?'

'One is Mr Harris, of Bermondsey, and the other is Mr Price, of this town,' said our clerk glibly. 'They are friends of mine, and gentlemen of experience, but they have been out of a place for some little time, and they hoped that perhaps you might find an opening for them in the company's employment.'

'Very possibly! Very possibly!' cried Mr Pinner, with a ghastly smile. 'Yes, I have no doubt that we shall be able to do something for you. What is your particular line, Mr Harris?'

'I am an accountant,' said Holmes.

'Ah, yes, we shall want something of the sort. And you, Mr Price?'

'A clerk,' said I.

'I have every hope that the company may accommodate you. I will let you know about it as soon as we come to any conclusion. And now I beg that you will go. For God's sake, leave me to myself!'

These last words were shot out of him, as though the constraint which he was evidently setting upon himself had suddenly and utterly burst asunder. Holmes and I glanced at each other, and Hall Pycroft took a step towards the table.

'You forget, Mr Pinner, that I am here by appointment to receive some directions from you,' said he.

'Certainly, Mr Pycroft, certainly,' the other answered in a calmer tone. 'You may wait here a moment, and there is no reason why your friends should not wait with you. I will be entirely at your service in three minutes, if I might trespass upon your patience so far.' He rose with a very courteous air, and bowing to us he passed out through a door at the farther end of the room, which he closed behind him.

'What now?' whispered Holmes. 'Is he giving us the slip?'

'Impossible,' answered Pycroft.

'Why so?'

'That door leads into an inner room.'

'There is no exit?'

'None.'

'Is it furnished?'

'It was empty yesterday.'

'Then what on earth can he be doing? There is something which I don't understand in this matter. If ever a man was three parts mad with terror, that man's name is Pinner. What can have put the shivers on him?'

'He suspects that we are detectives,' I suggested.

'That's it,' said Pycroft.

Holmes shook his head. 'He did not turn pale. He *was* pale when we entered the room,' said he. 'It is just possible that – '

His words were interrupted by a sharp rat-tat from the direction of the inner door.

'What the deuce is he knocking at his own door for?' cried the clerk.

Again and much louder came the rat-tat-tat. We all gazed expectantly at the closed door. Glancing at Holmes I saw his face turn rigid, and he leaned forward in intense excitement. Then suddenly came a low gurgling, gargling sound and a brisk drumming upon woodwork. Holmes sprang frantically across the room and pushed at the door. It was fastened on the inner side. Following his example, we threw ourselves upon it with all our weight. One hinge snapped, then the other, and down came the door with a crash. Rushing over it we found ourselves in the inner room.

It was empty.

But it was only for a moment that we were at fault. At one

corner, the corner nearest the room which we had left, there was a second door. Holmes sprang to it and pulled it open. A coat and waistcoat were lying on the floor, and from a hook behind the door, with his own braces round his neck, was hanging the managing director of the Franco-Midland Hardware Company. His knees were drawn up, his head hung at a dreadful angle to his body, and the clatter of his heels against the door made the noise which had broken in upon our conversation. In an instant I had caught him round the waist and held him up, while Holmes and Pycroft untied the elastic bands which had disappeared between the livid creases of skin. Then we carried him into the other room, where he lay with a slate-coloured face, puffing his purple lips in and out with every breath – a dreadful wreck of all that he had been but five minutes before.

'What do you think of him, Watson?' asked Holmes.

I stopped over him and examined him. His pulse was feeble and intermittent, but his breathing grew longer, and there was a little shivering of his eyelids which showed a thin white slit of ball beneath.

'It has been touch and go with him,' said I, 'but he'll live now. Just open that window and hand me the water carafe.' I undid his collar, poured the cold water over his face, and raised and sank his arms until he drew a long natural breath.

'It's only a question of time now,' said I, as I turned away from him.

Holmes stood by the table with his hands deep in his trouser pockets and his chin upon his breast.

'I suppose we ought to call the police in now,' said he; 'and yet I confess that I like to give them a complete case when they come.'

'It's a blessed mystery to me,' cried Pycroft, scratching his head. 'Whatever they wanted to bring me all the way up here for, and then – '

'Pooh! All this is clear enough,' said Holmes impatiently. 'It is this last sudden move.'

'You understand the rest, then?'

'I think that is fairly obvious. What do you say, Watson?'

I shrugged my shoulders.

'I must confess that I am out of my depths,' said I.

'Oh, surely, if you consider the events at first they can only point to one conclusion.'

'What do you make of them?'

'Well, the whole thing hinges upon two points. The first is the making of Pycroft write a declaration by which he entered the service of this preposterous company. Do you not see how very suggestive that is?'

'I am afraid I miss the point.'

'Well, why did they want him to do it? Not as a business matter, for these arrangements are usually verbal, and there was no earthly business reason why this should be an exception. Don't you see, my young friend, that they were very anxious to obtain a specimen of your handwriting, and had no other way of doing it?'

'And why?'

'Quite so. Why? When we answer that, we have made some progress with our little problem. Why? There can be only one adequate reason. Someone wanted to learn to imitate your writing, and had to procure a specimen of it first. And now if we pass on to the second point, we find that each throws a light upon the other. That point is the request made by Pinner that you should not resign your place, but should leave the manager of this important business in the full expectation that a Mr Hall Pycroft, whom he had never seen, was about to enter the office upon the Monday morning.'

'My God!' cried our client, 'what a blind beetle I have been!'

'Now you see the point about the handwriting. Suppose that

someone turned up in your place who wrote a completely different hand from that in which you had applied for the vacancy, of course the game would have been up. But in the interval the rogue learned to imitate you, and his position was therefore secure, as I presume that nobody in the office had ever set eyes upon you?'

'Not a soul,' groaned Hall Pycroft.

'Very good. Of course, it was of the utmost importance to prevent you from thinking better of it, and also to keep you from coming into contact with anyone who might tell you that your double was at work in Mawson's office. Therefore they gave you a handsome advance on your salary, and ran you off to the Midlands, where they gave you enough work to do to prevent your going to London, where you might have burst their little game up. That is all plain enough.'

'But why should this man pretend to be his own brother?'

'Well, that is pretty clear also. There are evidently only two of them in it. The other is personating you at the office. This one acted as your engager, and then found that he could not find you an employer without admitting a third person into his plot. That he was most unwilling to do. He changed his appearance as far as he could, and trusted that the likeness, which you could not fail to observe, would be put down to a family resemblance. But for the happy chance of the gold stuffing your suspicions would probably have never been aroused.'

Hall Pycroft shook his clenched hands in the air. 'Good Lord!' he cried. 'While I have been fooled in this way, what has this other Hall Pycroft been doing at Mawson's? What should we do, Mr Holmes? Tell me what to do!'

'We must wire to Mawson's.'

'They shut at twelve on Saturdays.'

'Never mind; there may be some doorkeeper or attendant – '

'Ah, yes; they keep a permanent guard there on account of the value of the securities that they hold. I remember hearing it talked of in the City.'

'Very good, we shall wire to him, and see if all is well, and if a clerk of your name is working there. That is clear enough, but what is not so clear is why at sight of us one of the rogues should instantly walk out of the room and hang himself.'

'The paper!' croaked a voice behind us. The man was sitting up, blanched and ghastly, with returning reason in his eyes, and hands which rubbed nervously at the broad red band which still encircled his throat.

'The paper! Of course!' yelled Holmes, in a paroxysm of excitement. 'Idiot that I was! I thought so much of our visit that the paper never entered my head for an instant. To be sure, the secret must lie there.' He flattened it out on the table, and a cry of triumph burst from his lips.

'Look at this, Watson!' he cried. 'It is a London paper, an early edition of the *Evening Standard*. Here is what we want. Look at the headlines – "CRIME IN THE CITY. MURDER AT MAWSON AND WILLIAMS. GIGANTIC ATTEMPTED ROBBERY. CAPTURE OF THE CRIMINAL." Here, Watson, we are all equally anxious to hear it, so kindly read it aloud to us.'

It appeared from its position in the paper to have been the one event of importance in town, and the account of it ran in this way:

> A desperate attempt at robbery, culminating in the death of one man and the capture of the criminal, occurred this afternoon in the City. For some time back Mawson and Williams, the famous financial house, have been the guardians of securities which amount in the aggregate to a sum of considerably over a million sterling. So conscious was the manager of the responsibility which devolved upon him in consequence of the great interests at stake, that safes of the very latest construction have been employed, and an armed watchman has been left day and night in the building. It

appears that last week a new clerk, named Hall Pycroft, was engaged by the firm. This person appears to have been none other than Beddington, the famous forger and cracksman, who, with his brother, has only recently emerged from a five years' spell of penal servitude. By some means, which are not yet clear, he succeeded in winning, under a false name, this official position in the office, which he utilized in order to obtain mouldings of various locks, and a thorough knowledge of the position of the strong-room and the safes.

It is customary at Mawson's for the clerks to leave at midday on Saturday. Sergeant Tuson, of the City Police, was somewhat surprised therefore to see a gentleman with a carpet-bag come down the steps at twenty minutes past one. His suspicions being aroused, the sergeant followed the man, and with the aid of Constable Pollock succeeded, after a most desperate resistance, in arresting him. It was at once clear that a daring and gigantic robbery had been committed. Nearly a hundred thousand pounds' worth of American railway bonds, with a large amount of scrip in other mines and companies, were discovered in the bag. On examining the premises the body of the unfortunate watchman was found doubled up and thrust into the largest of the safes, where it would not have been discovered until Monday morning had it not been for the prompt action of Sergeant Tuson. The man's skull had been shattered by a blow from a poker, delivered from behind. There could be no doubt that Beddington had obtained entrance by pretending that he had left something behind him, and having murdered the watchman, rapidly rifled the large safe, and then made off with his booty. His brother, who usually works with him, has not appeared in this job, as far as can at present be ascertained, although the police are making energetic inquiries as to his whereabouts.

'Well, we may save the police some little trouble in that direction,' said Holmes, glancing at the haggard figure huddled up by

'GLANCING AT THE HAGGARD FIGURE.'

the window. 'Human nature is a strange mixture, Watson. You see that even a villain and a murderer can inspire such affection that his brother turns to suicide when he learns that his neck is forfeited. However, we have no choice as to our action. The doctor and I will remain on guard, Mr Pycroft, if you will have the kindness to step out for the police.'

The Adventure of the Crooked Man

One summer night, a few months after my marriage, I was seated by my own hearth smoking a last pipe and nodding over a novel, for my day's work had been an exhausting one. My wife had already gone upstairs, and the sound of the locking of the door some time before told me that the servants had also retired. I had risen from my seat and was knocking out the ashes of my pipe, when I suddenly heard the clang of the bell.

I looked at the clock. It was a quarter to twelve. This could not be a visitor at so late an hour. A patient, evidently, and possibly an all-night sitting. With a wry face I went out into the hall and opened the door. To my astonishment, it was Sherlock Holmes who stood upon my step.

'Ah, Watson,' said he, 'I hoped that I might not be too late to catch you.'

'My dear fellow, pray come in.'

'You look surprised, and no wonder! Relieved, too, I fancy! Hum! you still smoke the Arcadia mixture of your bachelor days, then! There's no mistaking that fluffy ash upon your coat. It's easy to tell that you've been accustomed to wear a uniform, Watson; you'll never pass as a pure-bred civilian as long as you keep that habit of carrying your handkerchief in your sleeve. Could you put me up tonight?'

'With pleasure.'

'You told me that you had bachelor quarters for one, and I see that you have no gentleman visitor at present. Your hat-stand proclaims as much.'

'I shall be delighted if you will stay.'

'Thank you. I'll find a vacant peg, then. Sorry to see that

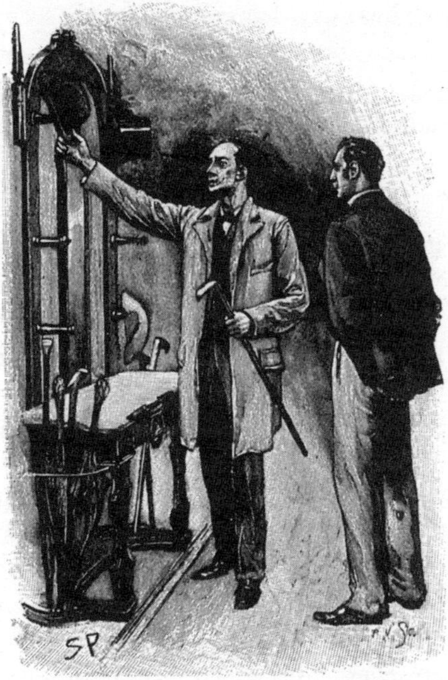

'I'LL FILL A VACANT PEG, THEN.'

you've had the British workman in the house. He's a token of evil. Not the drains, I hope?'

'No, the gas.'

'Ah! He has left two nail marks from his boot upon your linoleum just where the light strikes it. No, thank you, I had some supper at Waterloo, but I'll smoke a pipe with you with pleasure.'

I handed him my pouch, and he seated himself opposite to me, and smoked for some time in silence. I was well aware that nothing but business of importance could have brought him to me at such an hour, so I waited patiently until he should come round to it.

'I see that you are professionally rather busy just now,' said he, glancing keenly across at me.

'Yes, I've had a busy day,' I answered. 'It may seem very foolish in your eyes,' I added, 'but really I don't know how you deduced it.'

Holmes chuckled to himself.

'I have the advantage of knowing your habits, my dear Watson,' said he. 'When your round is a short one you walk, and when it is a long one you use a hansom. As I perceive that your boots, although used, are by no means dirty, I cannot doubt that you are at present busy enough to justify the hansom.'

'Excellent!' I cried.

'Elementary,' said he. 'It is one of those instances where the reasoner can produce an effect which seems remarkable to his neighbour, because the latter has missed the one little point which is the basis of the deduction. The same may be said, my dear fellow, for the effect of some of these little sketches of yours, which is entirely meretricious, depending as it does upon your retaining in your own hands some factors in the problem which are never imparted to the reader. Now, at present I am in the position of these same readers, for I hold in this hand several threads of one of the strangest cases which ever perplexed a man's brain, and yet I lack the one or two which are needful to complete my theory. But I'll have them, Watson, I'll have them!' His eyes kindled and a slight flush sprang into his thin cheeks. For an instant the veil had lifted upon his keen, intense nature, but for an instant only. When I glanced again his face had resumed that Red Indian composure which had made so many regard him as a machine rather than a man.

'The problem presents features of interest,' said he; 'I may even say very exceptional features of interest. I have already looked into the matter, and have come, as I think, within sight of my solution. If you could accompany me in that last step, you might be of considerable service to me.'

'I should be delighted.'

'Could you go as far as Aldershot tomorrow?'

'I have no doubt Jackson would take my practice.'

'Very good. I want to start by the 11.10 from Waterloo.'

'That would give me time.'

'Then, if you are not sleepy, I will give you a sketch of what has happened and of what remains to be done.'

'I was sleepy before you came. I am quite wakeful now.'

'I will compress the story as far as may be done without omitting anything vital to the case. It is conceivable that you may even have read some account of the matter. It is the supposed murder of Colonel Barclay, of the Royal Mallows, at Aldershot, which I am investigating.'

'I have heard nothing of it.'

'It has not excited much attention yet, except locally. The facts are only two days old. Briefly they are these:

'The Royal Mallows is, as you know, one of the most famous Irish regiments in the British Army. It did wonders both in the Crimea and the Mutiny, and has since that time distinguished itself upon every possible occasion. It was commanded up to Monday night by James Barclay, a gallant veteran, who started as a full private, was raised to commissioned rank for his bravery at the time of the Mutiny, and so lived to command the regiment in which he had once carried a musket.

'Colonel Barclay had married at the time when he was a sergeant, and his wife, whose maiden name was Miss Nancy Devoy, was the daughter of a former colour-sergeant in the same corps. There was, therefore, as can be imagined, some little social friction when the young couple (for they were still young) found themselves in their new surroundings. They appear, however, to have quickly adapted themselves, and Mrs Barclay has always, I understand, been as popular with the ladies of the regiment as her husband was with his brother officers. I may add that she was a woman of great beauty, and that even now, when she has been married for upwards of thirty years, she is still of a striking appearance.

'Colonel Barclay's family life appears to have been a uniformly happy one. Major Murphy, to whom I owe most of my facts, assures me that he has never heard of any misunderstanding between the pair. On the whole he thinks that Barclay's devotion to his wife was greater than his wife's to Barclay. He was acutely uneasy if he were absent from her for a day. She, on the other hand, though devoted and faithful, was less obtrusively affectionate. But they were regarded in the regiment as the very model of a middle-aged couple. There was absolutely nothing in their mutual relations to prepare people for the tragedy which was to follow.

'Colonel Barclay himself seems to have had some singular traits in his character. He was a dashing, jovial old soldier in his usual mood, but there were occasions on which he seemed to show himself capable of considerable violence and vindictiveness. This side of his nature, however, appears never to have been turned towards his wife. Another fact which had struck Major Murphy, and three out of five of the other officers with whom I conversed, was the singular sort of depression which came upon him at times. As the Major expressed it, the smile had often been struck from his mouth, as if by some invisible hand, when he had been joining in the gaieties and chaff of the mess table. For days on end, when the mood was on him, he had been sunk in the deepest gloom. This and a certain tinge of superstition were the only unusual traits in his character which his brother officers had observed. The latter peculiarity took the form of a dislike of being left alone, especially after dark. This puerile feature in a nature which was conspicuously manly had often given rise to comment and conjecture.

'The first battalion of the Royal Mallows (which is the old 117th) has been stationed at Aldershot for some years. The married officers live out of barracks, and the Colonel has during all this time occupied a villa called Lachine, about half a mile from the North Camp. The house stands in its own grounds, but the west side of it is not more than thirty yards from the high-road. A coachman and two maids form the staff of servants. These, with their master and mistress, were the sole occupants of Lachine, for the Barclays had no children, nor was it usual for them to have resident visitors.

'Now for the events at Lachine between nine and ten on the evening of last Monday.

'Mrs Barclay was, it appears, a member of the Roman Catholic Church, and had interested herself very much in the establishment of the Guild of St George, which was formed in connection with the Watt Street Chapel for the purpose of supplying the poor with cast-off clothing. A meeting of the Guild had been held that evening at eight, and Mrs Barclay had hurried over her dinner in order to be present at it. When leaving the house, she was heard by the coachman to make some commonplace remark to her husband, and to assure him that she would be back before long. She then called for Miss Morrison, a young lady who lives in the next villa, and the two went off together to their meeting. It lasted forty minutes, and at a quarter past nine Mrs Barclay returned home, having left Miss Morrison at her door as she passed.

'There is a room which is used as a morning-room at Lachine. This faces the road, and opens by a large glass folding door on to the lawn. The lawn is thirty yards across, and is only divided from the highway by a low wall with an iron rail above it. It was into this room that Mrs Barclay went upon her return. The blinds were not down, for the room was seldom used in the evening, but Mrs Barclay herself lit the lamp and then rang the bell, asking Jane Stewart, the housemaid, to bring her a cup of tea, which was quite contrary to her usual habits. The Colonel had been sitting in the dining-room, but hearing that his wife had returned, he joined her in the morning-room. The coachman saw him cross the hall, and enter it. He was never seen again alive.

'The tea which had been ordered was brought up at the end of ten minutes, but the maid, as she approached the door, was surprised to hear the voices of her master and mistress in furious altercation. She knocked without receiving any answer, and even turned the handle, but only to find that the door was locked upon the inside. Naturally enough, she ran down to tell the cook, and the two women with the coachman came up into the hall and listened to the dispute which was still raging. They all agree that only two voices were to be heard, those of Barclay and his wife. Barclay's remarks were subdued and abrupt, so that none of them were audible to the listeners. The lady's, on the other hand, were most bitter, and, when she raised her voice, could be plainly heard. "You coward!" she repeated over and over again. "What can be done now? Give me back my life. I will never so much as breathe the same air as you again! You coward! You coward!" Those were scraps of her conversation, ending in a sudden dreadful cry in the man's voice, with a crash, and a piercing scream from the woman. Convinced that some tragedy had occurred, the coachman rushed to the door and strove to force it, while scream after scream issued from within. He was unable, however, to make his way in, and the maids were too distracted with fear to be of any assistance to him. A sudden thought struck him, however, and he ran through the hall door and round to the lawn, upon which the long french windows opened. One side of the window was open, which I understand was quite usual in the summer-time, and he passed without difficulty into the room. His mistress had ceased to scream, and was stretched insensible upon a couch, while with his feet tilted over the side of an armchair, and his head upon the ground near the corner of the fender, was lying the unfortunate soldier, stone dead, in a pool of his own blood.

'Naturally the coachman's first thought, on finding that he could do nothing for his master, was to open the door. But here an unexpected and singular difficulty presented itself. The key was not on the inner side of the door, nor could he find it anywhere in the room. He went out again, therefore, through the window, and having obtained the help of a policeman and of a medical man, he returned. The lady, against whom naturally the strongest suspicion rested, was removed to her room, still in a state of insensibility. The Colonel's body was then placed upon the sofa, and a careful examination made of the scene of the tragedy.

'The injury from which the unfortunate veteran was suffering was found to be a ragged cut, some two inches long, at the back part of his head, which had evidently been caused by a violent blow from a blunt weapon. Nor was it difficult to guess what that weapon may have been. Upon the floor, close to the body, was lying a singular club of hard carved wood with a bone handle. The Colonel possessed a varied collection of weapons brought from the different countries in which he had fought, and it is conjectured by the police that this club was among his trophies. The servants deny having seen it before, but among the numerous curiosities in the house it is possible that it may have been overlooked. Nothing else of importance was discovered in the room by the police, save the inexplicable fact that neither upon Mrs Barclay's person, nor upon that of the victim, nor in any part of the room was the missing key to be found. The door had eventually to be opened by a locksmith from Aldershot.

'That was the state of things, Watson, when upon the Tuesday morning I, at the request of Major Murphy, went down to Aldershot to supplement the efforts of the police. I think you will acknowledge that the problem was already one of interest, but my observations soon made me realize that it was in truth much more extraordinary than would at first sight appear.

'Before examining the room I cross-questioned the servants, but only succeeded in eliciting the facts which I have already stated. One other detail of interest was remembered by Jane Stewart, the housemaid. You will remember that on hearing the sound of the quarrel she descended and returned with the other servants. On that first occasion, when she was alone, she says that the voices of her master and mistress were sunk so low that she could hear hardly anything, and judged by their tones, rather than their words, that they had fallen out. On my pressing her, however, she remembered that she heard the word "David" uttered twice by the lady. The point is of the utmost importance as guiding us towards the reason of the sudden quarrel. The Colonel's name, you remember, was James.

'There was one thing in the case which had made the deepest impression both upon the servants and the police. This was the contortion of the Colonel's face. It had set, according to their account, into the most dreadful expression of fear and horror which a human countenance is capable of assuming. More than one person fainted at the mere sight of him, so terrible was the effect. It was quite certain that he had foreseen his fate, and that it had caused him the utmost horror. This, of course, fitted in well enough with the police theory, if the Colonel could have seen his wife making a murderous attack upon him. Nor was the fact of the wound being on the back of his head a fatal objection to this, as he might have turned to avoid the blow. No information could be got from the lady herself, who was temporarily insane from an acute attack of brain fever.

'From the police I learned that Miss Morrison, who, you remember, went out that evening with Mrs Barclay, denied having any knowledge of what it was which had caused the ill-humour in which her companion had returned.

'Having gathered these facts, Watson, I smoked several pipes over them, trying to separate those which were crucial from others which were merely incidental. There could be no question that the most distinctive and suggestive point in the case was the singular disappearance of the door key. A most careful search had failed to discover it in the room. Therefore, it must have been taken from it. But neither the Colonel nor the Colonel's wife could have taken it. That was perfectly clear. Therefore a third person must have entered the room. And that third person could only have come through the window. It seemed to me that a careful examination of the room and the lawn might possibly reveal some traces of this mysterious individual. You know my methods, Watson. There was not one of them which I did not apply to the inquiry. And it ended by my discovering traces, but very different ones from those which I had expected. There had been a man in the room, and he had crossed the lawn coming from the road. I was able to obtain five very clear impressions of his footmarks – one on the roadway itself, at the point where he had climbed the low wall, two on the lawn, and two very faint ones upon the stained boards near the window where he had entered. He had apparently rushed across the lawn, for his toe marks were much deeper than his heels. But it was not the man who surprised me. It was his companion.'

'His companion!'

Holmes pulled a large sheet of tissue paper out of his pocket and carefully unfolded it upon his knee.

'WHAT DO YOU MAKE OF THAT?'

'What do you make of that?' he asked.

The paper was covered with tracings of the footmarks of some small animal. It had five well-marked footpads, an indication of long nails, and the whole print might be nearly as large as a dessert spoon.

'It's a dog,' said I.

'Did you ever hear of a dog running up a curtain? I found distinct traces that this creature had done so.'

'A monkey, then?'

'But it is not the print of a monkey.'

'What can it be, then?'

'Neither dog, nor cat, nor monkey, nor any creature that we are familiar with. I have tried to reconstruct it from the measurements. Here are four prints where the beast has been standing motionless. You see that it is no less than fifteen inches from fore-foot to hind. Add to that the length of neck and head, and you get a creature not much less than two feet long – probably more if there is any tail. But now observe this other measurement. The animal has been moving, and we have the length of its stride. In each case it is only about three inches. You have an indication, you see, of a long body with very short legs attached to it. It has not been considerate enough to leave any of its hair behind it. But its general shape must be what I have indicated, and it can run up a curtain and is carnivorous.'

'How do you deduce that?'

'Because it ran up the curtain. A canary's cage was hanging in the window, and its aim seems to have been to get at the bird.'

'Then what was the beast?'

'Ah, if I could give it a name it might go a long way towards solving the case. On the whole it was probably some creature of the weasel or stoat tribe – and yet it is larger than any of these that I have seen.'

'But what had it to do with the crime?'

'That also is still obscure. But we have learned a good deal, you perceive. We know that a man stood in the road looking at the quarrel between the Barclays – the blinds were up and the room lighted. We know also that he ran across the lawn, entered the room, accompanied by a strange animal, and that he either struck the Colonel, or, as is equally possible, that the Colonel fell down from sheer fright at the sight of him, and cut his head on the corner of the fender. Finally, we have the curious fact that the intruder carried away the key with him when he left.'

'Your discoveries seem to have left the business more obscure than it was before,' said I.

'Quite so. They undoubtedly showed that the affair was much deeper than was at first conjectured. I thought the matter over, and I came to the conclusion that I must approach the case from another aspect. But really, Watson, I am keeping you up, and I might just as well tell you all this on our way to Aldershot tomorrow.'

'Thank you, you've gone rather too far to stop.'

'It was quite certain that when Mrs Barclay left the house at half past seven she was on good terms with her husband. She was never, as I think I have said, ostentatiously affectionate, but she was heard by the coachman chatting with the Colonel in a friendly fashion. Now, it was equally certain that immediately on her return she had gone to the room in which she was least likely to see her husband, had flown to tea, as an agitated woman will, and, finally, on his coming in to her, had broken into violent recriminations. Therefore, something had occurred between seven-thirty and nine o'clock which had completely altered her feelings towards him. But Miss Morrison had been with her during the whole of that hour and a half. It was absolutely certain, therefore, in spite of her denial, that she must know something of the matter.

'My first conjecture was that possibly there had been some passages between this young woman and the old soldier, which the former had now confessed to the wife. That would account for the angry return and also for the girl's denial that anything had occurred. Nor would it be entirely incompatible with most of the words overheard. But there was the reference to David, and there was the known affection of the Colonel for his wife to weigh against it, to say nothing of the tragic intrusion of this other man, which might, of course, be entirely disconnected with what had gone before. It was not easy to pick one's steps, but on the whole I was inclined to dismiss the idea that there had been anything between the Colonel and Miss Morrison, but more than ever convinced that the young lady held the clue as to what it was which had turned Mrs Barclay to hatred of her husband. I took the obvious course, therefore, of calling upon Miss Morrison, of explaining to her that I was perfectly certain that she held the facts in her possession, and of assuring her that her friend, Mrs Barclay, might find herself in the dock upon a capital charge unless the matter were cleared up.

'Miss Morrison is a little, ethereal slip of a girl, with timid eyes and blonde hair, but I found her by no means wanting in shrewdness and common sense. She sat thinking for some time after I had spoken, and then turning to me with a brisk air of resolution, she broke into a remarkable statement, which I will condense for your benefit.

' "I promised my friend that I would say nothing of the matter, and a promise is a promise," said she. "But if I can really help her when so serious a charge is made against her, and when her own mouth, poor darling, is closed by illness, then I think I am absolved from my promise. I will tell you exactly what happened on Monday evening.

' "We were returning from the Watt Street Mission, about a quarter to nine o'clock. On our way we had to pass through Hudson Street, which is a very quiet thoroughfare. There is only one lamp in it upon the left-hand side, and as we approached this lamp I saw a man coming towards us with his back very bent, and something like a box slung over one of his shoulders. He appeared to be deformed, for he carried his head low, and walked with his knees bent. We were passing him when he raised his face to look at us in the circle of light thrown by the lamp, and as he did so he stopped and screamed out in a dreadful voice, 'My God, it's Nancy!' Mrs Barclay turned as white as death, and would have fallen down had the dreadful-looking creature not caught hold of her. I was going to call for the police, but she, to my surprise, spoke quite civilly to the fellow.

'"'I thought you had been dead this thirty years, Henry,' said she, in a shaking voice.

'"'So I have,' said he and it was awful to hear the tones that he said it in. He had a very dark, fearsome face, and a gleam in his eyes that comes back to me in my dreams. His hair and whiskers were shot with grey, and his face was all crinkled and puckered like a withered apple.

'"'Just walk on a little way, dear,' said Mrs Barclay. 'I want to have a word with this man. There is nothing to be afraid of.' She tried to speak boldly, but she was still deadly pale, and could hardly get her words out for the trembling of her lips.

'"I did as she asked me, and they talked together for a few minutes. Then she came down the street with her eyes blazing, and I saw the crippled wretch standing by the lamp-post and shaking his clenched fists in the air, as if he were mad with rage. She never said a word until we were at the door here, when she took me by the hand and begged me to tell no one what had happened. 'It is an old acquaintance of mine who has come down in the world,' said she. When I promised her that I would say nothing she kissed me, and I have never seen her since. I have told you now the whole truth, and if I withheld it from the police it is because I did not realize then the danger in which my dear friend stood. I know that it can only be to her advantage that everything should be known."

'There was her statement, Watson, and to me, as you can imagine, it was like a light on a dark night. Everything which had been disconnected before began at once to assume its true place, and I had a shadowy presentiment of the whole sequence of events. My next step obviously was to find the man who had produced such a remarkable impression upon Mrs Barclay. If he were still in Aldershot it should not be a very difficult matter. There are not such a very great number of civilians, and a deformed man was sure to have attracted attention. I spent a day in the search, and by evening – this very evening, Watson – I had run him down. The man's name is Henry Wood, and he lives in lodgings in the same street in which the ladies met him. He has only been five days in the place. In the character of a registration agent I had a most interesting gossip with his landlady. The man is by trade a conjurer and performer, going round the canteens, after nightfall, and giving a little entertainment at each. He carries some creature about with him in his box, about which the landlady seemed to be in considerable trepidation, for she had never seen an animal like it. He uses it in some of his tricks, according to her account. So much the woman was able to tell me, and also that it was a wonder the man lived, seeing how twisted he was, and that he spoke in a strange tongue sometimes, and that for the last two nights she had heard him groaning and weeping in his bedroom. He was all right as far as money went, but in his deposit he had given her what looked like a bad florin. She showed it to me, Watson, and it was an Indian rupee.

'So now, my dear fellow, you see exactly how we stand and why it is I want you. It is perfectly plain that after the ladies parted from this man he followed them at a distance, that he saw the quarrel between husband and wife through the window, that he rushed in, and that the creature which he carried in his box got loose. That is all very certain. But he is the only person in this world who can tell us exactly what happened in that room.'

'And you intend to ask him?'

'Most certainly – but in the presence of a witness.'

'And I am the witness?'

'If you will be so good. If he can clear the matter up, well and good. If he refuses, we have no alternative but to apply for a warrant.'

'But how do you know he will be there when we return?'

'You may be sure that I took some precautions. I have one of my Baker Street boys mounting guard over him who would stick to him like a burr, go where he might. We shall find him in Hudson Street tomorrow, Watson; and meanwhile I should be the criminal myself if I kept you out of bed any longer.'

It was midday when we found ourselves at the scene of the tragedy, and, under my companion's guidance, we made our way at once to Hudson Street. In spite of his capacity for concealing his emotions I could easily see that Holmes was in a state of suppressed excitement, while I was myself tingling with that half-sporting, half-intellectual pleasure which I invariably experienced when I associated myself with him in his investigations.

'This is the street,' said he, as he turned into a short thoroughfare lined with plain, two-storeyed brick houses – 'Ah! here is Simpson to report.'

'He's in all right, Mr Holmes,' cried a small street Arab, running up to us.

'Good, Simpson!' said Holmes, patting him on the head. 'Come along, Watson. This is the house.' He sent in his card with a message that he had come on important business, and a moment later we were face to face with the man whom we had come to see. In spite of the warm weather he was crouching over a fire and the little room was like an oven. The man sat all twisted and huddled in his chair in a way which gave an indescribable impression of deformity, but the face which he turned towards us, though worn and swarthy, must at some time have been remarkable for its beauty. He looked suspiciously at us now out of yellow-shot bilious eyes, and, without speaking or rising, he waved towards two chairs.

'Mr Henry Wood, late of India, I believe?' said Holmes, affably. 'I've come over this little matter of Colonel Barclay's death.'

'What should I know about that?'

'That's what I wanted to ascertain. You know, I suppose, that unless the matter is cleared up, Mrs Barclay, who is an old friend of yours, will in all probability be tried for murder?'

The man gave a violent start.

'I don't know who you are,' he cried, 'nor how you come to know what you do know, but will you swear that this is true that you tell me?'

'Why, they are only waiting for her to come to her senses to arrest her.'

'My God! Are you in the police yourself?'

'No.'

'What business is it of yours, then?'

'It's every man's business to see justice done.'

'You can take my word that she is innocent.'

'Then you are guilty?'

'MR HENRY WOOD, I BELIEVE?'

'No, I am not.'

'Who killed Colonel James Barclay, then?'

'It was a just Providence that killed him. But mind you this, that if I had knocked his brains out, as it was in my heart to do, he would have had no more than his due from my hands. If his own guilty conscience had not struck him down, it is likely enough that I might have had his blood upon my soul. You want me to tell the story? Well, I don't know why I shouldn't, for there's no cause for me to be ashamed of it.

'It was in this way, sir. You see me now with my back like a camel and my ribs all awry, but there was a time when Corporal Henry Wood was the smartest man in the 117th Foot. We were in India then, in cantonments, at a place we'll call Bhurtee. Barclay, who died the other day, was sergeant in the same company as myself, and the belle of the regiment – aye, and the finest girl that ever had the breath of life between her lips – was Nancy Devoy, the daughter of the colour-sergeant. There were two men who loved her, and one whom she loved; and you'll smile when you look at this poor thing huddled before the fire, and hear me say that it was for my good looks that she loved me.

'Well, though I had her heart her father was set upon her marrying Barclay. I was a harum-scarum, reckless lad, and he had had an education, and was already marked for the sword-belt. But the girl held true to me, and it seemed that I would have had her, when the Mutiny broke out, and all hell was loose in the country.

'We were shut up in Bhurtee, the regiment of us, with half a battery of artillery, a company of Sikhs, and a lot of civilians and women-folk. There were ten thousand rebels round us, and they were as keen as a set of terriers round a rat cage. About the second week of it our water gave out, and it was a question whether we could communicate with General Neill's column, which was moving up country. It was our only chance, for we could not hope to fight our way out with all the women and children, so I volunteered to go out and warn General Neill of our danger. My offer was accepted, and I talked it over with Sergeant Barclay, who was supposed to know the ground better than any other man, and who drew up a route by which I might get through the rebel lines. At ten o'clock the same night I started off upon my journey. There were a thousand lives to save, but it was of only one that I was thinking when I dropped over the wall that night.

'My way ran down a dried-up watercourse, which we hoped would screen me from the enemy's sentries, but as I crept round the corner of it I walked right into six of them, who were crouching down in the dark waiting for me. In an instant I was stunned with a blow, and bound hand and foot. But the real blow was to my heart and not to my head, for as I came to and listened to as much as I could understand of their talk, I heard enough to tell me that my comrade, the very man who had arranged the way I was to take, had betrayed me by means of a native servant into the hands of the enemy.

'Well, there's no need for me to dwell on that part of it. You know now what James Barclay was capable of. Bhurtee was relieved by Neill next day, but the rebels took me away with them in their retreat, and it was many a long year before ever I saw a white face again. I was tortured, and tried to get away, and was captured and tortured again. You can see for yourselves the state in which I was left. Some of them that fled into Nepal took me with them, and then afterwards I was up past Darjeeling. The hill-folk up there murdered the rebels who had me, and I became their slave for a time until I escaped, but instead of going south I had to go north, until I found myself among the Afghans. There I wandered about for many a year, and at last came back to the Punjab, where I lived mostly among the natives, and picked up a living by the conjuring tricks that I had learned. What use was it for me, a wretched cripple, to go back to England, or to make myself known to my old comrades? Even my wish for revenge would not make me do that. I had rather that Nancy and my old pals should think of Harry Wood as having died with a straight back, than see him living and crawling with a stick like a chimpanzee. They never doubted that I was dead, and I meant that they never should. I heard that Barclay had married Nancy, and that he was rapidly rising in the regiment, but even that did not make me speak.

'But when one gets old, one has a longing for home. For years I've been dreaming of the bright green fields and the hedges of England. At last I determined to see them before I died. I saved enough to bring me across, and then I came here where the soldiers are, for I know their ways, and how to amuse them, and so earn enough to keep me.'

'Your narrative is most interesting,' said Sherlock Holmes. 'I have already heard of your meeting with Mrs Barclay and your mutual recognition. You then, as I understand, followed her home and saw through the window an altercation between her husband and her, in which she doubtless cast his conduct to you in his teeth. Your own feelings overcame you, and you ran across the lawn, and broke in upon them.'

'I did, sir, and at the sight of me he looked as I have never seen a man look before, and over he went with his head on the fender. But he was dead before he fell. I read death on his face as plain as I can read that text over the fire. The bare sight of me was like a bullet through his guilty heart.'

'And then?'

'Then Nancy fainted, and I caught up the key of the door from her hand, intending to unlock it and get help. But as I was doing it it seemed to me better to leave it alone and get away, for the thing might look black against me, and anyway my secret would be out if I were taken. In my haste I thrust the key into my pocket, and dropped my stick while I was chasing Teddy, who had run up the curtain. When I got him into his box, from which he had slipped, I was off as fast as I could run.'

'Who's Teddy?' asked Holmes.

The man leaned over and pulled up the front of a kind of hutch in the corner. In an instant out there slipped a beautiful reddish-brown creature, thin, and lithe, with the legs of a stoat, a long thin nose, and a pair of the finest red eyes that ever I saw in an animal's head.

'It's a mongoose!' I cried.

'Well, some call them that, and some call them ichneumon,' said the man. 'Snake-catcher is what I call them, and Teddy is amazing quick on cobras. I have one here without the fangs, and Teddy catches it every night to please the folk in the canteen. Any other point, sir?'

'Well, we may have to apply to you again if Mrs Barclay should prove to be in serious trouble.'

'In that case, of course, I'd come forward.'

'But if not, there is no object in raking up this scandal against a dead man, foully as he has acted. You have, at least, the satisfaction of knowing that for thirty years of his life his conscience bitterly reproached him for his wicked deed. Ah, there goes Major Murphy on the other side of the street. Good-bye, Wood; I want to learn if anything has happened since yesterday.'

We were in time to overtake the Major before he reached the corner.

'Ah, Holmes,' he said, 'I suppose you have heard that all this fuss has come to nothing?'

'What, then?'

'The inquest is just over. The medical evidence showed conclusively that death was due to apoplexy. You see, it was quite a simple case after all.'

'Oh, remarkably superficial,' said Holmes, smiling. 'Come, Watson, I don't think we shall be wanted in Aldershot any more.'

'There's one thing,' said I, as we walked down to the station; 'if the husband's name was James, and the other was Henry, what was this talk about David?'

'That one word, my dear Watson, should have told me the whole story had I been the ideal reasoner which you are so fond of depicting. It was evidently a term of reproach.'

'Of reproach?'

'Yes, David strayed a little now and then, you know, and on one occasion in the same direction as Sergeant James Barclay. You remember the small affair of Uriah and Bathsheba? My Biblical knowledge is a trifle rusty, I fear, but you will find the story in the first or second of Samuel.'

The Adventure of the Solitary Cyclist

From the years 1894 to 1901 inclusive, Mr Sherlock Holmes was a very busy man. It is safe to say that there was no public case of any difficulty in which he was not consulted during those eight years, and there were hundreds of private cases, some of them of the most intricate and extraordinary character, in which he played a prominent part. Many startling successes and a few unavoidable failures were the outcome of this long period of continuous work. As I have preserved very full notes of all these cases, and was myself personally engaged in many of them, it may be imagined that it is no easy task to know which I should select to lay before the public. I shall, however, preserve my former rule, and give the preference to those cases which derive their interest not so much from the brutality of the crime as from the ingenuity and dramatic quality of the solution. For this reason I will now lay before the reader the facts connected with Miss Violet Smith, the solitary cyclist of Charlington, and the curious sequel of our investigation, which culminated in unexpected tragedy. It is true that the circumstances did not permit of any striking illustration of those powers for which my friend was famous, but there were some points about the case which made it stand out in those long records of crime from which I gather the material for these little narratives.

On referring to my notebook for the year 1895, I find that it was upon Saturday, April 23rd, that we first heard of Miss Violet Smith. Her visit was, I remember, extremely unwelcome to Holmes, for he was immersed at the moment in a very abstruse and complicated problem concerning the peculiar persecution to which John Vincent Harden, the well-known tobacco millionaire, had been subjected. My friend, who loved above all things precision and concentration of thought, resented anything which distracted his attention from the matter in hand. And yet without harshness, which was foreign to his nature, it was impossible to refuse to listen to the story of the young and beautiful woman, tall, graceful and queenly, who presented herself at Baker Street late in the evening and implored his assistance and advice. It was vain to urge that his time was already fully occupied, for the young lady had come with the determination to tell her story, and it was evident that nothing short of force could get her out of the room until she had done so. With a resigned air and a somewhat weary smile, Holmes begged the beautiful intruder to take a seat and to inform us what it was that was troubling her.

'At least it cannot be your health,' said he, as his keen eyes darted over her; 'so ardent a bicyclist must be full of energy.'

'MY FRIEND TOOK THE LADY'S UNGLOVED HAND AND EXAMINED IT.'

She glanced down in surprise at her own feet, and I observed the slight roughening of the side of the sole caused by the friction of the edge of the pedal.

'Yes, I bicycle a good deal, Mr Holmes, and that has something to do with my visit to you today.'

My friend took the lady's ungloved hand and examined it with as close an attention and as little sentiment as a scientist would show to a specimen.

'You will excuse me, I am sure. It is my business,' said he, as he dropped it. 'I nearly fell into the error of supposing that you were typewriting. Of course, it is obvious that it is music. You observe the spatulate finger end, Watson, which is common to both professions? There is a spirituality about the face, however' – he gently turned it towards the light – 'which the typewriter does not generate. This lady is a musician.'

'Yes, Mr Holmes, I teach music.'

'In the country, I presume, from your complexion.'

'Yes, sir; near Farnham, on the borders of Surrey.'

'A beautiful neighbourhood, and full of the most interesting associations. You remember, Watson, that it was near there that we took Archie Stamford, the forger. Now, Miss Violet, what has happened to you near Farnham, on the borders of Surrey?'

The young lady, with great clearness and composure, made the following curious statement:

'My father is dead, Mr Holmes. He was James Smith, who conducted the orchestra at the old Imperial Theatre. My mother and I were left without a relation in the world except one uncle, Ralph Smith, who went to Africa twenty-five years ago, and we have never had a word from him since. When Father died we were left very poor, but one day we were told that there was an advertisement in *The Times* inquiring for our whereabouts. You can imagine how excited we were, for we thought that someone had left us a fortune. We went at once to the lawyer whose name was given in the paper. There we met two gentlemen, Mr Carruthers and Mr Woodley, who were home on a visit from South Africa. They said that my uncle was a friend of theirs, that he died some months before in poverty in Johannesburg, and that he had asked them with his last breath to hunt up his relations and see that they were in no want. It seemed strange to us that Uncle Ralph, who took no notice of us when he was alive, should be so careful to look after us when he was dead; but Mr Carruthers explained that the reason was that my uncle had just heard of the death of his brother, and so felt responsible for our fate.'

'Excuse me,' said Holmes; 'when was this interview?'

'Last December – four months ago.'

'Pray proceed.'

'Mr Woodley seemed to me to be a most odious person. He was for ever making eyes at me – a coarse, puffy-faced, red-moustached young man, with his hair plastered down on each side of his forehead. I thought that he was perfectly hateful – and I was sure that Cyril would not wish me to know such a person.'

'Oh, Cyril is his name!' said Holmes, smiling.

The young lady blushed and laughed.

'Yes, Mr Holmes; Cyril Morton, an electrical engineer, and we hope to be married at the end of the summer. Dear me, how *did* I get talking about him? What I wished to say was that Mr Woodley was perfectly odious, but that Mr Carruthers, who was a much older man, was more agreeable. He was a dark, sallow, clean-shaven, silent person; but he had polite manners and a pleasant smile. He inquired how we were left, and on finding that we were very poor he suggested that I should come and teach music to his only daughter, aged ten. I said that I did not like to leave my mother, on which he suggested that I should go home to her every weekend, and he offered me a hundred a year, which was certainly splendid pay. So it ended by my accepting, and I went down to Chiltern Grange, about six miles from Farnham. Mr Carruthers was a widower, but he had engaged a lady-housekeeper, a very respectable, elderly person, called Mrs Dixon, to look after his establishment. The child was a dear, and everything promised well. Mr Carruthers was very kind and very musical, and we had most pleasant evenings together. Every weekend I went home to my mother in town.

'The first flaw in my happiness was the arrival of the red-moustached Mr Woodley. He came for a visit of a week, and oh, it seemed three months to me! He was a dreadful person, a bully to everyone else, but to me something infinitely worse. He made odious love to me, boasted of his wealth, said that if I married him I would have the finest diamonds in London, and finally, when I would have nothing to do with him, he seized me in his arms one day after dinner – he was hideously strong – and he swore that he would not let me go until I had kissed him. Mr Carruthers came in, and tore him off from me, on which he turned upon his own host, knocking him down and cutting his face open. That was the end of his visit, as you can imagine. Mr Carruthers apologized to me next day, and assured me that I should never be exposed to such an insult again. I have not seen Mr Woodley since.

'And now, Mr Holmes, I come at last to the special thing which has caused me to ask your advice today. You must know that every Saturday forenoon I ride on my bicycle to Farnham Station in order to get the 12.22 to town. The road from Chiltern Grange is a lonely one, and at one spot it is particularly so, for it lies for over a mile between Charlington Heath upon one side and the woods which lie round Charlington Hall upon the other. You could not find a more lonely tract of road anywhere, and it is quite rare to meet so much as a cart, or a peasant, until you reach the high-road near Crooksbury Hill. Two weeks ago I was passing this place when I chanced to look back over my shoulder, and about two hundred yards behind me I saw a man, also on a bicycle. He seemed to be a middle-aged man, with a short, dark beard. I looked back before I reached Farnham, but the man was gone, so I thought no more about it. But you can imagine how surprised I was, Mr Holmes, when on my return on the Monday I saw the same man on the same stretch of road. My astonishment was increased when the incident occurred again, exactly as before, on the following Saturday and Monday. He always kept his distance, and did not molest me in any way, but still it certainly was very odd. I mentioned it to Mr Carruthers, who seemed interested in what I said, and told me that he had ordered a horse and trap, so that in future I should not pass over these lonely roads without some companion.

'The horse and trap were to have come this week, but for some reason they were not delivered, and again I had to cycle to the station. That was this morning. You can think that I looked out when I came to Charlington Heath, and there, sure enough, was the man, exactly as he had been the two weeks before. He always kept so far from me that I could not clearly see his face, but it was certainly someone whom I did not know. He was dressed in a dark suit with a cloth cap. The only thing about his face that I could clearly see was his dark beard. Today I was not alarmed, but I was filled with curiosity, and I determined to find out who he was and what he wanted. I slowed down my machine, but he slowed down his. Then I stopped altogether, but he stopped also. Then I laid a trap for him. There is a sharp turning of the road, and I pedalled very quickly round this, and then I stopped and waited. I expected him to shoot round and pass me before he could stop. But he never appeared. Then I went back and looked round the corner. I could see a mile of road, but he was not on it. To make it the more extraordinary there was no side-road at this point down which he could have gone.'

Holmes chuckled and rubbed his hands.

'This case certainly presents some features of its own,' said he. 'How much time elapsed between your turning the corner and your discovery that the road was clear?'

'Two or three minutes.'

'Then he could not have retreated down the road, and you say that there are no side-roads?'

'None.'

'Then he certainly took a footpath on one side or the other.'

'It could not have been on the side of the heath or I should have seen him.'

'So by the process of exclusion we arrive at the fact that he made his way towards Charlington Hall, which, as I understand, is situated in its own grounds on one side of the road. Anything else?'

'Nothing, Mr Holmes, save that I was so perplexed that I felt I should not be happy until I had seen you and had your advice.'

Holmes sat in silence for some little time.

'Where is the gentleman to whom you are engaged?' he asked at last.

'He is in the Midland Electric Company, at Coventry.'

'He would not pay you a surprise visit?'

'Oh, Mr Holmes! As if I should not know him!'

'Have you had any other admirers?'

'Several before I knew Cyril.'

'And since?'

'There was this dreadful man, Woodley, if you can call him an admirer.'

'No one else?'

Our fair client seemed a little confused.

'Who was he?' asked Holmes.

'Oh, it may be a mere fancy of mine; but it has seemed to me sometimes that my employer, Mr Carruthers, takes a great deal of interest in me. We are thrown rather together. I play his accompaniments in the evening. He has never said anything. He is a perfect gentleman. But a girl always knows.'

'Ha!' Holmes looked grave. 'What does he do for a living?'

'He is a rich man.'

'No carriages or horses?'

'Well, at least he is fairly well-to-do. But he goes into the City two or three times a week. He is deeply interested in South African gold shares.'

'You will let me know any fresh development, Miss Smith. I am very busy just now, but I will find time to make some inquiries into your case. In the meantime, take no step without letting me know. Goodbye, and I trust that we shall have nothing but good news from you.'

'It is part of the settled order of Nature that such a girl should have followers,' said Holmes, as he pulled at his meditative pipe, 'but for choice not on bicycles in lonely country roads. Some secretive lover, beyond all doubt. But there are curious and suggestive details about the case, Watson.'

'That he should appear only at that point?'

'Exactly. Our first effort must be to find who are the tenants of Charlington Hall. Then, again, how about the connection between Carruthers and Woodley, since they appear to be men of such different types? How came they *both* to be so keen upon looking up Ralph Smith's relations? One more point. What sort of a *ménage* is it which pays double the market price for a governess, but does not keep a horse although six miles from the station? Odd, Watson – very odd.'

'You will go down?'

'No, my dear fellow, *you* will go down. This may be some trifling intrigue, and I cannot break my other important research for the sake of it. On Monday you will arrive early at Farnham; you will conceal yourself near Charlington Heath; you will observe these facts for yourself, and act as your own judgement advises. Then, having inquired as to the occupants of the Hall, you will come back to me and report. And now, Watson, not another word of the matter until we have a few solid stepping stones on which we may hope to get across to our solution.'

We had ascertained from the lady that she went down upon

the Monday by the train which leaves Waterloo at 9.50, so I started early and caught the 9.13. At Farnham Station I had no difficulty in being directed to Charlington Heath. It was impossible to mistake the scene of the young lady's adventure, for the road runs between the open heath on one side, and an old yew hedge upon the other, surrounding a park which is studded with magnificent trees. There was a main gateway of lichen-studded stone, each side-pillar surmounted by mouldering heraldic emblems; but besides this central carriage-drive I observed several points where there were gaps in the hedge and paths leading through them. The house was invisible from the road, but the surroundings all spoke of gloom and decay.

The heath was covered with golden patches of flowering gorse, gleaming magnificently in the light of the bright spring sunshine. Behind one of these clumps I took up my position, so as to command both the gateway of the Hall and a long stretch of the road upon either side. It had been deserted when I left it, but now I saw a cyclist riding down it from the opposite direction to that in which I had come. He was clad in a dark suit, and I saw that he had a black beard. On reaching the end of the Charlington grounds he sprang from his machine and led it through a gap in the hedge, disappearing from my view.

A quarter of an hour passed and then a second cyclist appeared. This time it was the young lady coming from the station. I saw her look about her as she came to the Charlington hedge. An instant later the man emerged from his hiding place, sprang upon his bicycle, and followed her. In all the broad landscape those were the only moving figures, the graceful girl sitting very straight upon her machine and the man behind her bending low over his handle-bar, with a curiously furtive suggestion in every movement. She looked back at him and slowed her pace. He slowed also. She stopped. He at once stopped, too, keeping two hundred yards behind her. Her next movement was as unexpected as it was spirited. She suddenly whisked her wheels round and dashed straight at him! He was as quick as she, however, and darted off in desperate flight. Presently she came back up the road again, her head haughtily in the air, not deigning to take further notice of her silent attendant. He had turned also, and still kept his distance until the curve of the road hid them from my sight.

I remained in my hiding-place, and it was well that I did so, for presently the man reappeared, cycling slowly back. He turned in at the Hall gates and dismounted from his machine. For some minutes I could see him standing among the trees. His hands were raised, and he seemed to be settling his necktie. Then he mounted his bicycle and rode away from me down the drive towards the Hall. I ran across the heath and peered through the trees. Far away I could catch glimpses of the old grey building with its bristling Tudor chimneys, but the drive ran through a dense shrubbery, and I saw no more of my man.

However, it seemed to me that I had done a fairly good morning's work, and I walked back in high spirits to Farnham. The local house agent could tell me nothing about Charlington Hall, and referred me to a well-known firm in Pall Mall. There I halted on my way home, and met with courtesy from the representative. No, I could not have Charlington Hall for the summer. I was just too late. It had been let about a month ago. Mr Williamson was the name of the tenant. He was a respectable elderly gentleman. The polite agent was afraid he could say no more, as the affairs of his clients were not matters which he could discuss.

Mr Sherlock Holmes listened with attention to the long report which I was able to present to him that evening, but it did not elicit that word of curt praise which I had hoped for and should have valued. On the contrary, his austere face was even more severe than usual as he commented upon the things that I had done and the things that I had not.

'Your hiding-place, my dear Watson, was very faulty. You should have been behind the hedge; then you would have had a close view of this interesting person. As it is you were some hundreds of yards away, and can tell me even less than Miss Smith. She thinks she does not know the man; I am convinced she does. Why, otherwise, should he be so desperately anxious that she should not get so near him as to see his features? You describe him as bending over the handle-bar. Concealment again, you see. You really have done remarkably badly. He returns to the house, and you want to find out who he is. You come to a London house agent!'

'What should I have done?' I cried, with some heat.

'Gone to the nearest public house. That is the centre of country gossip. They would have told you every name, from the master to the scullery-maid. Williamson! It conveys nothing to my mind. If he is an elderly man he is not this active cyclist who springs away from that athletic young lady's pursuit. What have we gained by your expedition? The knowledge that the girl's story is true. I never doubted it. That there is a connection between the cyclist and the Hall. I never doubted that either. That the Hall is tenanted by Williamson. Who's the better for that? Well, well, my dear sir, don't look so depressed. We can do little more until next Saturday, and in the meantime I may make one or two inquiries myself.'

Next morning we had a note from Miss Smith, recounting shortly and accurately the very incidents which I had seen, but the pith of the letter lay in the postscript:

> I am sure that you will respect my confidence, Mr Holmes, when I tell you that my place here has become difficult owing to the fact that my employer has proposed marriage to me. I am convinced that his feelings are most deep and most honourable. At the same time my promise is, of course, given. He took my refusal very seriously, but also very gently. You can understand, however, that the situation is a little strained.

'Our young friend seems to be getting into deep waters,' said Holmes thoughtfully, as he finished the letter. 'The case certainly presents more features of interest and more possibility of development than I had originally thought. I should be none the worse for a quiet, peaceful day in the country, and I am inclined to run down this afternoon and test one or two theories which I have formed.'

Holmes's quiet day in the country had a singular termination, for he arrived at Baker Street late in the evening with a cut lip and a discoloured lump upon his forehead, besides a general air of dissipation which would have made his own person the fitting object of a Scotland Yard investigation. He was immensely tickled by his own adventures, and laughed heartily as he recounted them.

'I get so little active exercise that it is always a treat,' said he. 'You are aware that I have some proficiency in the good old British sport of boxing. Occasionally it is of service. Today, for example, I should have come to very ignominious grief without it.'

I begged him to tell me what had occurred.

'I found that country pub which I had already recommended to your notice, and there I made my discreet inquiries. I was in the bar, and a garrulous landlord was giving me all that I wanted. Williamson is a white-bearded man, and he lives alone with a small staff of servants at the Hall. There is some rumour that he is or has been a clergyman; but one or two incidents of his short residence at the Hall struck me as peculiarly unecclesiastical. I have already made some inquiries at a clerical agency, and they tell me that there *was* a man of that name in orders whose career has been a singularly dark one. The landlord further informed me that there are usually weekend visitors – "a warm lot, sir" – at the Hall, and especially one gentleman with a red moustache, Mr Woodley by name, who was always there. We had got as far as this when who should walk in but the gentleman himself, who had been drinking his beer in the taproom, and had heard the whole conversation. Who was I? What did I want? What did I mean by asking questions? He had a fine flow of language, and his adjectives were very vigorous. He ended a string of abuse by a vicious back-hander, which I failed to entirely avoid. The next few minutes were delicious. It was a straight left against a slogging ruffian. I emerged as you see me. Mr Woodley went home in a cart. So ended my country trip, and it must be confessed that, however enjoyable, my day on the Surrey border has not been much more profitable than your own.'

The Thursday brought us another letter from our client:

> You will not be surprised, Mr Holmes [said she], to hear that I am leaving Mr Carruthers' employment. Even the high pay cannot reconcile me to the discomforts of my situation. On Saturday I come up to town, and I do not intend to return. Mr Carruthers has got a trap, and so the dangers of the lonely road, if there ever were any dangers, are now over.
>
> As to the special cause of my leaving, it is not merely the strained situation with Mr Carruthers, but it is the reappearance of that odious man, Mr Woodley. He was always hideous, but he looks more awful than ever now, for he appears to have had an accident and he is much disfigured. I saw him out of the window, but I am glad to say I did not meet him. He had a long talk with Mr Carruthers, who seemed much excited afterwards. Woodley must be staying in the neighbourhood, for he did not sleep here, and yet I caught a glimpse of him again this morning slinking about in the shrubbery. I would sooner have a savage wild animal loose about the place. I loathe and fear him more than I can say. How *can* Mr Carruthers endure such a creature for a moment? However, all my troubles will be over on Saturday.

'So I trust, Watson, so I trust,' said Holmes gravely. 'There is some deep intrigue going on round that little woman, and it is our duty to see that no one molests her upon that last journey. I think, Watson, that we must spare time to run down together on Saturday morning, and make sure that this curious and inconclusive investigation has no untoward ending.'

I confess that I had not up to now taken a very serious view of the case, which had seemed to me rather grotesque and bizarre than dangerous. That a man should lie in wait for and follow a very handsome woman is no unheard-of thing, and if he had so little audacity that he not only dared not address her, but even fled from her approach, he was not a very formidable assailant. The ruffian Woodley was a very different person, but, except on the one occasion, he had not molested our client, and now he visited the house of Carruthers without intruding upon her presence. The man on the bicycle was doubtless a member of those weekend parties at the Hall of which the publican had spoken; but who he was or what he wanted was as obscure as ever. It was the severity of Holmes's manner and the fact that he slipped a revolver into his pocket before leaving our rooms which impressed me with the feeling that tragedy might prove to lurk behind this curious train of events.

A rainy night had been followed by a glorious morning, and the heath-covered countryside, with the glowing clumps of flowering gorse, seemed all the more beautiful to eyes which were weary of the duns and drabs and slate-greys of London. Holmes and I walked along the broad, sandy road inhaling the fresh morning air, and rejoicing in the music of the birds and the fresh breath of the spring. From a rise of the road on the shoulder of Crooksbury Hill we could see the grim Hall bristling out from amidst the ancient oaks, which, old as they were, were still younger than the building which they surrounded. Holmes pointed down the long tract of road which wound, a reddish-yellow band, between the brown of the heath and the budding green of the woods. Far away, a black dot, we could see a vehicle moving in our direction. Holmes gave an exclamation of impatience.

'I had given a margin of half an hour,' said he. 'If that is her trap she must be making for the earlier train. I fear, Watson, that she will be past Charlington before we can possibly meet her.'

From the instant that we passed the rise we could no longer see the vehicle, but we hastened onwards at such a pace that my sedentary life began to tell upon me, and I was compelled to fall behind. Holmes, however, was always in training, for he had inexhaustible stores of nervous energy upon which to draw. His springy step never slowed, until suddenly, when he was a hundred yards in front of me, he halted, and I saw him throw up his hand with a gesture of grief and despair. At the same instant an empty dog-cart, the horse cantering, the reins trailing, appeared round the curve of the road and rattled swiftly towards us.

'Too late, Watson; too late!' cried Holmes, as I ran panting to his side. 'Fool that I was not to allow for the earlier train! It's abduction, Watson – abduction! Murder! Heaven knows what!

'"TOO LATE, WATSON; TOO LATE!" CRIED HOLMES.'

Block the road! Stop the horse! That's right. Now jump in, and let us see if I can repair the consequences of my own blunder.'

We had sprung into the dog-cart, and Holmes, after turning the horse, gave it a sharp cut with a whip, and we flew back along the road. As we turned the curve the whole stretch of road between the Hall and the heath was opened up. I grasped Holmes's arm.

'That's the man!' I gasped.

A solitary cyclist was coming towards us. His head was down and his shoulders rounded as he put every ounce of energy that he possessed on to the pedals. He was flying like a racer. Suddenly he raised his bearded face, saw us close to him, and pulled up, springing from his machine. That coal-black beard was in singular contrast to the pallor of his face, and his eyes were as bright as if he had a fever. He stared at us and at the dog-cart. Then a look of amazement came over his face.

'Halloa! Stop there!' he shouted, holding his bicycle to block our road. 'Where did you get that dog-cart? Pull up, man!' he yelled, drawing a pistol from his side-pocket. 'Pull up, I say, or, by George, I'll put a bullet into your horse!'

Holmes threw the reins into my lap and sprang down from the cart.

'You're the man we want to see. Where is Miss Violet Smith?' he said in his quick, clear way.

'That's what I am asking you. You're in her dog-cart. You ought to know where she is.'

'We met the dog-cart on the road. There was no one in it. We drove back to help the young lady.'

'Good Lord! Good Lord! What shall I do?' cried the stranger, in an ecstasy of despair. 'They've got her, that hell-hound Woodley and the blackguard parson. Come, man, come, if you really are her friend. Stand by me and we'll save her, if I have to leave my carcass in Charlington Wood.'

He ran distractedly, his pistol in his hand, towards a gap in the hedge. Holmes followed him, and I, leaving the horse grazing beside the road, followed Holmes.

'This is where they came through,' said he, pointing to the marks of several feet upon the muddy path. 'Halloa! Stop a minute! Who's this in the bush?'

It was a young fellow about seventeen, dressed like an ostler, with leather cords and gaiters. He lay upon his back, his knees drawn up, a terrible cut upon his head. He was insensible, but alive. A glance at his wound told me that it had not penetrated the bone.

'That's Peter, the groom,' cried the stranger. 'He drove her. The beasts have pulled him off and clubbed him. Let him lie; we can't do him any good, but we may save her from the worst fate that can befall a woman.'

We ran frantically down the path, which wound among the trees. We had reached the shrubbery which surrounded the house when Holmes pulled up.

'They didn't go to the house. Here are their marks on the left – here, beside the laurel bushes! Ah, I said so!'

As he spoke a woman's shrill scream – a scream which vibrated with a frenzy of horror – burst from the thick green clump of bushes in front of us. It ended suddenly on its highest note with a choke and gurgle.

'This way! This way! They are in the bowling alley,' cried the stranger, darting through the bushes. 'Ah, the cowardly dogs! Follow me, gentlemen! Too late! too late! by the living Jingo!'

We had broken suddenly into a lovely glade of greensward surrounded by ancient trees. On the farther side of it, under the shadow of a mighty oak, there stood a singular group of three people. One was a woman, our client, drooping and faint, a handkerchief round her mouth. Opposite her stood a brutal, heavy-faced, red-moustached young man, his gaitered legs parted wide, one arm akimbo, the other waving a riding-crop, his whole attitude suggestive of a triumphant bravado. Between them an elderly, grey-bearded man, wearing a short surplice over a light tweed suit, had evidently just completed the wedding service, for he pocketed his Prayer Book as we appeared, and slapped the sinister bridegroom upon the back in jovial congratulation.

'They're married!' I gasped.

'Come, on!' cried our guide; 'come on!' He rushed across the glade, Holmes and I at his heels. As we approached, the lady staggered against the trunk of the tree for support. Williamson, the ex-clergyman, bowed to us with mock politeness, and the bully Woodley advanced with a shout of brutal and exultant laughter.

'You can take your beard off, Bob,' said he. 'I know you right enough. Well, you and your pals have just come in time for me to be able to introduce you to Mrs Woodley.'

Our guide's answer was a singular one. He snatched off the dark beard which had disguised him and threw it on the ground,

'AS WE APPROACHED, THE LADY STAGGERED AGAINST THE TRUNK OF THE TREE.'

disclosing a long, sallow, clean-shaven face below it. Then he raised his revolver and covered the young ruffian, who was advancing upon him with his dangerous riding-crop swinging in his hand.

'Yes,' said our ally, 'I *am* Bob Carruthers, and I'll see this woman righted if I have to swing for it. I told you what I'd do if you molested her, and, by the Lord, I'll be as good as my word!'

'You're too late. She's my wife!'

'No, she's your widow.'

His revolver cracked, and I saw the blood spurt from the front of Woodley's waistcoat. He spun round with a scream and fell upon his back, his hideous red face turning suddenly to a dreadful mottled pallor. The old man, still clad in his surplice, burst into such a string of foul oaths as I have never heard, and pulled out a revolver of his own, but before he could raise it he was looking down the barrel of Holmes's weapon.

'Enough of this,' said my friend coldly. 'Drop that pistol! Watson, pick it up! Hold it to his head! Thank you. You, Carruthers, give me that revolver. We'll have no more violence. Come, hand it over!'

'Who are you, then?'

'My name is Sherlock Holmes.'

'Good Lord!'

'You have heard of me, I see. I will represent the official police until their arrival. Here, you!' he shouted to the frightened groom, who had appeared at the edge of the glade. 'Come here. Take this note as hard as you can ride to Farnham.' He scribbled a few words upon a leaf from his notebook. 'Give it to the superintendent at the police-station. Until he comes, I must detain you all under my personal custody.'

The strong, masterful personality of Holmes dominated the tragic scene, and all were equally puppets in his hands. Williamson and Carruthers found themselves carrying the wounded Woodley into the house, and I gave my arm to the frightened girl. The injured man was laid on his bed, and at Holmes's request I examined him. I carried my report to where he sat in the old tapestry-hung dining-room with his two prisoners before him.

'He will live,' said I.

'What!' cried Carruthers, springing out of his chair. 'I'll go upstairs and finish him first. Do you tell me that the girl, that angel, is to be tied to Roaring Jack Woodley for life?'

'You need not concern yourself about that,' said Holmes. 'There are two very good reasons why she should under no circumstances be his wife. In the first place, we are very safe in questioning Mr Williamson's right to solemnize a marriage.'

'I have been ordained,' cried the old rascal.

'And also unfrocked.'

'Once a clergyman, always a clergyman.'

'I think not. How about the licence?'

'We had a licence for the marriage. I have it here in my pocket.'

'Then you got it by a trick. But in any case a forced marriage is no marriage, but it is a very serious felony, as you will discover before you have finished. You'll have time to think the point out during the next ten years or so, unless I am mistaken. As to you, Carruthers, you would have done better to keep your pistol in your pocket.'

'I begin to think so, Mr Holmes; but when I thought of all the precaution I had taken to shield this girl – for I loved her, Mr Holmes, and it is the only time that ever I knew what love was – it fairly drove me mad to think that she was in the power of the greatest brute and bully in South Africa, a man whose name is a holy terror from Kimberley to Johannesburg. Why, Mr Holmes, you'll hardly believe it, but ever since that girl has been in my employment I never once let her go past this house, where I knew these rascals were lurking, without following her on my bicycle just to see that she came to no harm. I kept my distance from her, and I wore a beard so that she should not recognize me, for she is a good and high-spirited girl, and she wouldn't have stayed in my employment long if she had thought that I was following her about the country roads.'

'Why didn't you tell her of her danger?'

'Because then, again, she would have left me, and I couldn't bear to face that. Even if she couldn't love me it was a great deal to me just to see her dainty form about the house, and to hear the sound of her voice.'

'Well,' said I, 'you call that love, Mr Carruthers, but I should call it selfishness.'

'Maybe the two things go together. Anyhow, I couldn't let her go. Besides, with this crowd about, it was well that she should have someone near to look after her. Then when the cable came I knew they were bound to make a move.'

'What cable?'

Carruthers took a telegram from his pocket.

'That's it!' said he. It was short and concise:

THE OLD MAN IS DEAD

'Hum!' said Holmes. 'I think I see how things worked, and I can understand how this message would, as you say, bring them to a head. But while we wait, you might tell me what you can.'

The old reprobate with the surplice burst into a volley of bad language.

'By Heaven,' said he, 'if you squeal on us, Bob Carruthers, I'll serve you as you served Jack Woodley! You can bleat about the girl to your heart's content, for that's your own affair, but if you round on your pals to this plain-clothes copper it will be the worst day's work that ever you did.'

'Your reverence need not be excited,' said Holmes, lighting a cigarette. 'The case is clear enough against you, and all I ask is a few details for my private curiosity. However, if there's any difficulty in your telling me I'll do the talking, and then you will see how far you have a chance of holding back your secrets. In the first place, three of you came from South Africa on this game – you, Williamson, you, Carruthers, and Woodley.'

'Lie number one,' said the old man; 'I never saw either of them until two months ago, and I have never been in Africa in my life, so you can put that in your pipe and smoke it, Mr Busybody Holmes!'

'What he says is true,' said Carruthers.

'Well, well, two of you came over. His reverence is our own home-made article. You had known Ralph Smith in South Africa. You had reason to believe he would not live long. You found out that his niece would inherit his fortune. How's that – eh?'

Carruthers nodded, and Williamson swore.

'She was next-of-kin, no doubt, and you were aware that the old fellow would make no will.'

'Couldn't read or write,' said Carruthers.

'So you came over, the two of you, and hunted up the girl. The idea was that one of you was to marry her, and the other have a share of the plunder. For some reason Woodley was chosen as the husband. Why was that?'

'We played cards for her on the voyage. He won.'

'I see. You got the young lady into your service, and there Woodley was to do the courting. She recognized the drunken brute that he was, and would have nothing to do with him. Meanwhile, your arrangement was rather upset by the fact that you had yourself fallen in love with the lady. You could no longer bear the idea of this ruffian owning her.'

'No, by George, I couldn't!'

'There was a quarrel between you. He left you in a rage, and began to make his own plans independently of you.'

'It strikes me, Williamson, there isn't very much that we can tell this gentleman,' cried Carruthers, with a bitter laugh. 'Yes, we quarrelled, and he knocked me down. I am level with him on that, anyhow. Then I lost sight of him. That was when he picked up with this outcast padre here. I found that they had set up housekeeping together at this place on the line that she had to pass the station. I kept my eye on her after that, for I knew there was some devilry in the wind. I saw them from time to time, for I was anxious to know what they were after. Two days ago Woodley came up to my house with this cable, which showed that Ralph Smith was dead. He asked me if I would stand by the bargain. I said I would not. He asked me if I would marry the girl myself and give him a share. I said I would willingly do so, but that she would not have me. He said, "Let us get her married first, and after a week or two she may see things a bit different." I said I would have nothing to do with violence. So he went off cursing, like the foul-mouthed blackguard that he was, and swearing that he would have her yet. She was leaving me this weekend, and I had got a trap to take her to the station, but I was so uneasy in my mind that I followed her on my bicycle. She had got a start, however, and before I could catch her the mischief was done. The first thing I knew about it was when I saw you two gentlemen driving back in her dog-cart.'

Holmes rose and tossed the end of his cigarette into the grate. 'I have been very obtuse, Watson,' said he. 'When in your report you said that you had seen the cyclist as you thought arrange his necktie in the shrubbery, that alone should have told me all. However, we may congratulate ourselves upon a curious and in some respects a unique case. I perceive three of the county constabulary in the drive, and I am glad to see that the little ostler is able to keep pace with them; so it is likely that neither he nor the interesting bridegroom will be permanently damaged by their morning's adventures. I think, Watson, that in your medical capacity you might wait upon Miss Smith and tell her that if she is sufficiently recovered we shall be happy to escort her to her mother's home. If she is not quite convalescent you will find that a hint that we were about to telegraph to a young electrician in the Midlands would probably complete the cure. As to you, Mr Carruthers, I think that you have done what you could to make amends for your share in an evil plot. There is my card, sir, and if my evidence can be of help to you in your trial it shall be at your disposal.'

In the whirl of our incessant activity it has often been difficult for me, as the reader has probably observed, to round off my narratives, and to give those final details which the curious might expect. Each case has been the prelude to another, and the crisis once over, the actors have passed for ever out of our busy lives. I find, however, a short note at the end of my manuscripts dealing with this case, in which I have put it upon record that Miss Violet Smith did indeed inherit a large fortune, and that she is now the wife of Cyril Morton, the senior partner of Morton and Kennedy, the famous Westminster electricians. Williamson and Woodley were both tried for abduction and assault, the former getting seven years and the latter ten. Of the fate of Carruthers I have no record, but I am sure that his assault was not viewed very gravely by the Court, since Woodley had the reputation of being a most dangerous ruffian, and I think that a few months were sufficient to satisfy the demands of justice.

The Adventure of the Noble Bachelor

The Lord St Simon marriage, and its curious termination, have long since ceased to be a subject of interest in those exalted circles in which the unfortunate bridegroom moves. Fresh scandals have eclipsed it, and their more piquant details have drawn the gossips away from this four-year-old drama. As I have reason to believe, however, that the full facts have never been revealed to the general public, and as my friend Sherlock Holmes had a considerable share in clearing the matter up, I feel that no memoir of him would be complete without some little sketch of this remarkable episode.

It was a few weeks before my own marriage, during the days when I was still sharing rooms with Holmes in Baker Street, that he came home from an afternoon stroll to find a letter on the table waiting for him. I had remained indoors all day, for the weather had taken a sudden turn to rain, with high autumnal winds, and the jezail bullet which I had brought back in one of my limbs as a relic of my Afghan campaign, throbbed with dull persistency. With my body in one easy chair and my legs upon another, I had surrounded myself with a cloud of newspapers, until at last, saturated with the news of the day, I tossed them all aside and lay listless, watching the huge crest and monogram upon the envelope upon the table, and wondering lazily who my friend's noble correspondent could be.

'Here is a very fashionable epistle,' I remarked as he entered. 'Your morning's letters, if I remember right, were from a fishmonger and a tide-waiter.'

'Yes, my correspondence has certainly the charm of variety,' he answered, smiling, 'and the humbler are usually the more interesting. This looks like one of those unwelcome social summonses which call upon a man either to be bored or to lie.'

He broke the seal, and glanced over the contents.

'Oh, come, it may prove to be something of interest after all.'

'Not social, then?'

'No, distinctly professional.'

'And from a noble client?'

'One of the highest in England.'

'My dear fellow, I congratulate you.'

'I assure you, Watson, without affectation, that the status of my client is a matter of less moment to me than the interest of his case. It is just possible, however, that that also may not be wanting in this new investigation. You have been reading the papers diligently of late, have you not?'

'It looks like it,' said I ruefully, pointing to a huge bundle in the corner. 'I have had nothing else to do.'

'HE BROKE THE SEAL AND GLANCED OVER THE CONTENTS.'

'It is fortunate, for you will perhaps be able to post me up. I read nothing except the criminal news and the agony column. The latter is always instructive. But if you have followed recent events so closely you must have read about Lord St Simon and his wedding?'

'Oh, yes, with the deepest interest.'

'That is well. The letter which I hold in my hand is from Lord St Simon. I will read it to you, and in return you must turn over these papers and let me have whatever bears upon the matter. This is what he says:

> My dear Mr Sherlock Holmes,
>
> Lord Backwater tells me that I may place implicit reliance upon your judgement and discretion. I have determined, therefore, to call upon you, and to consult you in reference to the very painful event which has occurred in connection with my wedding. Mr Lestrade, of Scotland Yard, is acting already in the matter, but he assures me that he sees no objection to your co-operation, and that he even thinks that it might be of some assistance. I will call at four o'clock in the afternoon, and should you have any other engagement at that time, I hope you will postpone it, as this is a matter of paramount importance.
>
> Yours faithfully,
> ROBERT ST SIMON

'It is dated from Grosvenor Mansions, written with a quill pen, and the noble lord has had the misfortune to get a smear of ink upon the outer side of his right little finger,' remarked Holmes, as he folded up the epistle.

'He says four o'clock. It is three now. He will be here in an hour.'

'Then I have just time, with your assistance, to get clear upon the subject. Turn over those papers, and arrange the extracts in their order of time, while I take a glance as to who our client is.' He picked a red-covered volume from a line of books of reference beside the mantelpiece. 'Here he is,' said he, sitting down and flattening it out upon his knee. '"Robert Walsingham de Vere St Simon, second son of the Duke of Balmoral" – Hum! "Arms: Azure, three caltrops in chief over a fess sable. Born in 1846." He's forty-one years of age, which is mature for marriage. Was Under-Secretary for the Colonies in a late Administration. The Duke, his father, was at one time Secretary for Foreign Affairs. They inherit Plantagenet blood by direct descent, and Tudor on the distaff side. Ha! Well, there is nothing very instructive in all this. I think I must turn to you, Watson, for something more solid.'

'I have very little difficulty in finding what I want,' said I, 'for the facts are quite recent, and the matter struck me as remarkable. I feared to refer them to you, however, as I knew that you had an inquiry on hand, and that you disliked the intrusion of other matters.'

'Oh, you mean the little problem of the Grosvenor Square furniture van. That is quite cleared up now – though, indeed, it was obvious from the first. Pray give me the results of your newspaper selections.'

'Here is the first notice which I can find. It is in the personal column of the *Morning Post*, and dates, as you see, some weeks back. "A marriage has been arranged," it says, "and will, if rumour is correct, very shortly take place, between Lord Robert St Simon, second son of the Duke of Balmoral, and Miss Hatty Doran, the only daughter of Aloysius Doran, Esq., of San Francisco, Cal., U. S.A. ." That is all.'

'Terse and to the point,' remarked Holmes, stretching his long thin legs towards the fire.

'There was a paragraph amplifying this in one of the society papers of the same week. Ah, here it is. "There will soon be a call for protection in the marriage market, for the present free-trade principle appears to tell heavily against our home product. One by one the management of the noble houses of Great Britain is passing into the hands of our fair cousins from across the Atlantic. An important addition has been made during the last week to the list of prizes which have been borne away by these charming invaders. Lord St Simon, who has shown himself for over twenty years proof against the little god's arrows, has now definitely announced his approaching marriage with Miss Hatty Doran, the fascinating daughter of a Californian millionaire. Miss Doran, whose graceful figure and striking face attracted much attention at the Westbury House festivities, is an only child, and it is currently reported that her dowry will run to considerably over the six figures, with expectancies for the future. As it is an open secret that the Duke of Balmoral has been compelled to sell his pictures within the last few years, and as Lord St Simon has no property of his own, save the small estate of Birchmoor, it is obvious that the Californian heiress is not the only gainer by an alliance which will enable her to make the easy and common transition from a Republican lady to a British title." '

'Anything else?' asked Holmes, yawning.

'Oh yes; plenty. Then there is another note in the *Morning Post* to say that the marriage would be an absolutely quiet one, that it would be at St George's, Hanover Square, that only half a dozen intimate friends would be invited, and that the party would return to the furnished house at Lancaster Gate which has been taken by Mr Aloysius Doran. Two days later – that is, on Wednesday last – there is a curt announcement that the wedding had taken place, and that the honeymoon would be passed at Lord Backwater's place, near Petersfield. Those are all the notices which appeared before the disappearance of the bride.'

'Before the what?' asked Holmes, with a start.

'The vanishing of the lady.'

'When did she vanish, then?'

'At the wedding breakfast.'

'Indeed. This is more interesting than it promised to be; quite dramatic, in fact.'

'Yes; it struck me as being a little out of the common.'

'They often vanish before the ceremony, and occasionally during the honeymoon; but I cannot call to mind anything quite so prompt as this. Pray let me have the details.'

'I warn you that they are very incomplete.'

'Perhaps we may make them less so.'

'Such as they are, they are set forth in a single article of a morning newspaper of yesterday, which I will read to you. It is headed, "Singular Occurrence at a Fashionable Wedding":

' "The family of Lord Robert St Simon has been thrown into the greatest consternation by the strange and painful episodes which have taken place in connection with his wedding. The ceremony, as shortly announced in the papers of yesterday, occurred on the previous morning; but it is only now that it has been possible to confirm the strange rumours which have been so persistently floating about. In spite of the attempts of the friends to hush the matter up, so much public attention has now been drawn to it that no good purpose can be served by affecting to disregard what is a common subject for conversation.

' "The ceremony, which was performed at St George's, Hanover Square, was a very quiet one, no one being present save the father of the bride, Mr Aloysius Doran, the Duchess of Balmoral, Lord Backwater, Lord Eustace and Lady Clara St Simon (the younger brother and sister of the bridegroom), and Lady Alicia Whittington. The whole party proceeded afterwards to the house of Mr Aloysius Doran, at Lancaster Gate, where breakfast had been prepared. It appears that some little trouble had been caused by a woman, whose name has not been ascertained, who endeavoured to force her way into the house after the bridal party, alleging that she had some claim upon Lord St Simon. It was only after a painful and prolonged scene that she was ejected by the butler and the footman. The bride, who had fortunately entered the house before this unpleasant interruption, had sat down to breakfast with the rest, when she complained of a sudden indisposition, and retired to her room. Her prolonged absence having caused some comment, her father followed her; but learned from her maid that she had only come up to her chamber for an instant, caught up an ulster and bonnet, and hurried down to the passage. One of the footmen declared that he had seen a lady leave the house thus apparelled: but had refused to credit that it was his mistress, believing her to be with the company. On ascertaining that his daughter had disappeared, Mr Aloysius Doran, in conjunction with the bridegroom, instantly put themselves into communication with the police, and very energetic inquiries are being made, which will probably result in a speedy clearing up of this very singular business. Up to a late hour last night, however, nothing had transpired as to the whereabouts of the missing lady. There are rumours of foul play in the matter, and it is said that the police have caused the arrest of the woman who had caused the original disturbance, in the belief that, from jealousy or some other motive, she may have been concerned in the strange disappearance of the bride." '

'And is that all?'

'Only one little item in another of the morning papers, but it is a suggestive one.'

'And it is?'

'That Miss Flora Millar, the lady who had caused the disturbance, has actually been arrested. It appears that she was formerly a *danseuse* at the Allegro, and that she had known the bridegroom for some years. There are no further particulars, and the whole case is in your hands now – so far as it has been set forth in the public press.'

'And an exceedingly interesting case it appears to be. I would not have missed it for worlds. But there is a ring at the bell, Watson, and as the clock makes it a few minutes after four, I have no doubt that this will prove to be our noble client. Do not dream of going, Watson, for I very much prefer having a witness, if only as a check to my own memory.'

'Lord Robert St Simon,' announced our page-boy, throwing open the door. A gentleman entered, with a pleasant, cultured face, high-nosed and pale, with something perhaps of petulance about the mouth, and with the steady, well-opened eye of a man whose pleasant lot it had ever been to command and to be obeyed. His manner was brisk, and yet his general appearance gave an undue impression of age, for he had a slight forward stoop, and a little bend of the knees as he walked. His hair, too, as he swept off his curly brimmed hat, was grizzled round the edges, and thin upon the top. As to his dress, it was careful to the verge of foppishness, with high collar, black frock-coat, white waistcoat, yellow gloves, patent-leather shoes, and light-coloured gaiters. He advanced slowly into the room, turning his head from left to right, and swinging in his right hand the cord which held his golden eye-glasses.

'Good day, Lord St Simon,' said Holmes, rising and bowing. 'Pray take the basket chair. This is my friend and colleague, Dr Watson. Draw up a little to the fire, and we shall talk this matter over.'

'A most painful matter to me, as you can most readily imagine, Mr Holmes. I have been cut to the quick. I understand you have already managed several delicate cases of this sort, sir, though I presume that they were hardly from the same class of society.'

'No, I am descending.'

'I beg pardon?'

'My last client of the sort was a king.'

'Oh, really! I had no idea. And which king?'

'The King of Scandinavia.'

'What! Had he lost his wife?'

'You can understand,' said Holmes suavely, 'that I extend to the affairs of my other clients the same secrecy which I promise to you in yours.'

'Of course! Very right! very right! I'm sure I beg pardon. As to my own case, I am ready to give you any information which may assist you in forming an opinion.'

'Thank you. I have already learned all that is in the public prints, nothing more. I presume that I may take it as correct – this article, for example, as to the disappearance of the bride.'

Lord St Simon glanced over it. 'Yes, it is correct, as far as it goes.'

'But it needs a great deal of supplementing before anyone could offer an opinion. I think that I may arrive at my facts most directly by questioning you.'

'Pray do so.'

'When did you first meet Miss Hatty Doran?'

'In San Francisco, a year ago.'

'You were travelling in the States?'

'Yes.'

'Did you become engaged then?'

'No.'

'But you were on a friendly footing?'

'I was amused by her society, and she could see that I was amused.'

'Her father is very rich?'

'He is said to be the richest man on the Pacific Slope.'

'And how did he make his money?'

'In mining. He had nothing a few years ago. Then he struck gold, invested it, and came up by leaps and bounds.'

'Now, what is your own impression as to the young lady's – your wife's character?'

The nobleman swung his glasses a little faster and stared down into the fire. 'You see, Mr Holmes,' said he, 'my wife was twenty before her father became a rich man. During that time she ran free in a mining camp, and wandered through woods or mountains, so that her education has come from nature rather than from the school-master. She is what we call in England a tomboy, with a strong nature, wild and free, unfettered by any sort of traditions. She is impetuous – volcanic, I was about to say. She is swift in making up her mind, and fearless in carrying out her resolutions. On the other hand, I would not have given her the name which I have the honour to bear' (he gave a little stately cough) 'had I not thought her to be at bottom a noble woman. I believe she is capable of heroic self-sacrifice, and that anything dishonourable would be repugnant to her.'

'Have you her photograph?'

'I brought this with me.' He opened a locket, and showed us the full face of a very lovely woman. It was not a photograph, but an ivory miniature, and the artist had brought out the full effect of the lustrous black hair, the large dark eyes, and the exquisite mouth. Holmes gazed long and earnestly at it. Then he closed the locket and handed it back to Lord St Simon.

'The young lady came to London, then, and you renewed your acquaintance?'

'Yes, her father brought her over for this last London season. I met her several times, became engaged to her, and have now married her.'

'She brought, I understand, a considerable dowry.'

'A fair dowry. Not more than is usual in my family.'

'And this, of course, remains to you, since the marriage is a *fait accompli*?'

'I really have made no inquiries on the subject.'

'Very naturally not. Did you see Miss Doran on the day before the wedding?'

'Yes.'

'Was she in good spirits?'

'Never better. She kept talking of what we should do in our future lives.'

'Indeed. That is very interesting. And on the morning of the wedding?'

'She was as bright as possible – at least, until after the ceremony.'

'And did you observe any change in her then?'

'Well, to tell the truth, I saw then the first signs that I had ever seen that her temper was just a little sharp. The incident, however, was too trivial to relate, and can have no possible bearing upon the case.'

'Pray let us have it, for all that.'

'Oh, it is childish. She dropped her bouquet as we went towards the vestry. She was passing the front pew at the time, and it fell over into the pew. There was a moment's delay, but the gentleman in the pew handed it up to her again, and it did not appear to be the worse for the fall. Yet, when I spoke to her of the matter, she answered me abruptly; and in the carriage, on our way home, she seemed absurdly agitated over this trifling cause.'

'Indeed. You say that there was a gentleman in the pew. Some of the general public were present, then?'

'THE GENTLEMAN IN THE PEW HANDED IT UP TO HER.'

'Oh, yes. It is impossible to exclude them when the church is open.'

'This gentleman was not one of your wife's friends?'

'No, no; I call him a gentleman by courtesy, but he was quite a common-looking person. I hardly noticed his appearance. But really I think that we are wandering rather far from the point.'

'Lady St Simon, then, returned from the wedding in a less cheerful frame of mind than she had gone to it. What did she do on re-entering her father's house?'

'I saw her in conversation with her maid.'

'And who is her maid?'

'Alice is her name. She is an American, and came from California with her.'

'A confidential servant?'

'A little too much so. It seemed to me that her mistress allowed her to take great liberties. Still, of course, in America they look upon these things in a different way.'

'How long did she speak to this Alice?'

'Oh, a few minutes. I had something else to think of.'

'You did not overhear what they said?'

'Lady St Simon said something about "jumping a claim". She was accustomed to use slang of the kind. I have no idea what she meant.'

'American slang is very expressive sometimes. And what did your wife do when she had finished speaking to her maid?'

'She walked into the breakfast-room.'

'On your arm?'

'No, alone. She was very independent in little matters like that. Then, after we had sat down for ten minutes or so, she rose hurriedly, uttered some words of apology, and left the room. She never came back.'

'But this maid Alice, as I understand, deposes that she went to her room, covered her bride's dress with a long ulster, put on a bonnet, and went out.'

'Quite so. And she was afterwards seen walking into Hyde Park in company with Flora Millar, a woman who is now in custody, and who had already made a disturbance at Mr Doran's house that morning.'

'Ah, yes. I should like a few particulars as to this young lady, and your relations to her.'

Lord St Simon shrugged his shoulders, and raised his eyebrows. 'We have been on a friendly footing for some years – I may say on a *very* friendly footing. She used to be at the Allegro. I have not treated her ungenerously, and she has no just cause of complaint against me, but you know what women are, Mr Holmes. Flora was a dear little thing, but exceedingly hot-headed, and devotedly attached to me. She wrote me dreadful letters when she heard that I was to be married, and to tell the truth the reason why I had the marriage celebrated so quietly was that I feared lest there might be a scandal in the church. She came to Mr Doran's door just after we returned, and she endeavoured to push her way in, uttering very abusive expressions towards my wife, and even threatening her, but I had foreseen the possibility of something of the sort, and I had given instructions to the servants, who soon pushed her out again. She was quiet when she saw that there was no good in making a row.'

'Did your wife hear all this?'

'No, thank goodness, she did not.'

'And she was seen walking with this very woman afterwards?'

'Yes. That is what Mr Lestrade, of Scotland Yard, looks upon as so serious. It is thought that Flora decoyed my wife out, and laid some terrible trap for her.'

'Well, it is a possible supposition.'

'You think so, too?'

'I did not say a probable one. But you do not yourself look upon this as likely?'

'I do not think Flora would hurt a fly.'

'Still, jealousy is a strange transformer of characters. Pray what is your own theory as to what took place?'

'Well, really, I came to seek a theory, not to propound one. I have given you all the facts. Since you ask me, however, I may say that it has occurred to me as possible that the excitement of this affair, the consciousness that she had made so immense a social stride, had the effect of causing some little nervous disturbance in my wife.'

'In short, that she had become suddenly deranged?'

'Well, really, when I consider that she has turned her back – I will not say upon me, but upon so much that many have aspired to without success – I can hardly explain it in any other fashion.'

'Well, certainly that is also a conceivable hypothesis,' said Holmes, smiling. 'And now, Lord St Simon, I think that I have nearly all my data. May I ask whether you were seated at the breakfast-table so that you could see out of the window?'

'We could see the other side of the road, and the Park.'

'Quite so. Then I do not think that I need detain you any longer. I shall communicate with you.'

'Should you be fortunate enough to solve this problem,' said our client, rising.

'I have solved it.'

'Eh? What was that?'

'I say that I have solved it.'

'Where, then, is my wife?'

'That is a detail which I shall speedily supply.'

Lord St Simon shook his head. 'I am afraid that it will take wiser heads than yours or mine,' he remarked, and bowing in a stately, old-fashioned manner, he departed.

'It is very good of Lord St Simon to honour my head by putting it on a level with his own,' said Sherlock Holmes, laughing. 'I think that I shall have a whisky and soda and a cigar after all this cross-questioning. I had formed my conclusions as to the case before our client came into the room.'

'My dear Holmes!'

'I have notes of several similar cases, though none, as I

remarked before, which were quite as prompt. My whole examination served to turn my conjecture into a certainty. Circumstantial evidence is occasionally very convincing, as when you find a trout in the milk, to quote Thoreau's example.'

'But I have heard all that you have heard.'

'Without, however, the knowledge of pre-existing cases which serves me so well. There was a parallel instance in Aberdeen some years back, and something on very much the same lines at Munich the year after the Franco-Prussian War. It is one of these cases – but hullo, here is Lestrade! Good afternoon, Lestrade! You will find an extra tumbler upon the sideboard, and there are cigars in the box.'

The official detective was attired in a pea-jacket and cravat, which gave him a decidedly nautical appearance, and he carried a black canvas bag in his hand. With a short greeting he seated himself, and lit the cigar which had been offered to him.

'What's up, then?' asked Holmes, with a twinkle in his eye. 'You look dissatisfied.'

'And I feel dissatisfied. It is this infernal St Simon marriage case. I can make neither head nor tail of the business.'

'Really! You surprise me.'

'Who ever heard of such a mixed affair? Every clue seems to slip through my fingers. I have been at work upon it all day.'

'And very wet it seems to have made you,' said Holmes, laying his hand upon the arm of the pea-jacket.

'Yes, I have been dragging the Serpentine.'

'In heaven's name, what for?'

'In search of the body of Lady St Simon.'

Sherlock Holmes leaned back in his chair and laughed heartily.

'Have you dragged the basin of the Trafalgar Square fountain?' he asked.

'Why? What do you mean?'

'Because you have just as good a chance of finding this lady in the one as in the other.'

Lestrade shot an angry glance at my companion. 'I suppose you know all about it,' he snarled.

'Well, I have only just heard the facts, but my mind is made up.'

'Oh, indeed! Then you think that the Serpentine plays no part in the matter?'

'I think it very unlikely.'

'Then perhaps you will kindly explain how it is that we found this in it?' He opened his bag as he spoke, and tumbled on to the floor a wedding dress of watered silk, a pair of white satin shoes, and a bride's wreath and veil, all discoloured and soaked in water. 'There,' said he, putting a new wedding-ring upon the top of the pile. 'There is a little nut for you to crack, Master Holmes.'

'Oh, indeed,' said my friend, blowing blue rings into the air. 'You dragged them from the Serpentine?'

'No. They were found floating near the margin by a park-keeper. They were identified as her clothes, and it seemed to me that if the clothes were there the body would not be far off.'

'By the same brilliant reasoning, every man's body is to be found in the neighbourhood of his wardrobe. And pray what did you hope to arrive at through this?'

'At some evidence implicating Flora Millar in the disappearance.'

'I am afraid you will find it difficult.'

'Are you indeed, now?' cried Lestrade, with some bitterness. 'I am afraid, Holmes, that you are not very practical with your deductions and your inferences. You have made two blunders in as many minutes. This dress does implicate Miss Flora Millar.'

'And how?'

'In the dress is a pocket. In the pocket is a card-case. In the card-case is a note. And here is the very note.' He slapped it down upon the table in front of him. 'Listen to this. "You will see me when all is ready. Come at once, F.H.M." Now my theory all along has been that Lady St Simon was decoyed away by Flora Millar, and that she, with confederates no doubt, was responsible for her disappearance. Here, signed with her initials, is the very note which was no doubt quietly slipped into her hand at the door, and which lured her within their reach.'

'Very good, Lestrade,' said Holmes, laughing. 'You really are very fine indeed. Let me see it.' He took up the paper in a listless way, but his attention instantly became riveted, and he gave a little cry of satisfaction. 'This is indeed important,' said he.

'Ha, you find it so?'

'Extremely so. I congratulate you warmly.'

Lestrade rose in his triumph and bent his head to look. 'Why,' he shrieked, 'you're looking on the wrong side.'

'On the contrary, this is the right side.'

'The right side? You're mad! Here is the note written in pencil over here.'

'And over here is what appears to be a fragment of a hotel bill, which interests me deeply.'

'There's nothing in it. I looked at it before,' said Lestrade. ' "Oct. 4th, rooms 8s., breakfast 2s. 6d., cocktail 1s., lunch 2s. 6d., glass sherry 8d." I see nothing in that.'

'Very likely not. It is most important all the same. As to the note, it is important also, or at least the initials are, so I congratulate you again.'

'I've wasted time enough,' said Lestrade, rising. 'I believe in hard work, and not in sitting by the fire spinning fine theories. Good day, Mr Holmes, and we shall see which gets to the bottom of the matter first.' He gathered up the garments, thrust them into the bag, and made for the door.

'Just one hint to you, Lestrade,' drawled Holmes, before his rival vanished; 'I will tell you the true solution of the matter. Lady St Simon is a myth. There is not, and there never has been, any such person.'

Lestrade looked sadly at my companion. Then he turned to

me, tapped his forehead three times, shook his head solemnly, and hurried away.

He had hardly shut the door behind him, when Holmes rose and put on his overcoat. 'There is something in what the fellow says about outdoor work,' he remarked, 'so I think, Watson, that I must leave you to your papers for a little.'

It was after five o'clock when Sherlock Holmes left me, but I had no time to be lonely, for within an hour there arrived a confectioner's man with a very large flat box. This he unpacked with the help of a youth whom he had brought with him, and presently, to my very great astonishment, a quite epicurean little cold supper began to be laid out upon our humble lodging-house mahogany. There were a couple of brace of cold wood-cock, a pheasant, a *pâté de foie gras* pie, with a group of ancient and cobwebby bottles. Having laid out all these luxuries, my two visitors vanished away, like the genii of the *Arabian Nights*, with no explanation save that the things had been paid for, and were ordered to this address.

Just before nine o'clock Sherlock Holmes stepped briskly into the room. His features were gravely set, but there was a light in his eye which made me think that he had not been disappointed in his conclusions.

'They have laid the supper, then,' he said, rubbing his hands.

'You seem to expect company. They have laid for five.'

'Yes, I fancy we may have some company dropping in,' said he. 'I am surprised that Lord St Simon has not already arrived. Ha! I fancy that I hear his step now upon the stairs.'

It was indeed our visitor of the morning who came bustling in, dangling his glasses more vigorously than ever, and with a very perturbed expression upon his aristocratic features.

'My message reached you, then?' asked Holmes.

'Yes, and I must confess that the contents startled me beyond measure. Have you good authority for what you say?'

'The best possible.'

Lord St Simon sank into a chair, and passed his hand over his forehead.

'What will the Duke say,' he murmured, 'when he hears that one of the family has been subjected to such a humiliation?'

'It is the purest accident. I cannot allow that there is any humiliation.'

'Ah, you look on these things from another standpoint.'

'I fail to see that anyone is to blame. I can hardly see how the lady could have acted otherwise, though her abrupt method of doing it was undoubtedly to be regretted. Having no other, she had no one to advise her at such a crisis.'

'It was a slight, sir, a public slight,' said Lord St Simon, tapping his fingers upon the table.

'You must make allowance for this poor girl, placed in so unprecedented a position.'

'I will make no allowance. I am very angry indeed, and I have been shamefully used.'

'I think I heard a ring,' said Holmes. 'Yes, there are steps on the landing. If I cannot persuade you to take a lenient view of the matter, Lord St Simon, I have brought an advocate here who may be more successful.' He opened the door and ushered in a lady and gentleman. 'Lord St Simon,' said he, 'allow me to introduce you to Mr and Mrs Francis Hay Moulton. The lady, I think, you have already met.'

At the sight of these newcomers our client had sprung from his seat, and stood very erect, with his eyes cast down and his hand thrust into the breast of his frock-coat, a picture of offended dignity. The lady had taken a quick step forward and had held out her hand to him, but he still refused to raise his eyes. It was as well for his resolution, perhaps, for her pleading face was one which it was hard to resist.

'You're angry, Robert,' said she. 'Well, I guess you have every cause to be.'

'Pray make no apology to me,' said Lord St Simon bitterly.

'A PICTURE OF OFFENDED DIGNITY.'

'Oh, yes, I know that I treated you real bad, and that I should have spoken to you before I went; but I was kind of rattled, and from the time when I saw Frank here again, I just didn't know what I was doing or saying. I only wonder that I didn't fall down and do a faint right there before the altar.'

'Perhaps, Mrs Moulton, you would like my friend and me to leave the room while you explain this matter?'

'If I may give an opinion,' remarked the strange gentleman, 'we've had just a little too much secrecy over this business already. For my part, I should like all Europe and America to hear the rights of it.' He was a small, wiry, sunburned man, with a sharp face and alert manner.

'Then I'll tell our story right away,' said the lady. 'Frank here and I met in '81, in McQuire's camp, near the Rockies, where Pa was working a claim. We were engaged to each other, Frank and I; but then one day father struck a rich pocket, and made a pile, while poor Frank here had a claim that petered out and came to nothing. The richer Pa grew, the poorer was Frank; so at last Pa wouldn't hear of our engagement lasting any longer, and he took me away to 'Frisco. Frank wouldn't throw up his hand, though; so he followed me there, and he saw me without Pa knowing anything about it. It would only have made him mad to know, so we just fixed it all up for ourselves. Frank said that he would go and make his pile, too, and never come back to claim me until he had as much as Pa. So then I promised to wait for him to the end of time, and pledged myself not to marry anyone else while he lived. "Why shouldn't we be married right away, then," said he, "and then I will feel sure of you; and I won't claim to be your husband until I come back." Well, we talked it over, and he had fixed it all up so nicely, with a clergyman all ready in waiting, that we just did it right there; and then Frank went off to seek his fortune and I went back to Pa.

'The next that I heard of Frank was that he was in Montana, and then he went prospecting into Arizona, and then I heard of him from New Mexico. After that came a long newspaper story about how a miners' camp had been attacked by Apache Indians, and there was my Frank's name among the killed. I fainted dead away, and I was very sick for months after. Pa thought I had a decline, and took me to half the doctors in 'Frisco. Not a word of news came for a year or more, so that I never doubted that Frank was really dead. Then Lord St Simon came to 'Frisco, and we came to London, and a marriage was arranged, and Pa was very pleased, but I felt all the time that no man on this earth would ever take the place in my heart that had been given to my poor Frank.

'Still, if I had married Lord St Simon, of course I'd have done my duty by him. We can't command our love, but we can our actions. I went to the altar with him with the intention that I would make him just as good a wife as it was in me to be. But you may imagine what I felt when, just as I came to the altar rails, I glanced and saw Frank standing looking at me out of the first pew. I thought it was his ghost at first; but, when I looked again, there he was still, with a kind of question in his eyes as if to ask me whether I were glad or sorry to see him. I wonder I didn't drop. I know that everything was turning round, and the words of the clergyman were just like the buzz of a bee in my ear. I didn't know what to do. Should I stop the service and make a scene in the church? I glanced at him again, and he seemed to know what I was thinking, for he raised his finger to his lips to tell me to be still. Then I saw him scribble on a piece of paper, and I knew he was writing me a note. As I passed his pew on the way out I dropped my bouquet over to him, and he slipped the note into my hand when he returned me the flowers. It was only a line asking me to join him when he made the sign to me to do so. Of course I never doubted for a moment that my first duty was now to him, and I determined to do just whatever he might direct.

'When I got back I told my maid, who had known him in California, and had always been his friend. I ordered her to say nothing, but to get a few things packed and my ulster ready. I know I ought to have spoken to Lord St Simon, but it was dreadful hard before his mother and all those great people. I just made up my mind to run away, and explain afterwards. I hadn't been at the table ten minutes before I saw Frank out of the window at the other side of the road. He beckoned to me, and then began walking into the Park. I slipped out, put on my things, and followed him. Some woman came talking something or other about Lord St Simon to me – seemed to me from the little I heard as if he had a little secret of his own before marriage also – but I managed to get away from her, and soon overtook Frank. We got into a cab together, and away we drove to some lodgings he had taken in Gordon Square, and that was my true wedding after all those years of waiting. Frank had been a prisoner among the Apaches, had escaped, came on to 'Frisco, found that I had given him up for dead and had gone to England, followed me there, and had come upon me at last on the very morning of my second wedding.'

'I saw it in a paper,' explained the American. 'It gave the name and the church, but not where the lady lived.'

'Then we had a talk as to what we should do, and Frank was all for openness, but I was so ashamed of it all that I felt as if I would like to vanish away and never see any of them again, just sending a line to Pa, perhaps, to show him that I was alive. It was awful of me to think of all those lords and ladies sitting round that breakfast-table, and waiting for me to come back. So Frank took my wedding clothes and things, and made a bundle of them so that I should not be traced, and dropped them away somewhere where no one should find them. It is likely that we should have gone on to Paris tomorrow, only that this good gentleman, Mr Holmes, came round to us this evening, though how he found us is more than I can think, and he showed us very clearly and kindly that I was wrong and that Frank was right, and that we should put ourselves in the wrong if we were so secret. Then he offered to give us a chance of talking to Lord St Simon alone, and so we came right away and I am very sorry if I have given you pain, and I hope that you do not think very meanly of me.'

Lord St Simon had by no means relaxed his rigid attitude, but had listened with a frowning brow and a compressed lip to this long narrative.

'Excuse me,' he said, 'but it is not my custom to discuss my most intimate personal affairs in this public manner.'

'Then you won't forgive me? You won't shake hands before I go?'

'Oh, certainly, if it would give you any pleasure.' He put out his hand and coldly grasped that which she extended to him.

'I had hoped,' suggested Holmes, 'that you would have joined us in a friendly supper.'

'I think that there you ask a little too much,' responded his lordship. 'I may be forced to acquiesce in these recent developments, but I can hardly be expected to make merry over them. I think that, with your permission, I will now wish you all a very good night.' He included us all in a sweeping bow, and stalked out of the room.

'Then I trust that you at least will honour me with your company,' said Sherlock Holmes. 'It is always a joy to me to meet an American, Mr Moulton, for I am one of those who believe that the folly of a monarch and the blundering of a minister in far-gone years will not prevent our children from being some day citizens of the same world-wide country under a flag which shall be a quartering of the Union Jack with the Stars and Stripes.'

'The case has been an interesting one,' remarked Holmes, when our visitors had left, 'because it serves to show very clearly how simple the explanation may be of an affair which at first sight seems to be almost inexplicable. Nothing could be more inexplicable. Nothing could be more natural than the sequence of events as narrated by this lady, and nothing stranger than the result when viewed, for instance, by Mr Lestrade of Scotland Yard.'

'You were not yourself at fault, then?'

'From the first, two facts were very obvious to me, the one that the lady had been quite willing to undergo the wedding ceremony, the other that she had repented of it within a few minutes of returning home. Obviously something had occurred during the morning, then, to cause her to change her mind. What could that something be? She could not have spoken to anyone when she was out, for she had been in the company of the bridegroom. Had she seen someone, then? If she had, it must be someone from America, because she had spent so short a time in this country that she could hardly have allowed anyone to acquire so deep an influence over her that the mere sight of him would induce her to change her plans so completely. You see we have already arrived, by a process of exclusion, at the idea that she might have seen an American. Then who could this American be, and why should he possess so much influence over her? It might be a lover; it might be a husband. Her young womanhood had, I knew, been spent in rough scenes, and under strange conditions. So far had I got before I ever heard Lord St Simon's narrative. When he told us of a man in a pew, of the change in the bride's manner, of so transparent a device of obtaining a note as the dropping of a bouquet, of her resort to her confidential maid, and of her very significant allusion to claim-jumping, which in miners' parlance means taking possession of that which another person has prior claim to, the whole situation became absolutely clear. She had gone off with a man, and the man was either a lover or was a previous husband, the chances being in favour of the latter.'

'And how in the world did you find them?'

'It might have been difficult, but friend Lestrade held information in his hands the value of which he did not himself know. The initials were of course of the highest importance, but more valuable still was it to know that within a week he had settled his bill at one of the most select London hotels.'

'How did you deduce the select?'

'By the select prices. Eight shillings for a bed and eightpence for a glass of sherry, pointed to one of the most expensive hotels. There are not many in London which charge at that rate. In the second one which I visited in Northumberland Avenue, I learned by an inspection of the book that Francis H. Moulton, an American gentleman, had left only the day before, and on looking over the entries against him, I came upon the very items which I had seen in the duplicate bill. His letters were to be forwarded to 226 Gordon Square, so thither I travelled, and being fortunate enough to find the loving couple at home, I ventured to give them some paternal advice, and to point out to them that it would be better in every way that they should make their position a little clearer, both to the general public and to Lord

St Simon in particular. I invited them to meet him here, and, as you see, I made him keep the appointment.'

'But with no very good results,' I remarked. 'His conduct was certainly not very gracious.'

'Ah! Watson,' said Holmes, smiling, 'perhaps you would not be very gracious either, if, after all the trouble of wooing and wedding, you found yourself deprived in an instant of wife and of fortune. I think that we may judge Lord St Simon very mercifully, and thank our stars that we are never likely to find ourselves in the same position. Draw your chair up, and hand me my violin, for the only problem which we have still to solve is how to while away these bleak autumnal evenings.'

The Adventure of the Missing Three-Quarter

We were fairly accustomed to receive weird telegrams at Baker Street, but I have a particular recollection of one which reached us on a gloomy February morning some seven or eight years ago and gave Mr Sherlock Holmes a puzzled quarter of an hour. It was addressed to him, and ran thus:

> Please await me. Terrible misfortune. Right wing three-quarter missing. Indispensable tomorrow. OVERTON

'Strand postmark, and dispatched ten thirty-six,' said Holmes, reading it over and over. 'Mr Overton was evidently considerably excited when he sent it, and somewhat incoherent in consequence. Well, well, he will be here, I dare say, by the time I have looked through *The Times*, and then we shall know all about it. Even the most insignificant problem would be welcome in these stagnant days.'

Things had indeed been very slow with us, and I had learned to dread such periods of inaction, for I knew by experience that my companion's brain was so abnormally active that it was dangerous to leave it without material upon which to work. For years I had gradually weaned him from that drug mania which had threatened once to check his remarkable career. Now I knew that under ordinary conditions he no longer craved for this artificial stimulus; but I was well aware that the fiend was not dead, but sleeping; and I have known that the sleep was a light one and the waking near when in periods of idleness I have seen the drawn look upon Holmes's ascetic face, and the brooding of his deep-set and inscrutable eyes. Therefore I blessed this Mr Overton, whoever he might be, since he had come with his enigmatic message to break that dangerous calm which brought more peril to my friend than all the storms of his tempestuous life.

As we expected, the telegram was soon followed by its sender, and the card of Mr Cyril Overton, of Trinity College, Cambridge, announced the arrival of an enormous young man, sixteen stone of solid bone and muscle, who spanned the doorway with his broad shoulders and looked from one of us to the other with a comely face which was haggard with anxiety.

'Mr Sherlock Holmes?'

My companion bowed.

'I've been down to Scotland Yard, Mr Holmes. I saw Inspector Stanley Hopkins. He advised me to come to you. He said the case, so far as he could see, was more in your line than in that of the regular police.'

'Pray sit down and tell me what is the matter.'

'It's awful, Mr Holmes, simply awful! I wonder my hair isn't grey. Godfrey Staunton – you've heard of him, of course? He's simply the hinge that the whole team turns on. I'd rather spare two from the pack and have Godfrey for my three-quarter line. Whether it's passing, or tackling, or dribbling, there's no one to touch him; and then, he's got the head and can hold us all together. What am I to do? That's what I ask you, Mr Holmes. There's Moorhouse, first reserve, but he is trained as a half, and he always edges right in on to the scrum instead of keeping out on the touch-line. He's a fine place-kick, it's true, but, then, he has no judgement, and he can't sprint for nuts. Why, Morton or Johnson, the Oxford fliers, could romp round him. Stevenson is fast enough, but he couldn't drop from the twenty-five line, and a three-quarter who can't either punt or drop isn't worth a place for pace alone. No, Mr Holmes, we are done unless you can help me to find Godfrey Staunton.'

My friend had listened with amused surprise to this long speech, which was poured forth with extraordinary vigour and earnestness, every point being driven home by the slapping of a brawny hand upon the speaker's knee. When our visitor was silent Holmes stretched out his hand and took down letter 'S' of his commonplace book. For once he dug in vain into that mine of varied information.

'There is Arthur H. Staunton, the rising young forger,' said he, 'and there was Henry Staunton, whom I helped to hang, but Godfrey Staunton is a new name to me.'

It was our visitor's turn to look surprised.

'Why, Mr Holmes, I thought you knew things,' said he. 'I suppose, then, if you have never heard of Godfrey Staunton you don't know Cyril Overton?'

Holmes shook his head good-humouredly.

'Great Scott!' cried the athlete. 'Why, I was first reserve for England against Wales, and I've skippered the 'Varsity all this

'"WHY, MR HOLMES, I THOUGHT YOU KNEW THING," SAID HE.'

year. But that's nothing. I didn't think there was a soul in England who didn't know Godfrey Staunton, the crack three-quarter, Cambridge, Blackheath, and five Internationals. Good Lord! Mr Holmes, where *have* you lived?'

Holmes laughed at the young giant's naïve astonishment.

'You live in a different world to me, Mr Overton, a sweeter and healthier one. My ramifications stretch out into many sections of society, but never, I am happy to say, into amateur sport, which is the best and soundest thing in England. However, your unexpected visit this morning shows me that even in that world of fresh air and fair play there may be work for me to do; so now, my good sir, I beg you to sit down and to tell me slowly and quietly exactly what it is that has occurred, and how you desire that I should help you.'

Young Overton's face assumed the bothered look of the man who is more accustomed to using his muscles than his wits; but by degrees, with many repetitions and obscurities which I may omit from his narrative, he laid his strange story before us.

'It's this way, Mr Holmes. As I have said, I am the skipper of the Rugger team of Cambridge 'Varsity, and Godfrey Staunton is my best man. Tomorrow we play Oxford. Yesterday we all came up and we settled at Bentley's private hotel. At ten o'clock I went round and saw that all the fellows had gone to roost, for I believe in strict training and plenty of sleep to keep a team fit. I had a word or two with Godfrey before he turned in. He seemed to me to be pale and bothered. I asked him what was the matter. He said he was all right – just a touch of headache. I bade him good night and left him. Half an hour later the porter tells me that a rough-looking man with a beard called with a note for Godfrey. He had not gone to bed, and the note was taken to his room. Godfrey read it and fell back in a chair as if he had been pole-axed. The porter was so scared that he was going to fetch me, but Godfrey stopped him, had a drink of water, and pulled himself together. Then he went downstairs, said a few words to the man who was waiting in the hall, and the two of them went off together. The last that the porter saw of them, they were almost running down the street in the direction of the Strand. This morning Godfrey's room was empty, his bed had never been slept in, and his things were all just as I had seen them the night before. He had gone off at a moment's notice with this stranger, and no word has come back from him since. I don't believe he will ever come back. He was a sportsman, was Godfrey, down to his marrow, and he wouldn't have stopped his training and let down his skipper if it were not for some cause that was too strong for him. No; I feel as if he were gone for good and we should never see him again.'

Sherlock Holmes listened with the deepest attention to this singular narrative.

'What did you do?' he asked.

'I wired to Cambridge to learn if anything had been heard of him there. I have had an answer. No one has seen him.'

'Could he have got back to Cambridge?'

'Yes, there is a late train – quarter-past eleven.'

'But so far as you can ascertain, he did not take it?'

'No, he has not been seen.'

'What did you do next?'

'I wired to Lord Mount-James.'

'Why to Lord Mount-James?'

'Godfrey is an orphan, and Lord Mount-James is his nearest relative – his uncle, I believe.'

'Indeed. This throws new light upon the matter. Lord Mount-James is one of the richest men in England.'

'So I've heard Godfrey say.'

'And your friend was closely related?'

'Yes, he was his heir, and the old boy is nearly eighty – cram full of gout, too. They say he could chalk his billiard-cue with his knuckles. He never allowed Godfrey a shilling in his life, for he is an absolute miser, but it will all come to him right enough.'

'Have you heard from Lord Mount-James?'

'No.'

'What motive could your friend have in going to Lord Mount-James?'

'Well, something was worrying him the night before, and if it was to do with money it is possible that he would make for his nearest relative who had so much of it, though from all I have heard he would not have much chance of getting it. Godfrey was not fond of the old man. He would not go if he could help it.'

'Well, we can soon determine that. If your friend was going to his relative Lord Mount-James, you have then to explain the visit of this rough-looking fellow at so late an hour, and the agitation that was caused by his coming.'

Cyril Overton pressed his hands to his head. 'I can make nothing of it!' said he.

'Well, well, I have a clear day, and I shall be happy to look into the matter,' said Holmes. 'I should strongly recommend you to make your preparations for your match without reference to this young gentleman. It must, as you say, have been an overpowering necessity which tore him away in such a fashion, and the same necessity is likely to hold him away. Let us step round together to this hotel, and see if the porter can throw any fresh light upon the matter.'

Sherlock Holmes was a past master in the art of putting a humble witness at his ease, and very soon, in the privacy of Godfrey Staunton's abandoned room, he had extracted all that the porter had to tell. The visitor of the night before was not a gentleman, neither was he a working man. He was simply what the porter described as a 'medium-looking chap'; a man of fifty, beard grizzled, pale face, quietly dressed. He seemed himself to be agitated. The porter had observed his hand trembling when he had held out the note. Godfrey Staunton had crammed the note into his pocket. Staunton had not shaken hands with the man in the hall. They had exchanged a few sentences, of which the porter had only distinguished the one word 'time'. Then they had hurried off in the manner described. It was just half-past ten by the hall clock.

'Let me see,' said Holmes, seating himself on Staunton's bed. 'You are the day porter, are you not?'

'Yes, sir; I go off duty at eleven.'

'The night porter saw nothing, I suppose?'

'No, sir; one theatre party came in late. No one else.'

'Were you on duty all day yesterday?'

'Yes, sir.'

'Did you take any message to Mr Staunton?'

'Yes, sir; one telegram.'

'Ah! that is interesting. What o'clock was this?'

'About six.'

'Where was Mr Staunton when he received it?'

'Here in his room.'

'Were you present when he opened it?'

'Yes, sir; I waited to see if there was an answer.'

'Well, was there?'

'Yes, sir. He wrote an answer.'

'Did you take it?'

'No; he took it himself.'

'But he wrote it in your presence?'

'Yes, sir. I was standing by the door, and he with his back turned at that table. When he had written it he said, "All right, porter, I will take this myself." '

'What did he write it with?'

'A pen, sir.'

'Was the telegraphic form one of these on the table?'

'Yes, sir; it was the top one.'

Holmes rose. Taking the forms, he carried them over to the window and carefully examined that which was uppermost.

'It is a pity he did not write in pencil,' said he, throwing them down again with a shrug of disappointment. 'As you have no doubt frequently observed, Watson, the impression usually goes through – a fact which has dissolved many a happy marriage. However, I can find no trace here. I rejoice, however, to perceive that he wrote with a broad-pointed quill pen, and I can hardly doubt that we will find some impression upon this blotting pad. Ah, yes, surely this is the very thing!'

He tore off a strip of the blotting-paper and turned towards us the following hieroglyphic:

Cyril Overton was much excited. 'Hold it to the glass,' he cried.

'That is unnecessary,' said Holmes. 'The paper is thin, and the reverse will give the message. There it is.' He turned it over, and we read:

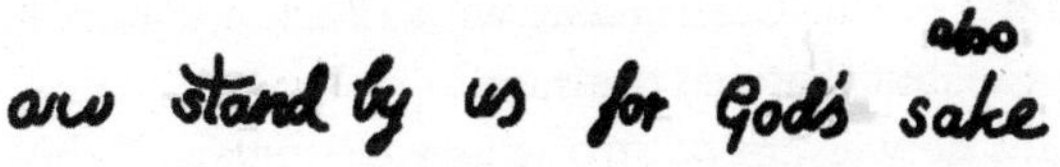

'So that is the tail end of the telegram which Godfrey Staunton dispatched within a few hours of his disappearance. There are at least six words of the message which have escaped us; but what remains – "Stand by us for God's sake!" – proves that this young man saw a formidable danger which approached him, and from which someone else could protect him. *"Us"*, mark you! Another person was involved. Who should it be but the pale-faced, bearded man who seemed himself in so nervous a state? What then, is the connection between Godfrey Staunton and the bearded man? And what is the third source from which each of them sought for help against pressing danger? Our inquiry has already narrowed down to that.'

'We have only to find to whom that telegram is addressed,' I suggested.

'Exactly, my dear Watson. Your reflection, though profound, had already crossed my mind. But I dare say it may have come to your notice that if you walk into a post-office and demand to see the counterfoil of another man's message there may be some disinclination on the part of the officials to oblige you. There is so much red tape in these matters! However, I have no doubt that with a little delicacy and finesse the end may be attained. Meanwhile, I should like in your presence, Mr Overton, to go through these papers which have been left upon the table.'

There were a number of letters, bills, and notebooks, which Holmes turned over and examined with quick, nervous fingers and darting, penetrating eyes. 'Nothing here,' he said at last. 'By the way, I suppose your friend was a healthy young fellow – nothing amiss with him?'

'Sound as a bell.'

'Have you ever known him ill?'

'Not a day. He has been laid up with a hack, and once he slipped his knee-cap, but that was nothing.'

'Perhaps he was not so strong as you suppose. I should think he may have had some secret trouble. With your assent I will put one or two of these papers in my pocket, in case they should bear upon our future inquiry.'

'One moment, one moment!' cried a querulous voice, and we looked up to find a queer little old man jerking and twitching in the doorway. He was dressed in rusty black, with a very broad-brimmed top-hat and a loose white necktie – the whole effect being that of a very rustic parson or of an undertaker's mute. Yet, in spite of his shabby and even absurd appearance, his voice had a sharp crackle, and his manner a quick intensity which commanded attention.

'Who are you, sir, and by what right do you touch this gentleman's papers?' he asked.

'"ONE MOMENT, ONE MOMENT!" CRIED A QUERULOUS VOICE.'

'I am a private detective, and I am endeavouring to explain his disappearance.'

'Oh, you are, are you? And who instructed you, eh?'

'This gentleman, Mr Staunton's friend, was referred to me by Scotland Yard.'

'Who are you, sir?'

'I am Cyril Overton.'

'Then it is you who sent me a telegram. My name is Lord Mount-James. I came round as quickly as the Bayswater bus would bring me. So you have instructed a detective?'

'Yes, sir.'

'And are you prepared to meet the cost?'

'I have no doubt, sir, that my friend Godfrey, when we find him, will be prepared to do that.'

'But if he is never found, eh? Answer me that!'

'In that case no doubt his family—'

'Nothing of the sort, sir!' screamed the little man. 'Don't look to me for a penny – not a penny! You understand that, Mr Detective! I am all the family that this young man has got, and I tell you that I am not responsible. If he has any expectations it is due to the fact that I have never wasted money, and I do not propose to begin to do so now. As to those papers with which you are making so free, I may tell you that in case there should be anything of any value among them you will be held strictly to account for what you do with them.'

'Very good, sir,' said Sherlock Holmes. 'May I ask in the meanwhile whether you have yourself any theory to account for this young man's disappearance?'

'No, sir, I have not. He is big enough and old enough to look after himself, and if he is so foolish as to lose himself I entirely refuse to accept the responsibility of hunting for him.'

'I quite understand your position,' said Holmes, with a mischievous twinkle in his eyes. 'Perhaps you don't quite understand mine. Godfrey Staunton appears to have been a poor man. If he has been kidnapped it could not have been for anything which he himself possesses. The fame of your wealth has gone abroad, Lord Mount-James, and it is entirely possible that a gang of thieves has secured your nephew in order to gain from him some information as to your house, your habits, and your treasure.'

The face of our unpleasant little visitor turned as white as his neckcloth.

'Heavens, sir, what an idea! I never thought of such villainy! What inhuman rogues there are in the world! But Godfrey is a fine lad – a staunch lad. Nothing would induce him to give his old uncle away. I'll have the plate moved over to the bank this evening. In the meantime spare no pains, Mr Detective. I beg you to leave no stone unturned to bring him safely back. As to money, well, so far as a fiver, or even a tenner, goes, you can always look to me.'

Even in his chastened frame of mind the noble miser could give us no information which could help us, for he knew little of the private life of his nephew. Our only clue lay in the truncated telegram, and with a copy of this in his hand Holmes set forth to find a second link for his chain. We had shaken off Lord Mount-James, and Overton had gone to consult with the other members of his team over the misfortune which had befallen them. There was a telegraph office at a short distance from the hotel. We halted outside it.

'It's worth trying, Watson,' said Holmes. 'Of course, with a warrant we could demand to see the counterfoils, but we have not reached that stage yet. I don't suppose they remember faces in so busy a place. Let us venture it.'

'I am sorry to trouble you,' said he in his blandest manner to the young woman behind the grating; 'there is some small mistake about a telegram I sent yesterday. I have had no answer, and I very much fear that I must have omitted to put my name at the end. Could you tell me if this was so?'

The young lady turned over a sheaf of counterfoils.

'What o'clock was it?' she asked.

'A little after six.'

'Whom was it to?'

Holmes put his finger to his lips and glanced at me. 'The last words in it were "for God's sake",' he whispered confidentially; 'I am very anxious at getting no answer.'

The young woman separated one of the forms.

'This is it. There is no name,' said she, smoothing it out upon the counter.

'Then that, of course, accounts for my getting no answer,' said Holmes. 'Dear me, how very stupid of me, to be sure! Good morning, miss, and many thanks for having relieved my mind.' He chuckled and rubbed his hands when we found ourselves in the street once more.

'Well?' I asked.

'We progress, my dear Watson, we progress. I had seven different schemes for getting a glimpse of that telegram, but I could hardly hope to succeed the very first time.'

'And what have you gained?'

'A starting-point for our investigation.' He hailed a cab. 'King's Cross Station,' said he.

'We have a journey, then?'

'Yes, I think we must run down to Cambridge together. All the indications seem to point in that direction.'

'Tell me,' I asked as we rattled up Gray's Inn Road, 'have you any suspicion yet as to the cause of the disappearance? I don't think that among all our cases I have known one where the motives were more obscure. Surely you don't really imagine that he may be kidnapped in order to give information against his wealthy uncle?'

'I confess, my dear Watson, that that does not appeal to me as a very probable explanation. It struck me, however, as being the one which was most likely to interest that exceedingly unpleasant old person.'

'It certainly did that. But what are your alternatives?'

'I could mention several. You must admit that it is curious and suggestive that this incident should occur on the eve of this important match, and should involve the only man whose presence seems essential to the success of the side. It may, of course, be coincidence, but it is interesting. Amateur sport is free from betting, but a good deal of outside betting goes on among the public, and it is possible that it might be worth someone's while to get at a player as the ruffians of the Turf get at a racehorse. There is one explanation. A second very obvious one is that this young man really is the heir of a great property, however modest his means may be at present, and it is not impossible that a plot to hold him for ransom might be concocted.'

'These theories take no account of the telegram.'

'Quite true, Watson. The telegram still remains the only solid thing with which we have to deal, and we must not permit our attention to wander away from it. It is to gain light upon the purpose of this telegram that we are now upon our way to Cambridge. The path of our investigation is at present obscure, but I shall be very surprised if before evening we have not cleared it up or made a considerable advance along it.'

It was already dark when we reached the old University city. Holmes took a cab at the station, and ordered the man to drive to the house of Dr Leslie Armstrong. A few minutes later we had stopped at a large mansion in the busiest thoroughfare. We were shown in, and after a long wait were admitted into the consulting-room, where we found the doctor seated behind his table.

It argues the degree in which I had lost touch with my profession that the name of Leslie Armstrong was unknown to me. Now I am aware that he is not only one of the heads of the medical school of the University, but a thinker of European reputation in more than one branch of science. Yet even without knowing his brilliant record one could not fail to be impressed by a mere glance at the man – the square, massive face, the brooding eyes under the thatched brows, and the granite moulding of the inflexible jaw. A man of deep character, a man with an alert mind, grim, ascetic, self-contained, formidable – so I read Dr Leslie Armstrong. He held my friend's card in his hand, and he looked up with no very pleased expression upon his dour features.

'I have heard your name, Mr Sherlock Holmes, and I am aware of your profession, one of which I by no means approve.'

'In that, doctor, you will find yourself in agreement with every criminal in the country,' said my friend quietly.

'So far as your efforts are directed towards the suppression of crime, sir, they must have the support of every reasonable member of the community, though I cannot doubt that the official machinery is amply sufficient for the purpose. Where your calling is more open to criticism is when you pry into the secrets of private individuals, when you rake up family matters which are better hidden, and when you incidentally waste the time of men who are more busy than yourself. At the present moment, for example, I should be writing a treatise instead of conversing with you.'

'No doubt, doctor; and yet the conversation may prove more important than the treatise. Incidentally I may tell you that we are doing the reverse of what you very justly blame, and that we are endeavouring to prevent anything like public exposure of private matters which must necessarily follow when once the case is fairly in the hands of the official police. You may look upon me simply as an irregular pioneer who goes in front of the regular force of the country. I have come to ask you about Mr Godfrey Staunton.'

'What about him?'

'You know him, do you not?'

'He is an intimate friend of mine.'

'You are aware that he has disappeared?'

'Ah, indeed!' There was no change of expression in the rugged features of the doctor.

'He left his hotel last night. He has not been heard of.'

'No doubt he will return.'

'Tomorrow is the 'Varsity football match.'

'I have no sympathy with these childish games. The young man's fate interests me deeply, since I know him and like him. The football match does not come within my horizon at all.'

'I claim your sympathy, then, in my investigation of Mr Staunton's fate. Do you know where he is?'

'Certainly not.'

'You have not seen him since yesterday?'

'No, I have not.'

'Was Mr Staunton a healthy man?'

'Absolutely.'

'Did you ever know him ill?'

'Never.'

Holmes popped a sheet of paper before the doctor's eyes. 'Then perhaps you will explain this receipted bill for thirteen guineas, paid by Mr Godfrey Staunton last month to Dr Leslie Armstrong, of Cambridge. I picked it out from among the papers upon his desk.'

The doctor flushed with anger.

'I do not feel that there is any reason why I should render an explanation to you, Mr Holmes.'

Holmes replaced the bill in his notebook.

'If you prefer a public explanation it must come sooner or later,' said he. 'I have already told you that I can hush up that which others will be bound to publish, and you would really be wiser to take me into your complete confidence.'

'I know nothing about it.'

'Did you hear from Mr Staunton in London?'

'Certainly not.'

'Dear me, dear me! – the post office again!' Holmes sighed wearily. 'A most urgent telegram was dispatched to you from London by Godfrey Staunton at six-fifteen yesterday evening – a telegram which is undoubtedly associated with his disappearance – and yet you have not had it. It is most culpable. I shall certainly go down to the office here and register a complaint.'

Dr Leslie Armstrong sprang up from behind his desk, and his dark face was crimson with fury.

'I'll trouble you to walk out of my house, sir,' said he. 'You can tell your employer, Lord Mount-James, that I do not wish to have anything to do either with him or with his agents. No, sir, not another word!' He rang the bell furiously. 'John, show these gentlemen out.' A pompous butler ushered us severely to the door, and we found ourselves in the street. Holmes burst out laughing.

'Dr Leslie Armstrong is certainly a man of energy and character,' said he. 'I have not seen a man who, if he turned his talents that way, was more calculated to fill the gap left by the illustrious Moriarty. And now, my poor Watson, here we are, stranded and friendless, in this inhospitable town, which we cannot leave without abandoning our case. This little inn just opposite Armstrong's house is singularly adapted to our needs. If you would engage a front room and purchase the necessaries for the night, I may have time to make a few inquiries.'

These few inquiries proved, however, to be a more lengthy proceeding than Holmes had imagined, for he did not return to the inn until nearly nine o'clock. He was pale and dejected, stained with dust, and exhausted with hunger and fatigue. A cold supper was ready upon the table, and when his needs were satisfied and his pipe alight he was ready to take that half-comic and wholly philosophic view which was natural to him when his affairs were going awry. The sound of carriage wheels caused him to rise and glance out of the window. A brougham and pair of greys under the glare of a gas-lamp stood before the doctor's door.

'It's been out three hours,' said Holmes; 'started at half-past six, and here it is back again. That gives a radius of ten or twelve miles, and he does it once, or sometimes twice, a day.'

'No unusual thing for a doctor in practice.'

'But Armstrong is not really a doctor in practice. He is a lecturer and a consultant, but he does not care for general practice, which distracts him from his literary work. Why, then, does he make these long journeys, which must be exceedingly irksome to him, and who is it that he visits?'

'His coachman –'

'My dear Watson, can you doubt that it was to him that I first applied? I do not know whether it came from his own innate depravity or from the promptings of his master, but he was rude enough to set a dog at me. Neither dog nor man liked the look of my stick, however, and the matter fell through. Relations were strained after that, and further inquiries out of the question. All that I have learned I got from a friendly native in the yard of our own inn. It was he who told me of the doctor's habits and of his daily journey. At that instant, to give point to his words, the carriage came round to the door.'

'Could you not follow it?'

'Excellent, Watson! You are scintillating this evening. The idea did cross my mind. There is, as you may have observed, a bicycle shop next to our inn. Into this I rushed, engaged a bicycle, and was able to get started before the carriage was quite out of sight. I rapidly overtook it, and then, keeping at a discreet distance of a hundred yards or so, I followed its lights until we were clear of the town. We had got well out on the country road when a somewhat mortifying incident occurred. The carriage stopped, the doctor alighted, walked swiftly back to where I had also halted, and told me in an excellent sardonic fashion that he feared the road was narrow, and that he hoped his carriage did not impede the passage of my bicycle. Nothing could have been more admirable than his way of putting it. I at once rode past the carriage, and, keeping to the main road, I went on for a few miles, and then halted in a convenient place to see if the carriage passed. There was no sign of it, however, and so it became evident that it had turned down one of several side-roads which I had observed. I rode back, but again saw nothing of the carriage, and now, as you perceive, it has returned after me. Of course, I had at the outset no particular reason to connect these journeys with the disappearance of Godfrey Staunton, and was only inclined to investigate them on the general grounds that everything which concerns Dr Armstrong is at present of interest to us; but, now that I find he keeps so keen a lookout upon anyone who may follow him on these excursions, the affair appears more important, and I shall not be satisfied until I have made the matter clear.'

'We can follow him tomorrow.'

'Can we? It is not so easy as you seem to think. You are not familiar with Cambridgeshire scenery, are you? It does not lend itself to concealment. All this country that I passed over tonight is as flat and clean as the palm of your hand, and the man we are following is no fool, as he very clearly showed tonight. I have wired to Overton to let us know any fresh London developments at this address, and in the meantime we can only concentrate our attention upon Dr Armstrong, whose name the obliging young lady at the office allowed me to read upon the counterfoil of Staunton's urgent message. He knows where that young man is – to that I'll swear – and if he knows, then it must be our fault if we cannot manage to know also. At present it must be admitted that the odd trick is in his possession, and, as you are aware, Watson, it is not my habit to leave the game in that condition.'

And yet the next day brought us no nearer to the solution of the mystery. A note was handed in after breakfast, which Holmes passed across to me with a smile.

> Sir [it ran] –
>
> I can assure you that you are wasting your time in dogging my movements. I have, as you discovered last night, a window at the back of my brougham, and if you desire a twenty-mile ride which will lead you to the spot from which you started, you have only to follow me. Meanwhile, I can inform you that no spying upon me can in any way help Mr Godfrey Staunton, and I am convinced that the best service you can do to that gentleman is to return at once to London and to report to your employer that you are unable to trace him. Your time in Cambridge will certainly be wasted.
>
> Yours faithfully,
> LESLIE ARMSTRONG

'An outspoken, honest antagonist is the doctor,' said Holmes. 'Well, well, he excites my curiosity, and I must really know more before I leave him.'

'His carriage is at his door now,' said I. 'There he is stepping into it. I saw him glance up at our window as he did so. Suppose I try my luck upon the bicycle?'

'No, no, my dear Watson! With all respect for your natural acumen, I do not think that you are quite a match for the worthy doctor. I think that possibly I can attain our end by some independent explorations of my own. I am afraid that I must leave you to your own devices, as the appearance of *two* inquiring strangers upon a sleepy countryside might excite more gossip than I care for. No doubt you will find some sights to amuse you in this venerable city, and I hope to bring back a more favourable report to you before evening.'

Once more, however, my friend was destined to be disappointed. He came back at night weary and unsuccessful.

'I have had a blank day, Watson. Having got the doctor's general direction, I spent the day in visiting all the villages upon that side of Cambridge, and comparing notes with publicans and other local news agencies. I have covered some ground: Chesterton, Histon, Waterbeach, and Oakington have each been explored, and have each proved disappointing. The daily appearance of a brougham and pair could hardly have been overlooked in such sleepy hollows. The doctor has scored once more. Is there a telegram for me?'

'Yes; I opened it. Here it is: "Ask for Pompey from Jeremy Dixon, Trinity College." I don't understand it.'

'Oh, it is clear enough. It is from our friend Overton, and is in answer to a question from me. I'll just send round a note to Mr Jeremy Dixon, and then I have no doubt that our luck will turn. By the way, is there any news of the match?'

'Yes, the local evening paper has an excellent account in its last edition. Oxford won by a goal and two tries. The last sentences of the description say: "The defeat of the Light Blues may be entirely attributed to the unfortunate absence of the crack International, Godfrey Staunton, whose want was felt at every instant of the game. The lack of combination in the three-quarter line and their weakness both in attack and defence more than neutralized the efforts of a heavy and hardworking pack." '

'Then our friend Overton's forebodings have been justified,' said Holmes. 'Personally I am in agreement with Dr Armstrong, and football does not come within my horizon. Early to bed tonight, Watson, for I foresee that tomorrow may be an eventful day.'

I was horrified by my first glimpse of Holmes next morning, for he sat by the fire holding his tiny hypodermic syringe. I associated that with the single weakness of his nature, and I feared the worst when I saw it glittering in his hand. He laughed at my expression of dismay, and laid it upon the table.

'No, no, my dear fellow, there is no cause for alarm. It is not upon this occasion the instrument of evil, but it will rather prove to be the key which will unlock our mystery. On this syringe I base all my hopes. I have just returned from a small scouting expedition, and everything is favourable. Eat a good breakfast, Watson, for I propose to get upon Dr Armstrong's trail today, and once on it I will not stop for rest or food until I run him to his burrow.'

'In that case,' said I, 'we had best carry our breakfast with us, for he is making an early start. His carriage is at the door.'

'Never mind. Let him go. He will be clever if he can drive where I cannot follow him. When you have finished come downstairs with me, and I will introduce you to a detective who is a very eminent specialist in the work that lies before us.'

When we descended I followed Holmes into the stableyard, where he opened the door of a loose-box and led out a squat, lop-eared, white-and-tan dog, something between a beagle and a foxhound.

'Let me introduce you to Pompey,' said he. 'Pompey is the pride of the local draghounds, no very great flier, as his build will show, but a staunch hound on a scent. Well, Pompey, you may not be fast, but I expect you will be too fast for a couple of middle-aged London gentlemen, so I will take the liberty of fastening this leather leash to your collar. Now, boy, come along, and show what you can do.' He led him across to the doctor's door. The dog sniffed round for an instant, and then with a shrill whine of excitement started off down the street, tugging at his leash in his efforts to go faster. In half an hour we were clear of the town and hastening down a country road.

'What have you done, Holmes?' I asked.

'A threadbare and venerable device, but useful upon occasion. I walked into the doctor's yard this morning and shot my syringe full of aniseed over the hind wheel. A draghound will follow aniseed from here to John o' Groats, and our friend Armstrong would have to drive through the Cam before he would shake Pompey off his trail. Oh, the cunning rascal! This is how he gave me the slip the other night.'

The dog had suddenly turned out of the main road into a grass-grown lane. Half a mile farther this opened into another broad road, and the trail turned hard to the right in the direction of the town, which we had just quitted. The road took a sweep to the south of the town and continued in the opposite direction to that in which we started.

'This detour has been entirely for our benefit, then?' said Holmes. 'No wonder that my inquiries among those villages led to nothing. The doctor has certainly played the game for all it is worth, and one would like to know the reason for such elaborate deception. This should be the village of Trumpington to the right of us. And, by Jove! here is the brougham coming round the corner! Quick, Watson, quick, or we are done!'

He sprang through a gate into a field, dragging the reluctant Pompey after him. We had hardly got under the shelter of the hedge when the carriage rattled past. I caught a glimpse of Dr Armstrong within, his shoulders bowed, his head sunk on his hands, the very image of distress. I could tell by my companion's graver face that he also had seen.

'I fear there is some dark ending to our quest,' said he. 'It cannot be long before we know it. Come, Pompey! Ah, it is the cottage in the field.'

There could be no doubt that we had reached the end of our journey. Pompey ran about and whined eagerly outside the gate, where the marks of the brougham's wheels were still to be seen. A footpath led across to the lonely cottage. Holmes tied the dog to the hedge, and we hastened onwards. My friend knocked at the little rustic door, and knocked again without response. And yet the cottage was not deserted, for a low sound came to our ears – a kind of drone of misery and despair, which was indescribably melancholy. Holmes paused irresolute, and then he glanced back at the road which we had just traversed. A brougham was coming down it, and there could be no mistaking those grey horses.

'By Jove, the doctor is coming back!' cried Holmes. 'That settles it. We are bound to see what it means before he comes.'

He opened the door, and we stepped into the hall. The droning sound swelled louder upon our ears, until it became one long, deep wail of distress. It came from upstairs. Holmes darted up, and I followed him. He pushed open a half-closed door, and we both stood appalled at the sight before us.

A woman, young and beautiful, was lying dead upon the bed. Her calm, pale face, with dim, wide-opened blue eyes, looked upwards from amid a great tangle of golden hair. At the foot of the bed, half sitting, half kneeling, his face buried in the clothes, was a young man, whose frame was racked by his sobs. So absorbed was he by his bitter grief that he never looked up until Holmes's hand was on his shoulder.

'Are you Mr Godfrey Staunton?'

'Yes, yes; I am – but you are too late. She is dead.'

The man was so dazed that he could not be made to understand that we were anything but doctors who had been sent to his assistance. Holmes was endeavouring to utter a few words of

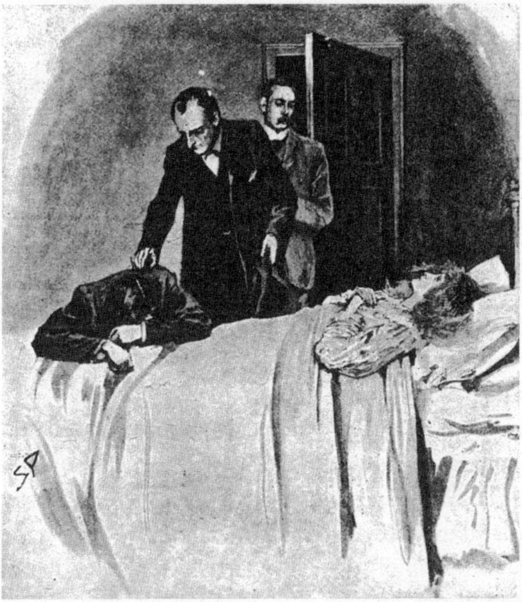

'HE NEVER LOOKED UP UNTIL HOLMES'S HAND WAS ON HIS SHOULDER.'

consolation, and to explain the alarm which had been caused to his friends by his sudden disappearance, when there was a step upon the stairs, and there was the heavy, stern, questioning face of Dr Armstrong at the door.

'So, gentlemen,' said he, 'you have attained your end, and have certainly chosen a particularly delicate moment for your intrusion. I would not brawl in the presence of death, but I can assure you that if I were a younger man your monstrous conduct would not pass with impunity.'

'Excuse me, Dr Armstrong, I think we are a little at cross purposes,' said my friend with dignity. 'If you could step downstairs with us we may each be able to give some light to the other upon this miserable affair.'

A minute later the grim doctor and ourselves were in the sitting-room below.

'Well, sir?' said he.

'I wish you to understand, in the first place, that I am not employed by Lord Mount-James, and that my sympathies in this matter are entirely against that nobleman. When a man is lost it is my duty to ascertain his fate, but having done so the matter ends so far as I am concerned; and so long as there is nothing criminal, I am much more anxious to hush up private scandals than to give them publicity. If, as I imagine, there is no breach of the law in this matter, you can absolutely depend upon my discretion and my co-operation in keeping the facts out of the papers!'

Dr Armstrong took a quick step forward and wrung Holmes by the hand.

'You are a good fellow,' said he. 'I had misjudged you. I thank heaven that my compunction at leaving poor Staunton all alone in this plight caused me to turn my carriage back, and so to make your acquaintance. Knowing as much as you do, the situation is very easily explained. A year ago Godfrey Staunton lodged in London for a time, and became passionately attached to his landlady's daughter, whom he married. She was as good as she was beautiful, and as intelligent as she was good. No man need be ashamed of such a wife. But Godfrey was heir to this crabbed old nobleman, and it was quite certain that the news of his marriage would have been the end of his inheritance. I knew the lad well, and I loved him for his many excellent qualities. I did all I could to help him to keep things straight. We did our very best to keep the thing from everyone, for when once such a whisper gets about it is not long before everyone has heard it. Thanks to this lonely cottage and his own discretion, Godfrey has up to now succeeded. Their secret was known to no one save to me and to one excellent servant who has at present gone for assistance to Trumpington. But at last there came a terrible blow in the shape of dangerous illness to his wife. It was consumption of the most virulent kind. The poor boy was half crazed with grief, and yet he had to go to London to play this match, for he could not get out of it without explanations which would expose the secret. I tried to cheer him up by a wire, and he sent me one in reply imploring me to do all I could. This was the telegram which you appear in some inexplicable way to have seen. I did not tell him how urgent the danger was, for I knew that he could do no good here, but I sent the truth to the girl's father, and he very injudiciously communicated it to Godfrey. The result was that he came straight away in a state bordering on frenzy, and has remained in the same state, kneeling at the end of her bed, until this morning death put an end to her sufferings. That is all, Mr Holmes, and I am sure that I can rely upon your discretion and that of your friend.'

Holmes grasped the doctor's hand.

'Come, Watson,' said he, and we passed from that house of grief into the pale sunlight of the winter day.

The Adventure of the Blue Carbuncle

I had called upon my friend Sherlock Holmes upon the second morning after Christmas, with the intention of wishing him the compliments of the season. He was lounging upon the sofa in a purple dressing-gown, a pipe-rack within his reach upon the right, and a pile of crumpled morning papers, evidently newly studied, near at hand. Beside the couch was a wooden chair, and on the angle of the back hung a very seedy and disreputable hard felt hat, much the worse for wear, and cracked in several places. A lens and a forceps lying upon the seat of the chair suggested that the hat had been suspended in this manner for the purpose of examination.

'You are engaged,' said I; 'perhaps I interrupt you.'

'Not at all. I am glad to have a friend with whom I can discuss my results. The matter is a perfectly trivial one' (he jerked his thumb in the direction of the old hat), 'but there are points in connection with it which are not entirely devoid of interest, and even of instruction.'

I seated myself in his armchair, and warmed my hands before his crackling fire, for a sharp frost had set in, and the windows were thick with the ice crystals. 'I suppose,' I remarked, 'that, homely as it looks, this thing has some deadly story linked on to it – that it is the clue which will guide you in the solution of some mystery, and the punishment of some crime.'

'No, no. No crime,' said Sherlock Holmes, laughing. 'Only one of those whimsical little incidents which will happen when you have four million human beings all jostling each other within the space of a few square miles. Amid the action and reaction of so dense a swarm of humanity, every possible combination of events may be expected to take place, and many a little problem will be presented which may be striking and bizarre without being criminal. We have already had experience of such.'

'So much so,' I remarked, 'that, of the last six cases which I have added to my notes, three have been entirely free of any legal crime.'

'Precisely. You allude to my attempt to recover the Irene Adler papers, to the singular case of Miss Mary Sutherland, and to the adventure of the man with the twisted lip. Well, I have no doubt that this small matter will fall into the same innocent category. You know Peterson, the commissionaire?'

'Yes.'

'It is to him that this trophy belongs.'

'It is his hat.'

'No, no; he found it. Its owner is unknown. I beg that you will look upon it, not as a battered billycock, but as an intellectual problem. And, first as to how it came here. It arrived upon Christmas morning, in company with a good fat goose, which is, I have no doubt, roasting at this moment in front of Peterson's fire. The facts are these. About four o'clock on Christmas morning, Peterson, who, as you know, is a very honest fellow, was returning from some small jollification, and was making his way homewards down Tottenham Court Road. In front of him he saw, in the gaslight, a tallish man, walking with a slight stagger, and carrying a white goose slung over his shoulder. As he reached the corner of Goodge Street a row broke out between this stranger and a little knot of roughs. One of the latter knocked off the man's hat, on which he raised his stick to defend himself and swinging it over his head, smashed the shop window behind him. Peterson had rushed forward to protect the stranger from his assailants, but the man, shocked at having broken the window and seeing an official-looking person in uniform rushing towards him, dropped his goose, took to his heels and vanished amid the labyrinth of small streets which lie at the back of Tottenham

Court Road. The roughs had also fled at the appearance of Peterson, so that he was left in possession of the field of battle, and also of the spoils of victory in the shape of this battered hat and a most unimpeachable Christmas goose.'

'Which surely he restored to their owner?'

'My dear fellow, there lies the problem. It is true that "For Mrs Henry Baker" was printed upon a small card which was tied to the bird's left leg, and it is also true that the initials "H. B." are legible upon the lining of this hat; but, as there are some thousands of Bakers, and some hundreds of Henry Bakers in this city of ours, it is not easy to restore lost property to any one of them.'

'What, then, did Peterson do?'

'He brought round both hat and goose to me on Christmas morning, knowing that even the smallest problems are of interest to me. The goose we retained until this morning, when there were signs that, in spite of the slight frost, it would be well that it should be eaten without unnecessary delay. Its finder has carried it off therefore to fulfil the ultimate destiny of a goose, while I continue to retain the hat of the unknown gentleman who lost his Christmas dinner.'

'Did he not advertise?'

'No.'

'Then, what clue could you have as to his identity?'

'Only as much as we can deduce.'

'From his hat?'

'Precisely.'

'But you are joking. What can you gather from this old battered felt?'

'Here is my lens. You know my methods. What can you gather yourself as to the individuality of the man who has worn this article?'

I took the tattered object in my hands, and turned it over rather ruefully. It was a very ordinary black hat of the usual round shape, hard and much the worse for wear. The lining had been of red silk, but was a good deal discoloured. There was no maker's name; but, as Holmes had remarked, the initials 'H. B.' were scrawled upon one side. It was pierced in the brim for a hat-securer, but the elastic was missing. For the rest, it was cracked, exceedingly dusty, and spotted in several places, although there seemed to have been some attempt to hide the discoloured patches by smearing them with ink.

'I can see nothing,' said I, handing it back to my friend.

'On the contrary, Watson, you can see everything. You fail, however, to reason from what you see. You are too timid in drawing your inferences.'

'Then, pray tell me what it is that you can infer from this hat?'

He picked it up, and gazed at it in the peculiar introspective fashion which was characteristic of him. 'It is perhaps less suggestive than it might have been,' he remarked, 'and yet there are a few inferences which are very distinct, and a few others which represent at least a strong balance of probability. That the man was highly intellectual is of course obvious upon the face of it, and also that he was fairly well-to-do within the last three years, although he has now fallen upon evil days. He had foresight, but has less now than formerly, pointing to a moral retrogression, which, when taken with the decline of his fortunes, seems to indicate some evil influence, probably drink, at work upon him. This may account also for the obvious fact that his wife has ceased to love him.'

'My dear Holmes!'

'He has, however, retained some degree of self-respect,' he continued, disregarding my remonstrance. 'He is a man who leads a sedentary life, goes out little, is out of training entirely, is middle-aged, has grizzled hair which he has had cut within the last few days, and which he anoints with lime-cream. These are the more patent facts which are to be deduced from his hat. Also, by the way, that it is extremely improbable that he has gas laid on in his house.'

'You are certainly joking, Holmes.'

'Not in the least. Is it possible that even now when I give you these results you are unable to see how they are attained?'

'I have no doubt that I am very stupid; but I must confess that I am unable to follow you. For example, how did you deduce that this man was intellectual?'

For answer Holmes clapped the hat upon his head. It came right over the forehead and settled upon the bridge of his nose. 'It is a question of cubic capacity,' said he: 'a man with so large a brain must have something in it.'

'The decline of his fortunes, then?'

'This hat is three years old. These flat brims curled at the edge came in then. It is a hat of the very best quality. Look at the band of ribbed silk, and the excellent lining. If this man could afford to buy so expensive a hat three years ago, and has had no hat since, then he has assuredly gone down in the world.'

'Well, that is clear enough, certainly. But how about the foresight, and the moral retrogression?'

Sherlock Holmes laughed. 'Here is the foresight,' said he, putting his finger upon the little disc and loop of the hat-securer. 'They are never sold upon hats. If this man ordered one, it is a sign of a certain amount of foresight, since he went out of his way to take this precaution against the wind. But since we see that he has broken the elastic, and has not troubled to replace it, it is obvious that he has less foresight now than formerly, which is a distinct proof of a weakening nature. On the other hand, he has endeavoured to conceal some of these stains upon the felt by daubing them with ink, which is a sign that he has not entirely lost his self-respect.'

'Your reasoning is certainly plausible.'

'The further points, that he is middle-aged, that his hair is grizzled, that it has been recently cut, and that he uses lime-cream, are all to be gathered from a close examination of the lower part of the lining. The lens discloses a large number of hair-ends, clean cut by the scissors of the barber. They all appear to be adhesive, and there is a distinct odour of lime-cream. This dust, you will observe, is not the gritty, grey dust of the street, but the fluffy brown dust of the house, showing that it has been hung up indoors most of the time; while the marks of moisture upon the inside are proof positive that the wearer perspired very freely, and could, therefore, hardly be in the best of training.'

'But his wife – you said that she had ceased to love him.'

'This hat has not been brushed for weeks. When I see you, my dear Watson, with a week's accumulation of dust upon your hat, and when your wife allows you to go out in such a state, I shall fear that you also have been unfortunate enough to lose your wife's affection.'

'But he might be a bachelor.'

'Nay, he was bringing home the goose as a peace-offering to his wife. Remember the card upon the bird's leg.'

'You have an answer to everything. But how on earth do you deduce that the gas is not laid on in the house?'

'One tallow stain, or even two, might come by chance; but, when I see no less than five, I think that there can be little doubt that the individual must be brought into frequent contact with burning tallow – walks upstairs at night probably with his hat in one hand and a guttering candle in the other. Anyhow, he never got tallow stains from a gas jet. Are you satisfied?'

'Well, it is very ingenious,' said I, laughing; 'but since, as you said just now, there has been no crime committed, and no harm done save the loss of a goose, all this seems to be rather a waste of energy.'

Sherlock Holmes had opened his mouth to reply, when the door flew open, and Peterson the commissionaire rushed into the compartment with flushed cheeks and the face of a man who is dazed with astonishment.

'The goose, Mr Holmes! The goose, sir!' he gasped.

'Eh! What of it, then? Has it returned to life, and flapped off through the kitchen window?' Holmes twisted himself round upon the sofa to get a fairer view of the man's excited face.

'See here, sir! See what my wife found in its crop!' He held out his hand, and displayed upon the centre of the palm a brilliantly scintillating blue stone, rather smaller than a bean in size, but of such purity and radiance that it twinkled like an electric point in the dark hollow of his hand.

Sherlock Holmes sat up with a whistle. 'By Jove, Peterson,' said he, 'this is treasure-trove indeed! I suppose you know what you have got?'

'A diamond, sir! A precious stone! It cuts into glass as though it were putty.'

'It's more than a precious stone. It's *the* precious stone.'

'Not the Countess of Morcar's blue carbuncle?' I ejaculated.

'Precisely so. I ought to know its size and shape, seeing that I

'SEE WHAT MY WIFE FOUND IN ITS CROP'

have read the advertisement about it in *The Times* every day lately. It is absolutely unique, and its value can only be conjectured, but the reward offered of a thousand pounds is certainly not within a twentieth part of the market price.'

'A thousand pounds! Great Lord of mercy!' The commissionaire plumped down into a chair, and stared from one to the other of us.

'That is the reward, and I have reason to know that there are sentimental considerations in the background which would induce the Countess to part with half of her fortune if she could but recover the gem.'

'It was lost, if I remember aright, at the Hotel Cosmopolitan,' I remarked.

'Precisely so, on the 22nd of December, just five days ago. John Horner, a plumber, was accused of having abstracted it from the lady's jewel-case. The evidence against him was so strong that the case has been referred to the Assizes. I have some account of the matter here, I believe'. He rummaged amid his newspapers, glancing over the dates, until at last he smoothed one out, doubled it over, and read the following paragraph:

'"Hotel Cosmopolitan Jewel Robbery. John Horner, 26, plumber, was brought up upon the charge of having upon the 22nd inst., abstracted from the jewel-case of the Countess of Morcar the valuable gem known as the blue carbuncle. James Ryder, upper-attendant at the hotel, gave his evidence to the effect that he had shown Horner up to the dressing-room of the Countess of Morcar upon the day of the robbery, in order that he might solder the second bar of the grate, which was loose. He had remained with Horner some little time but had finally been called away. On returning he found that Horner had disappeared, that the bureau had been forced open, and that the small morocco casket in which, as it afterwards transpired, the Countess was accustomed to keep her jewel, was lying empty upon the dressing-table. Ryder instantly gave the alarm, and Horner was arrested the same evening; but the stone could not be found either upon his person or in his rooms. Catherine Cusack, maid to the Countess, deposed to having heard Ryder's cry of dismay on discovering the robbery, and to having rushed into the room, where she found matters were as described by the last witness. Inspector Bradstreet, B Division, gave evidence as to the arrest of Horner, who struggled frantically, and protested his innocence in the strongest terms. Evidence of a previous conviction for robbery having been given against the prisoner, the magistrate refused to deal summarily with the offence, but referred it to the Assizes. Horner, who had shown signs of intense emotion during the proceedings, fainted away at the conclusion, and was carried out of court."

'Hum! So much for the police court,' said Holmes thoughtfully, tossing aside his paper. 'The question for us now to solve is the sequence of events from a rifled jewel-case at one end to the crop of a goose in Tottenham Court Road at the other. You see, Watson, our little deductions have suddenly assumed a much more important and less innocent aspect. Here is the stone; the stone came from the goose, and the goose came from Mr Henry Baker, the gentleman with the bad hat and all the other characteristics with which I have bored you. So now we must set ourselves very seriously to finding this gentleman, and ascertaining what part he has played in this little mystery. To do this, we must try the simplest means first, and these lie undoubtedly in an advertisement in all the evening papers. If this fails, I shall have recourse to other methods.'

'What will you say?'

'Give me a pencil, and that slip of paper. Now, then: "Found at the corner of Goodge Street, a goose and a black felt hat. Mr Henry Baker can have the same by applying at 6.30 this evening at 221B Baker Street." That is clear and concise.'

'Very. But will he see it?'

'Well, he is sure to keep an eye on the papers, since, to a poor man, the loss was a heavy one. He was clearly so scared by his mischance in breaking the window, and by the approach of Peterson, that he thought of nothing but flight; but since then he must have bitterly regretted the impulse which caused him to drop his bird. Then, again, the introduction of his name will cause him to see it, for everyone who knows him will direct his attention to it. Here you are, Peterson, run down to the advertising agency, and have this put in the evening papers.'

'In which, sir?'

'Oh, in the *Globe, Star, Pall Mall, St James's Gazette, Evening News, Standard, Echo*, and any others that occur to you.'

'Very well sir, and this stone?'

'Ah, yes. I shall keep the stone. Thank you. And, I say, Peterson, just buy a goose on your way back, and leave it here with me, for we must have one to give to this gentleman in place of the one which your family is now devouring.'

When the commissionaire had gone, Holmes took up the stone and held it against the light. 'It's a bonny thing,' said he. 'Just see how it glints and sparkles. Of course it is a nucleus and focus of crime. Every good stone is. They are the devil's pet baits. In the larger and older jewels every facet may stand for a bloody deed. This stone is not yet twenty years old. It was found in the banks of the Amoy River in Southern China, and is remarkable in having every characteristic of the carbuncle, save that it is blue in shade, instead of ruby red. In spite of its youth, it has already a sinister history. There have been two murders, a vitriol-throwing, a suicide, and several robberies brought about for the sake of this forty-grain weight of crystallized charcoal. Who would think that so pretty a toy would be a purveyor to the gallows and the prison? I'll lock it up in my strong-box now, and drop a line to the Countess to say that we have it.'

'Do you think this man Horner is innocent?'

'I cannot tell.'

'Well, then, do you imagine that this other one, Henry Baker, had anything to do with the matter?'

'It is, I think, much more likely that Henry Baker is an absolutely innocent man, who had no idea that the bird which he was carrying was of considerably more value than if it were made of solid gold. That, however, I shall determine by a very simple test, if we have an answer to our advertisement.'

'And you can do nothing until then?'

'Nothing.'

'In that case I shall continue my professional round. But I shall come back in the evening at the hour you have mentioned, for I should like to see the solution of so tangled a business.'

'Very glad to see you. I dine at seven. There is a woodcock, I believe. By the way, in view of recent occurrences, perhaps I ought to ask Mrs Hudson to examine its crop.'

I had been delayed at a case, and it was a little after half-past six when I found myself in Baker Street once more. As I approached the house I saw a tall man in a Scotch bonnet, with a coat which was buttoned up to his chin, waiting outside in the bright semicircle which was thrown from the fanlight. Just as I arrived, the door was opened, and we were shown up together to Holmes's room.

'Mr Henry Baker, I believe,' said he, rising from his armchair, and greeting his visitor with the easy air of geniality which he could so readily assume. 'Pray take this chair by the fire, Mr Baker. It is a cold night, and I observe that your circulation is more adapted for summer than for winter. Ah, Watson, you have just come at the right time. Is that your hat, Mr Baker?'

'Yes, sir, that is undoubtedly my hat.'

He was a large man, with rounded shoulders, a massive head, and a broad, intelligent face, sloping down to a pointed beard of grizzled brown. A touch of red in nose and cheeks, with a slight tremor of his extended hand, recalled Holmes's surmise as to his habits. His rusty black frock-coat was buttoned right up in front, with the collar turned up, and his lank wrists protruded from his sleeves without a sign of cuff or shirt. He spoke in a low staccato fashion, choosing his words with care, and gave the impression generally of a man of learning and letters who had had ill-usage at the hands of fortune.

'We have retained these things for some days,' said Holmes, 'because we expected to see an advertisement from you giving your address. I am at a loss to know now why you did not advertise.'

Our visitor gave a rather shamefaced laugh. 'Shillings have not been so plentiful with me as they once were,' he remarked. 'I had no doubt that the gang of roughs who assaulted me had carried off both my hat and the bird. I did not care to spend more money in a hopeless attempt at recovering them.'

'Very naturally. By the way, about the bird – we were compelled to eat it.'

'To eat it!' Our visitor half rose from his chair in his excitement.

'Yes; it would have been no use to anyone had we not done so. But I presume that this other goose upon the sideboard, which is about the same weight and perfectly fresh, will answer your purpose equally well?'

'Oh, certainly, certainly!' answered Mr Baker, with a sigh of relief.

'Of course, we still have the feathers, legs, crop, and so on of your own bird, if you so wish –'

The man burst into a hearty laugh. 'They might be useful to me as relics of my adventure,' said he, 'but beyond that I can hardly see what use the *disjecta membra* of my late acquaintance are going to be to me. No, sir, I think that, with your permission, I will confine my attentions to the excellent bird which I perceive upon the sideboard.'

Sherlock Holmes glanced sharply across at me with a slight shrug of his shoulders.

'There is your hat, then, and there your bird,' said he. 'By the way, would it bore you to tell me where you got the other one from? I am somewhat of a fowl fancier, and I have seldom seen a better-grown goose.'

'Certainly, sir,' said Baker, who had risen and tucked his newly gained property under his arm. 'There are a few of us who frequent the Alpha Inn near the Museum – we are to be found in the Museum itself during the day, you understand. This year our good host, Windigate by name, instituted a goose-club, by which, on consideration of some few pence every week, we were to receive a bird at Christmas. My pence were duly paid, and the rest is familiar to you. I am much indebted to you, sir, for a Scotch bonnet is fitted neither to my years nor my gravity.' With a comical pomposity of manner he bowed solemnly to both of us, and strode off upon his way.

'So much for Mr Henry Baker,' said Holmes, when he had

'HE BOWED SOLEMNLY TO BOTH OF US.'

closed the door behind him. 'It is quite certain that he knows nothing whatever about the matter. Are you hungry, Watson?'

'Not particularly.'

'Then I suggest that we turn our dinner into a supper, and follow up this clue while it is still hot.'

'By all means.'

It was a bitter night, so we drew on our ulsters and wrapped cravats about our throats. Outside, the stars were shining coldly in a cloudless sky, and the breath of the passers-by blew out into smoke like so many pistol shots. Our footfalls rang out crisply and loudly as we swung through the doctors' quarter, Wimpole Street, Harley Street, and so through Wigmore Street into Oxford Street. In a quarter of an hour we were in Bloomsbury at the Alpha Inn, which is a small public-house at the corner of one of the streets which run down into Holborn. Holmes pushed open the door of the private bar, and ordered two glasses of beer from the ruddy-faced, white-aproned landlord.

'Your beer should be excellent if it is as good as your geese,' he said.

'My geese!' The man seemed surprised.

'Yes. I was speaking only half an hour ago to Mr Henry Baker, who was a member of your goose-club.'

'Ah! yes, I see. But you see, sir, them's not our geese.'

'Indeed! Whose, then?'

'Well, I got the two dozen from a salesman in Covent Garden.'

'Indeed! I know some of them. Which was it?'

'Breckinridge is his name.'

'Ah! I don't know him. Well, here's your good health, landlord, and prosperity to your house. Good night!

'Now for Mr Breckinridge,' he continued, buttoning up his coat, as we came out into the frosty air. 'Remember, Watson, that though we have so homely a thing as a goose at one end of this chain, we have at the other a man who will certainly get seven years' penal servitude, unless we can establish his innocence. It is possible that our inquiry may but confirm his guilt; but, in any case, we have a line of investigation which has been missed by the police, and which a singular chance has placed in our hands. Let us follow it out to the bitter end. Faces to the south, then, and quick march!'

We passed across Holborn, down Endell Street, and so through a zigzag of slums to Covent Garden Market. One of the largest stalls bore the name of Breckinridge upon it and the proprietor, a horsey-looking man with a sharp face and trim side-whiskers, was helping a boy to put up the shutters.

'Good evening, it's a cold night,' said Holmes.

The salesman nodded, and shot a questioning glance at my companion.

'Sold out of geese, I see,' continued Holmes, pointing at the bare slabs of marble.

'Let you have five hundred tomorrow morning.'

'That's no good.'

'Well, there are some on the stall with the gas flare.'

'Ah, but I was recommended to you.'

'Who by?'

'The landlord of the Alpha.'

'Ah, yes; I sent him a couple of dozen.'

'Fine birds they were, too. Now where did you get them from?'

To my surprise the question provoked a burst of anger from the salesman.

'Now then, mister,' said he, with his head cocked and his arms akimbo, 'what are you driving at? Let's have it straight, now.'

'It is straight enough. I should like to know who sold you the geese which you supplied to the Alpha.'

'Well, then, I shan't tell you. So now!'

'Oh, it is a matter of no importance; but I don't know why you should be so warm over such a trifle.'

'Warm! You'd be as warm, maybe, if you were pestered as I

am. When I pay good money for a good article there should be an end of the business; but it's "Where are the geese?" and "Who did you sell the geese to?" and "What will you take for the geese?" One would think they were the only geese in the world, to hear the fuss that is made over them.'

'Well, I have no connection with any other people who have been making inquiries,' said Holmes carelessly. 'If you won't tell us the bet is off, that is all. But I'm always ready to back my opinion on a matter of fowls, and I have a fiver on it that the bird I ate is country bred.'

'Well, then, you've lost your fiver, for it's town bred,' snapped the salesman.

'It's nothing of the kind.'

'I say it is.'

'I don't believe you.'

'D'you think you know more about fowls than I, who have handled them ever since I was a nipper? I tell you, all those birds that went to the Alpha were town bred.'

'You'll never persuade me to believe that.'

'Will you bet, then?'

'It's merely taking your money, for I know that I am right. But I'll have a sovereign on with you, just to teach you not to be obstinate.'

The salesman chuckled grimly. 'Bring me the books, Bill,' said he.

The small boy brought round a small thin volume and a great greasy-backed one, laying them out together beneath the hanging lamp.

'Now then, Mr Cocksure,' said the salesman, 'I thought that I was out of geese, but before I finish you'll find that there is still one left in my shop. You see this little book?'

'Well?'

'That's the list of the folk from whom I buy. D'you see? Well, then, here on this page are the country folk, and the numbers after their names are where their accounts are in the big ledger. Now, then! You see this other page in red ink? Well, that is a list of my town suppliers. Now, look at that third name. Just read it out to me.'

'Mrs Oakshott, 117 Brixton Road – 249,' read Holmes.

'Quite so. Now turn that up in the ledger.'

Holmes turned to the page indicated. 'Here you are, "Mrs Oakshott, 117 Brixton Road, egg and poultry supplier." '

'Now, then, what's the last entry?'

' "December 22. Twenty-four geese at 7s. 6d." '

'Quite so. There you are. And underneath?'

' "Sold to Mr Windigate of the Alpha at 12s." '

'What have you to say now?'

Sherlock Holmes looked deeply chagrined. He drew a sovereign from his pocket and threw it down upon the slab, turning away with the air of a man whose disgust is too deep for words. A few yards off he stopped under a lamp-post, and laughed in the hearty, noiseless fashion which was peculiar to him.

'When you see a man with whiskers of that cut and the "Pink 'Un" protruding out of his pocket, you can always draw him by a bet,' said he. 'I dare say that if I had put a hundred pounds down in front of him that man would not have given me such complete information as was drawn from him by the idea that he was doing me on a wager. Well, Watson, we are, I fancy, nearing the end of our quest, and the only point which remains to be determined is whether we should go on to this Mrs Oakshott tonight, or whether we should reserve it for tomorrow. It is clear from what that surly fellow said that there are others besides ourselves who are anxious about the matter, and I should – '

His remarks were suddenly cut short by a loud hubbub which broke out from the stall which we had just left. Turning round we saw a little rat-faced fellow, standing in the centre of the circle of yellow light which was thrown by the swinging lamp, while

Breckinridge the salesman, framed in the door of his stall, was shaking his fists fiercely at the cringing figure.

'I've had enough of you and your geese,' he shouted. 'I wish you were all at the devil together. If you come pestering me any more with your silly talk I'll set the dog at you. You bring Mrs Oakshott here and I'll answer her, but what have you to do with it? Did I buy the geese off you?'

'No; but one of them was mine all the same,' whined the little man.

'Well, then, ask Mrs Oakshott for it.'

'She told me to ask you.'

'Well, you can ask the King of Proosia, for all I care. I've had enough of it. Get out of this!' He rushed fiercely forward, and the inquirer flitted away into the darkness.

'Ha, this may save us a visit to Brixton Road,' whispered Holmes. 'Come with me, and we will see what is to be made of this fellow.' Striding through the scattered knots of people who lounged round the flaring stalls, my companion speedily overtook the little man and touched him upon the shoulder. He sprang round, and I could see in the gaslight that every vestige of colour had been driven from his face.

'Who are you, then? What do you want?' he asked in a quavering voice.

'You will excuse me,' said Holmes blandly, 'but I could not help overhearing the questions which you put to the salesman just now. I think that I could be of assistance to you.'

'You? Who are you? How could you know anything of the matter?'

'My name is Sherlock Holmes. It is my business to know what other people don't know.'

'But you can know nothing of this?'

'Excuse me, I know everything of it. You are endeavouring to trace some geese which were sold by Mrs Oakshott, of Brixton

Road, to a salesman named Breckinridge, by him in turn to Mr Windigate, of the Alpha, and by him to his club, of which Mr Henry Baker is a member.'

'Oh, sir, you are the very man whom I have longed to meet,' cried the little fellow, with outstretched hands and quivering fingers. 'I can hardly explain to you how interested I am in this matter.'

Sherlock Holmes hailed a four-wheeler which was passing. 'In that case we had better discuss it in a cosy room rather than in this windswept market-place,' said he. 'But pray tell me, before we go further, who it is that I have the pleasure of assisting.'

The man hesitated for an instant. 'My name is John Robinson,' he answered, with a sidelong glance.

'No, no; the real name,' said Holmes sweetly. 'It is always awkward doing business with an alias.'

A flush sprang to the white cheeks of the stranger. 'Well, then,' said he, 'my real name is James Ryder.'

'Precisely so. Head attendant at the Hotel Cosmopolitan. Pray step into the cab, and I shall soon be able to tell you everything which you would wish to know.'

The little man stood glancing from one to the other of us with half-frightened, half-hopeful eyes, as one who is not sure whether he is on the verge of a windfall or of a catastrophe. Then he stepped into the cab, and in half an hour we were back in the sitting-room at Baker Street. Nothing had been said during our drive, but the high, thin breathing of our new companion, and the claspings and unclaspings of his hands, spoke of the nervous tension within him.

'Here we are!' said Holmes cheerily, as we filed into the room. 'The fire looks very seasonable in this weather. You look cold, Mr Ryder. Pray take the basket chair. I will just put on my slippers before we settle this little matter of yours. Now, then! You want to know what became of those geese?'

'Yes, sir.'

'Or rather, I fancy, of that goose. It was one bird, I imagine, in which you were interested – white, with a black bar across the tail.'

Ryder quivered with emotion. 'Oh, sir,' he cried, 'can you tell me where it went to?'

'It came here.'

'Here?'

'Yes, and a most remarkable bird it proved. I don't wonder that you should take an interest in it. It laid an egg after it was dead – the bonniest, brightest little blue egg that was ever seen. I have it here in my museum.'

Our visitor staggered to his feet, and clutched the mantelpiece with his right hand. Holmes unlocked his strong-box, and held up the blue carbuncle, which shone out like a star, with a cold, brilliant, many-pointed radiance. Ryder stood glaring with a drawn face, uncertain whether to claim or to disown it.

'The game's up, Ryder,' said Holmes quietly. 'Hold up, man, or you'll be into the fire. Give him an arm back into his chair, Watson. He's not got blood enough to go in for felony with impunity. Give him a dash of brandy. So! Now he looks a little more human. What a shrimp it is, to be sure!'

For a moment he had staggered and nearly fallen, but the brandy brought a tinge of colour into his cheeks, and he sat staring with frightened eyes at his accuser.

'I have almost every link in my hands, and all the proofs which I could possibly need, so there is little which you need tell me. Still, that little may as well be cleared up to make the case complete. You had heard, Ryder, of this blue stone of the Countess of Morcar's?'

'It was Catherine Cusack who told me of it,' said he, in a crackling voice.

'I see. Her ladyship's waiting-maid. Well the temptation of sudden wealth so easily acquired was too much for you, as it has been for better men before you; but you were not very scrupulous in the means you used. It seems to me, Ryder, that there is the making of a very pretty villain in you. You knew that this man Horner, the plumber, had been concerned in some such matter before, and that suspicion would rest the more readily upon him. What did you do, then? You made some small job in my lady's room – you and your confederate Cusack – and you managed that he should be the man sent for. Then, when he had left, you rifled the jewel-case, raised the alarm, and had this unfortunate man arrested. You then – '

Ryder threw himself down suddenly upon the rug, and clutched at my companion's knees. 'For God's sake, have mercy!' he shrieked. 'Think of my father! Of my mother! It would break their hearts. I never went wrong before! I never will again. I swear it. I'll swear it on a Bible. Oh, don't bring it into court! For Christ's sake, don't!'

'Get back into your chair!' said Holmes sternly. 'It is very well to cringe and crawl now, but you thought little enough of this poor Horner in the dock for a crime of which he knew nothing.'

'I will fly, Mr Holmes. I will leave the country, sir. Then the charge against him will break down.'

'Hum! We will talk about that. And now let us hear a true account of the next act. How came the stone into the goose, and how came the goose into the open market? Tell us the truth, for there lies your only hope of safety.'

Ryder passed his tongue over his parched lips. 'I will tell you it just as it happened, sir,' said he. 'When Horner had been arrested, it seemed to me that it would be best for me to get away with the stone at once, for I did not know at what moment the police might not take it into their heads to search me and my room. There was no place about the hotel where it would be safe. I went out, as if on some commission, and I made for my sister's house. She had married a man named Oakshott, and lived in Brixton Road, where she fattened fowls for the market. All the way there every man I met seemed to me to be a policeman or a detective, and for all that it was a cold night, the sweat was pouring down my face before I came to the Brixton Road. My sister asked me what was the matter, and why I was so pale; but I told her that I had been upset by the jewel robbery at the hotel. Then I went into the backyard, and smoked a pipe, and wondered what it would be best to do.

'I had a friend once called Maudsley, who went to the bad, and has just been serving his time in Pentonville. One day he had met me, and fell into talk about the ways of thieves and how they could get rid of what they stole. I knew that he would be true to me, for I knew one or two things about him, so I made up my mind to go right on to Kilburn, where he lived, and take him into my confidence. He would show me how to turn the stone into money. But how to get to him in safety? I thought of the agonies I had gone through in coming from the hotel. I might at any moment be seized and searched, and there would be the stone in my waistcoat pocket. I was leaning against the wall at the time, and looking at the geese which were waddling about round my feet, and suddenly an idea came into my head which showed me how I could beat the best detective that ever lived.

'My sister had told me some weeks before that I might have the pick of her geese for a Christmas present, and I knew that she was always as good as her word. I would take my goose now, and in it I would carry my stone to Kilburn. There was a little shed in the yard, and behind this I drove one of the birds, a fine big one, white, with a barred tail. I caught it and, prising its bill open, I thrust the stone down its throat as far as my finger could reach. The bird gave a gulp, and I felt the stone pass along its gullet and down into its crop. But the creature flapped and struggled, and out came my sister to know what was the matter. As I turned to speak to her the brute broke loose, and fluttered off among the others.

' "Whatever were you doing with that bird, Jem?" says she.

' "Well," said I, "you said you'd give me one for Christmas, and I was feeling which was the fattest."

'"Oh," says she, "we've set yours aside for you. Jem's bird, we call it. It's the big, white one over yonder. There's twenty-six of them, which makes one for you, and one for us, and two dozen for the market."

'"Thank you, Maggie," says I; "but if it is all the same to you I'd rather have that one I was handling just now."

'"The other is a good three pound heavier," she said, "and we fattened it expressly for you."

'"Never mind. I'll have the other, and I'll take it now," said I.

'"Oh, just as you like," said she, a little huffed. "Which is it you want, then?"

'"That white one, with the barred tail, right in the middle of the flock."

'"Oh, very well. Kill it and take it with you."

'Well, I did what she said, Mr Holmes, and I carried the bird all the way to Kilburn. I told my pal what I had done, for he was a man that it was easy to tell a thing like that to. He laughed until he choked, and we got a knife and opened the goose. My heart turned to water, for there was no sign of the stone, and I knew that some terrible mistake had occurred. I left the bird, rushed back to my sister's, and hurried into the backyard. There was not a bird to be seen there.

'"Where are they all, Maggie?" I cried.

'"Gone to the dealer's."

'"Which dealer's?"

'"Breckinridge, of Covent Garden."

'"But was there another with a barred tail?" I asked, "the same as the one I chose?"

'"Yes, Jem, there were two barred-tailed ones, and I could never tell them apart."

'Well, then, of course, I saw it all, and I ran off as hard as my feet would carry me to this man Breckinridge; but he had sold the lot at once, and not one word would he tell me as to where they had gone. You heard him yourselves tonight. Well, he has

'HE BURST INTO CONVULSIVE SOBBING.'

always answered me like that. My sister thinks that I am going mad. Sometimes I think that I am myself. And now – now I am myself a branded thief, without ever having touched the wealth for which I sold my character. God help me! God help me!' He burst into convulsive sobbing, with his face buried in his hands.

There was a long silence, broken only by his heavy breathing, and by the measured tapping of Sherlock Holmes's fingertips upon the edge of the table. Then my friend rose, and threw open the door.

'Get out!' said he.

'What, sir! Oh, heaven bless you!'

'No more words. Get out!'

And no more words were needed. There was a rush, a clatter upon the stairs, the bang of a door, and the crisp rattle of running footfalls from the street.

'After all, Watson,' said Holmes, reaching up his hand for his clay pipe, 'I am not retained by the police to supply their deficiencies. If

Horner were in danger it would be another thing, but this fellow will not appear against him, and the case must collapse. I suppose that I am committing a felony, but it is just possible that I am saving a soul. This fellow will not go wrong again. He is too terribly frightened. Send him to gaol now, and you make him a gaol-bird for life. Besides, it is the season of forgiveness. Chance has put in our way a most singular and whimsical problem, and its solution is its own reward. If you will have the goodness to touch the bell, Doctor, we will begin another investigation, in which also a bird will be the chief feature.'

The Adventure of the Copper Beeches

To the man who loves art for its own sake,' remarked Sherlock Holmes, tossing aside the advertisement sheet of the *Daily Telegraph*, 'it is frequently in its least important and lowliest manifestations that the keenest pleasure is to be derived. It is pleasant to me to observe, Watson, that you have so far grasped this truth that in these little records of our cases which you have been good enough to draw up, and, I am bound to say, occasionally to embellish, you have given prominence not so much to the many *causes célèbres* and sensational trials in which I have figured, but rather to those incidents which may have been trivial in themselves, but which have given room for those faculties of deduction and of logical synthesis which I have made my special province.'

'And yet,' said I, smiling, 'I cannot quite hold myself absolved from the charge of sensationalism which has been urged against my records.'

'You have erred, perhaps,' he observed, taking up a glowing cinder with the tongs, and lighting with it the long cherrywood pipe which was wont to replace his clay when he was in a disputatious rather than a meditative mood – 'you have erred, perhaps, in attempting to put colour and life into each of your statements, instead of confining yourself to the task of placing upon record that severe reasoning from cause to effect which is really the only notable feature about the thing.'

'It seems to me that I have done you full justice in the matter,' I remarked with some coldness, for I was repelled by the egotism which I had more than once observed to be a strong factor in my friend's singular character.

'TAKING UP A GLOWING CINDER WITH THE TONGS.'

'No, it is not selfishness or conceit,' said he, answering, as was his wont, my thoughts rather than my words. 'If I claim full justice for my art, it is because it is an impersonal thing – a thing beyond myself. Crime is common. Logic is rare. Therefore it is upon the logic rather than upon the crime that you should dwell. You have degraded what should have been a course of lectures into a series of tales.'

It was a cold morning of the early spring, and we sat after breakfast on either side of a cheery fire in the old room in Baker Street. A thick fog rolled down between the lines of dun-coloured houses, and the opposing windows loomed like dark, shapeless blurs, through the heavy yellow wreaths. Our gas was lit, and shone on the white cloth, and glimmer of china and metal, for the table had not been cleared yet. Sherlock Holmes had been silent all the morning, dipping continuously into the advertisement columns of a succession of papers, until at last, having apparently given up his search, he had emerged in no very sweet temper to lecture me upon my literary shortcomings.

'At the same time,' he remarked, after a pause, during which he had sat puffing at his long pipe and gazing down into the fire, 'you can hardly be open to a charge of sensationalism, for out of these cases which you have been so kind as to interest yourself in, a fair proportion do not treat of crime, in its legal sense, at all. The small matter in which I endeavoured to help the King of Bohemia, the singular experience of Miss Mary Sutherland, the problem connected with the man with the twisted lip, and the incident of the noble bachelor, were all matters which are outside the pale of the law. But in avoiding the sensational, I fear that you may have bordered on the trivial.'

'The end may have been so,' I answered, 'but the methods I hold to have been novel and of interest.'

'Pshaw, my dear fellow, what do the public, the great unobservant public, who could hardly tell a weaver by his tooth or a compositor by his left thumb, care about the finer shades of analysis and deduction! But, indeed, if you are trivial, I cannot blame you, for the days of the great cases are past. Man, or at least criminal man, has lost all enterprise and originality. As to my own little practice, it seems to be degenerating into an agency for recovering lost lead pencils and giving advice to young ladies from boarding-schools. I think that I have touched bottom at last, however. This note I had this morning marks my zero point, I fancy. Read it!' He tossed a crumpled letter across to me.

It was dated from Montague Place upon the preceding evening, and ran thus:

Dear Mr Holmes –

I am very anxious to consult you as to whether I should or should not accept a situation which has been offered to me as governess. I shall call at half-past ten tomorrow, if I do not inconvenience you.

Yours faithfully,
VIOLET HUNTER

'Do you know the young lady?' I asked.

'Not I.'

'It is half-past ten now.'

'Yes, and I have no doubt that is her ring.'

'It may turn out to be of more interest than you think. You remember that the affair of the blue carbuncle, which appeared to be a mere whim at first, developed into a serious investigation. It may be so in this case also.'

'Well, let us hope so! But our doubts will very soon be solved, for here, unless I am much mistaken, is the person in question.'

As he spoke the door opened, and a young lady entered the room. She was plainly but neatly dressed, with a bright, quick face, freckled like a plover's egg, and with the brisk manner of a woman who has had her own way to make in the world.

'You will excuse my troubling you, I am sure,' said she, as my companion rose to greet her; 'but I have had a very strange experience, and as I have no parents or relations of any sort from whom I could ask advice, I thought that perhaps you would be kind enough to tell me what I should do.'

'Pray take a seat, Miss Hunter. I shall be happy to do anything that I can to serve you.'

I could see that Holmes was favourably impressed by the manner and speech of his new client. He looked her over in his searching fashion, and then composed himself with his lids drooping and his fingertips together to listen to her story.

'I have been a governess for five years,' said she, 'in the family of Colonel Spence Munro, but two months ago the Colonel received an appointment at Halifax, in Nova Scotia, and took his children over to America with him, so that I found myself without a situation. I advertised and I answered advertisements, but without success. At last the little money which I had saved began to run short, and I was at my wits' end as to what I should do.

'There is a well-known agency for governesses in the West End called Westaway's, and there I used to call about once a week in order to see whether anything had turned up which might suit me. Westaway was the name of the founder of the business, but it is really managed by Miss Stoper. She sits in her own little office, and the ladies who are seeking employment wait in an ante-room, and are then shown in one by one, when she consults her ledgers, and sees whether she has anything which would suit them.

'Well, when I called last week I was shown into the little office as usual, but I found that Miss Stoper was not alone. A prodigiously stout man with a very smiling face, and a great heavy chin which rolled down in fold upon fold over his throat, sat at her elbow with a pair of glasses on his nose, looking very earnestly at the ladies who entered. As I came in he gave quite a jump in his chair, and turned quickly to Miss Stoper:

' "That will do," said he; "I could not ask for anything better. Capital! Capital!" He seemed quite enthusiastic and rubbed his hands together in the most genial fashion. He was such a comfortable-looking man that it was quite a pleasure to look at him.

' "You are looking for a situation, miss?" he asked.

' "Yes, sir."

' "As governess?"

' "Yes, sir."

' "And what salary do you ask?"

' "I had four pounds a month in my last place with Colonel Spence Munro."

' "Oh, tut, tut! sweating – rank sweating!" he cried, throwing his fat hands out into the air like a man who is in a boiling passion. "How could anyone offer so pitiful a sum to a lady with such attractions and accomplishments?"

'"My accomplishments, sir, may be less than you imagine," said I. "A little French, a little German, music and drawing – "

'"Tut, tut!" he cried. "This is all quite beside the question. The point is, have you or have you not the bearing and deportment of a lady? There it is in a nutshell. If you have not, you are not fitted for the rearing of a child who may some day play a considerable part in the history of the country. But if you have, why, then how could any gentleman ask you to condescend to accept anything under the three figures? Your salary with me, madam, would commence at a hundred pounds a year."

'You may imagine, Mr Holmes, that to me, destitute as I was, such an offer seemed almost too good to be true. The gentleman, however, seeing perhaps the look of incredulity upon my face, opened a pocket-book and took out a note.

'"It is also my custom," said he, smiling in the most pleasant fashion until his eyes were just two shining slits amid the white creases of his face, "to advance to my young ladies half their salary beforehand, so that they may meet any little expenses of their journey and their wardrobe."

'It seemed to me that I had never met so fascinating and so thoughtful a man. As I was already in debt to my tradesmen, the advance was a great convenience, and yet there was something unnatural about the whole transaction which made me wish to know a little more before I quite committed myself.

'"May I ask where you live, sir?" said I.

'"Hampshire. Charming rural place. The Copper Beeches, five miles on the far side of Winchester. It is the most lovely country, my dear young lady, and the dearest old country house."

'"And my duties, sir? I should be glad to know what they would be."

'"One child – one dear little romper just six years old. Oh, if you could see him killing cockroaches with a slipper! Smack!

smack! smack! Three gone before you could wink!" He leaned back in his chair and laughed his eyes into his head again.

'I was a little startled at the nature of the child's amusement, but the father's laughter made me think that perhaps he was joking.

' "My sole duties, then," I asked, "are to take charge of a single child?"

' "No, no, not the sole, not the sole, my dear young lady," he cried. "Your duty would be as I am sure your good sense would suggest, to obey any little commands which my wife might give, provided always that they were such commands as a lady might with propriety obey. You see no difficulty, heh?"

' "I should be happy to make myself useful."

' "Quite so. In dress now, for example! We are faddy people, you know – faddy, but kind-hearted. If you were asked to wear any dress which we might give you, you would not object to our little whim. Heh?"

' "No," said I, considerably astonished at his words.

' "Or to sit here, or sit there, that would not be offensive to you?"

' "Oh, no."

' "Or to cut your hair quite short before you come to us?"

'I could hardly believe my ears. As you may observe, Mr Holmes, my hair is somewhat luxuriant, and of a rather peculiar tint of chestnut. It has been considered artistic. I could not dream of sacrificing it in this off-hand fashion.

' "I am afraid that that is quite impossible," said I. He had been watching me eagerly out of his small eyes and I could see a shadow pass over his face as I spoke.

' "I am afraid that it is quite essential," said he. "It is a little fancy of my wife's, and ladies' fancies, you know, madam, ladies' fancies must be consulted. And so you won't cut your hair?"

' "No, sir, I really could not," I answered firmly.

' "Ah, very well; then that quite settles the matter. It is a pity, because in other respects you would really have done very nicely. In that case, Miss Stoper, I had best inspect a few more of your young ladies."

'The manageress had sat all this while busy with her papers without a word to either of us, but she glanced at me now with so much annoyance upon her face that I could not help suspecting that she had lost a handsome commission through my refusal.

'"Do you desire your name to be kept upon the books?" she asked.

'"If you please, Miss Stoper."

'"Well, really, it seems rather useless, since you refuse the most excellent offers in this fashion," said she sharply. "You can hardly expect us to exert ourselves to find another such opening for you. Good day to you, Miss Hunter." She struck a gong upon the table, and I was shown out by the page.

'Well, Mr Holmes, when I got back to my lodgings and found little enough in the cupboard, and two or three bills upon the table, I began to ask myself whether I had not done a very foolish thing. After all, if these people had strange fads, and expected obedience on the most extraordinary matters, they were at least ready to pay for their eccentricity. Very few governesses in England are getting a hundred a year. Besides, what use was my hair to me? Many people are improved by wearing it short, and perhaps I should be among the number. Next day I was inclined to think that I had made a mistake, and by the day after I was sure of it. I had almost overcome my pride, so far as to go back to the agency and inquire whether the place was still open, when I received this letter from the gentleman himself. I have it here, and I will read it to you:

> The Copper Beeches, near Winchester
>
> Dear Miss Hunter,
>
> Miss Stoper has very kindly given me your address, and I write from here to ask you whether you have reconsidered your

decision. My wife is very anxious that you should come, for she has been much attracted by my description of you. We are willing to give thirty pounds a quarter, or £120 a year, so as to recompense you for any little inconvenience which our fads may cause you. They are not very exacting after all. My wife is fond of a particular shade of electric blue, and would like you to wear such a dress indoors in the morning. You need not, however, go to the expense of purchasing new, as we have one belonging to my dear daughter Alice (now in Philadelphia) which would, I should think, fit you very well. Then, as to sitting here or there, or amusing yourself in any manner indicated, that need cause you no inconvenience. As regards your hair, it is no doubt a pity, especially as I could not help remarking its beauty during our short interview, but I am afraid that I must remain firm upon this point, and I only hope that the increased salary may recompense you for the loss. Your duties, as far as the child is concerned, are very light. Now do try to come, and I shall meet you with the dog-cart at Winchester. Let me know your train.

Yours faithfully,
JEPHRO RUCASTLE

'That is the letter which I have just received, Mr Holmes, and my mind is made up that I will accept it. I thought, however, that before taking the final step, I should like to submit the whole matter to your consideration.'

'Well, Miss Hunter, if your mind is made up, that settles the question,' said Holmes, smiling.

'But you would not advise me to refuse?'

'I confess that it is not the situation which I should like to see a sister of mine apply for.'

'What is the meaning of it all, Mr Holmes?'

'Ah, I have no data. I cannot tell. Perhaps you have yourself formed some opinion?'

'Well, there seems to me to be only one possible solution. Mr Rucastle seemed to be a very kind, good-natured man. Is it not possible that his wife is a lunatic, that he desires to keep the matter quiet for fear she should be taken to an asylum, and that he humours her fancies in every way in order to prevent an outbreak.'

'That is a possible solution – in fact, as matters stand, it is the most probable one. But in any case it does not seem to be a nice household for a young lady.'

'But the money, Mr Holmes, the money!'

'Well, yes, of course, the pay is good – too good. That is what makes me uneasy. Why should they give you £120 a year, when they could have their pick for £40? There must be some strong reason behind.'

'I thought that if I told you the circumstances you would understand afterwards if I wanted your help. I should feel so much stronger if I felt that you were at the back of me.'

'Oh, you may carry that feeling away with you. I assure you that your little problem promises to be the most interesting which has come my way for some months. There is something distinctly novel about some of the features. If you should find yourself in doubt or in danger – '

'Danger! What danger do you foresee?'

Holmes shook his head gravely. 'It would cease to be a danger if we could define it,' said he. 'But at any time, day or night, a telegram would bring me down to your help.'

'That is enough.' She rose briskly from her chair with the anxiety all swept from her face. 'I shall go down to Hampshire quite easy in my mind now. I shall write to Mr Rucastle at once, sacrifice my poor hair tonight, and start for Winchester tomorrow.' With a few grateful words to Holmes she bade us both good night, and bustled off upon her way.

'At least,' said I, as we heard her quick, firm step descending the stairs, 'she seems to be a young lady who is very well able to take care of herself.'

'And she would need to be,' said Holmes gravely; 'I am much mistaken if we do not hear from her before many days are past.'

It was not very long before my friend's prediction was fulfilled. A fortnight went by, during which I frequently found my thoughts turning in her direction, and wondering what strange side-alley of human experience this lonely woman had strayed into. The unusual salary, the curious conditions, the light duties, all pointed to something abnormal, though whether a fad or a plot, or whether the man were a philanthropist or a villain, it was quite beyond my powers to determine. As to Holmes, I observed that he sat frequently for half an hour on end, with knitted brows and an abstracted air, but he swept the matter away with a wave of his hand when I mentioned it. 'Data! data! data!' he cried impatiently. 'I can't make bricks without clay.' And yet he would always wind up by muttering that no sister of his should ever have accepted such a situation.

The telegram which we eventually received came late one night, just as I was thinking of turning in, and Holmes was settling down to one of those all-night researches which he frequently indulged in, when I would leave him stooping over a retort and a test-tube at night, and find him in the same position when I came down to breakfast in the morning. He opened the yellow envelope, and then, glancing at the message, threw it across to me.

'Just look up the trains in Bradshaw,' said he, and turned back to his chemical studies.

The summons was a brief and urgent one.

> Please be at the Black Swan Hotel at Winchester at midday tomorrow [it said]. Do come! I am at my wits' end.
>
> HUNTER

'Will you come with me?' asked Holmes, glancing up.

'I should wish to.'

'Just look it up, then.'

'There is a train at half-past nine,' said I, glancing over my Bradshaw. 'It is due at Winchester at 11.30.'

'That will do very nicely. Then perhaps I had better postpone my analysis of the acetones, as we may need to be at our best in the morning.'

By eleven o'clock the next day we were well upon our way to the old English capital. Holmes had been buried in the morning papers all the way down, but after we had passed the Hampshire border he threw them down, and began to admire the scenery. It was an ideal spring day, a light blue sky, flecked with little fleecy white clouds drifting across from west to east. The sun was shining very brightly, and yet there was an exhilarating nip in the air, which set an edge to a man's energy. All over the countryside, away to the rolling hills around Aldershot, the little red and grey roofs of the farmsteadings peeped out from amidst the light green of the new foliage.

'Are they not fresh and beautiful?' I cried, with all the enthusiasm of a man fresh from the fogs of Baker Street.

But Holmes shook his head gravely.

'Do you know, Watson,' said he, 'that it is one of the curses of a mind with a turn like mine that I must look at everything with reference to my own special subject. You look at these scattered houses, and you are impressed by their beauty. I look at them, and the only thought which comes to me is a feeling of their isolation, and of the impunity with which crime may be committed there.'

'Good heavens!' I cried. 'Who would associate crime with these dear old homesteads?'

'They always fill me with a certain horror. It is my belief, Watson, founded upon my experience, that the lowest and vilest alleys in London do not present a more dreadful record of sin than does the smiling and beautiful countryside.'

'You horrify me!'

'But the reason is very obvious. The pressure of public opinion can do in the town what the law cannot accomplish. There is no lane so vile that the scream of a tortured child, or the thud of a drunkard's blow, does not beget sympathy and indignation among the neighbours, and then the whole machinery of justice is ever so close that a word of complaint can set it going, and there is but a step between the crime and the dock. But look at these lonely houses, each in its own fields, filled for the most part with poor ignorant folk who know little of the law. Think of the deeds of hellish cruelty, the hidden wickedness which may go on, year in, year out, in such places, and none the wiser. Had this lady who appeals to us for help gone to live in Winchester, I should never have had a fear for her. It is the five miles of country which makes the danger. Still, it is clear that she is not personally threatened.'

'No. If she can come to Winchester to meet us she can get away.'

'Quite so. She has her freedom.'

'What *can* be the matter, then? Can you suggest no explanation?'

'I have devised seven separate explanations, each of which would cover the facts as far as we know them. But which of these is correct can only be determined by the fresh information which we shall no doubt find waiting for us. Well, there is the tower of the Cathedral, and we shall soon learn all that Miss Hunter has to tell.'

The Black Swan is an inn of repute in the High Street, at no distance from the station, and there we found the young lady waiting for us. She had engaged a sitting-room, and our lunch awaited us upon the table.

'I am so delighted that you have come,' she said earnestly, 'it is so kind of you both; but indeed I do not know what I should do. Your advice will be altogether invaluable to me.'

'Pray tell us what has happened to you.'

'I will do so, and I must be quick, for I have promised Mr Rucastle to be back before three. I got his leave to come into town this morning, though he little knew for what purpose.'

'Let us have everything in its due order.' Holmes thrust his long thin legs out towards the fire, and composed himself to listen.

'In the first place, I may say that I have met, on the whole, with no actual ill-treatment from Mr and Mrs Rucastle. It is only fair to them to say that. But I cannot understand them, and I am not easy in my mind about them.'

'What can you not understand?'

'Their reasons for their conduct. But you shall have it all just as it occurred. When I came down Mr Rucastle met me here, and drove me in his dog-cart to Copper Beeches. It is, as he said, beautifully situated, but it is not beautiful in itself, for it is a large square block of a house, whitewashed, but all stained and streaked with damp and bad weather. There are grounds round it, woods on three sides, and on the fourth a field which slopes down to the Southampton high-road, which curves past about a hundred yards from the front door. This ground in front belongs to the house, but the woods all round are part of Lord Southerton's preserves. A clump of copper beeches immediately in front of the hall door has given its name to the place.

'I was driven over by my employer, who was as amiable as ever, and was introduced by him that evening to his wife and the child. There was no truth, Mr Holmes, in the conjecture which seemed to us to be probable in your rooms at Baker Street. Mrs Rucastle is not mad. I found her to be a silent, pale-faced woman, much younger than her husband, not more than thirty, I should think, while he can hardly be less than forty-five. From their conversation I have gathered that they have been married about seven years, that he was a widower, and that his only child by the first wife was the daughter who has gone to Philadelphia. Mr Rucastle told me in private that the reason why she had left them was that she had an unreasoning aversion to her stepmother. As the daughter would not have been less than twenty, I can quite imagine that her position must have been uncomfortable with her father's young wife.

'Mrs Rucastle seemed to me to be colourless in mind as well as in feature. She impressed me neither favourably nor the reverse. She was a nonentity. It was easy to see that she was passionately devoted both to her husband and to her little son. Her light grey eyes wandered continually from one to the other, noting every little want and forestalling it if possible. He was kind to her also in his bluff, boisterous fashion, and on the whole they seemed to be a happy couple. And yet she had some secret sorrow, this woman. She would often be lost in deep thought, with the saddest look upon her face. More than once I have surprised her in tears. I have thought sometimes that it was the disposition of her child which weighed upon her mind, for I have never met so utterly spoilt and so ill-natured a little creature. He is small for his age, with a head which is quite disproportionately large. His whole life appears to be spent in an alternation between savage fits of passion and gloomy intervals of sulking. Giving pain to any creature weaker than himself seems to be his one idea of amusement, and he shows quite remarkable talent in planning the capture of mice, little birds, and insects. But I would rather not talk about the creature, Mr Holmes, and, indeed, he has little to do with my story.'

'I am glad of all details,' remarked my friend, 'whether they seem to you to be relevant or not.'

'I shall try not to miss anything of importance. The one unpleasant thing about the house, which struck me at once, was the appearance and conduct of the servants. There are only two, a man and his wife. Toller, for that's his name, is a rough, uncouth man, with grizzled hair and whiskers, and a perpetual smell of drink. Twice since I have been with them he has been quite drunk, and yet Mr Rucastle seemed to take no notice of it. His wife is a very tall and strong woman with a sour face, as silent as Mrs Rucastle, and much less amiable. They are a most unpleasant couple, but fortunately I spend most of my time in the nursery and my own room, which are next to each other in one corner of the building.

'For two days after my arrival at the Copper Beeches my life was very quiet; on the third, Mrs Rucastle came down just after breakfast and whispered something to her husband.

' "Oh yes," said he, turning to me, "we are very much obliged to you, Miss Hunter, for falling in with our whims so far as to cut your hair. I assure you that it has not detracted in the tiniest iota from your appearance. We shall now see how the electric-blue dress will become you. You will find it laid out upon the bed in your room, and if you would be so good as to put it on we should both be extremely obliged."

'The dress which I found waiting for me was of a peculiar shade of blue. It was of excellent material, a sort of beige, but it bore unmistakable signs of having been worn before. It could not have been a better fit if I had been measured for it. Both Mr and Mrs Rucastle expressed a delight at the look of it which seemed quite exaggerated in its vehemence. They were waiting for me in the drawing-room, which is a very large room, stretching along the entire front of the house, with three long windows reaching down to the floor. A chair had been placed close to the central window, with its back turned towards it. In this I was asked to sit, and then Mr Rucastle, walking up and down on the other side of the room, began to tell me a series of the funniest stories that I have ever listened to. You cannot imagine how comical he was, and I laughed until I was quite weary. Mrs Rucastle, however, who has evidently no sense of humour, never so much as smiled, but sat with her hands in her lap, and a sad, anxious look upon her face. After an hour or so Mr Rucastle suddenly remarked that it was time to commence the duties of the day, and that I might change my dress, and go to little Edward in the nursery.

'Two days later this same performance was gone through under exactly similar circumstances. Again I changed my dress, again I sat in the window, and again I laughed very heartily at the funny stories of which my employer had an immense repertoire, and which he told inimitably. Then he handed me a yellow-backed novel, and, moving my chair a little sideways, that my own shadow might not fall upon the page, he begged me to read aloud to him. I read for about ten minutes, beginning in the heart of a chapter, and then suddenly, in the middle of a sentence, he ordered me to cease and change my dress.

'You can easily imagine, Mr Holmes, how curious I became as to what the meaning of this extraordinary performance could possibly be. They were always very careful, I observed, to turn my face away from the window, so that I became consumed with the desire to see what was going on behind my back. At first it seemed to be impossible, but I soon devised a means. My hand mirror had been broken, so a happy thought seized me, and I concealed a little of the glass in my handkerchief. On the next occasion, in the midst of my laughter, I put my handkerchief up to my eyes, and was able with a little management to see all that there was behind me. I confess that I was disappointed. There was nothing.

'At least, that was my first impression. At the second glance, however, I perceived that there was a man standing in the Southampton road, a small bearded man in a grey suit, who seemed to be looking in my direction. The road is an important highway, and there are usually people there. This man, however, was leaning against the railings which bordered our field, and was looking earnestly. I lowered my handkerchief, and glanced at Mrs Rucastle to find her eyes fixed upon me with a most searching gaze. She said nothing, but I am convinced that she had divined that I had a mirror in my hand, and had seen what was behind me. She rose at once.

'"Jephro," said she, "there is an impertinent fellow upon the road there who stares up at Miss Hunter."

'"No friend of yours, Miss Hunter?" he asked.

'"No; I know no one in these parts."

'"Dear me! How very impertinent! Kindly turn round, and motion him to go away."

'"Surely it would be better to take no notice?"

'"No, no, we should have him loitering here always. Kindly turn round, and wave him away like that."

'I did as I was told, and at the same instant Mrs Rucastle drew down the blind. That was a week ago, and from that time I have not sat again in the window, nor have I worn the blue dress, nor seen the man in the road.'

'Pray continue,' said Holmes. 'Your narrative promises to be a most interesting one.'

'You will find it rather disconnected, I fear, and there may prove to be little relation between the different incidents of which I speak. On the very first day I was at Copper Beeches, Mr Rucastle took me to a small outhouse which stands near the kitchen door; as we approached it I heard the sharp rattling of a chain, and the sound as of a large animal moving about.

'"Look in here!" said Mr Rucastle, showing a slit between two planks. "Is he not a beauty?"

'I looked through, and was conscious of two glowing eyes, and of a vague figure huddled up in the darkness.

'"Don't be frightened," said my employer, laughing at the start which I had given. "It's only Carlo, my mastiff. I call him mine, but really old Toller, my groom, is the only man who can do anything with him. We feed him once a day, and not too much then, so that he is always as keen as mustard. Toller lets him loose every night, and God help the trespasser whom he lays his fangs upon.

For goodness' sake don't you ever on any pretext set your foot over the threshold at night, for it is as much as your life is worth."

'The warning was no idle one, for two nights later I happened to look out of my bedroom window about two o'clock in the morning. It was a beautiful moonlight night, and the lawn in front of the house was silvered over and almost as bright as day. I was standing wrapt in the peaceful beauty of the scene, when I was aware that something was moving under the shadow of the copper beeches. As it emerged into the moonshine I saw what it was. It was a giant dog, as large as a calf, tawny-tinted, with hanging jowl, black muzzle, and huge projecting bones. It walked slowly across the lawn and vanished into the shadow upon the other side. That dreadful silent sentinel sent a chill to my heart, which I do not think that any burglar could have done.

'And now I have a very strange experience to tell you. I had, as you know, cut off my hair in London, and I had placed it in a great coil at the bottom of my trunk. One evening, after the child was in bed, I began to amuse myself by examining the furniture of my room and by rearranging my own little things. There was an old chest of drawers in the room, the two upper ones empty and open, the lower one locked. I had filled the two first with my linen and as I had still much to pack away I was naturally annoyed at not having the use of the third drawer. It struck me that it might have been fastened by a mere oversight, so I took out my bunch of keys and tried to open it. The very first key fitted to perfection, and I drew the drawer open. There was only one thing in it, but I am sure that you would never guess what it was. It was my coil of hair.

'I took it up and examined it. It was of the same peculiar tint, and the same thickness. But then the impossibility of the thing obtruded itself upon me. How *could* my hair have been locked in the drawer? With trembling hands I undid my trunk, turned out the contents and drew from the bottom my own hair. I laid the

'I TOOK IT UP AND EXAMINED IT.'

two tresses together, and I assure you they were identical. Was it not extraordinary? Puzzle as I would, I could make nothing at all of what it meant. I returned the strange hair to the drawer, and I said nothing of the matter to the Rucastles as I felt that I had put myself in the wrong by opening a drawer which they had locked.

'I am naturally observant as you may have remarked, Mr Holmes, and I soon had a pretty good plan of the whole house in my head. There was one wing, however, which appeared not to be inhabited at all. A door which faced that which led into the quarters of the Tollers opened into this suite, but it was invariably locked. One day, however, as I ascended the stair, I met Mr Rucastle coming out through this door, his keys in his hand, and a look on his face which made him a very different person to the round jovial man to whom I was accustomed. His cheeks were red, his brow was all crinkled with anger, and the veins stood out at his temples with passion. He locked the door, and hurried past me without a word or a look.

'This aroused my curiosity; so when I went out for a walk in the grounds with my charge, I strolled round to the side from which I could see the windows of this part of the house. There were four of them in a row, three of which were simply dirty, while the fourth was shuttered up. They were evidently all deserted. As I strolled up and down, glancing at them occasionally, Mr Rucastle came out to me, looking as merry and jovial as ever.

' "Ah!" said he, "you must not think me rude if I passed you without a word, my dear young lady. I was preoccupied with business matters."

'I assured him that I was not offended. "By the way," said I, "you seem to have quite a suite of spare rooms up there, and one of them has the shutters up."

' "Photography is one of my hobbies," said he. "I have made my dark-room up there. But, dear me! what an observant young lady we have come upon. Who would have believed it? Who would have ever believed it?" He spoke in a jesting tone, but there was no jest in his eyes as he looked at me. I read suspicion there, and annoyance, but no jest.

'Well, Mr Holmes, from the moment that I understood that there was something about that suite of rooms which I was not to know, I was all on fire to go over them. It was not mere curiosity, though I have my share of that. It was more a feeling of duty – a feeling that some good might come from my penetrating to this place. They talk of woman's instinct; perhaps it was woman's instinct which gave me that feeling. At any rate, it was there; and I was keenly on the look-out for any chance to pass the forbidden door.

'It was only yesterday that the chance came. I may tell you that, besides Mr Rucastle, both Toller and his wife find something to do in these deserted rooms, and I once saw him carrying a large black linen bag with him through the door. Recently he has been drinking hard, and yesterday evening he was drunk; and, when I came upstairs, there was a key in the door. I have no doubt at all that he had left it there. Mr and Mrs Rucastle were both downstairs, and the child was with them, so that I had an admirable opportunity. I turned the key gently in the lock, opened the door, and slipped through.

'There was a little passage in front of me, unpapered and uncarpeted, which turned at a right angle at the farther end. Round this corner were three doors in a line, the first and third of which were open. They each led into an empty room, dusty and cheerless, with two windows in the one, and one in the other, so thick with dirt that the evening light glimmered dimly through them. The centre door was closed, and across the outside of it had been fastened one of the broad bars of an iron bed, padlocked at one end to a ring in the wall, and fastened at the other with stout cord. The door itself was locked as well, and the key was not there. This barricaded door corresponded clearly with the shuttered window outside, and yet I could see by the glimmer from beneath it that the room was not in darkness. Evidently there was a skylight which let in light from above. As I stood in the passage gazing at this sinister door, and wondering what secret it might veil, I suddenly heard the sound of steps within the room, and saw a shadow pass backwards and forwards against the little slit of dim light which shone out from under the door. A mad, unreasoning terror rose up in me at the sight, Mr Holmes. My overstrung nerves failed me suddenly, and I turned and ran – ran as though some dreadful hand were behind me, clutching at the skirt of my dress. I rushed down the passage, through the door, and straight into the arms of Mr Rucastle, who was waiting outside.

'"So," said he, smiling, "it was you, then. I thought it must be when I saw the door open."

'"Oh, I am so frightened!" I panted.

'"My dear young lady! my dear young lady!" – you cannot

think how caressing and soothing his manner was – "and what has frightened you, my dear young lady?"

'But his voice was just a little too coaxing. He overdid it. I was keenly on my guard against him.

' "I was foolish enough to go into the empty wing," I answered. "But it is so lonely and eerie in this dim light that I was frightened and ran out again. Oh, it is so dreadfully still in there!"

' "Only that?" said he, looking at me keenly.

' "Why, what do you think?" I asked.

' "Why do you think that I lock this door?"

' "I am sure that I do not know."

' "It is to keep people out who have no business there. Do you see?" He was still smiling in the most amiable manner.

' "I am sure if I had known – "

' "Well, then, you know now. And if you ever put your foot over that threshold again – " here in an instant the smile hardened into a grin of rage, and he glared down at me with the face of a demon, "I'll throw you to the mastiff."

'I was so terrified that I do not know what I did. I suppose that I must have rushed past him into my room. I remember nothing until I found myself lying on my bed trembling all over. Then I thought of you, Mr Holmes. I could not live there longer without some advice. I was frightened of the house, of the man, of the woman, of the servants, even of the child. They were all horrible to me. If I could only bring you down all would be well. Of course I might have fled from the house, but my curiosity was almost as strong as my fears. My mind was soon made up. I would send you a wire. I put on my hat and cloak, went down to the office, which is about half a mile from the house, and then returned, feeling very much easier. A horrible doubt came into my mind as I approached the door lest the dog might be loose, but I remembered that Toller had drunk himself into a state of insensibility that evening, and I knew that he was the only one in the household who had any influence with the savage creature, or who would venture to set him free. I slipped in in safety, and lay awake half the night in my joy at the thought of seeing you. I had no difficulty in getting leave to come into Winchester this morning, but I must be back before three o'clock, for Mr and Mrs Rucastle are going on a visit, and will be away all the evening, so that I must look after the child. Now I have told you all my adventures, Mr Holmes, and I should be very glad if you could tell me what it all means, and, above all, what I should do.'

Holmes and I had listened spellbound to this extraordinary story. My friend rose now, and paced up and down the room, his hands in his pockets, and an expression of the most profound gravity upon his face.

'Is Toller still drunk?' he asked.

'Yes. I heard his wife tell Mrs Rucastle that she could do nothing with him.'

'That is well. And the Rucastles go out tonight?'

'Yes.'

'Is there a cellar with a good strong lock?'

'Yes, the wine cellar.'

'You seem to me to have acted all through this matter like a brave and sensible girl, Miss Hunter. Do you think that you could perform one more feat? I should not ask it of you if I did not think you a quite exceptional woman.'

'I will try. What is it?'

'We shall be at the Copper Beeches by seven o'clock, my friend and I. The Rucastles will be gone by that time, and Toller will, we hope, be incapable. There only remains Mrs Toller, who might give the alarm. If you could send her into the cellar, on some errand, and then turn the key upon her, you would facilitate matters immensely.'

'I will do it.'

'Excellent! We shall then look thoroughly into the affair. Of course there is only one feasible explanation. You have been brought there to personate someone, and the real person is imprisoned in this chamber. That is obvious. As to who this prisoner is, I have no doubt that it is the daughter, Miss Alice Rucastle, if I remember right, who was said to have gone to America. You were chosen, doubtless, as resembling her in height, figure, and the colour of your hair. Hers had been cut off very possibly in some illness through which she has passed, and so, of course, yours had to be sacrificed also. By a curious chance you came upon her tresses. The man in the road was, undoubtedly, some friend of hers – possibly her fiancé – and no doubt as you wore the girl's dress, and were so like her, he was convinced from your laughter, whenever he saw you, and afterwards from your gesture, that Miss Rucastle was perfectly happy, and that she no longer desired his attentions. The dog is let loose at night to prevent him from endeavouring to communicate with her. So much is fairly clear. The most serious point in the case is the disposition of the child.'

'What on earth has that to do with it?' I ejaculated.

'My dear Watson, you as a medical man are continually gaining light as to the tendencies of a child by the study of the parents. Don't you see that the converse is equally valid. I have frequently gained my first real insight into the character of parents by studying their children. This child's disposition is abnormally cruel, merely for cruelty's sake, and whether he derives this from his smiling father, as I should suspect, or from his mother, it bodes evil for the poor girl who is in their power.'

'I am sure that you are right, Mr Holmes,' cried our client. 'A thousand things come back to me which make me certain that you have hit it. Oh, let us lose not an instant in bringing help to this poor creature.'

'We must be circumspect, for we are dealing with a very cunning man. We can do nothing until seven o'clock. At that hour we shall be with you, and it will not be long before we solve the mystery.'

We were as good as our word, for it was just seven when we

reached the Copper Beeches, having put up our trap at a wayside public house. The group of trees, with their dark leaves shining like burnished metal in the light of the setting sun, were sufficient to mark the house even had Miss Hunter not been standing smiling on the doorstep.

'Have you managed it?' asked Holmes.

A loud thudding noise came from somewhere downstairs. 'That is Mrs Toller in the cellar,' said she. 'Her husband lies snoring on the kitchen rug. Here are his keys, which are the duplicates of Mr Rucastle's.'

'You have done well indeed!' cried Holmes, with enthusiasm. 'Now lead the way, and we shall soon see the end of this black business.'

We passed up the stair, unlocked the door, followed on down a passage, and found ourselves in front of the barricade which Miss Hunter had described. Holmes cut the cord and removed the transverse bar. Then he tried the various keys in the lock, but without success. No sound came from within, and at the silence Holmes's face clouded over.

'I trust that we are not too late,' said he. 'I think, Miss Hunter, that we had better go in without you. Now, Watson, put your shoulder to it, and we shall see whether we cannot make our way in.'

It was an old rickety door and gave at once before our united strength. Together we rushed into the room. It was empty. There was no furniture save a little pallet bed, a small table, and a basketful of linen. The skylight above was open, and the prisoner gone.

'There has been some villainy here,' said Holmes; 'this beauty has guessed Miss Hunter's intentions, and has carried his victim off.'

'But how?'

'Through the skylight. We shall soon see how he managed it.' He swung himself up on to the roof. 'Ah, yes,' he cried, 'here's the end of a long light ladder against the eaves. That is how he did it.'

'But it is impossible,' said Miss Hunter, 'the ladder was not there when the Rucastles went away.'

'He has come back and done it. I tell you that he is a clever and dangerous man. I should not be very much surprised if this were he whose step I hear now upon the stair. I think, Watson, that it would be as well for you to have your pistol ready.'

The words were hardly out of his mouth before a man appeared at the door of the room, a very fat and burly man, with a heavy stick in his hand. Miss Hunter screamed and shrunk against the wall at the sight of him, but Sherlock Holmes sprang forward and confronted him.

'You villain,' said he, 'where's your daughter?'

The fat man cast his eyes round, and then up at the open skylight.

'"YOU VILLAIN!" SAID HE. "WHERE'S YOUR DAUCHTER?"'

'It is for me to ask you that,' he shrieked, 'you thieves! Spies and thieves! I have caught you, have I? You are in my power. I'll serve you!' He turned and clattered down the stairs as hard as he could go.

'He's gone for the dog!' cried Miss Hunter.

'I have my revolver,' said I.

'Better close the front door,' cried Holmes, and we all rushed down the stairs together. We had hardly reached the hall when we heard the baying of a hound and then a scream of agony, with a horrible worrying sound which it was dreadful to listen to. An elderly man with a red face and shaking limbs came staggering out at a side door.

'My God!' he cried. 'Someone has loosed the dog. It's not been fed for two days. Quick, quick, or it'll be too late!'

Holmes and I rushed out, and round the angle of the house, with Toller hurrying behind us. There was the huge famished brute, its black muzzle buried in Rucastle's throat, while he writhed and screamed upon the ground. Running up, I blew its brains out, and it fell over with its keen white teeth still meeting in the great creases of his neck. With much labour we separated them, and carried him, living but horribly mangled, into the house. We laid him upon the drawing-room sofa, and having dispatched the sobered Toller to bear the news to his wife, I did what I could to relieve his pain. We were all assembled round him when the door opened, and a tall, gaunt woman entered the room.

'Mrs Toller!' cried Miss Hunter.

'Yes, miss. Mr Rucastle let me out when he came back before he went up to you. Ah, miss, it is a pity you didn't let me know what you were planning, for I would have told you that your pains were wasted.'

'Ha!' said Holmes, looking keenly at her. 'It is clear that Mrs Toller knows more about this matter than anyone else.'

'Yes, sir, I do, and I am ready enough to tell what I know.'

'Then pray sit down, and let us hear it, for there are several points on which I must confess that I am still in the dark.'

'I will soon make it clear to you,' said she; 'and I'd have done so before now if I could ha' got out from the cellar. If there's police-court business over this, you'll remember that I was the one that stood your friend, and that I was Miss Alice's friend too.

'She was never happy at home, Miss Alice wasn't, from the time that her father married again. She was slighted like, and had no say in anything; but it never really became bad for her until after she met Mr Fowler at a friend's house. As well as I could learn, Miss Alice had rights of her own by will, but she was so quiet and patient, she was, that she never said a word about them, but just left everything in Mr Rucastle's hands. He knew he was safe with her; but when there was a chance of a husband coming forward, who would ask for all that the law could give him, then her father thought it time to put a stop on it. He wanted her to sign a paper so that whether she married or not, he could use her money. When she wouldn't do it, he kept on worrying her until she got brain fever, and for six weeks was at death's door. Then she got better at last, all worn to a shadow, and with her beautiful hair cut off; but that didn't make no change in her young man, and he stuck to her as true as man could be.'

'Ah,' said Holmes, 'I think that what you have been good enough to tell us makes the matter fairly clear, and that I can deduce all that remains. Mr Rucastle, then, I presume, took to this system of imprisonment?'

'Yes, sir.'

'And brought Miss Hunter down from London in order to get rid of the disagreeable persistence of Mr Fowler.'

'That was it, sir.'

'But Mr Fowler, being a persevering man, as a good seaman should be, blockaded the house, and having met you, succeeded by certain arguments, metallic or otherwise, in convincing you that your interests were the same as his.'

'Mr Fowler was a very kind-spoken, free-handed gentleman,' said Mrs Toller serenely.

'And in this way he managed that your good man should have no want of drink, and that a ladder should be ready at the moment when your master had gone out.'

'You have it, sir, just as it happened.'

'I am sure we owe you an apology, Mrs Toller,' said Holmes, 'for you have certainly cleared up everything which puzzled us. And here comes the country surgeon and Mrs Rucastle, so I think, Watson, that we had best escort Miss Hunter back to Winchester, as it seems to me that our *locus standi* now is rather a questionable one.'

And thus was solved the mystery of the sinister house with the copper beeches in front of the door. Mr Rucastle survived, but was always a broken man, kept alive solely through the care of his devoted wife. They still live with their old servants, who probably know so much of Rucastle's past life that he finds it difficult to part from them. Mr Fowler and Miss Rucastle were married, by special licence, in Southampton the day after their flight, and he is now the holder of a Government appointment in the Island of Mauritius. As to Miss Violet Hunter, my friend Holmes, rather to my disappointment, manifested no further interest in her when once she had ceased to be the centre of one of his problems, and she is now the head of a private school at Walsall, where I believe that she has met with considerable success.